The Dark That Begins

The Light of Darkness Book One

Steve Pantazis

SP Books

Written by Steve Pantazis

Cover artwork by germancreative

Map design by Steve Pantazis

Interior artwork by Samsul Hidayat

Published by SP Books

To my wife, my love, my one and only
To my father, whose wisdom shaped my life
To my mother, who taught me to believe in myself

Contents

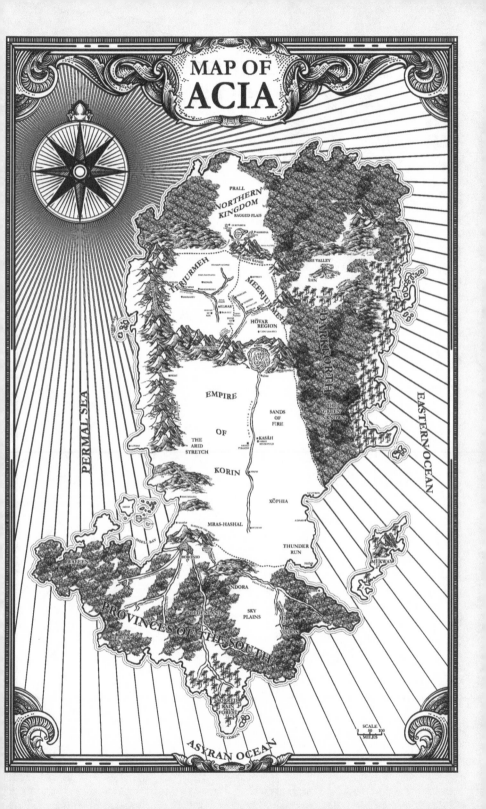

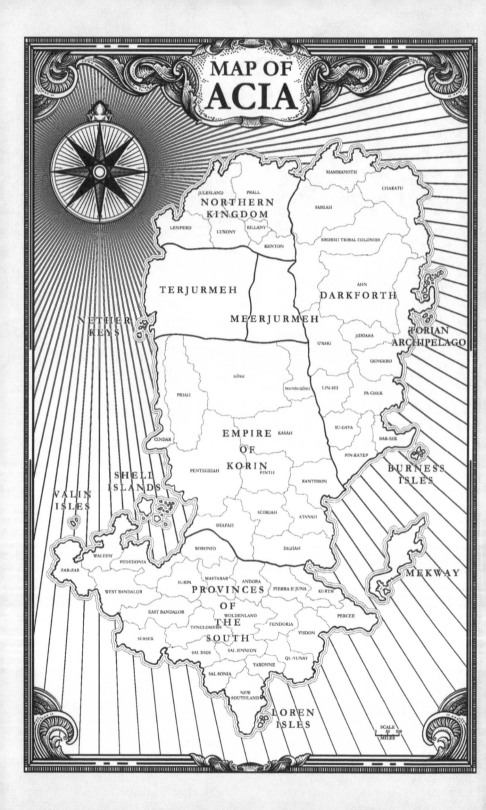

Terjurmeh & Meerjurmeh

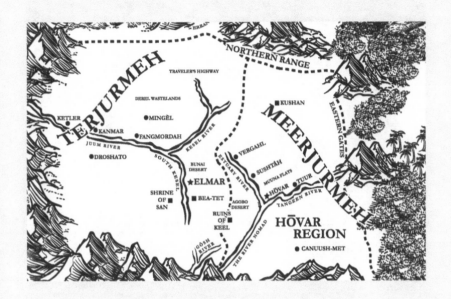

Northern Kingdom

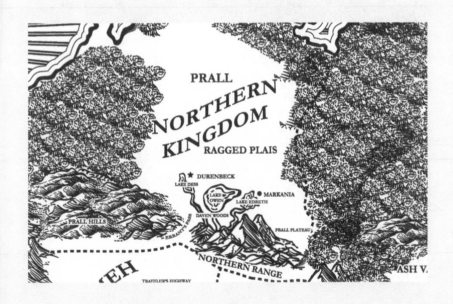

DARKFORTH

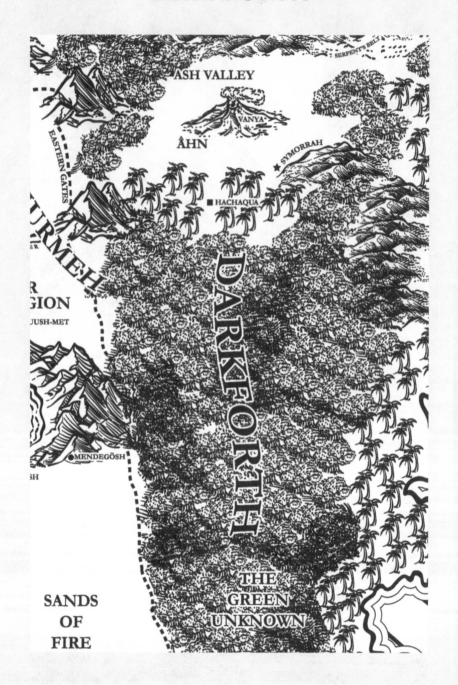

EMPIRE OF KORIN

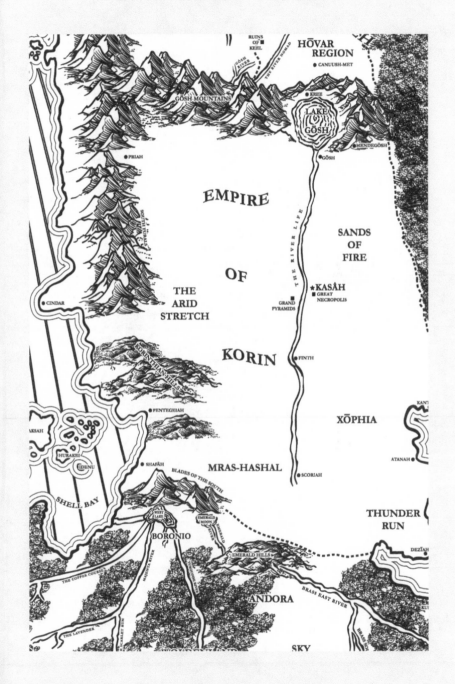

PROVINCES OF THE SOUTH

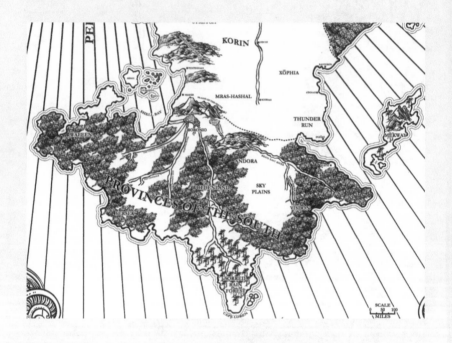

Foreword by the Author

I T BEGAN WITH A map.

Not a very impressive map, mind you.

Just a humble piece of paper with a couple of countries scrawled by hand—Terjurmeh to the west and Meerjurmeh to the east—ringed by mountains and separated from each other by a vast desert. Cities dotted the rivers that gave life to these countries, and I wondered who might live there.

Were they a kind people? Were they savage? What were their cultures like? Were there gods in this ancient world? Who were the heroes and who were the foes? What magic abounded in these realms? What other lands were there?

I'd grown up reading Tolkien and other luminaries of fantasy. I wanted a world readers could sink their teeth into. I wanted a story where the stakes were high and the consequences even higher.

When I turned my scrawled map into a watercolor painting that covered an entire continent, I knew I had something big.

I had six domains at my fingertips waiting to come alive: two desert nations at odds with each other, alongside a kingdom, an empire, a federation of provinces, and a treacherous land where no one dared to go.

My imagination soared.

From this one map came a world on the brink of war, a prophecy that would decide the fate of entire civilizations, and the making of the ultimate struggle between good and evil.

In other words, the making of an epic.

The Light of Darkness is a series that spans nine novels. I chose the title because I believe there is always light in the darkness—you just need to seek it out.

So, too, must my heroes find the bravery and fortitude to shine in the dark.

Otherwise, how else can they triumph over evil when the odds are stacked against them, when the shadow of doom tries to swallow them whole, when the black hand of fate conspires against them?

I promise you this: our heroes face a perilous mountain.

With each book, the mountain grows steeper, the pinnacle more difficult to reach, the risk of falling that much greater.

Will our heroes reach the summit and prevail? Or will they tumble into the nether reaches of darkness, forever lost?

Let us find out the answers to our questions, starting with Book 1, *The Dark That Begins*.

Thank you for embarking on this epic journey with me.

May you find your own light along the way.

Petrah

T HE BOY HID AMONG the golden barley grass as the sun dipped in the west, careful to keep his head below the tips of the swaying grain, lest he risk getting caught. Getting caught, he was certain, would be the end of him.

He was wary of the fieldworkers with the sickles, but more concerned about the armed men with the hungry eyes watching them with the daggers belted about the waists of their tunics. They twisted their blades with restless hands, as if looking for trouble.

Past the field, the boy glimpsed a stone farmhouse and fancy manor, with trees and a river beyond. The rest of the land was comprised of amber fields that sweetened the air. He'd waited all afternoon in the merciless heat, hoping the workers and guards would go away so he could sneak into the farmhouse. He licked his chapped lips and held a hand over his grumbling belly. If he was right, he'd find food and drink inside the farmhouse. But if he was wrong—

No. He'd seen one worker wipe crumbs from his beard, and another sip from a full waterskin that had been flat before she went into the house.

I'm right, he thought. *I have to be.*

The boy twirled a straw of loose barley between his fingers, trying to recall how he got here. He worked the steps backward in his mind. He'd awoken in this spot, facing the clear sky without a stitch of clothing on his person. Before that—

What happened before he woke up?

He searched for the answer but came up short.

It prompted more questions.

What was this place?

What happened to his clothes?

Where was his family?

The harder he searched his thoughts, the more questions he had.

He looked down at the fresh scar just below his breastbone. It didn't hurt when he ran his finger over the angry pink line. How did it get there?

The boy caught his breath when the one question—the most important one—stumped him.

"My name," he whispered. "What's my name?"

He squeezed his eyes shut and plugged his ears with his fingers, as if doing so might help, but the only thing that came to mind was his age. He was eleven. Why couldn't he remember anything else?

The commotion of voices grabbed his attention. He held his breath and dared a peek. Workers headed toward the sinking sun, and armed men trailed behind. Were they done for the day?

The boy waited until they were gone, until he was sure they wouldn't come back. Candlelight flickered to life through the windows of the manor as the sky turned shades of orange and purple. The farmhouse, with its solitary window, thankfully remained dark.

Go, he told himself. *Go now.*

He dashed through the barley field, across the dirt path, and stopped when he got behind the farmhouse. With hands flat against the stone wall of the building—still warm from the sun—and heart pounding in his chest, he listened. He heard nothing but the sound of his breathing.

He slunk along the wall until he found the door the workers had used. A light tug on the handle ensured it was open. His heart was pounding so strongly that he could feel the pulse in his ears.

Open the door. Just pull.

The door squealed open to the heavy scent of milled grain. He held onto the handle, listening to make sure no one was inside, that no one heard the creak of the hinges. When he let go, the door stayed open.

Murk and shadows flooded the space, but the single window let in just enough light to guide him along a walkway toward an open room filled with tools for fieldwork. He examined a bucket with the ladle sticking out. It sat on a table in the middle of the room. He dipped the ladle and sniffed the liquid, then took a cautious sip. Water. He drank ladle after ladle until he coughed and sputtered from swallowing too greedily, then drank some more.

With his thirst sated, the hunger pangs took over.

His nose picked up a pleasing, nutty aroma coming from the right. A skinny door revealed a larder with packed shelves. He could barely make out the items, but there appeared to be endless jars. Their cool glass clinked as he pushed several aside. He was determined to find the source of the delightful scent. With a careless shove, a jar fell, landing on the hard ground. It bounced loudly but didn't break.

The boy froze. A tense moment passed. But then hunger took over and his hands continued their search until he found the glorious treasure: a wheel of cheese.

He hefted it and carried it to the table with the bucket. The outside of the wheel's skin was waxy, but the middle was soft and edible. He dug his fingers into the fleshy center, rewarded with crumbles that he stuffed into his mouth, salty and tangy. He licked his fingers clean and gouged out another chunk.

A voice caught him off guard. He dropped the cheese.

He turned to see a man with a heavy gut staring at him. Another man, late in his years, shuffled after him, carrying a lamp. The second man pointed and said something to the boy, but the boy couldn't understand him, not even when the man raised his voice.

They were bigger than him.

Stronger than him.

But were they faster?

The boy bolted for the exit.

The man with the gut lunged with his hands out and missed. The man with the lamp tried to block the way. When he shifted left, the boy dodged to the right and sprinted past him. In seconds, the boy was out the door. He ran up the dirt road opposite from where the workers had gone, feet slapping over packed dirt and hard pebbles.

Shouts and a high-pitched whistle sounded behind him.

Then barking.

A look over his shoulder revealed torchlight. A second look revealed fast-moving shadows.

The boy cut left, toward the river. Maybe if he got in the water—

If he got in the water, could he swim?

Would he drown?

The barking grew louder.

With each stride over the rough, dry ground, each strained breath, each pump of the arms, they gained on him.

No, no, no.

He ran faster.

His lungs burned and his muscles ached, but the river was close. So close. He cleared the trees and—

Snarling, shaggy beasts cut off his escape. The pair of dogs growled and snapped their vicious jaws, ready to spring should the boy attempt to flee.

The boy was no fool.

He stood his ground until his pursuers arrived with their torches. They yelled at him in their foreign tongue, but he didn't need to translate their words to understand what he'd known all along: getting caught would be the end of him.

The man with the greasy jowls and cruel eyes ordered the boy fettered and locked in a shed for the night.

The next day, the boy went before a magistrate.

The day after, he was sold into slavery.

Four years later, as a slave in the city of Kanmar, he was fluent in their language, but he still couldn't remember his past. Nor could he remember his name.

But the slavers gave him one.

It was a name that would remain with him for as long as he survived their wrath.

A name in the old tongue that described the unique color of his eyes—a color none had seen before in all of Kanmar, perhaps the world—blue as the sky itself.

Petrah.

They named him Petrah.

Chapter 1

Slave

THE SAVAGE SNAP OF the whip split the air the instant before it struck flesh.

Petrah winced as the slave tied up to the post in the middle of the large stone quarry cried out. He barely knew the man, but he knew his name was Aggren and that he was being whipped because of Petrah.

Not all of it was Petrah's fault.

Sure, Petrah had tripped and fallen on the march to the quarry, disrupting the flow of the hundred-slave column and earning the ire of the Draadi, the slave masters.

But Aggren had acted on his own, breaking the nose of the nasty-tempered Draad who'd kicked Petrah while he was on the ground. Petrah would have endured the beating; it wasn't his first. He might have limped for a few days and wheezed from the tender ribs, but he would have healed in time.

But Aggren?

The man's life was forfeit, and for what? To come to the aid of a fifteen-year-old nobody?

Now, Aggren was on display for the throng of city slaves to witness in the blistering heat of the quarry where they toiled. Petrah tasted their foul perspiration on his tongue. Their rankness filled the shimmering air, his own no doubt a part of it. He was accustomed to the odor of unwashed bodies, but today's heat proved particularly suffocating.

The slaves would learn the consequence of Aggren's actions, and Aggren would lose his life in exchange.

He's going to die for nothing, Petrah thought.

Would anyone remember the man's death on the morrow?

Or would they forget, as they always did?

The Draadi made the slaves bunch together in the late-afternoon heat and face the impending execution. Petrah packed in with the sorry lot of them—gaunt men and women, broken spirits, right around one hundred twenty at last count.

The slave masters tied Aggren up to the T-shaped post with cords of leather. They pulled his arms taut to either side by his wrists, exposing the sharp outlines of his ribs and scars from past whippings. Spools of brown hair fell to his sweat-slicked shoulders.

When the Draadi announced his punishment, it knocked the breath from Petrah's lungs.

Aggren would receive an unthinkable twenty lashes, then disembowelment. The slaves had similar reactions to Petrah's: tremors, fearful murmurings, eyes searching among themselves for solace, but only finding the same quivering lips, hands over mouths, and quiet sobs. Death wasn't foreign by any means, but this was barbaric.

Just to teach us a lesson. As if we've not had enough.

Another crack of the whip and a mournful cry from Aggren, and Petrah flinched again.

At eight lashes, Aggren's lathered back was a crisscross of angry lacerations. If the gods were good, he'd pass out before the Draadi gutted him.

The slave master whom Aggren assaulted stood to the side of the post, watching the flogging with a self-satisfied smile, despite his broken nose and the blood pooling beneath his blackening eye. He was the same slave master who'd kicked Petrah, a hateful creature who took pleasure in the pain of others.

A Draad named Meska.

Aggren groaned, head drooping.

You should have let Meska beat me senseless. Now look at you.

The whip struck Aggren again, and Petrah turned away. He couldn't stand to watch anymore.

I'll show them justice. I'll make them pay.

He clenched his fists as the stink of sweat and rage filled him. The slave masters watched the whipping while laughing at Aggren's misfortune. Two more joined their brethren, leaving a platter of half-eaten grapes, cured meats, and bread on a stone table.

Petrah eyed the food.

Wouldn't it be something if he robbed them of their meal?

He imagined the saltiness of the meat, the aroma of wheat in the bread, the squish of fruit in his mouth. He could stand at their abandoned table and devour everything on it just as they devoured Aggren's misery. Or take what he could grab and share it with the others. The slaves would riot and scramble over each other. They'd fight one another for scraps, forcing the Draadi to stop. He'd save Aggren's life.

No, it would just stall the inevitable.

Unless he did something drastic.

Like incite the slaves to rebellion. Or encourage them to attack their masters. One hundred twenty against a handful of armed Draadi.

Or, or . . .

Why not flee? The Draadi couldn't catch them all. They could flee the quarry, run to the river, and swim to the opposite bank. Some would drown, others get caught, a few slain. They could take their chances.

Would it be worth it?

Petrah saw only sluggish, miserable souls around him. This sorry lot couldn't do anything, even if whipped to action.

No, there would be no rebellion today.

On impulse and without regard for his own safety, Petrah moved behind the congregation of slaves, hidden from the Draadi enthralled by

Aggren's misfortune. His cellmate, Tan, gave him a quizzical look, and his other cellmate, Kruush, blinked as if to warn him not to be so reckless.

Petrah ignored them.

He kept his head down and threaded his way to the table with the food, careful to avoid bumping into anyone or drawing unnecessary attention.

What are you doing?

He was quick to answer his own question: *taking from them.*

Petrah would take from the masters, just as they took from him.

He chose the bread, not because it was his first choice, but because it was the smartest choice. The heady scent of the salted beef would give him away for sure, and the grapes were too fragile and might burst. The loaf of bread was soft, cloven in half. He could take one half, leave the other, and conceal his trophy within the folds of his tunic.

Which is precisely what he did.

With the bread secured, he melded in with the slaves. A few odd looks and a head shake from Kruush, but nothing more. His act of thievery was a tiny victory against his oppressors.

For you, Aggren.

Aggren hung limply from his bindings now. Meska lifted the man's chin and slapped his face. Aggren remained unconscious. Meska cursed, but it didn't stop him from drawing his knife.

Petrah shut his eyes, but his ears caught the wet slash of the blade. The cheers of the Draadi confirmed the deed.

The slaver's gong resonated shortly after in the dry air, signaling an end to the brutal day. Petrah fell in line with the other disheartened slaves, careful to hide his prize from prying eyes. Aggren's death hung heavily on his conscience.

Even as regret seeped into his thoughts for his brash stupidity, Petrah tightened his grip on his tunic. It wasn't like he could undo his action.

Stay invisible.

His old cellmate, Antelle, had often warned him to keep his head down. *If they don't notice you, they don't bother you. And if they don't bother you, you live to see another day.*

It was a shame what those heathens had done to Antelle, just as it was a shame what they had done to Aggren. Was San, the God of Shadows, that cruel?

The Draadi marched the slaves single file out of the quarry onto the dirt-packed streets of Kanmar. The slave masters wore simple beige tunics, leather sandals, heavy leather belts, and the notorious crimson sashes running diagonally over their chests. In contrast, the slaves were barefoot and grimed and wore linen tunics tied about the waist. Black, triangular tattoos marked their ankles as the property of Kanmar.

The city itself was an array of temples, homes, and public buildings mostly constructed of stone or mud bricks, which came in plentiful supply from the surrounding desert.

Dusk cast long shadows across the great outer wall, a towering line of limestone and granite blocks silhouetted against the saffron sky, punctuated by pylons and watchtowers. The Temple of Nahn greeted them from the south with its nine minarets and grand rotunda, the one piece of beauty Petrah could always appreciate.

The haggard lot wended through the most rundown section of the city with nothing but the sound of their bare feet on the hard ground.

This was their ritual of misery.

This was the endless cycle that blended one day's march to the next.

A skinny dog crossed ahead of them. Petrah envied the animal, free to go about its business.

They passed a beggar in rags sitting beside the road. Next to him huddled an emaciated young girl who couldn't have been over eight years old. Petrah had seen the pair many times and assumed them father and daughter. He paid little attention to them on most days. They'd remain silent like statues, the smart thing to do in the presence of Draadi.

Today, the girl's copper-toned face was so withdrawn, her arms so thin, it was as if she hadn't eaten a morsel in weeks. At least Petrah had daily rations.

For a moment, their eyes met.

She glanced at him from beneath filthy, burnt-umber bangs, her large, bright eyes filled with desperation. A dingy cord of once-white beads threaded around her throat, telling him she was of Mumooni descent, a race of Westerners from the mountains, not well received by the Ter-ju-rah of Kanmar, who looked down upon foreigners.

Petrah's hand instinctively squeezed the small mound of bread hidden within his tunic. He'd meant to share his bounty with his cellmates, but at least they'd eat tonight.

The girl, however . . .

Petrah eased the bread out from the folds of his tunic. With a flick of his wrist, he tossed it toward the girl.

The girl scampered on all fours to fetch it. Her movement earned several looks from the slaves in front of Petrah.

A Draad with scars and boils on his face and a double sash over his tunic, signifying his rank as the element leader, called to the front, "Hold the line!"

He strode up to the girl. The father tried to intervene, but the slave master pushed him away and snatched the bread from the girl. "Where did you get this?"

She simply looked up at him.

"I said, where did you get this?"

When she didn't answer, he backhanded her across the face.

"What about you, old man?"

The man's eyes flew wide, but he didn't dare speak.

Petrah started to step away from the line, but his cellmate Tan re-strained him and shook his head.

Tan was right: Petrah had done enough stupid things this day.

One more would earn him a hole out in the desert, next to Aggren.

The Draad turned to the slaves. "Who did this? Tell me, and you'll have double rations for a week. I'll even throw in the bread."

Petrah expected at least one person to betray him. His bravado fled his body, leaving his cheeks flushed, then cold. He waited for a fellow slave to call him out and accuse him of the crime. Even with their evening rations, the small bit of bread would be a feast. Surely, someone wanted to not go hungry tonight.

But no one called him out. Perhaps Aggren's death was enough for today.

"Fine, stay silent. Half rations until somebody confesses. We'll see how that suits you rats." The Draad ordered the column forward.

Petrah fluffed his tunic as he resumed his march. If they found crumbs on his person, he was finished.

The slaves entered a cavernous opening dug into the bedrock, like a colony of ants. It led to the Denrethi pits, the labyrinth of tunnels and holding cells built to house the city slaves. The catacombs were extensive, going on for miles, according to some, a warren of cells rumored to have enough capacity to hold double the current count of occupants.

The Draadi charged with staying on watch overnight had a cozy nook on the northeast side, past the supply cells. Not that Petrah got to visit the space. Nor did he care to.

Iron sconces lined the roughly hewn rock walls, holding lit brands. The burn of pitch did little to mask the stench of excrement and rot of decaying food. Petrah was used to sleeping in fetid conditions, but he never got used to that first hit of foul air. No wonder the Draadi on shift were always in an unpleasant mood. They had to breathe the same air as the slaves. At least it was cooler in the pits.

The procession turned right at the second tunnel intersection.

A waiting group of slaves wearing black cords of rope cinched about their waists opened cell doors for the marchers. They were the Jabah, an elevated segment of the slave population, tasked with maintaining the pits. They were granted liberties not allowed for those like Petrah, who wore the red. Unlike the exalted scarlet sashes of the slave masters, the dingy-red cords of the lowest slaves were a reminder that they would pay for their lives in blood.

By fours, the slaves broke away from the column and entered their respective windowless holding cells. Each cell sat behind a metal grate embedded into the bedrock, with a hinged iron door in the center. Some cells, like Petrah's, offered more privacy from the other slaves' quarters, with a rock wall on either side. But all the cells were cramped: four cots of straw and linen, touching end-to-end, and a refuse bucket with an accompanying mound of straw in the center for cleaning up. The cells were otherwise bare.

Petrah angled his body when he slept. Knocking over the bucket with his feet happened only once, and poor Tan had been the one to receive the ill-fated gift.

The number four was unlucky in Terjurmehan culture because it was one beyond the sacred number three. From Petrah's perspective, there were far worse things to consider than the number of wretches sharing their quarters with you.

One of the Jabah signaled to Petrah and his cellmates, and the four entered their cell.

As soon as they were in, the Jabahn locked the metal door and moved on to the next cell. The sweet fragrance of fresh hay offered a welcome respite from the putrid air.

Petrah plopped down onto his cot, exhausted. The act of sitting sent pinpricks of pain up his side from where Meska had kicked him.

I'm lucky nothing got broken.

But next time . . .

A tray of pungent cheese and old nuuma nuts waited for him and his companions on the floor of their cell, half the usual amount, as promised by the element leader.

Petrah poured himself a mug of oily water from the clay jug at the foot of his cot. His cellmates did the same. They ate, save for Petrah, whose stomach was in knots over Aggren. Petrah might not have been responsible for his death, but the man's blood was on his hands, and it would always be.

Slaves continued to file past the cell before disappearing down the corridor. Bringing up the rear were three Draadi. They looked into each cell, making sure the residents were where they belonged.

Before Petrah could avert his gaze, Meska made eye contact.

The Draad pulled his knife from his belt and slapped the blade against the cell bars. The metal rang. It was the knife he'd used to gut Aggren, still smeared with the slave's blood and flecks of viscera. Petrah swore he could smell it.

"I know it was you who took the bread. Confess, and I'll go easy." When Petrah said nothing, Meska said, "Oh, acting coy, are you? Thought you might get away with tossing the evidence? Thought I wouldn't notice?"

Petrah tried to relax his rigid posture, to show he wasn't guilty or concerned, but his body wouldn't let him.

"Have it your way, thief. Unlock the door."

A Jabahn unlocked the cell door.

Although Petrah had dusted the crumbs from his tunic, he couldn't be sure he'd done a thorough job.

He tensed as Meska entered the cell.

The slave master's breath reeked like dried piss. Shorter than Petrah by a foot, he was muscular, particularly in the neck, like the fighting dogs the Draadi wagered on. Aggren had made fine work of his face, leaving a horrendously crooked, broken nose, the bridge almost a full inch to the left, and dark bruising under the eyes. Aggren might be gone from this world, but Meska would remember him whenever he glanced at his ugly reflection.

Meska licked his lips, thirsty for more blood. "Go on now, thief, strip."

Petrah removed his tunic, trying not to let the slave master see him tremble.

Meska gave it a good shake and looked for evidence among the strands of hay littering the stone floor. Petrah held his breath, waiting for the Draad to rise victoriously with evidence in hand. He didn't.

Instead, he spat on the ground after it became obvious not a crumb was to be found.

Without warning, he punched Petrah in the gut.

Petrah doubled over. Sparks of flame danced across his watering eyes.

"Next time, you won't be so lucky. Next time, I'll gouge out those pretty blue eyes. You'll never see bread again. Now get dressed."

By the time Petrah had his tunic on, Meska was gone and the cell was locked. Petrah slumped against the stone wall. His ribs throbbed.

His cellmate, Kruush, shook his big, round head. "I swear, boy, you're going to get us killed. Have you no wits about you?"

"He didn't find anything, did he?" It hurt Petrah to even speak.

"That's beside the point. What happened to that slave today—"

"His name was Aggren."

"That could have happened to you. It could have happened to *us*. But you weren't thinking, were you?"

Petrah didn't want to acknowledge his theft was foolish beyond words, but Kruush missed the point. The homeless girl on the street was the victim—not him, not Kruush, not the others. Hadn't they seen her eyes when the Draad took the bread away from her—that frantic look of despair, knowing she would go hungry tonight?

All you had to do was toss the bread to her, and you couldn't even get that right.

"Kruush is spot on," Tan said. "What happens to one of us could happen to *all* of us. And what was that bit about trying to step out of the line? If I hadn't stopped you, then what?"

Then I'd be dead too.

But Petrah wouldn't concede and admit fault. Maybe it was the pain, but he spoke his mind. "I won't apologize for what I did. If I had to do it again, I would."

"You're a stubborn runt," Kruush said. His hazel eyes softened. "That said, I saw what you did, even if it was the most foolish thing I'd seen in a long time."

"I'll take that as a thank you," Petrah said. "And yes, it was foolish. Tan, I don't know what I was thinking. That poor girl, though . . ."

Tan's ever-cheerful and often mischievous smile worked its way to the surface like a ray of sunlight. "I saw you snatch the bread. That was gutsy. Well, stupid, actually."

"Stupid for sure," Petrah said. "I wanted to spite Meska and his comrades."

"And you would have too . . . if you'd held on to it. What were you planning on doing with that bread, anyway?"

"I would have shared it with you fine gentlemen, of course." Now it was Petrah's turn to smile.

Tan grinned in return. "See, Kruush? And you were of the mind to give him a thrashing."

Kruush snorted. "More than a thrashing. We're at half rations now, thank you very much. Petrah, I don't care if you've been here longer than Tan or me. I've endured almost two summers in this hellhole, and I can tell you that stealing bread to spite a Draad is a sure way to follow in the path of your dead friend. You're how old, sixteen, seventeen?"

"Fifteen."

"Gods, is that all? You're barely weaned off your mom's tit. I was born in thirty-three forty-eight. That's almost forty years ago. Trust me when I say I know a thing or two."

"More like *one* thing," Tan said with a smirk.

"Was I talking to you?" Kruush frowned. "Listen, Petrah, and listen well. I want my old life back. I was happy being a smuggler and good at it too. I want to live long enough to survive this place, you hear me? I'm a slave today, but tomorrow is a different day."

"You'll still be a slave," Petrah said, returning to his dark mood. "We all will. I'm here because they caught me stealing food. You're here because you got caught selling Korinian religious artifacts. Tan's here because he got caught in bed with the daughter of a general of the Fist Party."

"A very beautiful daughter," Tan said. "But, please, do go on."

"The point is, we're here because we're guilty. It doesn't matter if we think it's unfair. Even Jow-quu agrees."

Their fourth cellmate, Jow-quu, a man of infrequent words, nodded. "It's true."

Petrah went on, "So we best get used to this life, because the only way out of here is the afterlife."

Kruush puckered his brow. "I disagree, but enough bickering." He crunched on a mouthful of nuuma nuts, then pointed at Petrah's untouched cheese. "For a food thief, you're not very good at eating."

"I'm not hungry," Petrah said.

"You're already painfully thin. Or are all of you Northerners like that?"

"Better than being short and stocky like you Ter-jurah," Petrah said.

Kruush wrinkled his nose. "Keep thinking that. Tell him, Tan."

"I don't think he's that different from us," Tan said between bites. "How do you know he's a Northerner, anyway? He could very well be Terjurmehan like us."

"Petrah's different. Look at him. He's taller, thinner, lighter-skinned. We're squat, wide-faced, naturally darker." Petrah had noted the differences many times. Even Tan, who stood a couple of hands above Kruush, was shorter than Petrah. And while he wasn't stocky like Kruush, Tan's face still bore the roundness of the typical Ter-jurahn and had a complexion that was browned, not tanned by the sun like Petrah's.

"His eyes are different too," Tan said. "They're blue."

"Exactly. Who among our people has blue eyes? No one."

Petrah shrugged. "It still doesn't mean I'm from the North."

"Then we'll ask Jow-quu," Tan said. "Jow, do you think Petrah's from the Northern Kingdom?"

Jow-quu struggled to come up with a response. He blinked several times, but his mouth fumbled to form the words. He was perhaps Kruush's age but appeared much older, with a beard that had turned mostly gray, dark troughs under his eyes, and pronounced jowls whose folds looked of worn leather.

"Jow, you don't have to answer," Petrah said. "Right, gentlemen?"

Kruush exhaled. "Right. That damned sprushah we drink every morning will get us all in the end, I swear. Makes you forget things. I say we stop drinking it."

"We can't do that," Tan said. "They watch us. Besides, we couldn't work without it. It gives us energy and kills our hunger."

"And kills our minds too," Kruush said with a scowl. "Jow's been here ten years and look at him. No offense, Jow."

Jow-quu smiled. "It's all right."

"But I'm curious," Kruush said to Petrah. "Why does it affect us and not you?"

Petrah could never understand why sprushah had no effect on him. It was ironic; the memories of the past four years were as sharp as a Draad's blade, but everything before that was as dark as a moonless night. He remembered snippets of his past, or what he thought was his past, mostly through dreams.

Years of glimpsing fragments.

Of a woman he called "Mama," who told him to hide, run, and get away and never be found. No concept of who he was or where he came from.

Except for his age. That he was sure of.

He had a memory in the back of his mind of his mother telling him he'd been born the night of the summer solstice and that he was special because of it.

You are more precious than anyone else to me, she'd said. *And not just because you're my son. You're going to change the world; I know it.*

Her words . . . her voice—they seemed so real.

Had he dreamed them?

They're real to me.

Maybe that was enough.

"I don't know why it doesn't affect me," Petrah said. It was as truthful as any answer.

Kruush held up the last of his nuuma nuts. "It's sad how things just slip from memory. Take pujin. I remember how it tastes, how it smells, but for the life of me, I can't remember the name of my favorite tavern where they serve it. A few more years of being here, and I won't even remember the taste or smell."

Tan poked a fingernail between his teeth. "I've had pujin. It's mouth-watering good, best washed down with a draught of frothy ale. Too bad we'll never see the inside of a tavern again."

Kruush shot him a look. "Says who?"

"Says anyone with common sense."

Kruush glanced over his shoulder, then lowered his voice. "I disagree. We *will* see the inside of a tavern again."

"What are you getting at?"

"You *know* what."

Tan stifled a laugh. "I see the sprushah hasn't killed off your imagination."

Kruush popped the nut into his mouth. "Not at all."

Petrah didn't like this dangerous talk about escape. If the Draadi caught wind of it, Petrah and his cellmates would get strung up and flayed open. Death was the only escape from slavery. But Petrah didn't feel like arguing, not with his ribs growing more tender by the breath.

Jow-quu spoke up after a spell, his kind eyes not matching the troubled expression on his lips. "Petrah?"

"Yeah, Jow?"

"I'm sorry about what that Draad did to you. You didn't deserve it. You're a"—he closed his eyes for a moment and blinked—"a good person."

"So are you. Kruush and Tan as well. We're all family here. We mustn't forget that, even if the sprushah claims everything else, even if we dream up silly notions."

Kruush bobbed his head. "Aye. We're all we've got in this cursed place."

It wasn't long after that the night bells rang and the torches were snuffed, save for the few the Draadi needed for their patrols.

Petrah lay on his cot, careful to not put pressure on his tender ribs. Meska had done quite the job on him, but he would heal in time. There was no telling if the same could be said of Meska's godawful mess of a face.

Aggren fixed you good, you cur. You'll wake up every morning and remember him.

Petrah tried to hold on to the satisfaction, but he kept hearing the whip snap, kept seeing the rivulets of blood, kept thinking about Meska's wicked smile.

Why, Aggren? Why couldn't you have left things alone?

Petrah stared up at the shadowed bedrock. He absently rubbed the scar below his breastbone, once bright pink, now faded with time. He never found out how he'd gotten it, and he supposed he never would. It was a part of him, just like being a slave. His thoughts went from Aggren and his violent end to the girl in the street who'd been denied one good meal.

Our lives are theirs. It's a matter of time before we're all slaughtered.

He had always known this, but after today, it became painfully apparent.

Petrah tried to imagine himself in a field filled with the perfume of freshly harvested wheat and the stars shining above, alone, with only the chirp of cicadas to keep him company.

It didn't work.

All he could think of was the beggar's daughter and the desperation in her eyes.

Don't worry, he promised her. *Tomorrow, I'll steal you an entire loaf.*

Sleep slowly took him, melding wishful thinking into troubled slumber.

Chapter 2

Purgatory

THE PREDAWN COMMOTION OF the Jabah woke Petrah and his cellmates. The Jabah would clean the cells once the slaves left for the day, but for now, they were busy bringing food and water.

Petrah took his turn over the refuse bucket and returned to his cot, awaiting the morning meal. Running a hand through his unwashed, thick brown hair, he gave it a sniff. It smelled exactly as he expected: straw mixed with the odor of the pits. The Draadi permitted the slaves to bathe only once per week. Under the watchful eye of the slave masters, the Jabah would escort the slaves to a stagnant inlet along the Juum River so they could wash themselves in the mosquito-infested water. No matter how many times Petrah dipped his head in the river, he could never get rid of the oily residue on his scalp.

Nor the stink.

Petrah rubbed the sleep from his eyes, his sluggish mind replaying the last dream before he'd awoken.

He recalled hiding in a dark, confined space, listening to water drip. His mother, who was just out of sight, told him in a hushed voice to stay perfectly still. Screams of men and women followed. Even now, sitting on his cot, Petrah's skin prickled down his back and across his arms from the piercing wails and shrieks. A gut-wrenching silence had swallowed the cries in his dream. He'd emerged from his hiding spot and went outside into the cold, blustery air, where ravaged bodies were strewn everywhere.

They'd been butchered and bludgeoned. Their blood had mixed with the mud and frozen puddles of the village while huts burned beneath stormy skies, churning up columns of thick smoke.

Petrah pondered the strange place, the icy wasteland, and the ghastly sight of bodies, but couldn't make any sense of it. He'd only known heat and the furnace that was the sun. Were there such places where one needed to bundle up to stay warm?

In his dream, the sun was but a shadow, hidden by clouds. Metal structures jutted across the hazy skyline like faint ghosts: great buildings and monuments in ruins.

What were these things?

The howl of voices prompted Petrah to run as fast as he could. He slipped on mud as he glanced over his shoulder, catching sight of his pursuers behind him. They gave chase on foot and horseback, dressed in black armor, cloaks snapping in the wind. He never saw their faces, but he heard the frightful laughter of their leader.

It's only a dream. None of it is real, so forget all this nonsense.

It seemed real though.

Petrah flexed his hands and kneaded them brusquely, as if the bone-gnawing chill was still in his fingers.

The grind of stone wheels over the corridor floor caught Petrah's attention. A female Jabahn rolled a metal cart along the hallway. She stopped at each cell, collected the trays from the prior evening, and gave the slaves bowls of gruel—half-servings as promised by the Draadi. The stuff had a coarse texture and bland taste but was hearty.

Kruush was quick to exchange trays with the Jabahn. She took his empty tray, replacing it with one laden with bowls.

"Good morning, Ahleen," he said. "You look as pretty as ever, like the desert dawn." He smiled. Ahleen, upon seeing Petrah and his cellmates watching, blushed.

Petrah knew Ahleen well enough. She was eighteen, three years older than him, kind and caring and a beacon of brilliance in the Denrethi pits. It wasn't just her generous spirit that defined her. She had a slender build, bronzed skin, and a smallish nose frosted with freckles. Her irises were the color of sand at dusk, and she had long, brown hair, braided down the middle of her back. But it was her smile that made her a true gift. Petrah could describe it only as humble.

"You should take your food before it gets cold," she said to Kruush.

"I shall enjoy this feast, now that I know you've blessed it with your touch."

The redness in Ahleen's face deepened. She released her hold on the last bowl, but Kruush took her hand. Startled, she looked up at her smiling suitor.

"Someday, we'll dine freely and watch the sunrise together," Kruush said. "I promise this, just as the sun promises a new day."

Ahleen afforded him a delicate smile. A rosy hue stained her cheeks. "I have to go."

She withdrew her hand and turned to leave but stopped herself. She lowered her voice and spoke to Petrah.

"Petrah, I heard what you did for that girl. That was kind of you. I'm sorry about the half rations. None of you deserve that."

She moved her cart ahead.

Petrah breathed in her compliment as if it were upon a draft of fresh air. He smiled at his cellmates. "See that? The Jabah heard of my kindness." He had no idea his reckless act had reached so many ears. He'd been down on himself for risking his life and the life of the starving girl on the street. In the end, the girl was no better off. But if his deed inspired Jabah like Ahleen, maybe it wasn't fruitless.

Kruush took the stack of bowls to the center of the cell and placed them on the ground. "Gentlemen," he announced, "breakfast is served." He flashed Petrah an annoyed look. "What little there is of it."

The slaves used their hands to scoop up the thick mush. Petrah's stomach soured at the thought of food, haunted by his dream, but more so by the memory of seeing Aggren's body dragged across the ground, entrails and blood in his wake. Still, Petrah ate his share.

"Ahleen likes you," Tan said to Kruush. "Not a bad thing, considering the lovely life we lead."

Kruush licked the gruel from his fingers. "I hope she does. She's like sunshine in these hellish pits. I tell you, boys, if we ever get out of here, I'm going to take her with me and marry her."

Tan smiled somberly. "If . . ."

THE SLAVES LINED UP for their daily dose of sprushah in the early morning. A Draad watched over a Jabahn who ladled the bitter tea from a bucket, making sure each slave drank their allotment and not one drop less. Once the slaves finished, the Draadi led their respective groups to the day's work.

"Work" wasn't the way Petrah would have phrased it. It was sunup to sundown of back-breaking labor under the blistering summer sun, with the constant threat of the whip, on top of heat exhaustion.

And that was on a good day. If any of the slave masters were in a vindictive mood . . .

The Draadi escorted the slaves to a massive quarry dug fifty feet into the ground in a section of the city reserved solely for slave labor. It was one of several public works sites of its kind. The walls were sheer, with only two ways in or out: a staircase hewn into the side or a pulley-operated hoist platform constructed of wooden planks and scaffolding.

They used the hoist mostly for lifting and lowering supplies and finished products.

Petrah knew from Antelle's teachings that Kanmar was the largest of the three cities of Terjurmeh, as well as a trading port on the Juum River, which connected Kanmar to the city of Fangmordah, and merged with the South Kesel River, where the capital of Elmar lay. Kanmar was also the center of the desert nation's slave trade. There certainly was no shortage of slaves.

Antelle had been a good teacher, an older man like Jow-quu, who helped Petrah learn Jurmehan, the common tongue of the world. Petrah missed his kind eyes, steady voice, and warm smile. Antelle had often spoken of his son and how he wished he could see him again, if only for a moment. Did his son feel the same?

If Petrah had the opportunity to meet his father, he would gladly do so. But he didn't know who his father was, whether he was still with Petrah's mother, if he was anywhere in or near Kanmar, or if he was even alive. His father never appeared in Petrah's dreams. That didn't stop Petrah from wondering what kind of man his father might be, what he sounded like, and if he had blue eyes like Petrah.

In Petrah's imagination, his father was an older man who didn't speak much but nodded his encouragement and smiled with bright eyes the shade of the afternoon sky. A man who spoke softly and was as wise as Antelle and who would teach Petrah to be good and humble and honorable, like him. A man who loved his son beyond words, who would do anything to seek him out, and who would make Petrah proud to say, "You're my Papa."

Petrah feared his father was nothing like Antelle—perhaps the very opposite—but he wouldn't allow himself to think anything less of his father. Not today.

The light of day was barely visible, and the shadows were still long, blending the sand-colored stone and ground together into a fusion of murky colors.

The head Draad led the column of slaves down the stairs.

Stations made of waist-high granite blocks dotted the site floor, providing workers with workbenches for their projects, whether they were working leather for saddles or pounding out iron hoops for barrels. Dug into the side of the rock face on the west wall was a recessed area for the smithy and forge where over four hundred slaves toiled in the smoky heat, slaves from pits all over the city, fashioning an assortment of metal products.

"Look who's here," Kruush whispered to Petrah as they descended the steps.

Petrah saw a figure standing on the hoist platform. It was hard to make out any details, but the man's crooked posture made his identity unmistakable.

Garesh, the head Jabahn.

"What's *he* doing here?" Petrah whispered back.

Kruush shrugged.

Whatever reason Garesh was here wasn't good. He acted like a Draad, although he was only a Jabahn; and everyone hated him for it. As the liaison to the Draadi, he handled the higher-ranking slaves. His presence here was highly unusual.

Kruush and his cellmates walked to their stations in the middle of the quarry floor so they could get to work. Like the other stations, there was no overhead protection. By the time the afternoon rolled around, the sun would become unbearable.

Garesh raised his fists into the air. Whatever commotion or murmuring going on below ceased.

"Good morning, rats," he began. "I hope you had a good night's rest because you'll need it." His words were met by sprushah-induced, blank stares.

"There's a change of plans today. I want you mongrels to be on your best behavior, and I mean your *best behavior*. By the grace of San, you're going to witness unprecedented greatness in your miserable lives. Today we are entertaining two visitors of eminent importance, the Dark Arrow and the First Articulate of the Temple."

Petrah groaned. A visitation like this meant a stressful day for him and his cellmates.

"No one better screw up, or you'll end up like that insolent runt yesterday, so help me. And if the Dark Arrow gets offended, there's no telling whether you'll be breathing tomorrow. Now, here's what's going to happen . . ."

Garesh explained the day's events, everything from the announcement and formal entrance of the official party to the way the slaves would perform their duties in the company of greatness. "Get to work!"

The slaves went about their business. Kruush huffed and muttered something offensive, and Tan chuckled as he grabbed a belt he was making.

Petrah double-checked the dyed markings on a strip of marsh reed. The sky had lightened well enough for him to see the details. When he looked up at Jow-quu, he noticed his cellmate staring aimlessly past him. Jow-quu's left arm trembled as it often did when he had trouble focusing, which had become a frequent occurrence as of late. Today wasn't the day for getting caught standing idle.

"Jow." Petrah waited for a response, then reached over and tugged on his sleeve. "Jow?"

Jow-quu turned slowly to him with deadpan eyes. He flinched when he saw Petrah's hand.

"Easy," Petrah said.

"Sorry. I was just thinking about something, although I can't remember what it was."

"It's all right. Listen, I need you to pay attention today. It's very important. Can you do that for me?"

Jow-quu's eyes wandered as if he was losing his focus again, but then he said, "I'll do my best."

Petrah needed Jow-quu's very best. At least his cellmate's arm had stopped shaking. "Good. Now give me a hand with these shields."

AFTER THE MIDDAY MEAL break, the quarry started to heat up. The sun was at its zenith and there wasn't a cloud in the sky to block the dreadful rays.

Petrah and Jow-quu attached forearm straps to their shields. They finished their first shield when the slaver's gong sounded.

Everyone put down their tools and supplies.

A hush followed.

All around, the slaves remained fidgety.

Petrah could relate to the nervousness, as he had a difficult time keeping his hands from moving. The Draadi were on edge as well. A visit like this was rare, and the slave masters expected everyone to perform their duties without fault. Not even the Draadi were exempt from harsh punishment for making the slightest mistake.

A Draad appeared atop the west wall, and all eyes redirected.

Petrah recognized him as Zen, Draadlord, and the top of the Draad chain of command, his stature noted by the additional gold sash over his chest. He addressed the onlookers in a clear and powerful voice.

"Attention in the land. Citizens and slaves of Kanmar, prepare to receive your honored guests. Today, His Greatness, Manis-cor, Dark Arrow and City Protectorate, and His Holiness, Septamo, First Articulate from the Shrine of San, are in attendance of the slave works of Kanmar. May San bless their presence." The Draad pressed fist to chest in a ceremonial sign of departure and backed away.

Twelve soldiers with square-shaped, red linen headdresses formed a line along the edge of the west wall, placing the butts of their spears on the ground and holding them perfectly upright.

Petrah had never seen the likes of them before.

Two of the soldiers parted, and a man stepped between them. It was Manis-cor, wearing his infamous black soldier's uniform of a muscle cuirass and greaves, black tunic and belt with a short sword, and ceremonial cape. The cuirass was stamped with his party's crest of twin black arrows crossed with their barbed arrowheads pointing toward either shoulder.

When he walked onto the hoist platform, an unnatural quiet fell over the crowd.

Manis-cor was tall for a Ter-jurahn, even taller than Tan, but seemed far too young for someone of his position, early twenties by Petrah's estimate. Petrah had seen him only once before, which was plenty. There were many rumors flying about regarding the Dark Arrow's sadistic ways.

An older man appeared between the gap of soldiers atop the west wall.

In unison, everyone dropped their heads in reverence.

Petrah had no doubt this was Septamo, First Articulate of the Temple. He saw the large, triangular-shaped device suspended from the Articulate's neck just before dipping his chin. Only priests wore the holy serak. If the saying, *the bigger the serak, the mightier the priest* was true, Septamo was one of the mightiest. The man wielded more power than even the

Dark Arrow. To be in his presence was to be in the presence of San—the presence of the God of Shadows.

Antelle had taught Petrah about the hierarchy in the Terjurmehan Temple. There were five Articulates, each numbered by the order of their promotion. That meant Septamo had been in his position the longest. It also meant he was next in line to the Mighty One, the head of the Temple.

Septamo stepped down onto the hoist platform, trailed by three attendants who kept the hem of his crimson robe from touching the ground. Zen, Garesh, and a couple of senior Draadi joined the official party on the platform.

When the platform reached the bottom, the Draadlord Zen issued a command, and the entire assembly of slaves and Draadi dropped and prostrated, forehead to ground, as was customary in front of a high-ranking priest.

Petrah glimpsed Manis-cor step off the hoist platform and wait for Septamo to join him.

"Holy One," Manis-cor said, "you honor us with your presence. I present to you the finest slave works in all of Kanmar."

The Articulate gestured to the crowd. "Manis, I came here to see your works in operation, not at a standstill. Is everyone going to stay put?"

"Of course not. Zen, get these slaves to work."

"Back to work!" the Draadlord shouted. "Draadi, take to your stations."

Kruush handed Tan a pair of tongs. "It's about time we got going. My neck was getting stiff."

"No talking," said a Draad standing nearby.

Across the quarry, the Dark Arrow's party disappeared into the smithy.

Jow-quu, who wasn't faring well, concerned Petrah. His face was sallow, his breathing raspy, and he was shaking again.

Petrah chided him in a loud whisper. "Stop moving!"

Jow-quu continued to shake. Being stern wouldn't help.

Petrah gently placed his hands over Jow-quu's, steadying them. "Like that," he said. Jow-quu stopped trembling. "Now we're going to keep working on this shield. You hold it by its edges while I work on the strap, all right?"

A sharp snap rent the air.

Several stations down from Petrah and his cellmates, a Draad whipped a slave for some kind of misfortune. The official party continued to the next station without regard to the incident.

Petrah's throat went dry as they made their way to where he and his partner were working. Jow-quu was having trouble keeping a steady grip on their shield.

The panicky feeling in Petrah's gut grew stronger.

Before he knew it, the regal procession was upon them. He dared not look up as Manis-cor remarked about the shield-making process.

Don't let them get to you. They'll move on, and then they'll be gone.

Petrah's distracted thinking caused him to blunder.

Jow-quu somehow moved the shield off-center, and Petrah's hammer blow caught the edge. The shield flipped and landed noisily on the ground.

Petrah reached down.

Before he could grab the shield, something hard and cold slapped his shoulder. He glanced sidewise and saw the flat of a sword blade.

"Let your dog pick it up," Manis-cor instructed him.

The Dark Arrow lifted his sword, and Petrah rose slowly. Jow-quu, however, stayed where he was.

Come on, Jow, Petrah wanted to shout.

He gestured to his partner with a hand, but that earned him a kick to the back of the knee. Petrah barely caught his fall.

Manis-cor grabbed his shoulder and spoke into his ear. "Did I tell you to motion to your dog?" The wetness of the man's vile breath sent a shiver down his neck. "Tell your dog to pick up the shield."

Petrah told Jow-quu, but his partner didn't respond. "Pick it up," Petrah insisted. "Come on, Jow."

His oppressor's voice filled his ear again. "If your dog doesn't move right now, I will strike him down. He's embarrassing me in front of His Holiness. Do you understand?"

"Jow-quu! Come on, man, snap out of it." Petrah wanted to reach over and shake him. "Jow, for San's sake—"

The Dark Arrow cuffed Petrah across the head. "Shut up!" He then walked over to Jow-quu and signaled to a couple of Draadi. "Bring him to his knees."

Petrah watched helplessly as they forced his partner down.

Manis-cor pressed his boot against Jow-quu's neck and pushed his head to the ground. The Dark Arrow's sword came about. He backed off and lifted it overhead. In a second, the older slave would be dead.

But as the Dark Arrow tensed for release, Petrah blurted, "No!"

Manis-cor's swing wavered. His eyes registered disbelief. "*No?*"

In the only manner of apology he could conceive, Petrah dropped to one knee and placed his hands together.

"Forgive me, Your Greatness. I wished only to save his life." It was a waste of effort. Instead of one head, the Dark Arrow was about to have two. Didn't Aggren's death teach him anything?

Petrah's face flushed. Numbness crawled down his spine.

A voice of condemnation shouted in his mind. *Serves you right for interfering!*

Manis-cor pointed his sword at him. "Are you a free man now? Did I miss your release from bondage? No? I didn't think so. I shall not suffer the defiance of a slave. On your face!"

It was the command that executioners gave before they beheaded their prisoners.

Petrah dropped his other knee and lowered his forehead to the ground.

The heat of the sun beat down on the back of his neck. It would be the last thing he felt before his spinal column was severed.

The Dark Arrow angled his sword again.

This time, the First Articulate interrupted him.

"Wait."

Petrah's heart pounded in his chest as Septamo addressed the Dark Arrow.

"Back away, Manis. I wish to have a closer look at this one."

"Holy One?"

"I said I will have a closer look."

"But he offended you and defiled himself—"

"Manis, stop blathering! Back away so I can inspect the slave. I want to see his face before you lop it off." Petrah heard the Dark Arrow shuffle backward, and Septamo addressed him. "Sit up."

Petrah sat back on his haunches but stared down. Dust and grime caked his nose and forehead.

"Lift your head and wipe your face."

Petrah did as told. As forewarned by Garesh's morning speech, he kept his eyes averted. It was a capital crime for a slave to make eye contact with a clergyman.

Not that it mattered now.

"You're a strange-looking slave," the Articulate said. "I will give you permission to speak. Where are you from?"

"My lord?"

"Address me as *Holy One*, not '*my lord*.' I'm not a commoner. Now, tell me, where are you from?"

"I don't know, Holy One," Petrah said. It was the truth. "I can't remember. They say I'm from the North."

Septamo turned to Manis-cor. "He can't remember?"

"The city slaves drink sprushah, Holy One. It affects their minds on many levels."

"I see. He has a strange accent. Where do you suppose he's from?"

"From the North, as he claims," Manis-cor said. "His face is shaped like those of the Prallites, and he's tall and lean like them."

"Interesting. But his eyes—they're most unusual, wouldn't you say? They're blue."

Petrah couldn't help but glance up at that moment.

"You dare look upon me, slave?"

Petrah tried to turn away, but Septamo snapped his fingers, bringing Petrah's gaze back to his.

The skin on the Articulate's face was smooth, not weather-beaten like those around him, and his deep brown eyes bore the curiosity of a child examining a desert beetle digging into the sand, but they held the threat of a scorpion about to strike.

"It's too late now," Septamo said. "Once you've done it, you can't take it back. A transgression of this magnitude could earn a slave's death." The Articulate smiled, but it wasn't a friendly one. "You have eyes that remind me of the brightest blue topaz. I've never seen such a thing. Not in all my years and all my travels. Have you, Manis?"

"No, Holy One, not in my lifetime."

"It's a curious aberration, I must admit." Septamo turned his attention back to Petrah. "So, slave, you can't remember where you're from?"

"No, Holy One."

"Let's pretend you're from the North, as the Dark Arrow suggests. There are rich forestlands in the Northern Kingdom. Yet I've heard your king insists on using stone instead of wood to build his castles and keeps. What do you make of that?"

"I don't know, Holy One."

"I should like to find out if the rumor is true. It's been something my brethren and I have speculated on for some time. Shall I visit this country of yours and put the conjecture to bed?"

Petrah felt enormous pressure to answer correctly. "Yes, Holy One. I would visit if I were you."

"If *he were I*?" Septamo laughed heartily. "A slave advises the holy. How clever."

"How dare you!" Manis-cor tightened the grip on his sword and stepped closer.

Septamo raised a hand. "Manis, don't be such a thorn. I'm receiving a personal lesson in slave etiquette."

Septamo's demeanor became utterly serious.

He turned to Garesh. "The Temple requires these slaves to be put to death for offending a member of my station. What shall I do with them, Jabahn? Shall I have them put to death? Or shall I put *you* to death for not training your dogs?"

Garesh's face paled.

"Don't worry, Jabahn. Today is not your day to die. But tomorrow is a different day." To Manis-cor, Septamo said, "Do as you wish with these slaves. Only I ask you keep them intact. I may come back to visit this feisty one and learn more about his country . . . if he can remember. I want him alive. Understood?"

"As you wish, Holy One," Manis-cor said.

"Good. I have a desire to quit this place and find refreshment. The heat bothers me. Let us away."

The procession started off but not before Zen placed a firm hand on Garesh's shoulder. "I suggest you clean up your mess. Am I clear?"

The Jabahn nodded.

"Good. Carry on." Zen followed the official party.

Garesh called the closest Draad over. It was Meska, with his swollen nose and dark circles under his eyes. "Take the old one back to his cell. As for him"—he pointed at Petrah, who was still on his knees—"flog him until he passes out. Just make sure you don't kill him."

Meska smiled at Petrah. "Don't worry. We'll take real good care of this one."

Chapter 3

Plotting

I F PAIN WAS A sensation meant for the living, what was the equivalent for the dead?

Petrah dwelled on this as he hung naked facing a stone wall, his arms chained to large rings, manacles firmly clamped over swollen wrists, and feet drooped behind him. Although he couldn't find the strength to lift his head, he knew he was alone in this godforsaken place.

Surely, he was dead. His body was numb. There was no smell to speak of. Perhaps this was the afterlife.

An appropriate ending. I'm dead, and this is a dream.

Petrah winced as a stab of pain radiated up his back. Then the odor of dried blood hit him.

He wasn't quite dead yet.

Aggren had it easy. His end was final. But Petrah's?

This isn't a dream. It's a nightmare.

The memory of his flogging returned to him.

Before Petrah could think it through, he heard grating metal. Somewhere behind him, a door opened. It struck the wall with a hollow clang followed by the familiar shuffle of feet.

Two pairs of Draadi sandals.

"I bet he's still alive," one of them said.

"Let's see," said the other. It was Meska. Petrah cried out as a heel pressed into his back and pushed him forward. "He's alive."

Pain overwhelmed Petrah's senses. This wasn't the afterlife he had hoped for.

The men went to either side of his slumped body and unlocked the manacles. Petrah dropped to the cold floor.

Meska nudged him with a foot. "Get up."

"I think he's done for," the other said.

"He's just playing. Aren't you?" Meska kicked Petrah hard in the hip, but Petrah was too injured to do anything but let out a muffled cry. "Come on. We'll have to drag him."

"By San's ass, they don't pay me enough for this."

"Stop complaining and help me."

The Draadi grabbed the young slave by the wrists and dragged his limp body out of the chamber.

P ETRAH LAY FACE DOWN in his cell. He couldn't move. Everything was a haze.

He was flopped over his cot as they had left him: naked and filthy, arms and legs splayed. He tasted salt, but the flavor of iron was there too.

Blood.

A rat scurrying along the wall came up to his left hand, sniffed, and continued on. It obviously cared nothing for this broken thing of flesh and bone.

Minutes later, the cell door squealed open.

Someone padded over to where he was. The cell grew brighter.

Had Meska returned to finish him? It didn't smell like Meska. In fact, the smell was pleasant, like the desert air just after the sun climbed above the horizon.

A gentle hand lifted his chin. Petrah opened his eyes to see the slender shape of a woman standing over him.

"Ahleen," he said weakly.

She set down her oil lamp. "You must drink." Ahleen positioned the mouthpiece of a waterskin to his lips. "Open up and I'll squeeze."

The water was fresh and invigorating—not the nasty, oily stuff Petrah was accustomed to. His head cleared.

"That was good," he said. "Thank you."

Ahleen examined his wounds. "I'll be right back."

She returned, carrying a basket of supplies and a basin of water. She draped a loincloth over his backside. "I'm going to wash you. This has brine in it, so it might sting, but it will help disinfect. Just relax." She dipped a washcloth in the water and wrung it out. The water dripped in a melody of plunks. "Try not to move."

Ahleen hummed as she sponged his wounds with gentle finesse. The Draadi would have let him rot. This was a mighty gift.

"How does it look?" Petrah asked, biting down as the salty water burned his lacerations.

"I've seen worse. The cuts are bad, but not so deep that we need stitches." She continued to clean him with the gentlest touch.

Ahleen was new compared to other Jabah, having tended the pits for perhaps six months. Petrah spoke to her only during the tray exchange in the mornings or on the way to the river to bathe, as the Draadi forbade the slaves from conversing openly with the Jabah.

Today was an exception because the slave masters allowed the Jabah to care for slaves that had succumbed to injury or illness.

Whenever Ahleen came around, she was always kind to him and his fellow cellmates. Most Jabah were fair with the slaves, many having once worn the red, others born into their position. Petrah knew nothing of Ahleen's past, but he was certain of one thing: she was a jewel in the rough. Petrah could see why Kruush was smitten by her.

"Ahleen, may I ask you a question?"

She dipped the washcloth again and squeezed out the excess water. He liked the sound it made. "Sure."

"Before you were a Jabahn, were you, you know . . . ?"

"Free?"

"Yes."

"I've served since I was seven. I was a house slave before this. Then my mistress sold me to the city. She and my master ran up debts, so they could no longer afford a household full of slaves. Before that, I was with my father, but he was a thief, and he got caught. He bargained for his life. I was the price for his freedom."

"I'm sorry."

Ahleen ran her washcloth in slow, tender circles over his back. "I'm not ashamed, Petrah. You and I are both the property of others. That doesn't make us any less than those who crack the whip. It's just the path we're on. But I do dream of freedom sometimes."

Kruush had mentioned it too. Petrah didn't believe it was possible. Did Ahleen? "If you were free," he said, trying to imagine it was more than words, "what would you do?"

She paused, her washcloth resting on his shoulder blade. "What would I do? I would walk through Kanmar without concern. I'd stand in the streets well after sunset. I'd sing and dance and stay out all night and not worry about the Draadi looking for me. It would be a different life, Petrah. It would be . . . wonderful."

Petrah sometimes glimpsed himself standing on the road, watching the slaves march to the pits. He'd shake his head in pity, then breathe in the glorious nighttime air without fear of being beaten or denied rations.

But those thoughts would disappear the moment he realized where he was—stuck in his corner of servitude, a slave destined to live out his days fettered to his masters' will.

"You have a good imagination," he said. "It's far better than mine."

"My body and spirit long for more than imagining life outside these walls."

I long to be left alone and not whipped. Perhaps the two aren't so different. "One day, you'll have it. I've heard of Jabah being released from service. It's rare, but it's possible."

"Now who has the better imagination?" She chuckled. "You've been here a long time, four years. The sprushah ruins the mind, but you don't seem affected like the others. Do you suppose it's your Prallite blood?" She soaked her washcloth.

"If that's what I am." He hadn't intended to share the ignorance of his lineage, but he felt he could talk to Ahleen about anything. She listened, she cared, and that meant a lot to him. "Before my time here, I have no memory of who I was. It's blank in my mind. My earliest memory is from four years ago. I woke up in a field with no clothes, no belongings, not even a name. I don't remember how I got there or where I'm from."

"You remember nothing?" She dabbed his lower back. He flinched when she pressed into the inflamed wound.

Petrah had a faded semicircular scar above his right eyebrow, another reminder of an early life he couldn't recall. "Only my age. Strange, isn't it?"

She didn't say so, but it *was* strange. How could he know nothing else about himself? He winced again.

"Sorry."

"Don't be sorry. I deserve this."

"No, you don't. You saved Jow-quu's life. You deserve none of this." Before he could object, she asked, "Do you remember anything at all from your childhood?"

"I catch pieces of memories sometimes through my dreams. I hear my mother's voice, but I can't see her face. She seems so distant, like she never existed. But her voice is clear. Even now, I can hear her calling out to me."

"What does she say?"

"Sometimes she tells me to hide, other times to run as far away as possible and never come back. Nothing pleasant and nothing I care to remember."

"Petrah, that's terrible!"

"I think she was trying to protect me from someone."

"Your father?"

"Possibly, although he's never appeared in my dreams. I always imagined he died when I was young. Maybe he died in an accident or from poor health or something worse. Or maybe he's alive and well and nowhere to be found. I doubt I'll ever know."

Ahleen placed a light hand on Petrah's upper arm. "Perhaps it's better not knowing."

"Perhaps."

Ahleen dried his back with a towel. "I have some healing salve for your wounds. It'll keep you from getting infected." She opened a small jar and scooped out salve with her fingers. Petrah smelled jasmine and mint. It reminded him of the one time he'd worked the fields outside the city.

"Why are you doing this?" Petrah asked.

"If you were in my place, wouldn't you do the same?"

No one had ever asked him that. "Ahleen, I've known little kindness in my life, but today . . ."

"Today, it's your turn. Tomorrow, it could be mine. The other day, it was the girl you tried to help. You know kindness, Petrah."

I know how to cause trouble.

Petrah had failed the girl and her father. He'd cost Aggren his life and his fellow slaves half their rations. How was there kindness in those actions? He had promised to get the girl more bread to make up for his blunder.

But now, in this condition . . .

Ahleen spread a small line of salve along the lower part of his back. His skin tingled. "The Con-jurah say, 'Give to those as you would receive.' If I believe nothing else, Petrah, I believe that."

"The Con-jurah say that?"

"They're a good people, even if they don't believe in our god."

"I've never met a Con-jurahn. Meerjurmeh's across the desert, and the Ter-jurah hate them to their core. I heard their country is beautiful though."

Petrah tried to picture Meerjurmeh and its vast desert and colorful cities. The Con-jurah were age-old enemies of the Ter-jurah, split along religious lines. The Con-jurah believed in Jah, the God of Light, and the Ter-jurah believed in San, the God of Shadows. They both believed the gods started out as brothers, each nation professing their deity as the one, true god, the other as an unworthy impostor. Antelle had spoken of great battles between the peoples of both countries over their religious differences. The threat of war was ever present; and just as a Terjurmehan could rely on the sun rising each day, so could they rely on the fact that blood would be spilled over divisions of faith.

Ahleen finished daubing his back. The salve produced a warm, soothing feeling that numbed some of the pain. "Your wounds need to absorb the salve a little more before I can dress them. You have dried blood on your legs. Let me wash it off." Ahleen wrung out her washcloth.

"Ahleen, if you could have anything besides your freedom, what would it be?"

She washed the back of his left thigh. "To love and be loved in return. I can't imagine anything sweeter in the world than two people falling madly in love. Maybe I'm a dreamer or an opportunist at heart. Still, I think that would be enough to fill my life with what I need. Of course, I would love to have children. Lots and lots of children. What about you, Petrah? What do you desire above all?"

It wasn't freedom. That was a dream for fools.

"To not be treated like an animal or die under the snap of the whip," he said. "But I prefer your answer better. After all, what purpose does life serve if you live it halfway? You should have someone to share the quiet moments with. I want to be made whole, not die a half man."

"It will happen, Petrah. You're a good soul, with much to give. As long as your heart is open, you will find someone."

"That's the thing. I feel as if my heart is closed. Maybe it's this place, or maybe I'm just made that way." Petrah sighed. "Perhaps I'm a lost cause. Does that mean there's something wrong with me?"

"Of course not. It means you're hurt, and the only way to keep the hurt from getting worse is to shut it out, along with any feelings that might get trampled in the process. Don't give up, Petrah. You're not a lost cause. Love has a funny way of showing up when you least expect it. Trust me, I know."

Petrah mulled over her words as she cleaned the backs of his calves and feet. Her talk inspired a modicum of hope—hope that he could find peace with his life and draw out the sweetness and know contentment.

The Jabah love and marry. They find happiness and bear children. There is a way if you truly want it.

For now, all Petrah wanted was for the pain to recede.

Ahleen applied strips of fiber soaked with honey and animal fat. It smelled sugary, like clover.

On the second dressing, she giggled.

"What's so funny?"

"I was just thinking about Kruush. About a week ago, he cut his foot, and"—she subdued a laugh—"he cried like a baby when I bandaged him."

Petrah pictured the big oaf acting tough around the men and whimpering in front of her. "That figures. I always knew he was soft."

She applied another dressing. Then she bent forward and gave Petrah a peck on the cheek.

"What's that for?"

"For being a good patient. And for letting me pry. And for being a good friend to Kruush."

"You *do* like him."

She washed her hands. "Do I?"

"If that's not obvious, I don't know what is."

"Yes, I do like him, but . . ." she trailed off, dropping her gaze to the ground.

"I know. Such a thing is forbidden. They keep us ordinary slaves apart from you Jabah for a reason."

"A silly reason, but the law is clear."

"But if Kruush were to become a Jabahn . . ."

Ahleen smiled. "If it's San's will, then it'll happen. Now let me finish before they wonder about me."

T HE DIN OF SLAVES returning from the day's work disrupted the calm of the pits.

Petrah could hear the Draadi shouting in the halls and the sounds of cells opening. The potent odor of jasmine masked the stink of the slaves arriving home after another day of toiling in the sun.

The element leader marched past Petrah's cell, followed by the most miserable lot he had ever seen. It was the first time Petrah saw them from this perspective.

The slaves shuffled by, stiff-legged or limping, dirty and barefoot, wearing soiled and tattered tunics or just loincloths. Broken men and women, the dead among the living.

The door to Petrah's cell opened, and his cellmates entered.

Tan dropped by his side. "Thank the gods you're alive!"

"I'm not as easy to kill as the Draadi would like." Petrah then noticed Jow-quu. He had swollen cheeks, and his left eye was nearly swelled shut. "Jow?"

Jow-quu waved and sat as if nothing had happened.

"He's been with us," Kruush said. "Those bastards beat him brutally. Praise San, they broke nothing."

"And he's been working?" Petrah asked.

"Aye. Those sick dogs have no mercy. Come, let's see if we can get you dressed. Tan, give me a hand."

P ETRAH STRUGGLED THROUGH SUPPER, but between Kruush holding him upright and Tan feeding him, he finished. Bits of nuuma nut stuck to his teeth. The soft crumbles of cheese were his only comfort, their saltiness and strong aroma a welcome reprieve from his predicament.

Afterward, Kruush and Tan sat at the end of their cots and whispered to each other.

Petrah watched curiously, wondering what they were talking about. After a while, Kruush waved him over. Petrah slid along the edge of his cot, mindful of his soreness, and leaned forward.

"Listen up, young fella," Kruush said quietly. "Tan and I were having an important discussion. We want you to pay attention." Kruush glanced at the cell door before continuing. "You see what's going on around here. Who knows how long any of us will last? After what happened to Aggren, then you . . .

"The bottom line is, as soon as you're better, we're going to escape."

Petrah resisted laughing at the outlandish notion. "That's as ridiculous as the first time you suggested it. This is our lot in life. What happened to me was unfortunate and completely my doing."

"And Aggren?"

Petrah's face wilted. It took him everything to not curse Meska's name.

"Exactly my meaning," Kruush said. "There are two ways out of this life: stay here and die a slave, or leave and die a free man."

"You're talking about the impossible. No one leaves here, not alive. I thought you were jesting the other day."

"I wasn't jesting."

"Nor is it impossible," Tan added. "When the Draadi attend Temple service in the evening on San's Day, who's left to work the pits? A skeleton crew, right? That's when we escape. By the time anyone realizes it, we'll be long gone."

Petrah wanted to tell Tan and Kruush they'd both drank too much sprushah to think rationally. "But we're locked in these cages. Who has ever escaped? No, let me ask it this way: who has attempted to escape and made it or even survived?"

"That's beside the point," Tan said, ruffling his face.

"Is it?"

Kruush rubbed his hands together. "The Draadi think this place is a fortress. But a fortress always has a door . . . and a way out. Ahleen and two other Jabah, Raya and Hamed, are going to help us. My little darling located a secret passageway in the tunnels that leads directly to the marshes next to the Juum. The Draadi don't know about it, or perhaps they forgot about it, or maybe they think it's out of reach for the likes of us.

"Hamed will keep a lookout, Ahleen will guide us out, and Raya will meet us with a raft. Once we're on the raft, we're free."

The idea had merit, but it seemed too fantastic to Petrah to be attainable.

What would it be like to smell the open fields under the stars, to walk anywhere he wanted without the chance of being whipped, to wake up and sleep at will?

"How do we get past the handful of Draadi? Having a lookout won't cut it if the Draadi are still around."

"We haven't figured out all the details yet," Kruush said, frowning, "but we're working on it."

"That's what I thought." Petrah kept circling back in his mind to Aggren and how his fate might become theirs. With Meska, it would be only a matter of time before he did something to Petrah when no one was looking. "And Jow knows?"

Kruush flicked his wrist. "Don't worry about Jow. He'll follow us when the time comes."

"Which is . . . ?"

"Seeing you're a fine mess," Kruush said, "I'd say we need at least a week." The way Petrah's back felt, it would probably be closer to a month before he was well enough to do anything, *if* he did anything. "So, what do you say, laddie, are you with us?"

To be caught was to be killed.

Not only that, they would be executed in a public display that made Aggren's evisceration seem merciful. Petrah had seen it years ago, when a sorry pair of slaves thought themselves clever by killing a Draad and making a run for it. They had died slowly and painfully, the word *exaltu—traitor* in Old Jurmehan—carved into their foreheads as they were strung up as a monument for their fellow slaves to see on the march to and from the Denrethi pits, until they withered under the sun and the crows picked out their eyes.

Petrah adjusted in his seat, trying to find respite from the dozens of pinpricks that bit into his skin. The soreness was really settling in, making every movement painful and each adjustment a reminder that sleep would not be kind to him. There was only one answer he could think of to Kruush's question, an answer he hoped he wouldn't regret once the pain let up. "I'm in."

Kruush patted him on the knee. "Excellent. Try not to get into any trouble between now and then, all right?"

Petrah smirked. "Who, me?"

Chapter 4

Escape

THE WEEK PASSED AT an excruciatingly slow pace, but Petrah felt less pain each day. Ahleen continued to care for him while he convalesced in his cell, a bright spot to his otherwise dreary day.

But the longer he stayed put, the more jittery, irritated, and anxious he got. Was it the isolation? The lack of movement? The interminable quiet during the day?

Petrah smacked his lips. They were dry, and the water he drank couldn't quench his thirst.

"It's sprushah cravings," Ahleen said. "If you stay away from that dreadful stuff long enough, the cravings will go away."

Petrah had heard of the cravings but didn't know anyone who'd experienced it. He pulled his knees up to his chest and wrapped his arms around them to keep from shaking. "How long does it last?"

"A week."

"That long?" A few mouthfuls were all he needed. "Do you think you can get me some, a ladleful perhaps? I promise I'll sip on it and make it last."

"I'm sorry, Petrah, I can't. The Draadi watch over the supply."

Petrah didn't want to trouble Ahleen any more than he had. He tongued the inside of his cheek and found it dry. If it came down to it, could he wean himself off sprushah for good? Could his friends? "That's all right, I'll endure."

Ahleen gave him a smile that lifted his spirits. "I'll check on you later."

Petrah took his mind off his shakes that evening by watching Kruush flirt with Ahleen. He enjoyed their banter, their laughter, and their growing affection for each other. Tan added his own quips, and even Jow-quu laughed. The levity eased Petrah's dark mood.

But as the week progressed, an underlying tone of seriousness hung over them. It drew furtive glances among themselves whenever they spoke in secret, especially when they plotted their escape. At least their plan was coming together.

On the evening of San's Day, when most of the Draadi would be relieved of their post and at Temple for the night, Hamed would distract the few remaining Draadi on shift by setting fire to a storeroom full of hay bales outside the pits' main entrance and then calling for help. With the Draadi preoccupied by the fire, the pits would be deserted.

That would be Ahleen's signal.

Once they were out, they would head north, then west through the pits, eventually passing through an unpopulated section of the underground labyrinth. Ahleen said there was an entire area on the northwest side that contained a natural tunnel system. There wasn't any reason for the slave masters to wander there, which meant the chance of running into a Draad was greatly reduced.

After they met up with Raya, Raya would take them by raft along the bank of the Juum, help them disguise their appearances, and follow the river to the harbor. That would give them a significant lead over any Draadi searching the pits and the surrounding area. It would also give them options. Catching a ship to the nearest port of Fangmordah was the best option, but being on the run and coinless presented significant challenges. Of course, the biggest challenge was escaping the pits.

"We'll have to move quickly," Ahleen said. "The speedier our departure, the better our chances."

Kruush grinned. "Don't you worry about us. We'll be ready."

Tan bobbed his head and Jow-quu blinked in silent agreement, but Petrah questioned their readiness. "How can you be sure Raya will be waiting for us? What if he's not there? What if he can't make it?"

Kruush lost his grin, but Ahleen was steadfast when she looked Petrah in the eye and said, "He'll be there. He's dependable. So is Hamed."

Petrah was not convinced. While he shivered at the notion of breaking free from captivity, he couldn't shake the doubt clouding his thoughts. Was it the dryness in his mouth, a thirst only quenchable by that wretched sprushah? "They risk too much. I understand they want to help, but why do this for us? Why put their lives on the line?" He expected Ahleen to lose her steadfastness and cave into reservation, but her eyes caught the fire of the torchlight.

"They risk everything, yes. But they believe it is worth it. They believe our lives are worth something more. So do I."

That night, Petrah was restless, unable to find a comfortable position to sleep in and unable to stop wrestling with his doubts over their escape. He listened to his cellmates shift on their cots. Were they as anxious as he was about their escape?

A part of him—the hopeful part—told his mind their decision was the right one, no matter what the outcome. That dying for the chance at freedom was better than wasting away in captivity.

Sleep came eventually, but his dreams were cruel and unforgiving.

Petrah was hiding again. Wind howled past the triangular opening of the collapsed stone roof that afforded him meager refuge against the relentless cold. It was perhaps a temple, with toppled columns and a cloven statue of a bearded man in a tunic, his torso sheared clean from its base. Outside, the world appeared utterly bleak, a muddling of gray tones and bitter shadows.

Petrah listened and waited, not daring to leave the protection of his shelter.

Then a strange flicker caught his eye, angry red and orange against the broken stone. He peeked through the angular gap, tracing the flicker across the flagstone road dipping to his right. When he emerged, his eyes followed the glow along the road, veering south, where it dipped down a steep hill and across an open plain to its source: an entire city on fire, burning out of control. Numerous strange towers sprouted across the horizon, mammoth beasts of metal writhing in flame. The scarlet inferno bellowed plumes of smoke driven into the shape of anvils at their peaks where the wind flattened them as if cut by scythes.

Petrah wrapped his arms with his hands, bracing against the chill. What seemed like husks in the distance were in fact the corpses of victims consumed and blackened by the fire. Dozens, perhaps hundreds of bodies.

A whinny cut through the whoosh of fire and crackle of warping metal. The clop of hooves heralded the quick approach of riders on horseback.

Petrah ducked into his hiding spot.

The riders slowed.

Petrah waited for them to pass, but when they came upon the collapsed roof of stone, they stopped. Petrah glimpsed a single pair of black boots in stirrups against the flank of a massive warhorse. The horse snorted as if it knew Petrah lurked in the shadows, as if it could smell him. Petrah was boxed in by another section of roof that had fallen away. A sliver of a gap between the slabs of stone might allow him to squeeze through.

The man with the black boots dismounted. His heels struck the flagstone like a hammer on rock.

Petrah backed against the tiny gap, pushing against the immovable stone as the man knelt to peer inside. His armor was as black as the deepest night, but his eyes—his *eyes*—were as blue as the midday sky. A blue so intense they carved the shadows with molten light. Eyes that met Petrah's, shaping into a smile of recognition.

Petrah scrambled for the gap. He shoved his upper body into the space and grabbed the opposite edge of the stone to pull himself. He wriggled, but the gap was too narrow, and his left shoulder got caught.

A powerful hand clasped his foot, sending a shock of fear up his spine.

Petrah started to lose his purchase as he was dragged back. He clung with his fingers, desperate as he dug into the stone to anchor himself.

He kicked with his feet, striking air. He kicked again. And again. And—

Hit something solid and broke free.

Petrah squeezed through like a fish slipping between a tear in a fisherman's net.

He fell onto cobbles facing a square with a lone, circular tower, presiding over a mass of worshippers too innumerable for Petrah to count. Petrah couldn't see their faces, for their backs were to him and their heads were all shrouded in cowls. They shouted the man's name, over and over, sending a tremor through the ground and into Petrah's bones. They cheered for him as if he were their champion, their savior.

Aman.

That was what they called him.

A name Petrah didn't know.

The man's blue eyes burned like a pair of flames. They cast an unnatural light across the crowd. He searched everywhere, his fiery gaze ceaseless, until—

Until Petrah felt the frigid gaze fall upon his face.

The crowd hushed.

As one, the cowled heads turned toward Petrah.

No eyes, no faces, just a sea of empty hoods, yet Petrah could feel their stares drench him with a chill that wracked his body.

They stole toward him, gliding silently as a lengthening shadow.

Petrah backed away until he knocked into the section of fallen roof again. He tried to squeeze through the gap, to escape to the other side, to pull himself through before—

Hands caught his dangling feet.

They hauled him onto his back.

Then, as a tide of smothering blackness, they fell upon him.

Petrah awoke panting and clutching his chest.

In the dark of his cell, he saw blue firelight everywhere. As his eyes adjusted, the familiar gloom returned.

But the name Aman . . .

It thundered in his head.

And remained with him for the rest of the day.

THE DRAADI FORCED PETRAH back to the slave works after four long days. He guzzled the sprushah as if he had drunk nothing the entire week. The tremors went away within the hour.

Petrah was glad to have something to occupy his time. Despite his condition and battle with withdrawals, he'd kept himself out of trouble. Antelle would be proud of him. Petrah worked silently next to Jow-quu, who was battered but manageable.

And, fortunately, there weren't any more "official" visits.

AFTER PETRAH AND HIS cellmates bedded down for the evening on San's Day, like the other slaves, Ahleen showed up. Quietly, she unlocked their cell and snuck inside. From beneath her bulging tunic, she produced a sack and placed it on the floor. "I brought torches. We'll need them for the dark passages." The odor of pitch permeated the air.

Petrah had a hard time keeping still. From the uncertain looks cast by his cellmates, he assumed they were nervous too.

Kruush kept his voice low. "Is Hamed in place?"

"He is," Ahleen said. "I have to make one more round. When I come back, we'll wait. Once the Draadi sound the bells, we leave."

As the minutes passed, restlessness seeped in. Petrah picked at the scattered straw by his cot. Tan bobbed a nervous knee. Jow-quu kept licking his lips, then dosed off. Kruush frowned, grunted, then frowned even deeper, his worry lines rippling like desert sand. They flicked tense glances at one another, which added to the already topsy-turvy feeling in Petrah's stomach.

Kruush spoke up eventually. "I don't like it. She's taking too long." He stalked to the bars, looked out into the dark, and turned back to his cellmates. "We should never have let her—"

He quieted and turned at the sound of soft footsteps.

Ahleen's small hands gripped the cell door. "Get ready," she whispered.

Kruush grabbed the sack with the torches. Tan and Petrah roused Jow-quu.

The alarm bells rang, a discord that made Petrah jump.

Ahleen opened the door. "Let's go."

The five hurried along. They passed cells filled with sleeping slaves rousing in confusion. A few pointed or called out to them, but they rushed by, set on moving away from the slaves' quarters.

Petrah's heart raced. They were at a run now. After two turns, they cleared the slaves' quarters, about to head north.

A Draad rounded the corner. Petrah knocked into Jow-quu, who had stopped. The Draad went for his sword.

Kruush and Tan tackled him, but the Draad fought back, elbowing Tan as he tried to free his sword. Kruush hooked his arm around the man's throat, and the pair knocked into the wall. The impact freed the Draad, who was all muscle and fury.

Petrah lunged at him, catching the brute by his sash, but tripped over his foot. Petrah clung to the sash to keep from falling. The Draad wheeled, flinging Petrah off. Before the Draad could cry for help, Kruush cracked his jaw with a forearm, and Tan locked his arms around the man's midsection, using momentum to throw the Draad off balance. Petrah grabbed onto the belt, and the Draad fell onto his back.

Without mercy or thought, the trio kicked the Draad.

Savagely.

Brutally.

Until the Draad stopped fighting back and went limp.

"Enough!" Ahleen said.

They were all out of breath. Petrah's arms vibrated from the rush coursing his body.

"Help me hide him," Kruush said.

The tunnel branched. They chose the direction opposite from where they were going, and Tan and Petrah dragged the unconscious man to a dark, well-hidden alcove around the corner. They propped him up to make it look like he'd fallen asleep.

Then they were off again.

When they turned west, the ground became rougher and the bedrock more irregular, exactly as Ahleen had described. The air was more breathable here, free of the choking stink of sweat and human waste. It was also the last of the lighted passageways.

Petrah looked over his shoulder, chasing the receding shadows with his eyes.

There was no turning back now. No undoing what they'd committed. No way but ahead.

Not if they didn't want to end up hanging from nooses on a wall for all of Kanmar to witness.

Tan grabbed a torch from the sack and used the brand on the wall to light it. It flared and gave off the scent of burning pitch. They moved along the corridor with a purpose.

Chills danced up Petrah's neck whenever he saw a shadow from the torchlight move along the wall as if it were a slave master about to ambush them. At one point, they thought they heard shouts.

"Draadi?" Tan asked.

"Give it a moment," Kruush said.

A cool draft of fresh air filtered through a fissure somewhere above. Jow-quu tilted his head back, letting the breeze blow over his leathery face. He closed his eyes. At first, Petrah thought he might be crying.

He's more alive now than the entire time I've known him.

"Jow," Petrah whispered, "is everything all right?"

Jow-quu wiped the tears away with his knuckles. "I'm the best I've been in ages."

Petrah placed a hand of encouragement on his friend's shoulder. "Things will be different from here on out, you'll see."

"We've waited long enough," Ahleen said. "Keep moving."

They resumed their trek. After a bend in the tunnel, Tan stopped them. "What's that sound?"

They listened. "It doesn't sound like footsteps," Kruush said.

"I hear it too," Ahleen said. "A scraping sound."

"I thought these passages were deserted," Kruush said. "If that's not a Draad, what is it?"

"They *are* deserted. The sound seems to be coming from the direction we're going."

The bit of news was enough to unnerve the entire group.

Petrah scooted up to the intersection and peered ahead. The corridor lay dark. He whiffed the air. Was it his imagination or was there a feral smell? He tasted rot on his tongue, like meat that had gone bad.

"What now?" Petrah asked.

"If we're supposed to go left, then we go left," Kruush said. "If there's a Draad hanging about, we'll take care of him just like the other fellow. If there's something else, well . . ."

"We better get moving," Petrah said, thinking of the "something else."

The five headed into the dark. They maneuvered through the growing debris of stone, sediment, and stalagmites. Jumpy shadows danced all around the rocky formations from their torchlight.

A hiss had everyone stopping dead in their tracks. Tan pointed behind him. "Did you hear that?"

They listened. The hiss was sharper the second time but seemed to come from a different direction.

Kruush bumped into Petrah, then spun around. "Where's it coming from?"

"What if it's in front of us?" Petrah asked.

"It's not in front," Ahleen said.

Tan squeaked, "'It?' What do you mean by 'it'?"

"We don't have time for guesses," Kruush said. "Let's go."

The tunnel opened up into an enormous cavern about three stories in height. A pool of water spanned its width, and a large column of limestone rose out of the center to join the ceiling as a single pillar.

Ahleen stepped into the cool water first, and the others followed. Petrah had never seen or felt water like this. It ran up to his waistline at its deepest point and was starkly cold.

Once across, they wrung out their clothes.

There was a third hiss, then scraping.

Kruush cocked his head. "It's definitely got claws, whatever it is. Could it be a rat?"

"It would have to be a pretty big rat," Tan said. "And fast."

A growl sounded, faint but strong enough to set the hairs on the back of Petrah's neck on end.

"That's no rat," Ahleen said. "Only one animal growls and hisses like that. It's a river beast. Run!"

Petrah didn't need to ask what a river beast was to know their lives were in peril. He ran, just like the others, maneuvering the uneven ground as rocks and sharp protrusions stabbed at the soles of his feet.

The passage leading out from the large chamber wound to the left and tightened.

The ceiling also dipped sharply, confining the space, forcing Petrah to stoop as he ran. Behind them, the growling and scraping grew louder.

The tunnel ended with a sudden two-story drop. They skidded to a stop, but Tan tripped, dropped his torch, and plunged into the dark with a yelp.

Petrah heard a splash below him and saw Tan surface from a natural inlet fed from the marsh.

"I'm all right," he called up, spitting out water. At the far end of the cavern, a roughed-out hole bridged the pool, leading to the marsh outside.

Ahleen picked up the dropped torch and scrambled down a steep slope dug into the bedrock on their left side. The others hurried behind her, almost pushing into one another to get to the bottom. Their footfall mixed with the harsh scrape of claws.

When they reached the base of the incline, they quickly waded out into the water.

It was cool but not as cold as the cavern pool. The slick footing gave way, and Petrah's toes could no longer touch the bottom. He took the torch from Ahleen and trod water while she helped orient Jow-quu.

"Over here." Tan beckoned the group to swim over to him. The torchlight revealed bars running vertically, embedded into the narrow outlet that led to freedom. The rusted metal drove from the top of the semicircular opening into the water, where it disappeared from view.

Kruush anchored his feet against the bars and yanked with both hands. "It's stuck."

"I thought you told us this was the way out," Tan said gruffly.

"It is," Ahleen said. "But Raya was supposed to take care of the bars."

"Then where is he?"

"How should I know? Hurry, I can hear it getting closer." A throaty grunting accompanied the scraping, growing louder with each breath.

"Kruush," Tan said, "help me with these bars. Petrah, get us more light."

Petrah paddled with one arm, doing his best to keep the burning brand aloft. His shoulder ached from the exertion, but he'd be damned if he'd let his arm drop.

Kruush and Tan yanked on the bars. Jow-quu treaded water off to the side.

Petrah pointed with his torch. "Check if the bars run all the way down."

"They do," Tan said. "But they're rusted. Maybe we can break them. See the last bar? It's missing. If we can find it, we might use it as a lever."

Kruush took a deep breath and ducked under the water. Seconds later, he resurfaced, holding a slimy two-foot section of rusted metal. "Got it."

A growl echoed in the cavern. Everyone looked up.

"For the love of San," Kruush swore.

Atop the stone shelf, a large animal sniffed the air. It was as long and wide as a water buffalo, like the ones Petrah had seen grazing by the Juum, but was shaped like a lizard with a leathery hide and squat legs. Horns swept backward from its head, and quills protruded from the ridgeline of its back in a menacing fashion.

It flicked its tongue and hissed.

Ahleen motioned frantically. "Hurry!"

Tan grabbed part of the rod, and together he and Kruush tried to wedge the bars apart. Just as one bar started to give, their rusted lever broke in half.

Kruush smacked the water. "Damn it! Now what?"

"Look," Tan said. "We bent this one." He grabbed the bar and wriggled it. Sure enough, it moved just a little. "Let's try to get it out."

Petrah turned to see the river beast testing the edge of the precipice with a paw. It bunched its hindquarters.

"I think it might jump," he said. He handed Jow-quu his torch. "Keep this above the water."

He reached down and grabbed the slimy bar just below Tan's hands. He strained to keep his nose above the splashing water as they yanked on the bar together. The three were busy twisting it back and forth when a flickering light appeared through the bars outside the cavern.

"Raya!" Ahleen called.

"Ahleen!"

"Come quickly! We're trapped."

A raft with a suspended lantern pushed through a wall of reeds toward them. A man with dark hair and muscled arms used a long pole to propel himself forward. One last push, and the raft glided their way.

The river beast growled, scraping a claw along the edge of the stone as if deciding whether to jump.

Raya tossed a length of rope to them. "Pull me in."

Kruush reached through the bars and pulled the raft close while Raya grabbed a large hammer.

"One of you hold me in place, the other help me loosen the bars."

Kruush held while Tan worked the first bar.

Raya swung his hammer, pounding with all his might. The blows rang loudly.

Bit by bit, the bar gave way. The brittle metal broke, leaving its sections askew. Raya worked the next bar while the men wiggled the loose ends.

A big splash startled Petrah from behind.

The water bubbled.

"Jow, get over here!"

Petrah snatched the torch back from his partner and held it out in front of him. The water swilled threateningly around him from the creature's plunge. The river beast was still below the surface, but where?

"Come on, you blasted metal!" Kruush shouted. Only one bar was gone. They needed at least two more to fit through.

"Give me that piece of bar!" Petrah said. Tan handed him a foot-long section.

The river beast surfaced a dozen feet from the group, spraying water through its giant nostrils. Its head looked large enough to engulf Petrah up to his shoulders. It paddled cautiously with its webbed forelegs, tongue tasting the air. The stench of rotting flesh was overpowering.

With a burst of speed, it shot forward and unhinged its lower jaw as it erupted out of the water.

Petrah slashed at it with the bar, striking the creature on the snout. He followed up with a blow from his torch.

Cinders sparked on contact.

A wave of water pushed Petrah backward. His head dipped below the pool's surface for a second, but he kept the torch from going out.

When he spit out the water and shook it from his eyes, the river beast had swum toward the stone ramp in the rear of the cavern.

"Are you all right?" Ahleen asked Petrah.

"I don't know how long I can keep that thing away. Tan, how close are we?"

"We've got a bar-and-a-half free. Almost there."

The river beast fell back. It came about and pivoted its snout back and forth, as if searching for the best angle of attack. Then it dove beneath the water.

"Hurry!" Ahleen yelled.

"We're hurrying!" Kruush said.

"It's going to come from underneath. Oh, my god . . ."

Ahleen kicked wildly as a shadow glided up toward them.

The beast launched open-jawed out of the water.

Petrah stabbed with the point of his bar. It struck the side of the creature's head, penetrating a soft fleshy area, sending the animal into a mad thrashing fit.

Petrah hung on, but the river beast was too strong and dragged him underwater.

When he surfaced, he coughed up water, and his torch was gone, extinguished with a sizzle. It left them with just Raya's light from the other side of the bars.

"Where is it?" Ahleen asked, voice quavering. "I don't see it!"

Petrah coughed, then pointed. "Over there."

The river beast scampered onto a jutting ledge on the other end of the cavern. It used the wall to dislodge the section of bar that impaled its head and let out a mournful cry when it came loose. The gout of blood from the wound appeared black in the diminished light.

Kruush shouted, "We're clear! Everyone through." The exit looked like a misshapen mouth with missing teeth.

Ahleen went first through the opening, Tan second. Petrah made sure Jow-quu followed Tan. Raya helped them up while Kruush held the raft in place with the rope.

"Petrah, get your ass through!" Kruush ordered.

After a few strokes, Petrah reached the raft. Raya helped him aboard.

When Petrah turned around, he saw Kruush head their way, arms piercing the water in a mad swim. The water splashed up around him. Then a wave sent Kruush under.

He was gone.

"Kruush!" Ahleen cried.

She tried to dive after him, but Tan caught her.

"Let go of me! He needs me!"

"No!" Tan said. "It'll get you too."

"I don't care. I—" Ahleen faltered.

The swirl of water subsided. Kruush was nowhere to be seen.

"Watch out for that thing," Raya warned as he grabbed his pole. He shoved off.

Tan grabbed the hammer while Petrah tried to comfort Ahleen, who had one hand over her mouth, the other clutching his arm. The air reeked of silt and marsh water.

Raya pushed their craft away from the cavern. They needed to gain distance from the predator. "Do you see anything?"

"Nothing," Tan said, sounding as if the world had fallen away.

Petrah numbly watched the opening in the rock face shrink as water dribbled from his bedraggled form onto the lashed bamboo canes of Raya's raft. His chest tightened as he searched for a sign—any sign at all—that Kruush might be alive.

Just when he thought he'd looked everywhere, a splash caught his attention. "There, in the reeds!"

Kruush cleared the water, gasping for air.

Petrah shouted to him. "Over here!"

Kruush kicked with his feet, chopping through the water with his arms while Raya poled hard to get to him.

A growl sounded behind him, followed by the savage shudder of metal. The river beast was trying to squeeze through the opening.

Ahleen waved at Kruush. "Swim, damn it!"

The river beast thrashed side to side, dislodging another bar as it wiggled through the outlet. It cleared the gap with the wallop of its mass just as Kruush made it to the raft, then it submerged.

Petrah kneeled at the raft's edge. "Kruush, grab my hand."

Kruush reached up. It took both Petrah and Ahleen to drag him onto the raft. He lay on his back, heaving.

Raya pointed. "Someone grab that paddle. Bash the blasted thing if it comes too close. The rest of you, gather toward the center."

Petrah grabbed the paddle by Raya's feet while Tan held his hammer ready. Ahleen and Jow-quu huddled in the center over Kruush's water-logged body.

"Shush," Petrah said. "Listen."

The water was black and still for a moment. From all around, crickets chirped and frogs croaked and the stink of marsh water filled the air. The raft rocked gently. Petrah gripped the wood paddle like a club, balancing himself with wet feet planted wide on the slippery bamboo.

The river beast reared its head a body length from the raft and snorted water. It tested the air with its tongue and gaped its jaws, then swam forward warily. There was a gash close to its left eye, now swelled shut. Petrah had injured it, but the creature was no less dangerous.

"Get ready," Raya said.

When it got too close, Petrah swatted it.

He struck its snout with a thud.

The river beast snapped its head toward him and hissed. Petrah lurched sideways from the momentum, then steadied himself.

The beast opened its maw wide. Water dripped from rows of teeth made for crunching bone and ripping sinew and muscle. Slowly, it hinged its upper jaw shut. It snorted again, then turned its body and swam away. It disappeared into a bank of reeds on the far side.

Petrah exhaled. "I think it's gone."

Tan laid his hammer down. "Praise San, that was close."

"Those animals usually prey on cattle," Raya said. "It must have been hungry."

Kruush tapped Ahleen on the back. She was sitting on him. "Can I get up now?"

She gave him an elbow to the ribs and moved over.

"What's that for?" he said, coughing.

"For scaring me." She crossed her arms and turned away.

AFTER CREEPING THROUGH THE wetlands, Raya guided the raft
toward shore. He navigated the reed banks of the Juum River in a
slow and deliberate fashion, not so much for the stealth of their passing
as it was to stay away from the swift current out past the break. The Juum
was a wide river, the lifeblood of the country, with certain parts more
treacherous than others.

Raya pulled into a narrow inlet bordered by tall marsh grass. Crickets,
hidden from sight, sang their chorus into the night. He dropped into the
water alongside his craft and prompted his passengers to do the same.

"You don't think another one of those river beasts might be skulking
about, do you?" Tan asked.

"I doubt it," Raya said. "No big game around here."

The Jabahn grabbed a rope, and Kruush helped him beach the craft
on the muddy riverbank. He took his lantern and had the others follow
him.

The group walked behind their guide, sodden. Petrah staggered from
fatigue. *How much longer?* His body ached. They pushed through the tall
grass for several minutes until they reached a clearing with a mud hut in
the center.

Raya gestured for them to sit on the ground. "Wait here."

One by one, they dropped to the ground, exhausted.

The Jabahn entered the hut and returned with a water jug. "Drink up.
We'll eat something too, then we'll be on our way."

The escapees took their turn drinking their fill. Raya passed around a
woven straw pouch. "It's jerked beef—tough, but tasty."

The strong odor reminded Petrah of the cured meats the Draadi sometimes ate while the slaves worked the quarry. *San be good*, he thought, licking his lips.

Kruush took a bite of his strip of jerky. "This is wonderful. I'll sleep like a babe after eating this."

"You and me both," Tan said, tearing into his jerky.

Petrah could fall asleep sitting up, but this was his first night outdoors in years.

Look at the stars above. Stars!

He could cry, they were so beautiful.

I will stay awake and look at them until I can't keep my lids open any longer. And if they capture us in the morning, I won't care, because it will have been worth it.

"When do we get to the harbor?" Petrah asked.

"We continue downriver in a bit," Raya said. "We'll stop at first light, where I can get you cleaned up. I've got supplies and clothes for each of you. From there, we head to the harbor."

Tan wiped his hands. "Do you think it's safe on the water?"

"Safer than on land. The Draadi will send out multiple search parties. They'll scour the pits and comb the nearby streets. When they come up empty-handed, they'll alert the city watch. You don't want to be anywhere inside the city walls when that happens."

The Draadi would come out in force once they realized the fire was set intentionally. Petrah worried about what might happen to Raya and Hamed too. Both had taken a significant risk by helping them. Then there was the Draad they'd beaten unconscious. What if he succumbed to his wounds and died? "What about you?" Petrah asked Raya. "Won't you be missed?"

"Don't worry about me. I have more privilege than most . . . and fewer eyes looking my way. The important thing now is to get you out of here safely. To do that, we need to change your appearances. By the time I'm done with you, you won't recognize yourselves."

Petrah was thankful for Raya's assurance. "After we get to the harbor, what do we do?"

"One thing at a time. We'll talk about it when you're fresh of mind and body. For now, help me get the supplies onto the raft." Raya gave them all a much-needed smile of encouragement as they climbed back onto the raft. "Tomorrow's going to be your first day of freedom."

Chapter 5

Eastward Bound

PETRAH WAS THE FIRST one up. It was still dark, the sky clear above, birds tweeting among the thickets. The raft glided smoothly, parallel to the riverbank with the swoosh of its passing. He breathed in air redolent of marsh grass, thankful he wasn't in the pits. He'd not only escaped captivity, but the likes of Meska and his brood.

Raya pushed them along. His long, brown hair was tied off into a topknot. He was older than he'd appeared the night before, with deep laugh lines and a slight stoop. He wore a stained, ochre tunic. Petrah noticed for the first time he was missing part of his right pinky finger above the knuckle.

Petrah went over to Raya, careful not to throw the raft off with his weight. "Do you want me to take over?"

"I'm fine," Raya said. "How do you feel?"

"Sore and tired. But happy to be alive."

"You tossed a lot."

Petrah's dreams had been vivid.

He was running again, searching for his mother while dodging the men on horseback. He had run through ruined and buckling streets, all strange to him, and slipped into shadowed buildings of decaying metal and crumbling stone—searching, searching, but never finding, never resting.

Until they cornered him, hunting him on foot, men dressed in black and armed with swords.

Petrah remembered huddling, wedged between the ruins of a sandstone building, peering out as the leader stepped toward his hiding spot, crunching the loose gravel with his boots.

He recognized the boots, the armor, the fierce, blue eyes.

The man named Aman.

He had dark, almost black, curly hair and wore a black breastplate embossed with a fiery serpent stained with spattered blood. He dropped to one knee and angled his head so that he was looking directly at Petrah, his blue eyes ablaze.

From his lips came three words.

"I. See. You."

Petrah shook off the nightmare. He changed subjects. "Are you coming with us?"

"No, but I'll take you far enough to get you to safety," Raya said. "The Jabah are going to be questioned, me included. The Draadi will press for answers to find out who helped you escape. Some will get accused of abetting. They'll notice Ahleen among those missing. It won't be pretty. People will suffer. I fear most for Hamed."

Petrah feared for Hamed too. The fire had been a terrible idea. "I'm so sorry. If I would have known—"

"Don't apologize. I've made my choice. If they find me out, so be it. I'm not afraid of the afterlife."

Petrah didn't want to think about what might happen to Raya if the Draadi accused him of aiding him and his friends. "Has anyone escaped the pits?"

"Not that I'm aware of. The last time someone escaped, there was a citywide manhunt. They locked down all of Kanmar, the docks too. I don't think you want to know the outcome of that expedition. But this time, it will be different."

Petrah smiled wanly. The odds were against them. Anything was better than dying under the scorching sun with a whip snapping at the heels. "I hope so too."

I T WASN'T MUCH LONGER before the others stirred awake.

They said little as they helped themselves to berries and day-old bread. Petrah sat next to Jow-quu, whose hands shook as he tried to eat. He could see the frustration on Jow-quu's face.

"Don't worry," Petrah said. "You'll never have to drink sprushah again. From here on out, you are a free man, understood?"

Jow-quu smiled weakly. "Thank you, Petrah. For everything."

It broke Petrah's heart to see his cellmate in such distress. He hoped the shaking would go away with time and Jow-quu would regain his wits. Deep down, Petrah suspected the damage was permanent. He hoped he was wrong.

But he *was* worried about the sprushah cravings that would vex all of them. His cellmates had witnessed the plight firsthand. They knew what was coming their way.

After breakfast, Raya pulled into an inlet that hid them from the river. The tall grass provided ample cover.

"Strip down and get in the water. There's soap and scrubbing stones in the basket over there. Ahleen, I'll need help shaving and cutting hair."

"What about this?" Tan tapped the triangular tattoo on his ankle.

"Not to worry. I've got some special stuff for that."

Ahleen helped Raya groom the men. The sun had just begun to climb by the time they finished.

The men were unrecognizable from their former selves.

They wore clean, cotton tunics and leather sandals that made them look like ordinary citizens. Petrah didn't know what kind of stuff Raya applied to his ankle—only that it burned and made his eyes water. By the time the pain went away, the tattoo was miraculously gone. A faded triangle remained, the skin pinkish-red and slightly blistered.

"The blistering from the acid will disappear in a week or two," Raya said. "In a month, you won't remember you had anything there. Between now and then, try not to draw attention to yourselves."

After the men were done, Raya attended to Ahleen, who had washed in a secluded alcove. "Are you sure about the hair?"

Ahleen took her long, braided, brown hair in hand and looked forlornly at it. "I'm sure."

Raya cut the hair to shoulder length with the sharp edge of a cutting stone.

A touch of sadness crossed her face, but Kruush gave her a reassuring smile. "It looks well on you." Petrah and Tan nodded their assent.

"Ah, my handsome man," she said, running a hand over Kruush's smooth jaw. "You look like a prince among the fish."

"Aye," Kruush said. "A prince among the fish I am."

Raya had the group gather around. "I'm taking you as far as the city harbor. I believe your best chance for getting out of Kanmar undetected is aboard a ship, preferably one leaving today. You don't want to be seen traveling the river on a raft for any length of time, and I know you wouldn't make it very far on foot. Remember, if you're asked where you're from, say you're from Ketler. It's too obscure a village for anyone to question.

"The Draadi will hunt you. They will trace through the pits, find evidence of your escape, and follow the trail. We're gambling the city watch keeps its attention within the city. Hopefully, you'll be long gone before they realize you're not hiding in the pits or the city."

"How do we get aboard a ship?" Kruush asked. "We have no money."

"You'll have to get hired on as crew. Kanmar's got cargo ships coming and going all the time. And where there are ships, there are captains in need of crews." Raya smiled his encouragement. "Even novice ones."

R AYA STEERED HIS RAFT along the slower current near the shore-line.

The odor of mud hung thickly in the air, which was abuzz with small, flying insects. Reeds, fields, and tall groups of palms dotted the horizon. Workers tilled or tended crops on plantations. Every so often, the travelers would pass an irrigation canal running inland from the shore.

The journey took the better part of an hour to reach the city limits.

Buildings appeared along the coast, the smaller ones made of mud bricks, the larger ones sandstone.

Petrah's hope grew with each minute, but so did his apprehension. He fidgeted with the beige headscarf Ahleen helped him knot. She wore one too, but more in the conservative style, wrapped around her face to reveal just the bridge of her nose and her eyes. The others wore theirs around their necks, much in the fashion of local fishermen.

The longer they took, Petrah feared, the worse the outcome for Raya. How would he explain his disappearance? Petrah couldn't understand the man's reasoning for putting himself in harm's way. Maybe he felt so strongly about freeing a handful of slaves that it was worth risking his life. Petrah knew only that the man was selfless and kind beyond words.

The city finally came into view, with its towering west and south walls meeting at the river's edge. Soldiers patrolled the teeth-like parapets atop the walls, hazy and tiny from this far away. Petrah hoped they couldn't discern the travelers about to enter the harbor.

Raya angled the raft toward the harbor. The wharf comprised a series of piers made of wooden walkways atop stone pillars. There were a couple of dozen ships at port, mostly small boats with single masts and larger ones with double masts, along with a few that were wide and flat.

Petrah marveled at the watercraft. He'd seen boats on the river during his weekly baths as a slave and always wondered what it would be like to sail with the wind at your back and not a care in the world. At the far end of the wharf was a ship with a massive flat deck jutting out into the water.

"What's that?" Petrah asked, pointing.

"It's a cargo ship for high-tonnage loads," Kruush said.

"Do you think she needs a crew?"

Kruush cupped his mouth to keep from laughing. "She needs more than the likes of us."

A pylon with an opening the width of two dozen of Raya's rafts created an entry to the city. Beyond the titanic, slanted, stone towers, the streets teemed with activity: citizens, merchants selling wares and foodstuffs, children running about. The air carried the odors of salted fish, cooked meats, spices that tickled the nose, and the burn of incense.

The amalgamation of aromas made Petrah heady.

If Kanmar had such wonders, what did the port city of Fangmordah hold, or the nation's capital, the citadel city of Elmar? What of the greater world: the desert land of Meerjurmeh, the forested Northern Kingdom, the vast Empire of Korin? Antelle had spoken of these wondrous places, tiny hints of their richness and diverse cultures. Petrah wanted to experience them all.

Raya pulled Petrah aside. "Keep your headscarf on and mind where you show your face. You don't look Terjurmehan, and I don't want to attract any unnecessary attention, do you understand?"

Petrah thought of Antelle and how he would preach the same warning. Petrah dipped his chin.

The Jabahn maneuvered the raft alongside an open quay and secured it to a cleat. Gulls cried above them, flapping wings and hovering in the air.

Raya addressed his group. "I suggest you solicit the barge masters directly. I thought I might speak to the harbormaster on your behalf, but it's too risky. Kruush, you and Tan should go together to talk to the captains. Try to find someone moving out of port within the day, if possible. Remember, you're from Ketler."

"What about you?" Kruush asked.

"It's a bad idea if I go." Raya lifted the end of the black cord hanging from his waist. "You don't want a Jabahn with you while you offer your services, do you?"

Kruush and Tan worked the south side of the wharf. An hour later, they returned.

"Any luck?" Raya asked.

"No," Kruush said, flexing his jaw. "Everyone we talked to is either docked for repairs or in town on business. No one's heading out any time soon, and none of them needs a crew. Then we saw a pair of soldiers heckling a man with a donkey cart headed out of the city. A third inspected his cart as if searching for contraband."

"Did they spot you?"

"I don't think so. Maybe we should wait until later and try again."

"You can't afford to wait," Raya said. "You understand that, don't you?"

"I do," Kruush said.

"Have you checked the boats on the other side of the harbor?"

"Not yet."

"Well?"

Kruush sighed. "Aye, we best get to it. Come on, Tan."

After Kruush and Tan headed off, Raya said to the others, "Stay here and keep a low profile. I'm going to check for trouble and make sure there aren't any curious types asking questions or looking this way."

Petrah made sure to conceal his face with his headscarf as he sat beside Ahleen and Jow-quu.

No one spoke, except for Jow-quu, who pointed at the moored ships whose hulls reflected off the water and said, "The boats are nice."

Petrah shared a kind smile with his friend. "They are, aren't they? Maybe Kruush and Tan will find a really nice one for us." He added, "And one leaving sooner rather than later."

Raya came back to report he saw the same trio of soldiers as the ones Kruush and Tan had spotted, busy inspecting a wain laden with produce.

"No trouble then?" Petrah asked.

"Not yet," Raya said. "But your friends best hurry. Who knows how long things will remain calm?"

Petrah was relieved when Kruush and Tan returned. They were in high spirits.

"Good news," Kruush announced. "We found a barge in need of a crew. Turns out it's just the captain and his first mate on board."

Ahleen clapped her hands. "That's wonderful." Then she said, "But we don't have any experience."

"The captain says he needs three strong hands to load and unload goods bound for Fangmordah and to help as needed while onboard. I said we're green when it comes to crew work, but we're fast learners."

"And he accepted that?"

"I told him he could have five crew for the price of three, and he agreed."

"A smart negotiation," Raya said. "When do you leave?"

Kruush could hardly contain his smile. "Today."

R AYA SAID HIS GOODBYES. Ahleen tried to convince him to go
with them, but he wouldn't have it. In the end, she watched
teary-eyed as the Jabahn pushed off and headed upriver.

Petrah hoped the man would be spared from the wrath of the Draadi.
Raya was clever and resourceful. Petrah believed he would find a way.

Kruush led the group to their new home. The ship was outfitted with
two masts and rigged with lateen sails furled along obliquely sloping
yards. A scarlet bunting with several embroidered symbols hung over
the gunwale on the port side, showing that it was a trading vessel. A
small cabin rested on the aft portion of the craft, enough to sleep one or
two individuals. Petrah hoped for fair weather at night so he could sleep
under the stars.

The barge master waited on board with his first mate. They both wore
breeches, sandals, and linen shirts over their pants.

The barge master waved to the group. "Come up, come up."

Kruush walked up the ramp and onto the deck, followed by his comrades. He locked arms, hand to forearm, with the barge master, a man
named Monta-por. Tan followed suit and so did Jow-quu.

With Ahleen, the captain gently took her hand and bowed his head,
and she reciprocated the nod. The barge master seemed unsure what
to do when Petrah approached the gangway. "Greetings, stranger of the
land."

"Greetings, Captain." Petrah twisted his fingers together, uncomfortable with being called a stranger but understanding it was something he
was going to have to get used to.

Better than being called a slave.

The captain was wide in the face, like Kruush, and sported a full beard braided with beads. Petrah locked forearms with the captain, then his first mate. Both men smelled of the river.

When everyone was aboard, Monta-por gathered his new crew amidships.

"My name is Monta-por, but everyone calls me Mont. This is Jayeem, my first mate. Welcome aboard the *Kafta*. Her name means 'swift runner,' and I assure you, she's fast for a barge."

Jayeem was a wiry fellow with brown eyes and thick, wavy hair. A long scar ran down his cheek. Petrah had a hard time not staring.

"Souvenir," Jayeem said, tracing a finger over it.

Monta-por instructed the newcomers about the ship, their duties, destination, and what was to happen from there. When he finished, Kruush, Tan, and Jow-quu left with Jayeem to get their shipment, and Petrah and Ahleen stayed with Monta-por to prep the ship.

All the while, Petrah remained vigilant, keeping a lookout for trouble. He'd catch Ahleen glancing at the port entrance as well. At one point, two soldiers accompanied an officious-looking man with a mustachio down the wharf, thankfully away from where they were docked.

Petrah startled when Monta-por pointed at the man with the mustachio. "That's the harbormaster. He keeps this place running smoothly. Best to get on his good side."

The only side Petrah wanted the harbormaster on was the opposite end of the harbor.

Kruush and the others returned a couple of hours later with a pair of men directing an oxen-led train of wagons.

"Who are they?" Petrah asked.

"Members of the Commerce Guild," Monta-por said. "Can't do much without the guild's involvement."

Petrah furrowed his brow, not getting it.

Monta-por showed him a copper coin threaded among the beads in his beard. "See this? It means I'm a member of the Copper Shield Party. Our party controls the waterways, but the Silver Blade Party controls the Commerce Guild. Somehow, the two get along, and we transact civilly. Get it?"

Petrah didn't want to say *no*, so he simply said, "I think so."

"Good. Come on, time to get busy."

Monta-por had his crew form a line.

Together, they unloaded crates and sacks and stacked them at the foot of the gangplank. Ahleen insisted on helping, even though Jayeem told her she didn't need to.

"I have hands," she said. "I can work."

"But you're—" Jayeem started.

She cut him off. "A woman?"

Monta-por stepped in. "Let her help, Jayeem. She's able-bodied." He dipped his chin in Ahleen's direction. "Apologies for my friend. He's—how should I say . . . ?"

"Of a certain mindset," Ahleen said.

Monta-por grinned. "Yes, that."

Petrah thought Ahleen was a harder worker than all of them. She lifted the sacks with the same tenacity as any of the men. Jayeem came around, tipping his head and smiling as if to apologize for assuming she was any less capable than the others.

It took all afternoon for the crew to situate the shipment aboard the *Kafta*. Petrah enjoyed the hard work. It was his first job as a free man. He liked the feel of the bamboo crating, even its smell. He could easily acclimate to this new life.

But as the afternoon waned, Petrah glanced more frequently at the port entrance. He expected a contingent of soldiers to appear at any time.

Kruush placed a friendly hand on his shoulder and whispered into his ear. "Stop looking for problems. You're being obvious, and you're going to raise suspicion with our new captain."

Petrah backed off, keeping his eyes on the cargo and work at hand.

When the crew was done, they ate a simple meal of smoked fish and hardtack Monta-por had procured in Kanmar and went about leaving port.

Jayeem had Petrah help him push off the quay while the captain took position on the aft side of the deck near the tiller.

The craft creaked a little and then floated free and backward. After a few minutes, it cleared the dock.

Petrah let out a long breath. The tension bottled up inside him all morning released itself, unclenching the muscles in his arms, legs, and chest.

When they were far enough away from the harbor, he stopped worrying about getting caught and took in the river, which went for as far as he could see.

The swish of the water soothed Petrah. It reminded him of his weekly baths, the one time in the week when he'd stand waist-deep in the river, his unending servitude forgotten for the few minutes he could submerge his problems.

"The wind is good today," Jayeem told Petrah. "Not much work for us to do."

The barge accelerated as it headed downriver. The current and the wind were in their favor. Jayeem unfurled, hoisted, and sheeted in the smaller sail, and the ship picked up more speed.

"We should get to Fangmordah by tomorrow evening if the wind holds," Jayeem said.

"What do I do now?" Petrah asked.

"Sit down and rest. You've earned it."

Petrah settled against a crate. It was strange being told to rest.

After a minute, he glanced left and right out of habit, as if he were at his station in the slave works or in line waiting for his daily dose of sprushah. Eventually, the ship's rhythmic rise and fall relaxed him to where he could doze off.

When Petrah opened his eyes again, it was early evening.

The sun had disappeared behind the western horizon, and a cool breeze was settling in, bringing in the earthiness of the nearby mud bank. Jayeem stood on the starboard side of the craft, performing a maneuver to change the ship's position toward the center of the river.

"Oy, Petrah," Jayeem called. "Come here. I need your help with something."

Petrah lifted his sore body and went over to the first mate.

It felt good to be needed.

T HE SKY CHANGED FROM indigo to deep blue. They passed farmland that gave off the sweet smell of hay that had been curing in the sun.

Monta-por anchored the ship off the north coast of the Juum, alongside a bank of purplish-green reeds that rustled in the breeze. In the distance, a collection of freestanding stone statues in the shape of warriors caught the last light of day. They bore capes. Only one had a spear still intact in his grasp, the others, only splinters of stone.

Petrah was about to ask why the statues' heads were missing, when a strong aroma drew his attention away. Jayeem was setting out supper. They shared a meal of sheep's milk cheese and wheat bread aboard the ship. Petrah devoured his food. He'd never tasted soft, fresh cheese, only the rank, hard stuff the Jabah left him and his cellmates. The bread was chewy, its aroma heavenly.

Tan noticed his frown. "Why the long face?"

"It's just—" Petrah started. "It's that girl, the beggar's daughter in Kanmar. She was so hungry, and I—" *I messed up.*

Tan nodded. "Those devils could have left her alone, but they didn't. Don't worry, they'll have theirs coming to them."

Monta-por raised a piece of cheese he'd skewered with his knife. "When we unload, we can all go into town and have ourselves something proper to eat."

Petrah raised a brow. "Better than this?"

Monta-por laughed. "Far better. What do they feed you in Ketler, dust and sand?"

"Nuuma nuts," Tan said, smiling like an ass. Petrah thought it funny too, but Ahleen shook her head at the slave humor. Truth be told, Petrah wished to never see—or taste—another nuuma nut in his life.

Monta-por cracked a grin. "There it is then: you've been deprived. I'll see that changes."

"That's exactly what I was thinking," Kruush said, smiling with his mouth full.

Ahleen elbowed him. "Letting your stomach do the thinking for you again?"

"Always."

T HE CREW WEIGHED ANCHOR early in the morning and got on their way.

Petrah felt the jitters of sprushah cravings coming on as they set sail. He took his fill of water, but it couldn't quell the shakiness. He held out his hand, which trembled, then hid it when he caught Jayeem turning his way.

Ahleen shared a knowing look. She glanced over her shoulder at Jayeem and Monta-por, who were working the riggings, then kept her voice low as she spoke to Petrah. "Hang in there. I've spoken to Kruush and Tan, and they're feeling it too."

"It's worse in the mornings. We'll get over it. I'm more concerned about Jow-quu." His cellmate shivered as if he'd caught the chills from being underwater all night long.

"Want me to talk to him?"

"No, I'll do it."

Petrah sat beside Jow-quu. "How are you doing?"

"The wind is nice," Jow-quu said. "I missed it."

"Me too. Are you feeling all right?"

Jow-quu shrugged, then said, "My throat is dry. And my head—" He massaged his scalp.

"It's the sprushah cravings. The headaches and dryness will go away. Ahleen says it takes up to a week. The shaking will go away as well. Just be patient. But listen," Petrah said. "We're all here for you. If you need anything, just ask."

Jow-quu smiled, then turned back to watch the water.

ONCE AGAIN, THE WIND moved in their favor.

Jayeem adjusted the sails for running, and the craft picked up the pace.

After a while, the wind changed direction again, but this time Petrah anticipated Jayeem's maneuvers. The whole *sailing* thing was starting to make sense.

Occasionally, the *Kafta* passed fishing vessels and other craft. Crews often called out, and Monta-por would shout a greeting in return.

The coasts changed from flat and lush to high and rocky. The Juum widened the closer they came to port. On the near shore, the land flattened. Crop fields and groves appeared.

Petrah saw all manner of trees, many unfamiliar to him. Tan named them: olive, fig, avocado, lemon, orange.

"Orange is among my favorites," Tan said. "It's both tart and sweet—and juicy too. Gods, I miss the taste. Can you smell it? The air carries just a hint of citrus."

Petrah caught something on the wind, not sure if it was the orange Tan was referring to. There was a brightness to it, almost a tang. Petrah wished he could stop and pluck the ripe fruit and give it a taste. He was like a child who had never seen such wonders. He even forgot his sprushah cravings, which subsided considerably with the climbing sun.

The river narrowed, and the *Kafta* came close to the north shore. Petrah gestured to an area beyond the sandy riverbank where about twenty women worked in a field of waist-high grass, hunched over with straw baskets strapped to their backs. They used scythes to cut the stalks, then bent down to gather the grass and put them in their baskets while two guards armed with short swords on their belts looked on. "What do you suppose they're doing?"

"Harvesting barley or wheat," Jayeem said.

Petrah remembered the barley field he'd awoken in when he was eleven. He could still feel the sway of the golden grass against his face as he had crouched to remain hidden from the armed men who watched the workers tending the field. "Looks like hard work."

"They're slaves. They're used to it. See the red spots on their wrists? Tattoos."

Petrah squinted. He glimpsed what appeared to be red dots on their skin as they worked. He wanted to say something to Jayeem in defense of the slaves but remained quiet. He couldn't blame the helmsman for his prejudice. It was one more thing Petrah would have to get used to.

Jayeem continued. "Your people don't accept slavery, do they?"

Petrah got tongue-tied over what to say. "My people?"

"You're a Northerner, aren't you? You have the face of a Prallite."

Kruush butted in, saving Petrah from fumbling. "He is. A stubborn Prallite too." He winked, setting Petrah slightly at ease.

"That explains it," Jayeem said, flashing his teeth in a wide smile. "Prallites are finicky, if not pompous. No offense, Petrah." Petrah kept his mouth shut. It suited Jayeem well enough. "I blame it on your nobles. They like to indenture the poor, but call them serfs, not slaves. Your country is strange, Petrah. I've only encountered a handful of Northerners in my time, and they were always homesick, missing 'green country,' they would tell me. They missed the cooler clime of the Northern Kingdom, the pine-scented woods, the dignity of civilization. Dignity! Can you believe that? It's as if we Ter-jurah are animals. What's your opinion of our country?"

Petrah had known nothing but the desert. To imagine a place filled with trees was something to behold, for sure. Antelle had painted a picture in Petrah's mind of the Northern Kingdom, one filled with every shade of green Petrah could conceive. And skies of the clearest blue, with white-capped mountains in the background. Terjurmeh had only hills of rock and sand—nothing as tall as a mountain or as vibrant as Antelle had described.

Petrah wondered if he would ever get the chance to travel outside Terjurmeh in his lifetime.

Gods willing, I shall.

Prall was located north, beyond the vast desert, past hills and mountains. It wasn't a trek for the weak-willed.

For now, Terjurmeh would remain his home. Petrah would stay away from Kanmar, but he wasn't opposed to settling down in one of the other cities, Fangmordah perhaps, which Antelle had said bustled with industry, or head out into the desert with a tribe. Ahleen spoke highly of Meerjurmeh, but that, too, required travel across a great stretch of arid land.

"I like what I've seen so far," Petrah said to the first mate. Then, with a smile, he added, "And its people."

Jayeem reached over and slapped him jovially on the thigh. "Hah, good answer! Now we need to get you a Terjurmehan woman. Fangmordah boasts the finest whorehouses in the land. Of course, the Temple frowns on such establishments, but they pay a hefty fee, and well, there you have it. I can show you the better of the bunch. Unless you want a proper girl, of course."

Petrah's face flushed.

"I see," Jayeem said, acknowledging his virginity. "Perhaps you're too young for these things. How old did you say you were?"

"Fifteen."

"I was a year younger than you when I lost my innocence." Jayeem's eyes drifted off as if he were remembering a time long ago, his more inexperienced days. "It's best to wait, I suppose." He left it at that.

They stayed silent for a while.

Petrah listened to the barge cutting through the water, the creak of wood and rope, and the wind against the sails.

He thought about what Jayeem said about the Northern Kingdom and its people.

Antelle had spoken about the world as well, of the six domains that covered the continent: Terjurmeh in the center, Prall to the north, Meerjurmeh to the east, the Empire of Korin to the south, and toward the southern tip of Acia, the Provinces of the South.

Then there was Darkforth, farthest to the east and most enigmatic of all.

Antelle had said few traveled to Darkforth, and even fewer returned, likely swallowed up by its endless forests and jungles.

Petrah studied Jow-quu. His cellmate's troubled expression was as unknown as Darkforth. Jow-quu gazed out over the water, eyes looking hither then thither. Were there memories locked inside his mind, memories now surfacing after years of sprushah-induced haze, finally set free?

Petrah wanted to make small talk with his friend, but Jow-quu squeezed his eyes shut. When he opened them, Petrah caught a tear coursing down the rough fabric of his face.

Petrah looked away. He'd leave his friend be.

"So, what do you miss most about home?" Jayeem asked.

Petrah wasn't expecting the question, but he didn't want to sound foolish either. "I don't know. Maybe it's my family. Maybe it's some girl who once flirted with me. Maybe it's the sound of rain. I can't remember."

Jayeem leaned against the rail. "Aye, being far away makes you forget sometimes. I left home when I was eight. I miss my mother, I won't deny it. She had the kindest eyes. Eyes that warm your soul, you know?"

"Would you ever go back?"

"Probably not. I've done some terrible things in my life and earned a few reminders along the way." He pointed at the prominent scar on his cheek. "There's no going home for me, Petrah."

Petrah turned and leaned over the rail, looking at the ripples of the river. *Home, where even is home?* He mulled over the few memories he had—and the details of his dreams. But as he pondered his origin, the swirling eddies around the boat started to look like dark eyes, staring up at him, ready to draw him in.

I. See. You.

Chapter 6

Fangmordah

T HE CITY OF FANGMORDAH appeared off the north shore just as
evening set in.

Unlike Kanmar, which was surrounded by high walls, Fangmordah
was open. Although the city was smaller, Fangmordah's harbor was
twice Kanmar's size and housed an even greater array of vessels, including
a couple of ships Tan pointed out as war galleys. Jow-quu seemed especially taken by the city's splendor, lifting onto his tiptoes as he leaned
against the starboard railing.

Petrah shared in his friend's wonder. From their distance, the sounds
of the city blended. But the closer they got, the easier it became to distinguish them: the raucous calls from hawkers selling wares from stalls,
children hooting and chasing after each other, and the laughter of people
who'd never known the tribulations of slavery. All of it tugged at Petrah's
heart as if he'd yearned for it his entire life. This wasn't just a city; it was
a place that offered freedom. "Fangmordah's quite something, Jow. She
really is."

Damp eyes accompanied Jow-quu's smile while emotion frayed
his voice. "She's the most beautiful sight I've seen in"—he breathed
deeply—"in a long time. Do you see, Petrah? Do you see it?"

Petrah felt Jow-quu's welling of wonderment down to his bones. "I
see it, Jow. I see all of it."

Ahleen peered over Kruush's shoulder. "I do too. It's something to behold, especially from a ship, where you can take it all in."

Kruush reached back and took her hand. "We should all savor this moment."

Tan bobbed his head. "And bottle up the memory so we can relive it, time and again."

Jayeem untied the bunting on the port side to inform the harbormaster that a trading vessel was arriving. He then ran over to the bow and searched for an available quay.

He called out to the captain. "Number five."

"Number five," repeated the captain. "Bringing her about."

Jayeem ran back and adjusted the mainsail. "Petrah, can you lower the aft sail?"

Petrah took care of it. He didn't have to ponder the steps; he went through them with the ease of the wind tossing his hair.

"Good work, sailor," Jayeem said with a smile.

Petrah returned the smile and tipped his head.

Once the craft was dockside, a dockworker hailed the crew and called to moor the boat.

"All hands," shouted the captain to his crew. "Approach the gangway and be counted."

Kruush and the others gathered in place.

Monta-por looked over his crew, narrowing one eye. "Why are you all so jittery? Did you catch a bug or something?"

"They've been like this since we brought them on board," Jayeem said.

"They have, haven't they?"

Kruush spoke up for the crew. "You're right. We've been fighting something ever since Ketler. Got us all unsettled, but it'll pass. We landlubbers might appear weak, but we've got strong constitutions."

Monta-por laughed. "You hear that, Jayeem? They're landlubbers."

Jayeem eked out a grin. "Good thing we're not on the open ocean, eh, Captain?"

"Good thing. All right, landlubbers," Monta-por said. "Try to get your sea legs before we head to Elmar. I'd like a hale and healthy crew."

The dockworker whistled up.

Monta-por waved at him. "Oy, young man."

"Greetings, shipmaster. Welcome to Fangmordah. Name, business, and destination, please."

Monta-por relayed the information. The goods were to go to the city's Commerce Guild.

The dockworker presented Monta-por with a document, which he signed. With clearance granted, the crew disembarked.

Jayeem went to the end of the dock, where he met a cluster of boys that mobbed him as if he was giving away candies. He picked one and shooed the others away, and the pair returned to the ship. Jayeem gave the boy a sturdy pat on the back. "Everyone, this is Musta. He's going to watch our ship for us while we're out. Just like last time, right, Musta?"

Musta bobbed his head and grinned, showing a missing tooth.

Monta-por slipped the boy a coin. "When we get back, you get the rest. Now go sit over there." The boy plopped down on a crate. He couldn't have been more than ten or eleven, but he seemed experienced, with the same darting eyes that Petrah had seen among the younger slaves in Kanmar.

"We'll unload in the morning," Monta-por said to the others. "In the meantime, we're going into town to have ourselves a hot meal. Unless your ailment precludes you from eating." He fixed Petrah a significant look.

"We can eat," Petrah said, offering up a smile.

"That's what I was hoping. Very well, crew, let's go. Dinner's on me."

"Hear, hear!" Tan said.

Kruush nodded in agreement. "Aye, my stomach was thinking the same thing."

MONTA-POR LED HIS CREW through the busy streets of Fang-mordah. The unfamiliar sights and sounds mesmerized Petrah. Everywhere he looked, he saw something different: food carts, tents, shops, and people dressed in tunics, robes, and uniforms. City workers by the handful lit oil lamps affixed to bronze posts. In an instant, the city transformed into a nighttime metropolis.

The group followed Monta-por's lead along the winding dirt and cobblestone streets.

They passed a line of Mumooni tribeswomen balancing wicker baskets on top of their heads, their skin shades of copper and honey-brown, which was darker than the other denizens milling about. Rows of colored beads wrapped around their throats. The young beggar girl and her father, back in Kanmar, had been Mumooni. Petrah had seen others traveling with water jugs balanced over their shoulders in Kanmar, similar to these women.

Monta-por noted Petrah's curiosity. "You're taken by them."

"I like their beads," Petrah said. "So colorful."

"Do you know what the beads are for?"

The beggar girl in Kanmar had worn white beads. Petrah had assumed they were part of her culture, a simple decoration and nothing more. "No."

"They symbolize the experiences in these women's lives—their joys, struggles, and seminal moments. Each color has meaning."

"What does white mean?"

STEVE PANTAZIS

"White is a sign of virtue. The young wear white. But life changes; it always does. White turns to blue or amber or green. The young grow up and become women, but they never forget their past or where they belong. The Mumooni have a rich history and keep the traditions of their ancestors. I admire them." Monta-por tugged on his beard, knit with beads of its own. "It's a tragedy the Ter-jurah treat them so poorly. They came from the Fural Mountains to find a more prosperous life here in the East. Yet we oppress them. Shame on us."

Ahleen said Meerjurmeh was a much freer land, one that prohibited slavery. Had any Mumooni ventured there? Perhaps life would be better for them.

Perhaps for us too.

Petrah shelved the thought as his party reached a line of people standing in front of a kiosk. Monta-por had his crew form up behind him.

A priest wearing a crimson robe performed the holy sacrament. For each person in line, he dipped his thumb into a basin and rubbed a shiny, reddish liquid on the forehead in the shape of a triangle. Another man to his side held a collection tin for donations.

Petrah leaned over Kruush's shoulder. "What's he using?"

"Sercula: blood and oil. Very holy. If we're lucky, he's using the good stuff."

Petrah glanced back to see how Jow-quu was faring. The old slave had been quiet the entire trip. "You all right, Jow?"

Jow-quu nodded but said nothing. His hands trembled fiercely, and he appeared waxen in the lamplight.

Besides the withdrawals from the sprushah, Petrah wondered if their travel had taken its toll on his friend. He hoped, with time, the damage to Jow-quu's memories would reverse itself, or would at least allow him to hold a normal conversation, perhaps even give him the opportunity to assimilate into society as a productive citizen. Jow-quu was a diligent laborer. He deserved a second chance at life.

Hang in there, Jow. Everything will be better now, you'll see.

Petrah took his turn before the priest. The man had an unkind face with pockmarks embedded into his cheeks. He gave Petrah a distasteful look but dipped the index and middle fingers of his right hand into the brass bowl and marked Petrah's brow with the holy delta.

"With this blessed Sercula, I do thee anoint," he said. "San be with you."

The holy oil felt warm on Petrah's forehead, almost burning. His friends were all marked with the delta, glistening testaments to the faith of their nation.

Monta-por led his party down a busy street. "We're almost there."

Kruush grumbled something incoherent and rubbed his belly. Tan laughed but cut himself short when a patrol of soldiers appeared. They wore double black sashes over their chests in the shape of an X.

Petrah turned his head the other way. *Stay invisible.*

By the time the patrol was gone, the barge master halted his crew.

Outside an old tavern, a fabric standard hung from a protruding pole with an embroidered bird talon logo.

"Can you smell it, mates? That's the scent of heaven."

Petrah caught the aroma of something good. Kruush exchanged smiles with Tan.

Monta-por held up a hand. "I have but one request: respect me as your captain, but above all, respect this establishment. We're here to enjoy ourselves, nothing more. As for you, Petrah, no funny business. The locals don't take kindly to foreigners making a scene. Got it?"

"Got it," Petrah said. He had no plans to do anything but eat.

The travelers entered the tavern. An array of inviting odors, conversations, and music met them. Wooden tables occupied the busy dining room, and lanterns hung from metal pins wedged between stone blocks in the wall. A lady troubadour sang a feisty bar tune by the hearth of a fireplace, and the whole place clapped to the rhythm.

Monta-por led his crew to a solitary table in the rear, next to a pair of swinging doors leading to the kitchen. The captain had Petrah sit with his back to the crowd.

Monta-por spoke above the hubbub. "I think you'll be happy to know that Fangmordah has a reputation for making the best ale in the nation."

"Ah, ale," Kruush said dreamily. "The sound of it brings tears to my eyes."

A young man with a slight limp approached the table. "Good evening, gentlemen." Spotting Ahleen, he quickly added, "And lady. Welcome to the Silver Claw. My name is Jubar. Might I interest you in a round of ale?"

"You certainly may," Monta-por said. "Any specials tonight, Jubar?"

"Aye, Master. We've got manja on the spit. Very tender."

"Bring enough for everyone."

Kruush was quick to add, "Would you have pujin by any chance?" Petrah remembered Kruush's description of it as a flatbread stuffed with sizzling onions.

Jubar's eyes lit up. "Why, yes, we serve the best in the city."

"Then bring us two servings." Kruush looked at Monta-por, "If you don't mind."

"Of course not," Monta-por said. "We are here to feast, not nibble."

The server left.

The troubadour sang a crass ditty that had the crowd rattling their tables with the beat of their fists.

She's an ugly lass, who plays a tune or two
He's a silly lad, who dances like a fool
She's not a lady, but he doesn't care a bit
He'll keep a-drinkin' til she's a pretty lil' twit

The more he drinks, the more he thinks

I'll make her swoon tonight
They dittle here, they dittle there
They dittle everywhere

He loves her good, he loves her well
She's as fair as they come
Until the morn, he sees and thinks . . .
Good lord, what have I done?

The crowd roared and cheered.

Kruush pounded the table. "Now that's more like it!"

The server hobbled back, carrying a tray with mugs.

Monta-por gestured to the others. "Drink up."

Petrah smelled wood, citrus, and grass, then ventured a sip. He didn't know what to expect, but after swishing the liquid around his tongue, he noticed the bitter taste was offset by something sweet. It made him burp.

His next swallow was a gulp.

Kruush patted him on the back. "What do you think?"

Petrah wiped the foam from his mouth. "Not bad."

"Wait a bit," Tan said, smiling. "It gets better."

Petrah had no idea what Tan was referring to, but after a few minutes, he felt different, looser. It was a strange feeling, but a good one.

Jubar brought a large, steaming platter of manja while a serving girl set out a pair of unleavened loaves of piping-hot pujin, cheese, and dried fruits for the table. Petrah was giddy from the mouthwatering aromas.

"Don't be shy," Monta-por said. "Eat up!"

Petrah almost came to tears after taking his first bite of manja. The pork was fatty and salted to perfection.

The last time he had eaten anything cooked, it was a roasted rat.

Every morsel of manja was better than the previous: meaty, tender, and juicy. He licked the juices from his fingers. The pujin soaked up the drippings, adding flavor upon delicious flavor.

"What's this?" he asked, pointing to the small bowl of dip swimming in oil.

"Fama," Monta-por said. "It's made with mashed peas, nut paste, oil, and garlic. It's a nomad staple. The Con-jurah think theirs is the best, but ours is better. Dip your bread and see."

Petrah scooped up the creamy dip with a piece of flatbread. The flavor was rich and had a familiar nuttiness. "I taste nuuma nut."

"I taste it too. You don't have to eat it if you don't want it."

After being subjected to daily rations of nuuma nuts, Petrah decided to leave the fama for the others. It was flavorful, but if he didn't have to taste nuuma nuts again in his life, he'd be glad.

Petrah finished three more pieces of flatbread, but without the fama. His mouth danced with the caramelized sweetness of onions.

In the end, he had no choice but to loosen the sash about his waist and grab another piece.

Kruush was all smiles, Tan too.

After another round of ale, the group was in high spirits and chatting up a storm. Petrah had risked his life for this moment. A risk worth every ounce of fear, every moment of incarceration.

The troubadour finished another song, and the crowd cheered their approval.

She joined a rowdy table and was replaced by an older man with a heart-shaped, stringed instrument. He took a spot near the front of the tavern.

The minstrel settled atop a pile of cushions, tuned his instrument, and gave the audience a welcoming smile. He played a lively song, singing along in a deep, melodious voice. Monta-por joined the tavern crowd in thumping hands on the table to the rhythm of the music.

When the musician finished, everyone roused a cheer. He continued onto another song, something a little softer.

No one thumped their hands. Conversations resumed as if the minstrel weren't there.

"Hey," Tan whispered to Kruush. "Take a look."

Kruush glanced to where Tan gestured and made a face. "Gods, we don't need that."

Petrah peeked over his shoulder and saw six soldiers weaving their way through the crowd. They wore belted tunics covered with cuirasses and double sashes of black over their fronts, and they were armed with dirks and short swords.

Petrah turned back and motioned for Ahleen—who'd lifted out of her seat to get a better look—to sit down.

"Oy, you," spoke a man.

Monta-por and his companions looked up at once.

The man speaking had a triangular device affixed to his shoulders. Probably the leader of the squad. "You're sitting at our table."

"Sir, if you please," Monta-por said, "how about you let us finish our drinks, and we'll be off? We've been on the river all day."

The leader placed a firm hand on Petrah's shoulder and leaned forward. He stunk of sweat and oiled leather. "I don't care. Pay your bill and leave. This is our table, mate."

Monta-por nodded. "Aye, sir. Give us a moment to settle up." He signaled to Jubar, who limped over as fast as he could.

"That's two currah," Jubar said, looking as nervous as Petrah felt.

Monta-por produced a couple of silver, delta-shaped coins and handed them to the young man. He got up, nodded to his companions to follow suit, and moved past the soldiers.

When Ahleen tried to get through, the leader grabbed her arm. "Not you, sweetie. You can stay with us."

Ahleen pulled free from the man's grip. "I don't think so."

He squinched his face into something dark and dangerous. "I'm not asking. You sat at our table with these dogs. Now you're going to sit back down with us."

Ahleen attempted to leave, but the leader blocked her way. When she tried again, he backhanded her across the face.

Ahleen stumbled backward into Jow-quu, who caught her with an outstretched arm.

Kruush started toward the soldier, but Jayeem pulled him sideways. "Don't."

By now, the music had stopped.

The entire tavern turned its attention to the escalating situation. The anxious soldiers looked expectantly at their leader, hands firmly on the pommels of their swords.

Monta-por wedged himself between Ahleen and the soldier in charge. "Please, sir, the woman means no harm. What say you let me buy you boys a round of ale and call it a day?"

"Out of my way, fish," the leader said, shoving Monta-por aside.

One of his soldiers drew a dagger and pointed it at the barge master. Monta-por held up his hands and backed away.

The leader grabbed Ahleen by the hair and tugged hard, driving her to her knees. "Now, let's start again, shall we? I'm going to let go and you're going to behave, right?"

Ahleen was practically in tears, but she still shook her head.

Petrah wanted to clobber the man; take a leg off a chair and crack him across the back of his head. He glanced at the chair closest to him. It was too sturdy and too heavy to tear apart.

But the bread knife on the next table with the thick wood handle . . .

"No?" The squad leader took a fistful of hair and dragged Ahleen to her feet.

"Let go of me!" she cried.

Kruush was off to the side, livid but showing restraint, thanks to Jayeem. Monta-por's attempt to bribe the leader had failed, and there wasn't a thing Petrah or any of his friends could do about it, save watch, fight, or leave.

The patrons weren't too keen on the heavy-handed leader either. They grew restive and grumbled among themselves.

One came out of his seat, slightly sauced and swaying. "Leave her alone!"

"Yeah!" said his drunk friend. "Leave her alone."

Others murmured their complaints. The soldiers clasped the pommels of their swords, set with unease. The leader scowled. Petrah hoped he would lose interest and leave.

But then Jow-quu grabbed a carving blade from a nearby table, and Petrah's hopefulness fell out the bottom of his stomach.

"Jow, no!"

Jow-quu swung.

The knife pierced the squad leader's throat, sending him flailing to the ground. The man thrashed about, blood spurting.

Everyone watched in astonishment as the leader clutched his throat. Seconds later, he stopped moving.

Jow-quu dropped the knife and caught Petrah's gaze, like a child who knew he had done something wrong.

An instant later, the tavern erupted in chaos.

Patrons near the incident dodged to the side as soldiers became animated and drew weapons.

Chairs overturned, and plates and mugs crashed to the ground.

The momentum of the crowd shoved Petrah backward. In the bedlam, he lost sight of Ahleen.

Then, between bodies, he glimpsed the unthinkable.

"Jow!" Petrah cried.

A steel blade glinted in the lamplight for just a moment. Then it plunged forth.

Petrah heard a shriek and saw his friend arch backward in agony. When the soldier withdrew his blade, Jow-quu collapsed.

Petrah froze, but only for a moment.

Shouts erupted around him. Enraged patrons cursed at the soldiers and hurled trays, food, and mugs at them, drawing the ire and attention of the soldiers and adding to the confusion. The drunk patron who first spoke up grabbed a soldier by his sash while his companion swung at another and missed, only to get tackled from behind.

Petrah tried to push his way past the throng to get to Jow-quu, but Tan hauled him away.

"Petrah, we have to go. Now!"

"I can't just leave him!"

"If we don't get out of here, we're all dead. Move!"

Tan found a gap around the knot of people pushing, tripping, and shoving into one another and forced Petrah through the door.

Outside, patrons scattered in all directions. Jayeem waved his arms wildly from up the hill, and Tan sprinted toward him. The rest of the crew caught up, including Ahleen, who was crying.

"We have to head to the ship," Monta-por said. "This way!"

They ran. Petrah turned, but when he saw soldiers exit the tavern with their weapons drawn, he knew he couldn't do anything for his friend.

He cursed his misfortune and fled.

Chapter 7

Elmar

I T WAS JUST PAST midnight, and the dispirited crew sat aboard the *Kafta* under the light of a single lantern. When they'd returned to the ship, Monta-por had paid Musta extra to keep quiet.

"Not a word to anyone, do you understand?" he'd said to the boy. "Tomorrow morning, I need you to come back and keep a lookout for us just outside the entrance to the harbor." He told Musta his job was to watch for soldiers, and that if any showed up, got nosy, or had any questions, Musta was to say he hadn't seen anything or anyone they might be interested in. "You do whatever it takes to get rid of them. Do a good job, and I'll pay you double what I gave you today. Agreed?"

Musta agreed and then sped off.

Save for the intermittent creaking of a ship or the occasional burp of water from a fish breaking the surface, the harbor was mostly silent. Ahleen sat against a crate, hugging her knees to her chest while Kruush spoke to her softly, hand on her knee. Tan paced, sat down, stood up, then paced the deck again.

Petrah kept to himself in the shadowy part of the boat's stern. His eyes burned as tears welled up. Water-drenched wood mixed with the odor of the old canvas cover he was bunched against, a musty, sour smell.

Petrah absently picked at the canvas, fingers cold and mind numb. Jow-quu was the closest thing he had to family, and now he was gone.

Monta-por had the crew gather under the yellow curtain of light. Petrah remained in the back but listened to the captain talk.

"I know this is a difficult time to say anything. I can only imagine your loss. But we must discuss our next move. We're sitting on a lot of cargo that needs to be unloaded. If anyone's looking for us, it's going to be hard to do that. We'll stay aboard the ship until first light. Then I'll go into town and arrange for the cargo exchange to be done here so we can leave Fangmordah as soon as possible. I need everyone with me. Nod your heads that you understand."

The weary travelers concurred.

Monta-por jerked a thumb toward the stern. "Someone pass the word to our friend back there."

P ETRAH HAD A HARD time falling asleep. When he finally did, he dreamed—not of the usual hiding and fleeing, but of a place he'd never seen before.

An angry mass of swirling clouds rotated around a dark center, high above the peak of a naked mountain. Lightning lit the underside of the mass, brightening the gray sky, to reveal a desolate landscape of rock and scree. Below the mountain, a barren valley carved into an inhospitable, lifeless wasteland.

Petrah felt himself fly upward and forward, toward the peak.

An odd protrusion jutted from the mountainside near the top, shadowed, except when the lightning scorched the sky.

The forward flight slowed, and the shape took the form of a figure.

The sky flashed, revealing a gray robe and drawn cowl.

Another flash revealed a metal staff grasped in the left hand with a large loop on top and inscriptions running its length. The figure was as immobile as the mountain itself, as still as a statue at first.

Then it lifted its head, and Petrah saw the faint glow of two orbs radiating a soft, white light from within the cowl.

Petrah spoke first. "Where am I?"

The figure responded in a deep, almost inhuman, voice that carried a metallic, vibrating hum. "At the end of the world."

"Who are you?"

"I have many names. Your ancestors called us Watchers, for we were tasked to watch over mankind, to guide and shape you. We taught you how to sew and harvest, create industry and weapons of war, heal the sick, and tap into divine power. We showed you how to beautify your appearances, to be proud and independent, to learn the motion of the stars, to take of the earth, and to indulge your desires, so that you might know pleasure and pain. Before that, we lived in the Above, serving our Maker. I am the last of my kind, a servant of Truth.

"You also have many names."

"I know only one."

"Yes. They call you Petrah, because of your eyes. And what wondrous eyes you have."

"Do you know my other names?"

"There is the name your mother gave you and the name your father gave you. There is the name that was forged in the heavens, the name cursed by those you will betray, and the name the Maker has forbidden because you are not worthy of having it. Yes, I know your other names."

"Tell me who my mother is, my father, where I'm from, *who I am*."

The Watcher grasped his staff with both hands and dug his long, black fingernails into his knuckles. "My purpose is to guide you, Petrah, as I am a Watcher, and nothing more. I'm not here to reveal your names or your past. Seek those paths on your own."

"At least tell me what became of my mother. I can't remember what happened to her, or me, or how I got here. But you know, don't you?"

The Watcher said nothing.

"Why won't you tell me?"

Still, the Watcher remained silent.

"At least show me your face."

The Watcher raised his staff and drove it down with great force. The metal sparked and rang out as the shaft buried into the bedrock.

With his hands freed, the Watcher pulled back his cowl and draped it behind him. As he did so, the glow intensified and then winked out, revealing the face of a man, or at least something resembling a man.

He was young and old, handsome and terrible, light and dark—an impossible combination of contradictions, an impossible notion of humanity. The glowing orbs of his eyes were now dimmed, the pupils turned pitch black, unblinking and unswerving in their gaze, his skin, pale and smooth, and not a single hair on his scalp or brow.

"What are you?"

"I am reason," the Watcher said. "I am purpose. I am the keeper of secrets, the one who listens, and the one who waits. I am the Gatekeeper, just as you are the Key, Petrah."

"The key to what?"

"Give it time and you will see. But remember this: the gears of the cosmos turn on their own, and you with it. They cannot be bent, nor can they be stopped. They must persist, as it is written in the stars—no more, no less."

"I don't believe that. I'm a free man now. I can choose what I want."

"Then why couldn't you save your friend in the tavern if you had the power to choose?"

"I couldn't. I—" Petrah had no answer. He wanted to shout at this man, to tell him he tried, that he would have done something if he could have. But he couldn't, and that was the curse he'd have to live with.

"None of us can choose, Petrah. Jah, the Maker, created all, but He too is locked into the fate of what shall pass. The angels say it is the cruelest jest in history, for both Jah, the Maker, and San, the Father, are servants of destiny, as is humankind. Have comfort in knowing your place in the wheel of fate is both great and terrible."

"I want no part of it."

"You may believe you are at a crossroads, yet the path you choose will be the one already chosen for you.

"Now." The Watcher lifted his arms. "It is time for you to awaken."

"Not yet. Tell me who I am."

The view of the Watcher drifted away.

"Who am I?"

PETRAH AWOKE, WRESTLING WITH the canvas tarp draped over his body.

He threw it off and shot bolt upright.

He could feel the sheen of sweat on his brow, the puddle of moisture clinging to his chest, and the stale taste of flatbread and ale from the night before. Fork-tailed gulls hovered over a fishing vessel coming to port, crying shrilly.

Petrah licked his lips, craving that blasted sprushah again.

Ahleen came over to him. "Petrah, are you all right?"

Words from a dream lingered like the foul stench of bog water.

Who am I?

The question perched on the tip of his tongue, but Ahleen wouldn't know the answer.

"Sorry, I was just tangled up, that's all." He couldn't tell if Ahleen believed him.

"We're getting ready to exchange our goods. As soon as we're done, we're off. We could use your help."

A gull dove into the water beside the fishing boat. Petrah wished his life was that simple: riding the wind and hunting for food.

He rubbed the blistered acid burn on his ankle. It was itchy. He wanted to scratch it, but he remembered Raya telling him to leave it alone so that it wouldn't scar over.

"Petrah, you don't look well."

He imagined his skin the tint of wax and his aroma vulgar like day-old piss. He got to his feet. "Bad dreams, but I'm all right."

Ahleen rested her hand lightly on his shoulder. He appreciated the gentle touch. "I know how much Jow meant to you. He was a good man. I'm sorry for your loss, Petrah."

Petrah nodded, trying not to let her see his eyes, which grew damp. "He was family to me. If only I—" He couldn't say it. The Watcher had told him he didn't have a choice, that the outcome would have been the same. Why couldn't he have saved Jow-quu?

Because he saved us.

The Watcher was wrong.

Everyone had a choice.

Jow-quu had made his—a decision to save his friends. Petrah would honor his sacrifice.

"No, I'm being selfish," he said, admitting his foolishness. "What they did to you though . . ."

If Ahleen felt violated, she hid it well. "I'm shaken up, but I'm here—and whole. I'm eager to move on. I only wish we could have had a proper burial for Jow, someplace out in the desert, under a bluff perhaps, shielded from the wind."

"He would have liked that." Petrah jabbed a bare toe between a gap in the boards of the wood decking. The grain was rough. "He was a wonderful, kind-hearted man, Ahleen. The best I knew. He deserves to be honored."

He deserves to be laid to rest in a place where we could pay our respects. Not left behind in a bar and tossed out with the trash.

She made him look at her. "And we'll honor him every day with our thoughts and prayers. You know that, don't you?"

Petrah wiped his eyes. "Of course."

T HE CARGO TRADE WENT smoothly and without incident. The crew of the *Kafta* exchanged non-perishables for dried fruits, salted meats, pickled vegetables, and sacks of grain. They were to transport the goods to the Commerce Guild in the capital city of Elmar, where Monta-por would receive payment in coin.

Musta came through for Monta-por, diverting a pair of soldiers on patrol by giving them a made-up story about seeing a suspicious band of men a few blocks from the harbor to draw them away from the docks. He was all smiles and proud of his work. Monta-por tousled his hair and paid him double as promised.

By noon, the *Kafta* was on its way downriver, much to the crew's relief.

Tan and Jayeem engaged in mock swordplay on the deck, using swords with blunt edges.

"What are they doing?" Petrah asked Kruush as he sat atop the grain sacks in the early afternoon. The warm breeze comforted him, but it couldn't quell the sadness.

"Fencing," Kruush said. "Tan used to handle a sword for a living. He's a bit rusty, but not bad. Not bad at all."

"He looks pretty good to me. He's blocking everything Jayeem is throwing at him."

Kruush produced a crooked grin. "Bet you a gold till Jayeem's going soft on our friend. Look at Tan: he's winded."

Petrah had never seen a gold coin. He knew twelve silver currah equaled one electrum kant, and three kanta equaled one gold till. Even with their combined wages from this trip, they'd amass a quarter till in silver at most. "Make it a ruh, and you've got yourself a deal."

"One copper, eh? Fine. First to make contact wins." Kruush spit on his hand and Petrah shook it.

The silly bet lifted Petrah's wretched mood. He needed the distraction.

No sooner had they made the deal, Tan parried one of Jayeem's thrusts and swung about and smacked the helmsman on the back with the flat of his blade.

Petrah slapped his knees in victory. "Hah! You owe me."

Kruush raised an eyebrow. "That was fast." Then, with a smirk, he added, "One more round. Double or nothing."

Jayeem and Tan went at it again.

Petrah didn't know a thing about swordsmanship, but he noted the grace in their movements. One attacked, the other countered, and together they formed a dance.

Tan won.

"Beginner's luck," Kruush said, crossing his arms with a sour face.

Petrah flashed a fiendish smile. "You owe me two ruh now."

Kruush humphed. "So I do."

Jayeem and Tan readied their blades. Jayeem won the next two rounds, evening the score. The longer Petrah watched the duo with their swordplay, the more enthralled he became, anticipating their moves with a jab or slash of his hand and slapping his knee whenever one struck the other.

When Jayeem won the next round, Kruush grumbled and said, "I should be ahead by now."

"You should," Petrah said, but stopped short of rubbing it in his face. Instead, he asked, "Do you suppose Jayeem might show me how to use a sword?"

Kruush gave him a questioning look. "And why would you want to learn how to use a sword?"

"Because it's a good skill to learn. And besides," Petrah said, "I'm fascinated by it. So, what do you think? Should I ask?"

Kruush crossed his arms. "Go ahead. Don't blame me if he says no."

B UT JAYEEM SAID YES and agreed to instruct Petrah on the basics of sword fighting.

"You need to pay attention to me," Jayeem said. "Have you handled a weapon before?"

"Never."

"Good. Then you won't need to unlearn any bad habits."

During periods when the wind was steady, the helmsman taught his avid student amidships. Tan shadowed their moves with his hands while Kruush and Ahleen commented to each other and Monta-por looked on with an amused smile.

"The key is to have proper balance," Jayeem said. "You have to anticipate your opponent's next move even before he knows it."

"And if it's a 'she'?" Petrah asked.

Jayeem laughed at that, the scar on his face dancing. "Then you're in real trouble, my friend. Especially if she's beautiful." He returned to a more serious tone. "A word to the wise: never assume anything. You must be on guard. You must be vigilant and dogged in handling your adversary. Any less, and you're a dead man. Be patient and wait for the right opportunity to strike—or strike fast and hard, but don't overextend yourself foolishly. Above all, you must think with your mind, not your weapon. That's the mark of a good swordsman."

Petrah proved to be a fast learner, just as he was with sailing.

Soon, he could parry, riposte, lunge, and even feint, although he never got the better of Jayeem. Tan shadowed Petrah from a few feet away, matching him move for move. Petrah tried to concentrate on Jayeem, but Tan's swings and thrusts were a constant distraction. On one occasion, Jayeem landed a kick that knocked Petrah to the deck.

Jayeem pressed his blunt practice sword into Petrah's throat. "That's what happens when you don't pay attention."

Tan laughed at his misfortune. "You won't impress any bar maidens on the ground like that."

Petrah didn't appreciate Tan's ill-timed jab. He yielded, and Jayeem helped him up. "You kicked me. That wasn't fair."

"As my father once said, life's never fair. Your opponent will use the dirtiest of tricks to gain the advantage. So can you. All is fair in swordplay. Remember that. Are you ready to go some more?"

Petrah rubbed the spot where the blade had pushed into his throat. He wouldn't let Jayeem trick him again. Nor would he let Tan distract or make fun of him. He would show them both he was a worthy opponent. "Aye, ready."

T HE *KAFTA* REACHED THE citadel of Elmar early on the third day of travel. Monta-por guided his vessel toward the large harbor, and Jayeem and Petrah worked the sails.

The capital rose to the center of a wide hill like a step pyramid, each level encircled by towering, stone walls that started at the base and climbed upward in concentric rings.

Shrines, temples, villas, homes, and public buildings crowded each level in a variety of whites, tans, browns, and bone hues.

Petrah caught a whiff of cooked meats from the vendors within the city's walls. It made him hungry just as it made him sad, filling him with regrets about Jow-quu.

By the time the sun dipped below the horizon, the crew completed the delivery of their shipment to the Commerce Guild.

As promised, Monta-por disbursed payment.

Petrah opened the drawstrings of his pouch and peered inside in the dwindling light. He fingered the silver and copper triangular coins and wondered what he would do with them. Kruush handed him two ruh.

"I thought you were joking earlier," Petrah said.

"Joking? A bet's a bet, lad. If you'd lost, you better believe I'd be collecting. Now take these before I change my mind."

Petrah accepted payment and added it to his purse with a happy plunk.

"Jayeem and I are staying in Elmar for the rest of the week," Monta-por told the crew. "You're welcome to remain aboard. If you want to continue on with us, we'll make another delivery upriver. Money should be better this trip around. I just need to know your decision in the next day or two."

"That's a generous offer," Kruush said. "To be honest, Captain, we don't know what we're going to do. We'll make sure we give you an answer within the next couple of days."

Monta-por ran a hand through the beads in his beard. "Fair enough."

K RUUSH, TAN, AND PETRAH went into the city the next morning
so they could look for work. Ahleen remained behind.

Petrah thought it unfair that she couldn't go as well, considering she
was as capable as any of them, just as she was when she'd helped load their
shipment aboard the *Kafta* in Kanmar.

Petrah shared his opinion on the matter as they walked up a narrow,
winding street. "Ahleen should be with us."

"She should," Kruush said, "but she can't."

"Why not?"

"Because the merchants, guildsmen, and market makers are dominated by men. Men who stick to a thousand-year-old edict that robs women
of opportunities. It's as absurd as it is vexing. Trust me, I don't believe in
it. But I must abide by it."

If not for Ahleen's ingenuity and risk-taking, Petrah would still be a
slave, his friends too. "Absurd is right."

The street opened up to a major thoroughfare filled with pedestrians.
Everywhere Petrah looked, the avenue teemed with people. Petrah got
caught up in the bustle, the excitement, the constant motion.

The multi-tiered design of the citadel, though, confounded him.

Half a dozen ringed walls rose to the top of a hill, connected through
stairwells and gates. An array of buildings occupied the summit, including a rotunda and six minarets surrounding it.

One building, the largest of all of them, took his breath away.

It was a grand construct of spires, towers, and connecting spans made
of black granite. He moved between two merchants and their carts, filled
with the heady scent of dried tea leaves, to get a clearer view of the edifice.

"The rotunda is the Dome of San, the city's main temple," Kruush
said. "The big building across from it, with the black spines shooting

toward the sky, is the famous Den Gajjal, our country's capitol. It's also where the Iron Fist rules."

Petrah recognized the title of Iron Fist. It belonged to Andus-nai, the leader of the Fist, Terjurmeh's ruling party. Petrah recalled Manis-cor being called the Dark Arrow—and his party, the Black Arrow. There were many other parties, but only a few controlled the country.

"It's a pompous title."

"Aye, and a fitting one," Kruush said. "That man's got a stranglehold on the country. No wonder things are falling apart."

"Where are we headed?"

"A pub called the Red Hope. I've heard it's the best place to find out what's happening in the job market. There should be plenty of gossip to hear."

Tan leaned in between them. "And it's right around the corner from a brothel. One reputed to have the loveliest ladies in the land. Perhaps after our bit of business, we can make a visit."

Kruush rolled his eyes. "Only *you* would think of such base things."

Petrah colored at the idea they might end up at a whorehouse. "But I thought we were looking for work."

"Aye, we are," Kruush said, giving Tan the stink eye. "We won't be doing any philandering, I assure you."

"And if we can't find any work?" Petrah asked.

Kruush grinned. "There's always good ale to drink."

THE RED HOPE WAS a large establishment, nearly filled to capacity with workers and merchants. The ex-slaves were fortunate to find an open table.

Petrah settled into a chair made of cane shoots lashed together. He smelled unfamiliar spices from a stew cooking. His stomach rumbled.

"Be right back," Kruush said, vanishing into the crowd.

Petrah motioned after him. "Where's he going?"

Tan smacked his lips. "Finding something to drink, I hope." Then he said, "Knowing Kruush, he's all business."

Kruush returned minutes later, smiling.

"What's that for?" Petrah asked.

"Got some information to help us out, or should I say"—Kruush produced two coins and rubbed them together—"bought the information to help us out." When Petrah looked at him strangely, he replied, "That's how you speed things up, boy. Money can do just about anything."

"What did I tell you?" Tan said, drumming the table with his fingers. "All business."

Petrah didn't understand Kruush's comment. "What information did you buy?"

"Patience, young lad," Kruush said. "First, we eat and drink. Can't do business on an empty stomach, you know."

Tan grinned. "I'll second that!"

A SERVING BOY WITH dark freckles brought the men clay mugs filled with foamy ale, followed by a platter of cheeses, breads, and some type of stuffed vegetable.

Petrah poked at one of the vegetable rolls. The steam let out a meaty aroma that had him salivating. "What's this?"

"Soolechia-su," Kruush said. "Soolechia leaves stuffed with rice and ground meat. My mother made the best, but judging from the smell of these beauties, I'd say we're in for a treat. Dig in!"

Petrah took a nibble and discovered he liked it. The leaves themselves had no taste, only a pleasant chew that complimented the meat-and-rice mixture that brought out garlic and onion flavors with just the right touch of salt. A thick dipping sauce added a tang which danced on his tongue long after the first bite.

As he ate, Petrah noticed a tingling sensation in the back of his head. Every time he looked up, he saw the same man seated in the rear of the establishment. It was hard to make out his shadowed face this far away, but Petrah suspected the man was watching them.

Tan took a swig of ale and wiped his mouth. "What's the matter?"

"There's a man back there who keeps looking at us."

When Tan and Kruush started to turn their heads, Petrah quickly said, "Don't look!"

"Why not?" Kruush asked. "I thought you wanted us to see."

"I don't want to attract any unnecessary attention," Petrah said. "Or did you forget what happened in Fangmordah?"

"Pah, you're paranoid. Fangmordah was bad luck. I say our luck is about to change. So why don't we take a moment to relax and enjoy our food and drink? No one else is looking at us, are they?"

Everyone else was minding their business: eating, drinking, and talking. But the stranger in the back . . . "I don't like being watched, is all. It reminds me of the Draadi."

Kruush's face knotted into a scowl. "If there were any Draadi here, we'd know. Now, can we please finish our meal in peace?"

Petrah didn't want to keep arguing, so he said, "Fine, I'll leave it alone."

With a smirk, Tan said, "Maybe the man's related to Meska. That rat had a fancy for you."

Petrah frowned. "Not funny."

K RUUSH WAVED DOWN THE serving boy after their second round. "Young man, come here." Kruush took the boy's palm and placed a silver coin on it. "I need to buy the men at that far table another of whatever they're drinking."

The boy turned in the direction of three men dressed in long, white robes. An embroidered pattern of a hand was stitched over their right breasts. "Anything else, Master?"

"Yes. Tell them there's a party interested in doing business with them. Now, off with you."

The boy returned a few minutes later, carrying change.

"What did they say?" Kruush asked.

"They said that you should come back tomorrow about midday. Someone will be here who you can talk to. They said the man you'd meet would be dressed like them."

"Excellent! You did well, boy."

"Here's your change, Master."

Kruush closed the boy's fingers over the money. "Keep it."

The boy smiled with the intensity of the sun and ran off to clean a table.

"That was awfully generous," Tan said. "So, are you going to tell us what's happening?"

Kruush leaned over the table but kept his voice low. "The men at the far table are from the White Hand. Remember when I paid for some information earlier? The barkeep told me the party's looking to increase membership. That's big news."

Tan darted a glance at the men. "You want us to do business with the White Hand? Do you think that's wise right now, given our newness? Besides, they're not exactly well-liked among the parties. They have dealings with an enemy country. It's caused friction in the past. Or at least that's how it was before we, you know . . ."

"The White Hand is one of the top-ranked parties in Terjurmeh," Kruush said. "They've got the largest trade routes to Meerjurmeh. And yes, Meerjurmeh is an enemy of Terjurmeh, but it borders our nation, and where there are borders, there are opportunities. There's a lot of money to be made, especially on the import side."

"The border you're talking about is a vast desert," Tan said, drawing a box on the table with his finger as if making a map. "It's not like going from Kanmar to Fangmordah or Elmar. No river to connect the two countries. What would we trade, anyway?"

"Dusk."

Tan lifted a brow. "A spice?"

"A very special spice," Kruush said. "One that makes people a bit more spiritual, if you get my meaning. And it's expensive stuff. Only the wealthy can afford it. My partner and I tried to break into the market back in Kanmar before you-know-what happened."

Petrah couldn't help but interrupt. "Didn't Monta-por mention something about us going to war with Meerjurmeh?"

Kruush shrugged. "Money's money. When has a war ever changed that?"

Tan dragged a finger across the rough grain of the stone tabletop. "Dusk, you said?"

"Yes," Kruush said. "And much, much more. Our empty purses will burst a year from now. Think about it. Imagine being on the open road with no one to tell you what to do. We'd be our own persons. Ahleen would be safe from pigs like those who struck down our dear friend, Jow. Petrah, you would learn the skill of trade, and at such a young age too.

I'd teach you everything I know. You could be wealthy before you start your own family. Who gets an opportunity like that? Tan, you wouldn't have to go back to being a swordsman for some godforsaken tribe in the middle of the wastelands. Who knows, you might even find a pretty lass along the way. You might finally settle down and spit out a runt or two."

"I doubt that," Tan said. "But I'm always up for a pretty lass . . . or two."

There was weight to Kruush's words, yet Petrah found himself buoyant and dreaming of a different life, away from the scrutiny of soldiers on the lookout for escaped slaves. He'd experienced a lightness on the ship with Monta-por and Jayeem.

Could the open desert offer the same? Could he become a trader and embrace a life of travel and new experiences? Could he find someone like Ahleen to give the long road meaning?

His palms were damp, his fingertips cold, his face hot from all the thoughts swimming in his head. There was a lot to consider.

Kruush grinned brightly. "Tomorrow, boys, we change our destiny. Tomorrow, we begin a new life."

Chapter 8

Crossroads

T HE TRIO RETURNED TO the Red Hope the following day. Again, it was full.

Petrah picked up the aroma of charbroiled fish over the odor of un-washed men. It was far better than anything in the pits in Kanmar and tamer than the smells of the quarry, where smelt ore mingled with the heinous stink of his fellow slaves baking in the sun.

He held out a hand. The shakes were still there, but not as bad today. He looked forward to the morning when he woke up and didn't tremble or lick his lips and desire that godawful drink.

The others didn't seem as jittery as when they'd first boarded the *Kafta*. Nor did he catch them wringing their hands, bobbling their knees, or darting glances like they'd done in days past.

Kruush paid the same serving boy from the day before to keep an eye out for any members of the White Hand.

Sure enough, several trickled in an hour later.

The one whom Kruush was looking for took a table near the entrance. Kruush had the boy bring the man a draught of ale. The man made eye contact with Kruush and bowed his head, a sign of gratitude. He then pulled out the chair next to him and gestured.

Kruush stood. "All right, gents, it's time to find out what our friend can do for us. See you in a bit."

"I hope he doesn't take too long," Tan said after Kruush left. "I'm getting that hungry feeling again."

Petrah shook his head. "You two are always thinking with your stomachs. I'm surprised you're not twice your size."

Tan smacked his gut. "Give it some time, my friend. If we keep eating and drinking like this, we'll be triple our size soon enough. And if we get married . . . ?" He let out a hearty cheer.

"You, married?" Petrah doubted Tan knew the meaning of the word. "I thought you were excited to start collecting lasses."

"I was." Tan smiled guiltily. "But you never know. I'm fancying the serving girl over there. She'd make a good wife."

"You were fancying a different one yesterday."

"I suppose I was. Many a good wife to be had."

Kruush locked forearms with the White Hand member, an older man with a pointed gray beard.

Petrah asked Tan, "Do you think he's looking to do legitimate trade?"

"As opposed to . . . ?"

"Smuggling."

Tan frowned at him. "You heard what Kruush said yesterday. Why would you ask such a question?"

"Because of what he did before you-know-what-happened to him."

"Losing your freedom changes you. Kruush has Ahleen now and us. He wouldn't jeopardize his freedom. I know *I* won't."

"But he spoke about trading dusk yesterday. It sounds risky."

"Everything in life carries risk," Tan said. "You might cross the road and not make it to the other side."

Petrah huffed. "That's not what I meant, and you know it."

"What would you have me say? That joining the White Hand poses no risk? That we'll be bathing in silver and gold a year from now because of good fortune and our unmatched wits? No, there are no guarantees. And yes, trading dusk is a tricky bit of business. You have to grease the

right hands to get a shipment through. As Kruush said, there's more
to trading than dusk. We might not even get the opportunity to trade
it, so I wouldn't put much faith in the idea. Practically speaking, it'll
probably be something much more mundane. From my experience, even
mundane shipments require getting past guards and dealing with the
Commerce Guild and all sorts of wrangling, which could prove expensive. Sometimes, it's wiser to pay off the right people and avoid such
hassles."

"Isn't that smuggling?"

"Call it what you want, but it's how the world operates. You'll see."

Petrah released a heavy sigh. "I still don't get it."

"You won't," Tan said. "At least, not yet. But Kruush knows what he's
doing. Give it some time, and you'll learn it too."

Petrah dropped the subject, frustrated at his lack of understanding of
business dealings. Smuggling goods didn't sit well with him. They had
made Kruush a city slave for getting caught as a smuggler. Even if Kruush
wore the badge of the White Hand over his breast, would it legitimize his
dealings? Or would his actions jeopardize their freedom?

Petrah was just getting used to being a free man. He didn't want to risk
losing it. Nor did he want the bedrock of a cell to get in the way of him
looking at the stars at night.

But he was just an ignorant, young man. *I know nothing of the world.
I must change that.*

After a couple of minutes, he felt the same tingling sensation in the
back of his head as he had the day before.

Petrah looked up and over to the shadowed corner.

The mystery man from yesterday was sitting there again. Petrah still
couldn't make out his features, but he was definitely watching him. This
time, the man bowed his head. Petrah, not wanting to be rude, reciprocated. Was it the right response? After observing Kruush, it seemed like
the natural thing to do. He needed Tan's input.

"Our watchful friend from yesterday has returned," Petrah said. "He tipped his head at me, and I did the same back. Should I have done that?"

"Do you know what he wants?"

"No."

"Maybe he's being friendly, or maybe he's interested in you for some reason. My advice: don't engage. We don't need any trouble."

The mention of "trouble" had Petrah shifting uncomfortably in his seat. The mystery man, whoever he was, could be a spy for the city, perhaps a cutthroat looking for easy prey.

I should have known better. Why didn't I know better?

Before Petrah could chide himself further, the serving boy showed up.

"Pardon me, Master," he said to Petrah. "But the gentleman in the back has invited you to his table for refreshments."

Tan shook his head. He was saying *no*, but Petrah wanted to understand what the mystery man wanted. "Did the man say why?"

"Sorry, Master, he didn't."

Petrah looked at Tan, who wasn't happy. "What do you think?"

"You know what I think, but it's up to you. Tradition says it's rude to refuse an invitation, so there's that."

Kruush was still busy. It wasn't like they could leave. "I guess I'll find out what he wants."

"Just be careful."

P ETRAH FOLLOWED THE BOY to the back of the taproom, mindful of the other patrons. If the mystery man had friends of an ill sort, Petrah needed to be prepared to leave in a hurry. Tan would watch him, ready to act.

The man wants to talk to me, nothing more. How bad could it be?

The customers at the neighboring tables talked among themselves, paying scant attention to the fifteen-year-old. Petrah wished Jayeem was here. He'd have a sword on his person, just in case.

When they got to the table, the man tossed the boy a coin. The boy caught it, smiled, and left, leaving the two by themselves.

Petrah hadn't felt this uncomfortable since his last encounter with Meska. At least this man wasn't a Draad.

The man pointed at the chair opposite him. "Please."

Petrah sat. Only when the stranger leaned forward did his face become visible.

Petrah was surprised to see someone so well groomed. The man had a thin, trimmed mustache, short beard, and combed, dark brown hair to complement his olive complexion and deep bronze pupils. Everything about the man reflected poise and precision. He wore a pressed black robe with green stitching over his left breast, a depiction of a flame. Petrah didn't recognize the insignia but suspected it belonged to one Terjurmehan party or another.

"My name is Joriah. I asked you here so we could speak in private. Would you like some spring water?" He presented a clean mug to Petrah and put a hand on a clay jug sitting atop the table.

Petrah eyed the vessel. Is this what the serving boy meant by "refreshments?" He accepted anyway. "Yes, please."

Joriah filled Petrah's cup, then his own. Petrah waited for the man to drink before doing the same.

"You're suspicious of me. That's good. It reflects measured thinking, and measured thinking is important in my line of work."

"And what line of work is that?" Petrah didn't know if it was rude to speak out of turn. He knew nothing of Terjurmehan custom, just as he didn't know it was rude to refuse an invitation as a guest. Regardless, this man owed him an explanation.

"I'll get to my line of work in a moment," Joriah said. "But first, I'd like to ask you your name. A fair request, seeing I told you mine."

It was a fair request. "I'm Petrah."

The man studied Petrah's face. "A very clever name. 'Blue eyes' would be the translation. Your accent—it's unique. I can't quite place it." When Petrah didn't volunteer any information, Joriah continued. "You can relax. I'm not trying to pry. I was simply curious. I promise I'll say my piece, and then you can go back to your table." Petrah couldn't relax, at least not until he found out what this man wanted with a fifteen-year-old stranger. "What do you know of the Green Flame?"

"Nothing really, other than it's a political party."

"One of the most prominent, in fact. I've been with the party for many years. Our cause differs greatly from the others'."

Petrah didn't like where this was going. Antelle had said certain parties had fanatical followings. Was this one of them? "What's so special about it?"

"Our membership differentiates us. Unlike the other parties—take the White Hand, for instance—we only accept qualified individuals. We're a brotherhood, Petrah, and that means a lot these days."

So they *were* a fanatical organization.

Petrah tried to think of a way of saying "no thank you" without seeming impolite.

"I know that look," Joriah said, as if reading his thoughts. "You want to leave."

Petrah couldn't help himself. "I do."

"Hear me out, just a little longer. If you don't like what I have to tell you, then you can go, and you'll never hear from me again. What do you say?"

Petrah sank back into his seat. He'd hear the man out.

"I'll be frank, Petrah. We're looking to expand. We need prospects with potential. I think you're someone with potential."

"Potential for what?" It was as Petrah had suspected: Joriah was looking to recruit him. But for what purpose and to what end?

"Potential to learn, to excel, to make a difference. Determining someone's potential is tied to identifying certain characteristics of that person. There are ways to tell this beyond conventional means."

Petrah touched the back of his head, the spot where he had felt the strange tingling sensation.

"Yes," Joriah said, "you're beginning to understand. No one else in this establishment noticed, but you did. That sets you apart. I've been looking for someone like you."

Petrah doubted there was anything special about himself. Joriah was playing a mind trick on him, making him think that sensing someone's eyes on the back of their head was unique. Tan had probably felt it too but not said anything.

"What makes you think I'm interested? I'm seeking work, not to get involved in politics."

"You've got the wrong idea about us. Politics is but one facet of a party. You'd be involved in a very special program, something that could earn you respect, position, and even power in time. It would be more than just a job; it would be a vocation. It could elevate you in society. That's one thing a career with the White Hand could never achieve. Ask anyone when was the last time a trader rose in prominence. Ask anyone about the last time a member of the White Hand earned respect in the Great Council. Their members are good with coin, and that's fine and well. But what I'm offering goes far beyond anything your friend is brokering right now."

Petrah rubbed the scar above his right eyebrow. He didn't like that he was intrigued by Joriah's pitch and that it sounded better than Kruush's, even though Kruush's pitch yesterday had excited him. But he had doubts about Kruush's plan. Kruush had been a smuggler who'd gotten himself caught. Wasn't he proposing to go right back to the crimes that got him imprisoned—to "pay off the right people," as Tan had suggested? How was that a noble path?

But Joriah represented a party Petrah knew nothing about. To say yes to him would be to entertain the unknown, maybe do something he'd regret, and perhaps risk the freedom he'd fought so hard to win. It would also be saying goodbye to the people he cared about—his family.

I should say thank you, but no. I should tell Joriah goodbye.

But Petrah couldn't speak the words. Instead, his curiosity got the better of him. "What exactly would I be doing?"

For the first time since their meeting, Joriah smiled.

K RUUSH SLAMMED HIS MUG against the table. Foam and ale spilled over. "Are you joking, boy?"

It was late afternoon in the Red Hope, and many of the tables were empty.

Petrah had stayed with Joriah for the better part of an hour, listening to the man weave an exciting tale of the youth's prospective future as a mage apprentice and member of the Green Flame.

Petrah had heard of magi and their ability to tap into divine power. The highest members of the Temple had that power, leaders like Septamo, First Articulate. Joriah said this common ability among magi and priests tied the Green Flame to the Temple, forging a union between the two—one that distinguished the Green Flame from the other parties, and one that created unique opportunities for its magi to advance their status in society. Petrah had parted with Joriah, promising to let him know his decision the next day.

Kruush was far from receptive when Petrah returned and told them of Joriah's proposal. "You listen here, you naive little runt! I just got us a deal with the White Hand. The four of us, including Ahleen, who's not even here. Do you know how difficult that was? We're talking about a legitimate trade route from Terjurmeh to Meerjurmeh and a percentage of the business. That's huge. And here you are brokering a separate deal for yourself, some apprentice nonsense." Kruush crossed his arms, his face red with a hint of purple.

Petrah took a moment before responding. He knew Kruush would be mad, so he took it slow.

"First of all, I never agreed to join anything. I told Joriah that I would consider the offer and let him know tomorrow. And second, this apprenticeship is not some nonsense. It's an opportunity to become a magus within a well-respected organization."

"Oh, so you're an expert on parties now, is that it? Before you sat at that man's table, you had no idea what the Green Flame was. I've seen things, boy. Even with a chewed-up brain, I know krell dung when I smell it. And it stinks. You've been duped. Do you have any idea what you're going to be earning as some dog slave of an apprentice? Do you even know what liberties you'd be giving up? It will be just like you're back in the pits again, a puppet under a new master."

"The Green Flame is known for their extremism," Tan said. "I've always heard their members referred to as zealots. That's not a kind term."

Petrah didn't appreciate Kruush's tone or Tan's condemnation, but worse, he didn't like the fact his friends might be right. He had the urge to quaff a pint of ale and let it cleanse Joriah's sales pitch from his mind.

Kruush tossed the pouch Monta-por had given him onto the table. It lay flat. "There. Open it and see."

Petrah didn't have to open it. Its contents were gone. "I get the point."

"No, you don't. That pouch is empty because I used my share of the money to buy us this opportunity with the White Hand. That takes guts and sharp thinking, my friend. It also takes experience, which you lack. What have you done? Sit with some stranger and buy a story about becoming a mage? It's a life of servitude. You'll end up serving someone's political agenda or turning into a war puppet, expendable and replaceable. There's no glory in the Hall of Fools, my father used to say, and he was right."

Tan added his opinion. "I don't know much about apprenticeships, but I understand how these parties operate. Kruush is looking out for us. He wouldn't partner with the White Hand if it wasn't a smart move. We have to stick together. Three is a good number, Petrah. After all the crap we've been through, you know it's the right choice. Stay with us."

Petrah had thought his queasiness was because of his excitement. Now he understood it was because of his nerves . . . and his doubts. The allure of ale no longer appealed to him. In fact, the smell from the spilled puddle by Kruush's mug had him pushing back from his seat. "I'll think about it."

Both Kruush and Tan dropped their chins in disappointment. Petrah's answer wasn't the one they wanted to hear.

That was all anyone said until they got to the ship.

P ETRAH LEANED AGAINST THE barge's railing in the black of night, wistfully lost in troubling thoughts while his shipmates slept.

It wasn't just Joriah's offer. It was a combination of things that left him so restless.

Jow-quu's passing. The Watcher's deterministic warning. And now this—a decision to leave his only friends.

Petrah wished Joriah had never spoken to him. Yet Joriah's offer made sense. It snapped the missing puzzle piece of his life into place. Didn't that count for something?

Or am I just losing my mind?

That had to be it. First Aggren's death, then his flogging, then freedom, only to see his friend Jow-quu killed in front of him. And now . . . ?

And now I have to make the most important decision of my life.

Petrah kept going back and forth in his mind about the Green Flame and whether it was a good choice or a poor one, but Joriah had spoken to more than Petrah's desire to make something of his freedom.

Joriah had spoken to Petrah's desire to belong *someplace* in the world.

But Kruush, Tan, and Ahleen were family. What could be more important than family?

Kruush startled him. "Up past bedtime, eh?" He propped his forearms against the railing and inhaled deeply. "Ah, I love this time of day. Smell that? Sweetwater reeds. They give off their fragrance only at night."

Petrah breathed in the fragrant nighttime air. It carried a sweetness like the honeyed mead he'd sampled at the Red Hope. The faint light from the lamps along the pier made the whiskers of Kruush's stubbly chin appear longer than they were. Petrah was going to miss talking to his friend.

"Listen, Kruush, I didn't mean to—"

Kruush batted a hand. "You don't have to say anything. I'm not angry. A little disappointed, but not angry. I doubt I could persuade you any differently, but I know that stubborn mind of yours has already decided what to do. You Northerners are a trying, pigheaded lot."

Petrah chuckled. "I guess. What about Tan and Ahleen?"

"What about them? You're their little brother. Do they want to see their little brother leave?"

Petrah didn't answer. The dampness in his palms told him he might be making a terrible decision.

But he wasn't a slave anymore; he was free. Freedom meant he could choose whatever he wanted, didn't it? Even if it meant choosing the wrong thing?

"For whatever it's worth, lad, I have only one thing to say: watch your back. I know these cultish factions. The man standing on the lowest step gets his face kicked in, if you get what I mean. But, most important"—Kruush raised a finger—"stay true to yourself and remember who you are, always. Be the Petrah who escaped captivity, who risked his life for a better one, who stands strong and proud. Not the Petrah who fell for a dream and lost himself along the way. You understand what I'm telling you, don't you?"

Petrah understood. He wrung his hands while wrestling with Kruush's warning. Was he making the wrong decision by going with Joriah?

Kruush glanced at Petrah's fidgeting. "It's not too late to change your mind."

Petrah untangled his fingers and laid his hands on the railing.

Meeting Joriah couldn't be by chance. There had to be a reason he chose me.

That was it. It had to be! This wasn't chance; it was destiny.

But even as the revelation came to him, the excitement receded again. The confusion returned, reigniting the contested battle of choices in his mind.

Decide!

And he did.

Kruush picked up on it. He sighed wearily. "Very well, lad. I'll break the news to Ahleen in the morning. Don't be surprised if she tosses you overboard."

A HLEEN WAS TEARFUL, AS she was with Raya's departure, but she braved a smile and gave Petrah a hug. "Don't forget us, all right?"

Petrah, too overcome for words, returned the embrace.

Ahleen was his sister.

She would marry Kruush, and they would have children. Petrah would become an uncle. He liked the idea of being an uncle.

He wished Ahleen and Kruush much happiness together. Tan as well, scallywag that he was.

They'll be fine because they have each other. And that's more valuable than all the coin in the world.

Petrah fought back tears as Tan locked forearms with him. Kruush gave him a bear hug, almost squeezing the breath out of him.

"You'd better write," the big man said.

Petrah laughed. He couldn't write, just as Kruush couldn't read. "You've got it."

"I'll be keeping an eye on you, nonetheless," Kruush said. "When I'm not on a caravan route, that is. Stay healthy, lad, and remember what I told you."

Monta-por and Jayeem said their goodbyes as well. The first mate even gave his sparring partner a parting gift: a sword.

Not a practice sword, but a real one.

Petrah hefted the sword. It was short, made of forged steel, and two-edged for cutting, with a tapered point for stabbing. It had a cross guard that curved forward and a knobbed hilt with a red bead embedded into the pommel which Jayeem said was for luck. It came complete with a leather scabbard and oilstone.

Petrah ran his fingers over the cursive lettering punched into the blade.

"It reads *Neckcleaver* in the sailor's tongue of my grandfather's day," Jayeem said with a proud smile. "Every sword needs a name. That's hers, if perhaps morose. Believe me, I didn't name her. I would have called her *Wenchstealer*, but that's just me."

Petrah smiled at that. "This must have cost you a fortune. I can't accept it."

"Nonsense. And it didn't cost me a single copper. I won it in a wager, fair and square. Now the other fellow . . . Well, let's say he wasn't too happy to part with the old gal."

Petrah locked forearms in earnest. "Thank you for this."

"Just remember what I taught you and you'll keep your head," Jayeem said. "May she serve you well. Now, off with you before I dunk you in the river."

Petrah headed toward the city to meet his new employer. He walked briskly as Kruush, Ahleen, and Tan watched from the end of the wharf, not because he was in a hurry, but because he didn't want them to see the tears in his eyes.

A HLEEN RESTED HER HEAD on Kruush's shoulder as she watched Petrah fade into the crowd. When he was gone, she cried, and Kruush held her tight.

"It'll be all right, darling," he said. "He'll be just fine."

Chapter 9

Apprentice

PETRAH TRAVELED WITH JORIAH by horse-drawn coach to his private, hundred-acre estate in a secluded area south of the capital that hugged the South Kesel. A six-foot masonry wall overgrown with vegetation enclosed the vast property. Petrah kept peeking out the coach window, trying to find a beginning or end to the long wall. His hands grew fidgety in anticipation as the horses slowed.

The coach let them out by the main gate, whose twin doors of heavy iron grating created a break in the endless wall. Armed guards greeted them with the sigil of the Green Flame embossed on the brass buckles pinning their green capes. Petrah found a pleasing earthiness to the air, like freshly-tilled soil, a far cry from the smells of the city.

A shiver of excitement and hesitation ran through him as he passed through the gate. He flinched when the crossbar clanked in place, locking the gate behind him. Winding paths of dirt led in different directions, disappearing through the shrubs and trees that stretched everywhere he looked.

Joriah presented the estate. "Welcome to *Maseah*. It means 'green sanctuary' in the Old Jurmehan tongue. What do you think of her?"

"She's—" Petrah tried to find the right word. Among a grove of olives, small birds tweeted, filling the fragrant air with their song. "She's beautiful. And peaceful too."

"Maseah is a compound that serves not only as a residence but a stronghold for the Green Flame party. She's a place of learning unlike any other offered to aspiring magi by the parties, a jewel among schools, and very much a sanctuary, not just for the learned mind, but the soul. Come, I'll take you to your dormitory."

Joriah had Petrah walk to his right, the correct position of one subordinate in stature. He went on to explain the property was a natural run of grassland, brush, and reed banks enclosed on all sides by the perimeter wall, except for where the property bordered the river.

An on-site garrison of soldiers permanently housed in a barracks set apart from the students' dormitory protected the property.

Inlets from the South Kesel fed the marshy alcoves along its waterfront, which Joriah touted as superb spots for his mage apprentices to meditate and reflect on their studies.

They ducked under a twist of branches entangled overhead. "From here on out," Joriah said, "you will refer to me as 'Master.' The same with your instructors. I am Master Joriah to you, not Joriah, and I expect you to address me and my peers with proper title and respect. We are not friends, Petrah, nor are we equals. You belong to the Green Flame now. Do you understand?"

Petrah felt a hitch in his side, a slight tightening in the chest, and Kruush's warning in his mind, which he squashed, and said, "I understand."

"Good. I believe you'll be pleased with your room."

Petrah's new living quarters were a small room in the dormitory. The ten-by-ten area of cinderblock walls and rock slab floor was luxurious compared to what Petrah had endured for the past few years. It even came with its own window.

Home, Petrah thought. *This is home now.*

Master Joriah told Petrah that he would be at Maseah until his schooling was completed, but he didn't say for how long. Students would have to attain journeyman before being permitted to advance to the next stage of becoming a mage.

"The path of an aspiring mage is long and difficult," Master Joriah said. "But if you put in the work, listen to your masters, apply yourself, and prove your worth, you will be rewarded."

Petrah wrung his hands during the walk along the unfamiliar grounds of the giant property, fingertips cold and wet. If Master Joriah noticed, he kept it to himself. The man remained quiet much of the way, holding up a hand anytime Petrah started to ask a question.

That only added to Petrah's unease.

Now, standing in the doorway of his dorm room, Petrah expected Master Joriah to speak up. But the mage provided no introduction, no explanation of what Petrah was to do, just an order to don the white robe folded on his bed and to remain in his room until further notice.

For several days, that's what Petrah did. By the third morning, his sprushah cravings were gone.

An older, heavyset woman named Annia delivered trays of food and drink. She limped with a bad hip that rose and fell with her uneven cadence, and she smelled medicinal to Petrah, like a balm. She escorted him to the outhouse twice a day, where he could do his business.

In his room, Petrah could hear the voices of his dormmates as they passed his door, returning from class, or wherever it was they went, but he never saw them. He was eager to crack open his door and peek, to glimpse the faces of his fellow students.

He didn't.

Master Joriah had been specific about Petrah keeping his door closed, and Annia made sure it stayed that way.

The room's furnishings were minimal: bed, desk, cane chair, trunk for storage, prayer book, and tabletop oil lamp. On the wall hung a black, iron serak. The holy triangle served as the symbol of faith for the Ter-jurah, with the lidless eye of their god, San, in the center, a source of comfort for the pious. To Petrah, it was just another adornment. The furniture was worn and scratched, the acha wood frayed and falling apart. Despite Master Joriah taking away Petrah's old clothing, sandals, and money, he'd let the youth keep the bundled sword Jayeem had given him. It mystified Petrah, but he didn't question his new master.

He appreciated having something to call his own. The sword was his one possession in the world. As a slave, nothing had been his, not even the dirty loincloth issued to him by the Draadi.

On a partly-cloudy afternoon, Petrah retrieved the bundle with his sword and clutched it to his chest. The jute soothed him with its rough texture and the embedded scent of wood from Jayeem's boat.

Petrah missed his sparring partner, but not as much as his friends. He missed Kruush's gruff voice, Ahleen's gentle but firm spirit, and Tan's irreverence.

I'll see you all again.

Sitting here, alone and doubtful about his decision to join the Green Flame, he tried not to think of what he was missing by not being with his friends, but he couldn't help himself.

Had they started on their caravan route? What were they transporting, and to whom? Were they happy with the White Hand?

No answers, just more questions.

Petrah unsheathed Jayeem's sword and inspected it.

There were nicks along both edges, pockmarks on the cross guard, rust spots on the metal, and the leather binding of the handle showed wear from frequent use. The red bead set into the pommel had a couple of minor scratches but was otherwise in good condition. Petrah ran a finger along the centerline of the blade from tip to hilt.

"Your name is *Neckcleaver*," he whispered as he hefted it. Had it cleaved any necks? Jayeem hadn't said. Petrah laughed when he realized this sword was his. It was a truly special gift, now a remarkable possession, and one that Petrah never would have dreamed of having when he was a slave. Petrah fingered the point of the blade, wondering if he might ever need to use it.

Not today.

He sheathed it, put it back in its gunnysack, and stuck it in the trunk.

For days, Petrah did a lot of thinking, bored and alone.

He spent much of the time lying in bed or peering out the window above his desk. Or he would look at the serak on the wall while reflecting on things.

Petrah watched the swaying marsh grass and pictured life with his friends. It was too much time for reflection. He also thought of home—wherever it might be—and wondered if there were any aunts, uncles, or cousins he'd left behind as a child. Did anyone miss him?

Sometimes, he'd think about the horrible dreams that woke him up in the middle of the night.

His mother's pleas and cries would linger long after he'd awaken, and he'd hear the gallop of hooves of the horsemen chasing after him. The Watcher hadn't returned since the night of Jow-quu's death.

Petrah believed the dream was just his imagination at work, a lashing out for how he couldn't save Jow-quu's life, not some prophetic message about the future.

He would forge his own destiny.

I will make my life my own. I'll prove the Watcher wrong.

Petrah grew tired of being shut in. Why was he stuck in this room? What purpose did it serve? Why wouldn't Annia speak to him? Petrah wasn't sure if she was mute or just following orders. She used hand gestures to communicate: wait, walk, go there, stop, go back.

Petrah spoke to her anyway, complimenting her on her tunic and her hair, but she said nothing back to him.

"Be that way," he said. "I guess I'll just have to be nice to someone else."

When she didn't react to his comment, he sighed. Yet he couldn't fault her. She was a slave. Her curvy green tattoo on her left ankle was the shape of a torch flame. The Green Party owned her.

His own tattoo was gone, the blisters too, but a faint patch of skin over his ankle remained. It was little more than an oval of discolored skin one might mistake for an abrasion that was still healing.

He'd caught Annia looking at it, perhaps out of curiosity, but like everything else, she kept her opinion to herself.

By day four, Petrah found himself pacing his small room. He'd endured years of imprisonment, but he'd never suffered isolation, not to this extent. He was desperate for something besides the relentless chirp of crickets or Annia's unbearable silence. At least in the pits, he'd had his cellmates.

Petrah heard his dormmates talk or laugh as they passed his door. They sounded young. He listened to their conversations—snippets of mundane things, like what they might do on San's Day, a complaint about class, or a gag someone was planning.

On day five, Petrah was sitting at his desk midafternoon, watching a pair of spotted male chee-chee crabs on the ground outside his window, locked in an epic battle with entangled claws, when he heard a knock.

The door opened, and Master Joriah entered wearing his usual green-trimmed, black robe.

He closed the door, placed his hands behind him, and scrutinized his new student.

Petrah waited for the mage to say something. Like Annia, his lips remained pressed together. Why wouldn't he speak?

Petrah waited and waited.

Finally, he couldn't take it anymore. "Aren't you going to say something?"

Master Joriah placed a finger over his lips and shushed him. "You will not speak until spoken to, understood? You cannot begin your training until you're ready. You're not ready."

"But I—" Petrah tried to say.

The mage shut the door on him.

It wasn't until the following evening that he returned.

Petrah said nothing this time. He let the mage study him.

"Better," Master Joriah said and left.

The next evening, Petrah repeated his silence. He didn't move; he barely breathed. It was obvious what Master Joriah was doing: teaching him to be patient. It was Petrah's first lesson.

The minutes passed, but Petrah stayed where he was. He didn't even wipe the itch from where the perspiration was trickling down his forehead.

I won't let him win.

His patience paid off. Master Joriah rewarded him with a single inclination of the head. "You're almost ready."

S AN'S DAY ARRIVED, AND the smell of sun-warmed mud wafted into Petrah's room.

He heard footfalls.

Then a familiar knock.

Petrah turned around in his seat, expecting another test.

Master Joriah wasn't alone. He entered with a tall youth in tow who was dressed in a green robe.

The young man was around Petrah's age but exuded the air of someone much older, particularly in the way he looked about the room so studiously and the way his parted, sienna hair was brushed to the side with attentive precision. He stood beside the mage, stiff in posture, with his hands behind him.

Master Joriah nodded to Petrah after a wait. "You're ready." He then gestured to the young man in green. "This is Hamma, our lead apprentice. You will follow his instructions. Hamma, this is Petrah."

The youth gave Petrah a cursory nod, and Petrah did the same. It seemed to meet Master Joriah's satisfaction.

"Hamma will show you around Maseah today. In the evening, you will shave and wash up before you sit down to sup. Annia will help you. You start school tomorrow. Clear your mind and pray well tonight. I will see you later."

With that, Master Joriah departed, leaving Petrah alone with his lead apprentice.

Petrah saw determination in Hamma's sand-colored eyes, an unyieldingness that went well with his taut lips and olive-complected, oval face. Hamma was lean in physique and long waisted. Petrah imagined him a superb swimmer.

Petrah felt a brief tingling on the back of his scalp. He touched the area, but there was nothing there but unwashed hair.

"You will not speak unless spoken to," Hamma said with authority. "Put on your sandals and follow me."

Petrah tailed the youth out into the blinding light of day. It was refreshing to feel air on his face that didn't smell like the outhouse. Hamma kept his palms crossed behind his back, his gait steady and surefooted.

"Next to me," Hamma said, nudging to his right with his chin.

Petrah scuffled forward and took his place by Hamma's side, on the right, the same as he'd done with Master Joriah when he'd first arrived.

They walked along a dirt pathway that cut through patchy, brown grass, palm trees, bamboo with reddish-green leaves, and patches of fragrant purple flowers that gave off the aroma of sage and lavender. To the right, a wall of reeds obscured the view of the churning river. The walkway curved to the left. Two stone buildings appeared.

"What did Master Joriah tell you about Maseah?" Hamma asked.

"He said to stay away from where the soldiers train and sleep," Petrah said. "Not much else."

"We're fortunate the student buildings are in one area and the soldiers' barracks and training grounds are in a separate area. The masters don't tolerate trespassing." Hamma's tone lightened. "There are six of us with you. Six is a good number, Petrah. We are in San's grace again."

They walked over to the first building. It was domed and capped by a tall, golden metal spire.

"This is the library," Hamma said. "You'll be permitted to study here and research any of the tomes or scrolls in the stacks. We have one of the finest collections in Elmar. I'll show you inside later. First, I want to show you the student hall."

Petrah had heard wondrous things about libraries, of the scent of parchment and leather, decades, even centuries old, of the volumes of art and literature students and scholars pored over to enrich their minds, of the conversations spurred by a great many works. The idea of holding a book in his hands excited him as much as it frightened him. After all, he'd never seen one up close.

Hamma stretched his arm to the north as they walked. "Master Joriah has a villa yonder. I've been there twice. Consider yourself privileged if he ever invites you over for tea."

They entered the windowless student hall into a vestibule lit by candles set into sconces.

A pair of diorite statues guarded the entry, each the size of a grown Terjurmehan. The one on the left was a figure of a man dressed in a robe and blindfolded, the one on the right, a robed figure with his hood drawn. Both pointed outward in opposite directions.

"They are Qufah and Qufay," Hamma explained, "'the blind and the blinded.' As the masters teach us, the *blind may see, but not the blinded*."

Puzzling as it sounded, it made sense to Petrah.

"This way," Hamma said.

They descended a stairway underground and passed through a tunnel brightened by mounted oil lamps. The air was cooler down below.

The corridor opened into a semicircular auditorium. It was set up like an amphitheater, ascending in a stepped fashion, six rows up from the floor. Black curtains lined the back wall, and a granite podium occupied the floor's center. A cupola added another story of height above. Shadows danced along a mosaic of blue tiles from the flicker of oil lamps set along the walls.

After they climbed to the top, Hamma presented the room with a sweep of his arms. "This is the *canteem*. It's where the masters instruct us as a group. You're going to learn many aspects of the world in here: history, divinity, sociology, politics, and of course, the arcane arts. Master Nole does most of the teaching. Have you met him?"

"Not yet."

The room appeared much larger from up top. When Hamma spoke, his words seemed to originate from one side of the room and travel to the other. Petrah swiveled his head to discover its source.

"It's the acoustics," Hamma explained. "It's meant to amplify the instructors' voices from the podium below. Marvelous, isn't it?"

Petrah had experienced nothing like it. "Quite." Then he asked, "Where do we sit?"

"Down below, center seats. Three students in the first row, the other three behind them. You'll be in the first row with me. Each seat has its own swivel table that converts the chair into a desk, which is good, because we'll be taking lots of notes. So be prepared."

Petrah drew a sharp breath when he realized how close he'd be to the podium—and Master Nole. "We'll be in the front row?"

"Being in the front isn't so bad," Hamma said. "Although you should keep in mind Master Nole is absolute about things and not very forgiving. You're the new student. Don't give him a chance to make an example of you. That being said, don't let him intimidate you. He means well."

Petrah knew a thing or two about being made an example of. The Draadi had insisted on it. If he were smart, he would heed Hamma's advice. "What about the other seats?"

"Empty, but the masters are considering adding more students in a season or two, maybe even creating a separate journeyman school. For now, it's just the six of us, all apprentices of the arts."

Petrah decided sharing the space with so few students might be better. The smaller number felt special, making Master Joriah's selection of him that much more significant. "Where are the windows?"

"You won't find any in the entire building. Thought is pure when uninterrupted by sound or sunlight; less room for the mind to wander. How can we enlighten ourselves if we are constantly distracted?"

It was a valid question which prompted another. "Then why do we have windows in our dorm rooms?"

Hamma smiled, the first glimpse of a softer side. "Could you imagine the smell? We'd never be able to sleep." Petrah smiled at that as well. Hamma became serious again. "Don't forget, we're always being watched and not just by San. Windows serve more than ventilation, you know."

Petrah took another look at the seats below, this time letting go of his concerns and instead imagining himself learning from his wise instructors: the rich cultures of the world, famous events in history, heroes who shaped the past, the inner workings of the Temple, the secrets of the arcane arts. How many former slaves got to learn such wondrous things?

If only Kruush could see this. Then he'd agree, I've made the right decision.

His thickheaded friend would probably scoff at that, but he'd smile.

"So, Petrah, what do you make of our humble canteem?"

Petrah placed a hand over his chest. His heart was beating fast. How had he gotten so lucky to be here, to have this opportunity, to have a chance so few people got? But he had reservations, namely with his inability to read or write. At the slave works in Kanmar, he had tallied parts for making shields on strips of reed. The skills he needed here went far beyond that. Did Master Joriah know he lacked these skills? Petrah refused to let his inadequacies deprive him of the moment. "It's amazing, like nothing I've seen."

"When I saw it for the first time, I wanted to pinch my face and know this was real, not some dream."

Petrah asked one more question, a personal one he hoped would be all right. "Hamma, what made you want to become a mage?"

The lead apprentice stared off for a moment.

"When I was a child, our tribe traveled north from Elmar, across the Kesel and into the desert. One day, a sandstorm took us by surprise. The darkest, most terrible storm you'd ever seen. A vaellra, they called it. Another boy and I were separated from our tribe. We were lost and didn't know where to go. In our search for water and shelter, the boy died. I ended up alone, wandering aimlessly across the sands. I thought I was dead too. I guess I finally fainted, because the next thing I knew, I was in a tent being attended to by a tribesman. I'll never forget it, Petrah.

"The man who took me in was a Terad, the leader of the tribe. When I was strong enough, I asked him how he found me. He said he dreamed of me. When he awoke, he used his divine sight to seek me out. It was then that I knew what I wanted to be. I wanted to become a mage, like him. And here I am, two years into my apprenticeship. If all goes well, I'll become a journeyman in a year and attend a journeyman school in the city, where I will learn the advanced arts. Another four years, and I'll become a mage just like the man who saved my life."

Master Joriah never said anything about it taking seven years to become a mage. Petrah had assumed it happened at the end of his schooling. "That long?"

"It's not that long if you really think about it. And it's not that long if you really want it. The magi are well respected in Terjurmeh, Petrah. We are to become the *matya*, 'the glue that binds society.' The road to magehood is protracted but necessary. Don't forget, it was the magi who defended our lands over the centuries when our military strength faltered. Wars were won because of us. What could be more important?"

I T WAS LATE AFTERNOON when Petrah returned to the dormitory. He was weary from all the new information sloshing around in his head. Hamma told him to spend the rest of the afternoon in reflection.

Petrah rested on his bed. Before he knew it, reflection turned to sleep. It was just before suppertime when Annia arrived, rousing him with a chubby hand. He startled awake.

"What is it?"

"You must shave, Master." She could speak!

Petrah followed her to a shallow inlet where another slave was waiting, an old man so bony, he looked like he would crack if touched. He made sure Petrah was shaved and washed in time for the evening meal. With his white robe and sandals, Petrah felt every bit a free man.

Kruush, you should be here seeing this. Ahleen and Tan, you too!

Hamma fetched Petrah, and the two walked to dinner. Their destination was in a clearing, minutes from the dorm.

The dining area comprised a scullery made of mudbrick with a canvas awning attached to its open window. Through the kitchen window,

Petrah heard chopping and the clank of pots. The cooked smells were wonderful.

There were two tables under the awning. Master Joriah sat between a pair of men dressed in black robes at the table nearest to the scullery. Four white-robed adolescents sat at the opposing table.

All eyes fell upon Petrah at once.

He stopped, unsure of what to do. He'd been taught to avoid attention. Antelle had drummed it into his head. Attention fared poorly for a slave, especially when the Draadi were around. The men clad in black were a different kind of master, but Petrah couldn't stop the pounding in his chest.

The attention from the students didn't sit well with him either.

He was relieved when Hamma directed him to his seat and the others stopped staring. Hamma and Petrah sat across from each other at the corner of the student's table, Petrah with his back to the masters.

When they were settled into their seats, Petrah noted Hamma was the only one with a green robe. The other students wore white like Petrah.

Hamma clasped his hands and bowed his head. The students followed suit—Petrah too.

Hamma said a prayer, giving thanks to San, the one true god. At the conclusion, everyone made the holy sigil: the triangular dabs of the air with the thumb, forefinger, and middle finger pressed together. Hamma seemed pleased with Petrah's attentiveness to prayer.

The food was simple but tasty: fish stew with root vegetables. Petrah smelled mushrooms and carrots in the steaming broth. He longed for ale but figured it would be a while before he got to drink any again. Water would have to do for now. At least it wasn't the oily stuff that accompanied every meal in the Denrethi pits.

No one except the masters talked during supper.

Petrah heard their conversations, but the subject matter was far beyond anything he could follow, with the likes of politics and religion. A couple of times he felt a tingle in his temples or atop his head. When he moved his hand to touch the spot, he'd hear muffled snickers from one student or another.

"That's enough," Hamma said. No one did anything after that.

At the end of the meal, slaves removed the platters.

Master Joriah walked over and placed a hand on Petrah's shoulder. The touch startled him, but he remained locked in place.

"Everyone, this is Petrah," the mage said from behind.

Petrah forced himself to look at his classmates.

There was a mixture of expressions, most leaning toward the suspicious, which made his stomach tighten into a knot. The students were around his age, two boys and two girls.

"I want you to introduce yourselves," Master Joriah told them. "Tell Petrah your name and something about yourself."

First was Nuk, the boy farthest from Petrah. His hair swept low across his brow like a swath of barley at harvest time and was colored the same, and his hooked nose reminded Petrah of a spotted gull. He had a hard time making eye contact with Petrah but seemed excited to be in the apprenticeship program. "I've been here almost a year. My great-grandfather was a mage. He fought the Con-jurah but died before I was born. My father said I'm the only one among twelve grandchildren to learn the craft. I just hope to do my family proud." Then, with a shy smile, he said, "It's good to have you with us, Petrah."

Taline came next. She seemed to be the tallest of the group—wiry and with boyish features. She spoke in nervous bursts, which made it hard for Petrah to follow along. "—and I promised my mother I wouldn't let her down. You know, as a girl. Because we—well, I'm the only girl to be accepted into the apprenticeship program. I don't mean the only one here, because there's Ajoon, and, well—"

"Thank you, Taline, that's plenty," Master Joriah said with a stern smile. "Ajoon?"

Ajoon was the other girl. She was ordinary and pretty in the same breath, with short, brown hair and large eyes Petrah swore were different colors. She was smaller than Taline in stature, fuller in the face, and stockier too. "I'm just grateful to be here. I'm the first in my family to go to a school of any kind, so being at Maseah means a lot to me. My favorite place is the library. I love to read books, the older the better. I mean, what could be more amazing than reading a book written hundreds of years ago? It's—it's incredible." Ajoon smiled at Petrah. His cheeks warmed as her stare lingered. He was thankful when the next student introduced himself.

Miko differed from his peers. At first, Petrah thought it might be his angular jawline, which was uncharacteristic of the Ter-jurah and more in line with those of the Prallites, or the sharp ends of thick brown hair curling over his forehead like the talons of a raptor.

But as he spoke, Petrah could tell his demeanor set him apart from the others: authoritative and with the confidence of a natural-born leader. "Not a day passes that I'm not grateful for the day Master Joriah came to my home. I didn't know him or that he was there to test my aptitude for the arcane arts at my father's behest. He simply asked me what I wanted to be when I grew up. When I told him I wanted to be a mage, he didn't believe me. When I said I wanted to make a difference in society, he said I could do that by working under my father's tutelage for the Fist Party. When he told me becoming a mage was a life of sacrifice and ceaseless servitude, I didn't balk. I knew what I wanted to be. I still do. And yes, it is a life of sacrifice and ceaseless servitude, but it is so much more. I wouldn't give it up for anything." His dark, thoughtful eyes never left Petrah's, and the more he spoke, the more he chiseled the air with every word. "You've just arrived, so this is all new to you. Want my advice from someone who was in your place not too long ago? Study hard and listen to your betters. You'll be glad you did." Petrah didn't like the way Miko looked at him, nor did he like how he emphasized "betters" so strongly, as if Petrah answered to him. Hamma was the student leader, not Miko.

But Petrah kept quiet and simply tipped his head as if Miko had imparted sage guidance.

Master Joriah introduced the two adults seated at his table last, Masters Nole and Maglo. They couldn't be more different in appearance or personality.

Petrah had wondered what this authoritarian Master Nole looked like since Hamma first described him. Master Nole was utterly serious as predicted, lean and balding. He barely paid any attention to Petrah, although his beady eyes saw everything and everyone, Petrah was sure.

Petrah didn't know what to make of Master Maglo, who sat quietly while Master Joriah talked. It was hard not to stare at the mage. The man was considerably overweight, with bulging cheeks and a jolly double-chin, fat fingers covered in grease, and a mouth in a fixed open position like a fish out of water. He closed his mouth long enough to extend Petrah a friendly smile.

"It's San's Day," Master Joriah said to the students once the introductions were done. "Remember to pray tonight. San is our strength and our life. He is the Father, and we are his children. Blood to spirit."

"Blood to spirit," the students repeated.

Hamma ordered the White Robes to fall in line behind him.

Petrah was settling in place behind Ajoon, who offered him the spot with a friendly wave of her hand, when Miko shoved past him.

He gave Petrah a blistering glare.

Petrah's stomach curdled, not because of the glare, but because of the malicious intent. Miko wasn't anything like the others. He had a predator's air about him.

Petrah saw the spirit of a Draad in Miko.

Miko's demeaning look made Petrah want to drop to the back of the line.

And that's exactly where he ended up.

Chapter 10

Struggles

MORNING DAWNED WARM AND bright.

The students assembled at the dining area and ate quietly, heads down. The meal was a hearty porridge of oats and dried dates mixed with warmed sheep's milk and a hint of cinnamon. Petrah loved the smell of cinnamon and how it soothed him. He felt Miko's eyes on him as he ate but ignored him. Nothing would spoil his meal, not today.

After breakfast, Hamma marched the students to class. Petrah took up the rear again, mindful of Miko. They entered the canteem, the learning center Hamma had shown Petrah during their tour of Maseah. The canteem seemed larger today, more cavernous, with its cupola set so high above the upward sloping rows of seats. Petrah had the impression of being swallowed up by its windowless walls.

Master Nole sat in a tall chair on the podium, reading from a large tome resting atop the sloping surface of the lectern. He didn't look up as the students shuffled past, but Petrah imagined he was watching their every step.

I must be cautious with him, just as Hamma suggested.

The class took their seats, Miko in the first row, Nuk, Taline, and Ajoon behind him. Hamma waited for the four to get situated before directing Petrah to a vacant seat front and center, between Miko and himself.

Petrah glanced over his shoulder.

Taline and Nuk were oblivious to his presence, whispering among themselves, but Ajoon offered him a friendly smile. He liked the way she smiled at him.

Her smile vanished quickly.

It wasn't until Petrah turned around and saw Miko's harsh frown that he understood Miko to be the cause. Apparently, Miko didn't approve of anyone being nice to Petrah.

He's a Jabahn who thinks he's a Draad. Well, he's not.

Petrah looked down at the swivel table mounted on the right side of his chair. Hamma said it had a clever mechanism to move it out of the way and then fold down. On the table rested several items, including a clean sheet of parchment paper, a bottle of dark liquid, and a feather. He didn't know what to do with the feather or the black stuff. After waiting for Hamma to notice his helplessness, he gave up. He'd have to figure it out during class.

When the students were settled, Master Nole picked up a wooden pointer and moved to the front of the lectern. He tightened the sash about his robe and cleared his throat. "Good morning, class."

"Good morning, Master Nole," responded the students, all except for Petrah, who made a mental note not to miss the response tomorrow.

"I'd like to start off today with a simple but important question, something you should all know the answer to. Who can tell me what divine power is?"

Several hands raised.

Master Nole pointed. "Ajoon."

"Power of the spirit, Master."

The mage rapped the pointer against his palm. "Power of the spirit. Is that supposed to mean something?"

Ajoon's face flushed. She tried to come up with something else, but her complexion only got redder. Petrah thought her answer was a good one, but Taline and Nuk snickered, maybe in disagreement. Petrah had

THE DARK THAT BEGINS

the feeling Ajoon was an outsider as much as he was. It brought him a measure of comfort.

"It's not a bad answer," Master Nole said, easing up on her. "It's just open to misinterpretation. You could say divine power is power of the spirit, yes. But it's more than that. Divine power is the essence of the cosmos, *unseen energy* that we conduct through our living vessels by using our souls as conduits. It was made by Jah, the Creator, and perfected by San, the Father. We use our spirits to reach it. If you've ever seen fire or lightning, you've glimpsed it, wild and raw, waiting to be harnessed by those who can. And who can harness this power, class?"

Most hands went up, but Master Nole chose Taline.

She blurted the answer proudly. "Magi, Teradi, and Terad-mari."

"Yes, that's right," Master Nole said. "But is it not the case that angels use the same power?" Before anyone could put up a hand, he answered the question for them. "Yes, they use this power. Their perfection in its use is our model as mortals to emulate and duplicate without transcending flesh into spirit."

Master Nole stepped down from the podium and walked over to where his newest student sat. The mage's tall, narrow frame cast a treelike shadow against Petrah's desk.

"So, what do we do? What do magi, Teradi, and Terad-mari do?"

He towered over Petrah, making the initiate feel small and meek.

"Do they perform magic? Are they magicians weaving spells like those written in children's tales?" Master Nole leaned against the desk, inches from Petrah's face. "Do you think you might learn to harness such power someday, White Robe?"

In a jittery fashion, Petrah answered as best he could. "Yes, Master."

Master Nole smacked his rod against the tabletop. The sound echoed with unnerving vibration.

"You might say yes," he said, pointing his stick accusingly, "but you don't have a clue as to what it takes, do you?"

"No, Master."

"Then how would you go about it, White Robe? Do as the children's tales suggest and read a spell from a piece of parchment? Would that work? Or would the answer fall from the sky and strike you on your outlandish head?"

A couple of laughs came from the back row, but Master Nole's icy stare stifled them. He returned his attention to Petrah and continued. "The key, White Robe, is to detach yourself from your body. We do this through meditation and prayer, vocalization and willpower, not spells. In fact, there is no such thing as spell casting. Angels don't cast spells and neither do we. Purists would argue that magic doesn't exist either. They'd say it's divine power and nothing more and that magic is in the domain of fairytales. But what is divine power? Is it not magic? Is it not a form of the arcane arts? What term satisfies the curious mind? Miko?"

"Channeling, Master."

"Miko's correct. The practice is called channeling because we channel divine power in our craft. We create a divine conduit to draw power from the heavens. That's how it works. In channeling, we bring the bond between the body, spirit, and mind together to create a union between matter and energy. We call this bond 'unity.' We also speak words of power as the angels do, so one might consider that to be spellcasting, even though it is not."

Master Nole held up a rigid finger. "Think about it. Think about how we create these channels. You focus the mind. You separate body from spirit. With practice, you become so proficient, you learn to tune in with your detached self without meditation or putting yourself in a trance. It becomes natural, second nature. At which point you can summon it with a mere thought. Imagine that!"

Petrah tried to imagine it, but the idea of drawing power from the realm of angels baffled him. How could anyone do such a thing? Then he remembered the tingling in the back of his neck. At first, he'd thought it a phantom sensation. But it had been deliberate and aimed at him. Some-one knew how to invoke the sensation. Master Joriah knew how—the other students too.

And if I can't learn it?

That was Petrah's biggest fear since coming to Maseah: that Master Joriah had made a mistake in choosing him. How could Petrah learn how to tap into divine power? It seemed . . .

Unfathomable.

"But where do we begin?" Master Nole asked his students. "How do we take the first step toward enlightenment? Do we find the answers in the light?"

The class responded with head shakes and *nos*.

"Correct. Enlightenment and our path to magehood comes from the dark, the color of no color, the purest of all places. Without the dis-traction of light, we can bind with the dark and focus; we can lose the constraints of our flesh. It is the perfection I spoke of from the Father, to whom we pray every night. The knowledge to build mountains—and destroy them—it's all there."

Master Nole moved behind the lectern.

"Class, today's subject is the formation of the Temple. We're going to discuss how An-jurahn high priests of the Great War evolved into today's Articulates. Take this down for notes . . ."

"LIKE THIS," HAMMA SAID, positioning Petrah's fingers around the feather's shaft. When Petrah was sure the quill wouldn't fall, Hamma let go. "Now dip the nib into the inkwell. Don't submerge the whole thing like you did earlier. You'll just make another mess."

The two were sitting in the library. Sunshine streamed in through the louvers of an adjustable skylight. Although the masters preferred it shuttered, students could keep it open if it didn't disturb anyone else.

At this time, the place was vacant. The pair sat at a polished marble table at the center of the circular, single-roomed building. The walls were lined with bookshelves stuffed with books and tubes of scrolls from floor to ceiling. A giant serak was inlaid into the stone floor, its lines iridescent like mother-of-pearl.

Petrah was giddy from being surrounded by so many books. Never in his dreams had he imagined he'd be a free man, and certainly not in a place as magnificent as this. He rescinded his doubts from earlier. Ahleen would be proud of him.

With a shaky but cautious hand, Petrah dipped the tip of his quill into the inkwell, careful not to repeat the morning's disaster. Even Master Nole couldn't control the outburst from the students as Petrah chased after the fallen bottle of ink, kicking it each time it came within his grasp, spraying ink everywhere.

"Good," Hamma said. "Now try writing something."

Petrah wrote with the grace of a toddler, fingers twisted, knuckles almost white from the strain. It looked like he was stabbing the paper.

When he was done, scribbles remained.

Petrah had drawn with his finger in the dirt as a slave, symbols and characters from a distant childhood memory, but he didn't know what he was writing, only that it comforted him, as if his mother had taught him to inscribe such things. Considering it now, it seemed preposterous. How could he write if he couldn't read?

"What's that?"

"It's the first thing that came to my mind: the word *fire*."

Hamma pulled the parchment over to him. He leaned closer for a better look. "That's not *fire*. Are those characters supposed to be letters?"

Petrah shrugged. "I guess. How else would I write it?"

Hamma checked the sundial at the corner of the desk. "Never mind. We have to go to Master Maglo's for your first private lesson."

H AMMA LED PETRAH TO a building the new student hadn't seen before. Again, they went belowground. At the bottom of the stairs, a narrow passageway led to a single door.

"Go to the end and knock once," Hamma said. "Master Maglo will let you in."

When Hamma left, Petrah walked up to a brass door. It was embossed with intricate symbols. The runes reminded him of the Watcher's staff at first. Collecting himself, he knocked once.

"Enter," came the instructor's muffled voice.

Master Maglo's office was cluttered with books, papers, scrolls, tablets, and a whole assortment of tubes and wicker casings that smelled like tallow and old leather. The mage sat behind a table with a pair of candles burned down to nubs, his heavy frame slouched. An unlit oil lamp sat at the far corner of the table.

As soon as Petrah stepped forward, Master Maglo heaved his body upright and waved excitedly at the chair opposite him. "Sit, sit."

Petrah looked at the lopsided chair and wondered if he would fall. He didn't, although it creaked and wobbled back and forth.

"I haven't had a new student in a long time," Master Maglo said, cheeks swelled in excitement. "I have to tell you, it's quite invigorating to see a fresh face. I'm a bit rusty, so bear with me." Master Maglo reached for a cup beneath a mound of papers. He eyed the contents and shook it out before presenting it to his guest. "Water?"

Petrah accepted. The mage grabbed a jug and another cup. He poured them water.

"So, Petrah, is it?"

"Yes, Master."

Master Maglo pressed into a jowl with a stubby finger. "Odd name. *Blue* something . . . ?"

"'Blue eyes.'"

"Ah, there it is." He laughed heartily, and the soft flesh under his chin jiggled. The mage was a refreshing change from his counterparts. Petrah remained optimistically cautious and offered a sliver of a smile.

"So Petrah, tell me, what do you know of the divine?"

"Only what Master Nole told us in class today. He said that magi use it as a power source. He called it 'channeling.' He also mentioned 'unity'—the connection of the mind, body, and soul."

"Very important concepts. What else did he say?"

"That we should meditate and pray. Once we do that, it would come naturally."

Master Maglo seemed satisfied enough by the answer. "I'd say you know the philosophy behind the theory. Now I'll explain the theory behind the technique."

The mage went into detail about the spirit's link to the body and the way the mind could communicate with its incorporeal self to draw from the divine.

"If you remove any of the key elements—mind, body, or soul," Master Maglo said, "channeling fails. But if you bring them together in harmony, then you can achieve anything as a channeler."

Petrah asked, "Do I need to pray to tap into divine power?"

"Simply put: no."

"But Master Nole said you have to pray and meditate to detach yourself from your body. Then the soul can reach out into the spiritual realm to draw power."

"I think you misunderstood Master Nole's point," Master Maglo said. "Prayer allows you to deepen your beliefs and hone your spiritual connection. By doing that, you achieve a mindset that helps the channeler improve their focus, which helps them 'detach,' as we call it. But is prayer the method by which you tap into divine power? No. Does it make it easier? Yes. That was Master Nole's point. Think of it as a tool in a mage's toolkit."

Whenever Petrah stared at the serak in his room, his thoughts wandered. He doubted praying would help him focus.

Master Maglo went on. "Meditation is an even more effective tool. It accomplishes a similar effect to prayer, but on a deeper level. It sets the intention of the mind at its root. With the correct techniques—which I will teach you—you'll learn to attune the mind to reach the right frequency for our craft." The mage's lips unfurled into a smile. "That said, you should meditate *and* pray."

Petrah wrestled with his fingers. How did the other students grasp these concepts? How would he?

"Don't feel overwhelmed," Master Maglo said. "You're a beginner. I was in your place once. Skinnier, I'll admit, but just as unsure of myself and asking the universe the same question as you're probably thinking: 'Can I really do this?' The answer, unequivocally, is *yes*. Otherwise, you wouldn't be here, right?"

Petrah pushed his fingertips into the table to stop his fidgeting. "It's a lot to take in."

"It is," Master Maglo said. "But consider this: most people aren't suited to become magi. They lack the mental acuity. A craft such as ours takes focus and a natural affinity. Master Joriah saw this in you. Last night at dinner I noticed the same. Did you feel a slight tingling sensation on your scalp?"

Petrah assumed his classmates were behind it. "Several times. I've been wondering what that was."

"The correct term is *currata*, but we all call it a mind probe, a sort of psychic *hello*. The tingling feeling is your head saying hello back, even though you're not aware it's saying it."

"Is there a way to block it?"

"Oh, sure. It's not hard. I'll show you once you get the basics down. But don't think just because you block the hello someone doesn't know it. Anyway, we're getting ahead of ourselves.

"Let's focus today's lesson on technique. We'll start with the foundation of our craft: meditation."

MEDITATING PROVED MORE DIFFICULT than Petrah imagined. He spent days trying variations of Master Maglo's techniques to set his mind at rest, but to no avail. His mind wandered, which earned frowns and headshakes from the big mage.

"Maybe my office is a poor choice of environment for putting your mental state at ease," Master Maglo said. "Try meditating in your room before you go to sleep."

Petrah did, but the incessant buzzing of insects outside his window at night was a constant distraction. Even worse, he couldn't find the voice to pray.

It wasn't that he couldn't muster the words. It was the lack of faith.

San was the Father, the God of Shadows, and everyone gave their thanks and prayed to him for guidance and strength. Petrah had always felt untrue when he spoke the words of contrition, as his fellow slaves had done religiously on the occasions the Draadi let them gather for prayer.

Petrah kept his non-belief to himself.

He faked his gestures during dinner with the other students, something he hoped the masters would never find out.

On San's Day, Petrah looked for a transformation, a change in perspective on faith.

He assembled with his fellow students after the evening meal. The
masters escorted them into the city to attend Temple service. Petrah
hadn't seen Elmar in over two weeks, but this time it was different. He
was no longer a slave running from society.

He was *part* of society.

Was that enough to lift the barrier blocking his faith?

Master Joriah marched his pupils through Elmar's streets, accompanied by Masters Nole and Maglo. The students walked single file, Petrah
taking up the rear as usual.

They ran into other magi, some belonging to the Green Flame, others
to different parties, but all members of the Magi Guild, which seemed
to unify the brotherhood, despite their political differences. They wore
a variety of black robes, differentiated from one another by the color of
trim or insignia over their breasts.

As Petrah looked among them, he recalled from class that magi weren't
the only wielders of divine power. There were the Teradi, the tribal
leaders who became the heads of their families only after learning the
skills of the magus.

There were also the Terad-mari—a fancy term for priests—who all had
to learn how to harness divine power in order to advance from acolyte to
cleric to priest.

So it was with magi like Master Joriah, who started off as apprentices,
wearing the white robe, followed by the green, then the gray as journeymen, and finally, the black as a full-fledged channeler. Magi, Teradi, and
Terad-mari shared this path to enlightenment. But as Master Maglo had
said on Petrah's first day of class, meditation and prayer were important

tools for the channeler. Both of which, Petrah admitted, were regrettably elusive.

The Dome of San stood as a black granite structure overlooking the city. Six minarets rose skyward above a dome from a central courtyard where the devout assembled.

Master Joriah led his entourage into the enormous courtyard. Hundreds were already gathered, with dozens more filtering in. They stood patiently next to one another, their faces bathed in the red glow of crimson lamps jutting from the walls. The smoke of incense permeated the air, like smoldering acha wood and spice.

Petrah spotted a heavyset man alone on the balcony of the central minaret. Aman came to mind, plucked from a dream where worshippers gathered in a similar fashion to those around him, except they chanted the name of the warrior in black.

Here, the people remained quiet and observant.

Petrah was curious as to the heavyset man standing all by himself. He whispered in Hamma's ear. "Who's that?"

"Our city Seer, Baaka, one of the Sacred Nine. Remember what Master Nole taught you?"

Petrah remembered: five Articulates, three Seers, and the Mighty One, the papal head of the Temple. Collectively, they were called the Sacred Nine, the Pillars of the Temple. Master Nole said they were the most revered priests in Terjurmeh, if not the world. All citizens, even the Iron Fist, bowed before their holy edict.

The assemblage, now packed to capacity and numbering perhaps well over a thousand, with more spilling out into the street, fell silent.

The Seer let the hush last a minute before crying out a single word: "San-la!" Attend!

It was the first of two phrases in the call to prayer. The entire congregation moved fluidly to lower themselves to the ground and tuck their legs behind them. Petrah placed the palms of his hands out in front of him, flat against the ground. He bent his arms and leaned forward with the weight of his upper body to prostrate and touch his forehead to the ground, just as his neighbors did.

"*San-su!*" *Listen!*

Everyone rested back on their haunches, attentive, with palms on their thighs. Petrah was familiar with the phrases and attending postures. Even slaves partook in the holy service on San's Day.

Petrah wished the devotion of the surrounding attendees would rub off on him. He wanted to say a prayer for the dead: for Aggren, who had saved his life, and for Jow-quu, whose life he couldn't save.

They deserve to be remembered and to be at peace in the afterlife.

As much as Petrah tried, the belief wasn't in him.

Baaka spoke fervently, issuing a monologue that praised San, denounced Jah, and told of a day when Terjurmeh would unite the world under one religion. Even though Jah was the Maker, He was reviled by the Temple, considered a false god because He blinded His followers with light. He poisoned their minds with lies and false promises, and because they were blinded, they couldn't see the truth. But San spoke the truth. He dwelled among the shadows, away from the light and the lies. He was the one true god, the Father of Truth. For in the absence of light, the truth was plain for all to see.

Baaka's speech galvanized the crowd to a fever pitch of godly praise. Hamma was among them, his peers too—all absorbed by the fervor, shouting San's name into the night sky.

Petrah's shouts lacked the same fervency. He went through the motions to keep up pretenses, but his voice was hollow, lacking the spiritual conviction it needed. As he repeated San's name, he searched within for a sign of faith—anything at all—but came back empty-handed. He'd stared at the serak in his room for hours but never heard San's voice, never felt his presence, never experienced any fulfillment, rapture, or awakening of his spirit. The only thing he came away with was disappointment in his inability to believe.

If I can't believe in our god, what can I believe in?

Which prompted another question: was his lack of faith the reason he struggled to bring his body, mind, and soul in harmony?

Maybe it is.

If he couldn't achieve the unity Master Nole spoke of in class, then what chance did he have at becoming a channeler? And if he couldn't do something so basic as meditate—the foundation of their craft—then how long would he last as an apprentice at Maseah before Master Joriah decided he wasn't a good fit?

Petrah's heart sank, and his hopes of becoming a mage along with it.

MASTER JORIAH RELEASED THE students once they returned to Maseah from service. They were free to spend the rest of the night as they saw fit, as long as it involved prayer or meditation.

Petrah was restless. He didn't want to go back to his dorm room. Perhaps a walk would calm his troubled soul.

Petrah followed the sound of a nocturnal songbird to an inlet close to the dorm. A full moon brightened the nighttime sky, making the dark water gleam. The cooler air carried a dampness from the river and with it, the freshness of lilies. The inlet led from the shore into a shroud of grass, the water still except for a school of tiny, orange fish darting about beneath the surface by the bank.

Petrah took a seat on the wooden bench facing the water, then grabbed a fallen branch. He hunched over and mindlessly began scribing circles in the glistening silt.

"It's peaceful here, isn't it?" said someone from behind.

The voice startled Petrah, and he dropped the branch.

It was Miko. He walked around the bench. He was shorter than Petrah by a head, but he had all the trappings of a leader with the way he pinned his shoulders back and stuck out his chin. "May I sit?"

Petrah slid over. "Please."

Miko sat.

Petrah didn't like sitting so close to him, even though they sat next to each other in the canteem, but he thought it impolite if he refused. Miko stunk of Sercula. The triangle of anointing oil on his forehead glinted. The blood in the oil appeared black in the moonlight.

"Look at all the fish," Miko said, leaning forward to get a better look. "You chose a good spot. Let's see if I'm lucky."

He plunged his hand into the water. The fish scattered.

When Miko withdrew his clenched fist and opened it, there was nothing but sediment. "Someday, I'll catch one of them."

He rinsed his palm and shook the excess water before leaning back. Even in the moonlight, his eyes appeared like glossy coals, dark and watchful. "So, Petrah, what do you think of our school?"

Petrah answered carefully, not sure if Miko was probing for information or just being conversational. "It's good. I feel purpose here. The masters treat me well, and I'm still figuring things out."

"It's natural to struggle in the beginning."

"I wouldn't say I'm struggling exactly."

"No? I thought you were having issues with reading and writing." Miko shrugged. "Maybe I got that wrong."

Miko hadn't gotten it wrong, but Petrah didn't want to make a point of dwelling on it. "As I said, I'm still figuring things out."

"Listen to your instructors, and it'll happen. You'll find your way."

"I just need time to catch up, that's all," Petrah said, hopeful Miko's intentions were true. They had gotten off to a shaky start. Petrah wanted to give his fellow student the benefit of the doubt.

"Of course," Miko said. "A year ago, I was the new robe. Now it's you. Next year, it'll be somebody else. It's a cycle, like life itself." Miko used the hem of his robe to dry his hand. "Has Master Maglo taught you anything useful yet?"

"Meditation and breathing." Petrah didn't want to say that he'd yet to get anywhere with meditating.

"Oh. Just that, huh?" There was a glimmer of haughtiness in his voice. "I forget, that's what beginners learn. It seems so long ago to me."

Petrah put the question back on Miko. "How are your studies going?"

Miko reached down, grabbed a smooth stone from the silt, and threw it across the pond, skipping it along the surface. It disappeared into the marsh grass with a plunk. He then held out his hand and Petrah watched in amazement as the same stone rose from the water and glided through the air into his palm. "They go well."

"How did you do that?"

"That's nothing. I can do many things the masters don't know about. Soon, I'll surpass Hamma's skills, and they will be forced to give me the Green."

Petrah detested Miko's arrogance. Was he jealous of Hamma? Or did he think so highly of himself that he had to put everyone down? Petrah tried to keep the conversation civil. "Would you and Hamma both have green robes then?"

"Not with six students. Maybe they'll give him the Gray. Who knows? I'm not concerned about what happens to Hamma."

"My only wish is to do well in my studies and become a mage in due time."

"If that's what you believe, then you'll go nowhere. Your predecessor believed the same thing. Look what happened to him."

"My predecessor?"

"Yes, the boy whose position you've taken. You didn't hear about him?"

"No one told me."

"Let's just say his tenure here ended abruptly. Health issues, if you get my meaning." Miko patted Petrah callously on the back with the same vitriol that filled his words. He rose from his seat. "See you around."

Petrah watched his classmate leave . . . and shivered.

Chapter 11

Progress

M ASTER MAGLO TAPPED THE sheet of parchment. "What's this scribble?"

Petrah sat across from his instructor in the mage's underground office. It was a month since the apprentice had begun his formal training. Although summer was waning, time seemed to stand still.

This wasn't the first occasion Petrah's crabbed handwriting had been critiqued. Hamma had shown a local scholar visiting the school Petrah's writing, and the man had dismissed it as gibberish, claiming the letters were not even close to those the Prallites used for their alphabet.

"So what language is it?" the mage asked. "It's not Jurmehan, Korinian, Idarian, Machoo, or even that barbaric trash from the North."

"I don't know," Petrah said truthfully.

He had thought long and hard about the origin of his handwriting. What else could it be other than the original Prallite language—a derivative of the Idarian tongue, which had fallen out of favor centuries ago with the adoption of Jurmehan as the world's common language—if he were a Northerner as everyone believed?

The fact his writing was unrecognizable, even to a scholar, made Petrah doubt his belief that his mother had been his teacher or that the written language was that of an outdated tongue.

If not that, then what?

He strained to remember, but nothing emerged from before the day he woke up as an eleven-year-old in the barley field in Kanmar.

Perhaps no one had taught me. Perhaps I'm making this all up.

"What about your reading? You haven't been able to read a thing I've given you. What are we going to do about these things, hmm?"

"Hamma offered to help me with the reading, Master."

"And your writing?"

"I can still take notes."

Master Maglo turned the parchment around and pushed it across the desk. "Then tell me what you wrote here."

Petrah examined the writing. It was a set of notes he'd taken during class.

He held the sheet up to the candlelight to get a better look. The wick smoked something awful, making Petrah's eyes water and his nose clog up from the heavy odor. Still, he read the words.

"It says, 'The Year One is important to us because it marks the settlement of the An-jurah, our forefathers, on the east bank of the Kesel River. The An-jurahn settlers later became known as the Ter-jurah when—'"

"That's enough." Master Maglo puffed out his already inflated cheeks. "You can write, which is a relief, but this language . . . What is it? An ancient tongue? Something of your creation? A long-forgotten form of speech?" The mage tapped a finger against a bulging cheek. "What are we going to do? Master Nole says you are attentive in class, and I think you have good potential. But Master Joriah thinks we have a problem on our hands, and that means *you* have a problem."

Petrah started to panic, thinking all sorts of dreadful things, including expulsion. "But I can learn to read and write properly!" *I just need more time.*

Master Maglo pushed his finger into the dimple on his chin. It seemed to disappear like a finger poking into a meat pie. "It's not just that, Petrah. You're distracted all the time. Every lesson with you is a chore. I've given you three mantras to help with the meditation, and none of them seem to work. What's going on?"

"I don't know, Master. Maybe it's"—*maybe it's the dreams*—"maybe it's the noise at night. I can't concentrate."

"What noise?"

"Outside the dormitory. The insects—they buzz and buzz and never stop. The frogs and birds, too. I can't focus with all that noise." *I can't focus at all.*

The mage studied Petrah. He pointed a finger at the initiate's head. "Something's going on in there. I see the windows, but they're shuttered."

Master Maglo looked away for a moment, tapping a finger against his chin, deep in thought. When he returned his attention to Petrah, he said, "Let's try something. It's not exactly"—he glanced up—"conventional, but I think it will help. It's called *insurata*—the 'joining of minds.' Are you willing to try it?"

Petrah gave a hesitant *yes*.

"Sit still. I'm going to find out what's going on in that distracted mind of yours. Close your eyes. Don't fight me. Let me in."

Petrah's fingers trembled, but he followed Master Maglo's instructions and held his hands as still as possible.

A few seconds passed, and Petrah felt a prickle along his scalp, like the stabbing of fingernails, followed by a burst of vibration. His instinct was to block it out, but he resisted, giving in, as Master Maglo asked. His head rattled and his ears rang. He gripped the chair's armrests and tried to remain still.

Memories flickered in rapid succession, an abbreviated history of the past few years, whirling past in a matter of elongated breaths. It hurt to see so much.

Then it was over.

Petrah slanted in his chair, his equilibrium off.

The mage appeared transfixed. His eyes darted rapidly back and forth, as if assimilating a tidal wave of information. Master Maglo's eyes stopped moving. His face was flush, his forehead damp.

"That was a little much," he said, shaking his head as if to clear it. "I'm sorry, but I couldn't stop myself. I saw, I felt, I—they flogged you?" Master Maglo reached over, grabbed a rag from a reading stand, and dabbed his forehead while Petrah sat, petrified. "I think I found our problem. Unfortunately, it just got a lot bigger."

The secret was out. *Master Maglo knows!* "Master, I can explain—"

A pudgy hand stopped him. "No. This isn't good, Petrah. We don't train slaves to become magi."

"But I'm not a slave anymore!"

"No? They just let you go? The Draadi showed you to the door and said, 'Thanks for coming'? I don't think so. You're"—he dipped his head below the table—"well, I can't figure out whose property. It's too dark to see your ankle."

Petrah squirmed in his seat like a fish caught by giant paws. If he only would have refused Master Maglo's invasion into his mind. But how was he supposed to know the mage would see everything?

Because you should have known!

Master Maglo let out a troubled sigh. "We have a serious problem, Petrah. I must report this to Master Joriah."

"Don't!" Petrah begged. "Please!"

"What I want to know is how he didn't see it. He tested you for ability, yes? That ping we do where you feel it in the back of your head? That mind probe I spoke of?"

"Yes, but—"

"Yet he didn't investigate to find out just what sort of young man you are. He was so driven to find a sixth student, someone with the right mind for our craft, that he decided to bring you to Maseah without putting forth the diligence required. That's the problem here. He acted too quickly. Now we're in this fine mess. Sorry, Petrah. I can't just let this go."

"But—" Petrah fumbled over his words. "But what if you don't say anything?"

"You mean, keep quiet? Let it remain our little secret? Is that it?" Master Maglo shook his head. "Master Joriah will chain you up and ship you back if he finds out. He'll drown me for sure for knowing and keeping it to myself. So what do I do with you?"

Petrah's temples pounded as fingers of pressure wrapped themselves invisibly around his head. If they sent him back to the Draadi, his life was over.

"Master, please. You don't have to tell him. I won't say a word, I promise. I need this apprenticeship. I can't even begin to tell you how much. Don't say anything. Please!"

Master Maglo cupped his chin and rocked back and forth, staring off into the corner, plagued with indecisiveness. Seconds passed, one for every two of Petrah's heartbeats.

The mage stopped rocking.

"You've put me in a difficult position. If I say something, you're gone. Poof, the end of you. If I don't, I'm responsible if you're found out. I don't know . . ."

Petrah reached across the table, hands clasped. "I swear it on my life, I won't say anything. Please, Master."

Several more painful seconds ticked by.

Master Maglo's seriousness retreated. "I wish you could look at yourself in the mirror. Your beggar's face is quite something to behold."

Petrah couldn't decide whether the off-color remark was a good sign.

"Very well, Initiate Petrah, I'm going to do something that, despite my better judgment, might do me in the end: I'm going to keep my mouth shut. And, as you might have guessed, that's not something I'm gifted at doing."

Petrah let the tension out from his lungs. "Thank you, Master."

Master Maglo huffed, then sat rigid in his chair. "Don't thank me. I'm not at all happy to be privy to your secret. It's not like I can just make it disappear. Unless you know of a way. Do you?"

Petrah swallowed. Sweat tickled his brow. "I don't."

Master Maglo narrowed one eye and watched Petrah for a long, uncomfortable moment before saying, "I think we're done talking about this. We have a lesson to get on with. Shall we put this dark business behind us and focus on that?"

Petrah nodded spiritedly, glad to put the matter to rest.

"All right," Master Maglo said, easing back into his seat. "I will now teach you a special meditation technique, something to get through all that buzzing and those"—with a wink—"sleepless nights."

LEARNING TO READ AND write Jurmehan was impossible, but knowing he wouldn't be sent back to Kanmar kept Petrah's mood elevated.

"You're making progress," Hamma told him. "It's slow but steady. Be patient."

Slow was right. His biggest challenge remained meditation.

Petrah did as Master Maglo instructed to block out distractions. The most useful exercise, Petrah discovered, involved sitting on the floor of his room with his eyes shut and legs crossed after his classmates had gone to bed.

No sway, no leaning, no movement. He was to remain as a stone pillar, Master Maglo had said.

Petrah intoned a single syllable through pursed lips, low and deep, to set the "vibrational tone," as Master Maglo put it. From there, he chanted a mantra the mage called Silkworm—a slow, sinuous rise and fall of three syllables that transitioned seamlessly from one note to the next, like a worm inching along a leaf.

With his mantra set, Petrah emptied his mind of distractions. And then . . .

Stillness.

Perfect, absolute, clear quietude.

The room turned silent and invisible, and his body became light as a mote of dust.

Petrah repeated the meditation technique in Master Maglo's office.

The mage appraised him, then said, "You're almost there. Keep at it. I want you to achieve a meditative state in under a minute, and I want you to do so without chanting your mantra aloud."

Petrah practiced and repeated his meditation whenever he had the chance: at night, between his studies, secluded among the trees. The time it took to get into a meditative state went from the better part of an hour to right around a minute. He no longer needed to intone his mantra aloud. He could set the vibrational tone with his mind.

Master Maglo evaluated Petrah's progress in his office on the eve of San's Day. Petrah waited for the verdict with his hands tucked under his thighs, resisting the urge to bob his knee.

Master Maglo folded his hands on his desk. "The mind is ready, Petrah. Well done."

Petrah expelled a long breath of relief. "Thank you, Master."

"Now," Master Maglo said with a teasing smile, "are you ready to try something truly special?"

Petrah's neck tingled when he heard "special." He sat up tall in his seat. "What is it?"

The mage leaned over his desk as if to whisper a secret, but then he clasped his hands and said, "Come back to my office on the morrow, right after dawn, and you'll find out."

P ETRAH COULD HARDLY SLEEP a wink. He spent most of the night staring up at the ceiling of his room, wondering what Master Maglo had in store for him. A more advanced meditation technique? A channeling skill Master Nole had talked about in class? What did Master Maglo mean by "special"?

Petrah was back at the mage's office at first light, bleary-eyed but attentive and eager to find out the answer to his questions. His instructor appeared well rested. There was even a mysterious gleam to his eyes under the light of an oil lamp.

"I'm sure you're intrigued by why you're here on a day of rest when you could be still asleep," the mage began. "I assure you it will be worth it. I've been longing to try this with one of my newer students." He reached below his desk and produced a kerchief. "Here, use this as a blindfold. Tie it around your head and make sure it covers your eyes." He smiled and said, "No peeking."

Petrah did as he was told, making sure the kerchief was tied in a tight knot behind his head. He licked his dry lips and waited, breathing slowly. He allowed the steady breaths to counteract the claustrophobic stuffiness of the room closing in around him.

Master Maglo said, "I want you to listen to my voice and follow my instruction. Your task today is to feel with your mind. And by 'feel' I mean for you to make contact with the physical world with only your thoughts. And not only make contact, but explore it, touch it, and take hold of it as if using your hands. Do you think this is possible?"

Master Nole had given Petrah the impression that anything was possible for a channeler. "Yes."

"Let me clarify: do you believe *you* can make it possible?"

After mastering his mantra, Petrah was ready to take on the world. "Yes."

"Good. You said that with conviction. Let us proceed with our lesson. But first, a small test. How many fingers am I holding up?"

Petrah saw only the hint of orange against a field of black, which had to come from the lamp. He could see naught else. "I don't know."

"Guess anyway."

Petrah squinted but couldn't tell. "Three?"

"Wrong. I'm not even holding up my hand. Now, onto our lesson."

Petrah resisted folding his arms across his chest as a sign of annoyance. Did Master Maglo plan to make a game of this? He heard the mage shuffle through papers on his desk. Then Master Maglo said, "Ah, there it is," before additional rustling made it sound like he was clearing the papers aside. He then plopped something down on the desktop. It made a heavy thud. "Your task is to tell me what this object is I just laid before me. Would you care to throw out a casual guess based on the sound alone?"

Petrah gave it some thought. It didn't sound like a book. "Your hand?"

"Clever guess, but no, I'm not that cruel. This is an actual object, I promise." Before Petrah could offer another guess, Master Maglo said, "To unearth this quandary, you must silence your thoughts. You must meditate as you've learned and project your mind outward. Then the mind can be receptive to its surroundings. Go ahead and use Silkworm to put yourself in a trance. I'll give you one minute."

Petrah did as asked, and the office became quiet, almost distant.

"Can you hear me?"

"I can," Petrah said.

"I will begin by initiating a ping. Let me know when you feel it."

Petrah felt the buzz at the back of his head. "I feel it."

"I'm going to change the characteristics of the ping. It's going to be . . . different. What do you feel now?"

It was as if invisible fingers were prodding his nape. Petrah shivered at the cringy feel of it. "Fingertips?"

"Excellent. Now you try. While I'm connected to you, follow the tendril I've projected with my mind back to its source. You don't have to do anything but follow its length, much as if you were trying to cross a river blindfolded, holding on to a rope that's stretched across from one bank to the other. You know where you're starting from: dry land. Hold on to the rope, let it guide you, and tread through the water until you reach the opposite bank where the rope is tied off. Go ahead."

Petrah took hold of the tendril as Master Maglo suggested by cupping it with his mind. He found purchase, but as he started along its length, he lost his way.

"Try again."

The second time, Petrah followed the tendril of outstretched thought halfway before losing his way. The third time, he reached Master Maglo. He felt something soft and almost squishy at the end of the tendril. "That's my cheek," the mage said.

Petrah released his hold. "Sorry."

"That's all right. You did well enough. Try the desk next. Use the same technique you just used, but expand out from yourself as if you're the one leading the end of your rope into the water. Sense the water, the air, the mud underfoot. Do the same in this room. There's the floor beneath you, your chair, the desk in front, then me. Stop when you reach the desk. Can you feel the grain, the solidness, the flatness of the top, the grooved bevel on the side? Give it a few minutes."

Petrah sent his tendril out from his mind. He guided it down, then forward, until—

He laughed. "I feel it." He moved the tendril left and found the beveled edge the mage spoke of, then emptiness, which he assumed was where the desk ended. The flat plane of the desk proved not to be so flat, with lots of unfamiliar shapes forming obstacles.

"Move on to the object now. Where is it? What is it?"

Petrah's tendril of stretched thought wandered, but it got lost as it fell off the opposite edge of the desk. He tried several more times, then grunted in frustration.

He heard the scrape of the heavy item as it was being taken off the desktop. "Remove the blindfold," Master Maglo said. "You did well on your first attempt. Tomorrow, we'll try again."

That evening, Petrah repeated the exercise on the floor of his room, using his bedsheet as a blindfold. He tackled the familiar objects he knew well: his bed, his desk, the serak on the wall. The serak proved to be the easiest of the items to work with. It gave off a distinct, sharp feel to his mind. He also discovered the cold of the iron, the tiny pits in the metal's surface, then the angles the corners produced. He then contrasted the feel of the metal with that of wood, paper, masonry, and stone. Each surface differed. Each object had its own shape, its mix of curves, straight lines, and angles.

The next afternoon, Petrah was prepared.

"You look confident today," Master Maglo said, appraising his student. "Shall we try the blindfold again?"

With the kerchief over his eyes, and the sound of the heavy object being placed on the desk, Petrah began.

He entered a meditative state, then probed with his mind. Petrah felt the wood desk, which gave off a similar feel to the one in his dorm room. He navigated his tendril of thought over the desktop, rummaging through the papers scattered over its surface, until he found the object in the center. Unlike the sharp corners of the serak, this item was smooth. It didn't give off the ping of metal, but rather a different material. And it was dense. What could it be? Petrah's mind felt around the perimeter of the object, discovering it to be circular at its base. From anywhere along the circumference, the circle rose upward, then curved down to the other side, like a hill. He pinged the material. Not metal, not wood, not paper.

Then it occurred to him: glass!

Petrah smiled and folded his hands in his lap. "I know what it is."

"Go on. Tell me."

"A paperweight."

"Are you sure?"

Petrah felt it again, all of it. "Yes, that's my answer."

"Take off your blindfold. See for yourself."

When Petrah's eyes adjusted to the lamplight, he saw the object. It was indeed a glass paperweight, just like the one Master Nole kept on his lectern, with a green flame suspended in the middle.

Master Maglo stretched the corners of his lips into a big smile.

"Superb work, Petrah."

M ASTER NOLE PACED IN front of Petrah's desk in the canteem. It was week six of the apprentice's instruction.

"Who can tell me an appropriate divination technique for putting out a fire?"

The one thing Petrah realized about his instructor since the calamity on the first day was that the man was strict but fair. As long as the mage's students paid attention, his disciplinarian persona remained subdued.

But when things went wrong . . .

"I want you to imagine a cask of burning oil," Master Nole told his class. "Smell the charred wood, feel the heat, taste the fumes on your tongue. How would you snuff the flames without lifting a finger or submerging the cask in water?"

Several students raised their hands.

Master Nole picked Nuk to answer.

The shy fifteen-year-old stammered as he spoke, but exhibited fortitude. Petrah was impressed. The youth was working hard to overcome his fear of public speaking.

"Master, fire needs air, so I would find a way to remove it."

"How?"

"Create a vacuum. I've read that air can be displaced through pressure. Remove the air and the fire will die."

Master Nole placed the pointer against his lips. "It's an interesting notion, but I don't think it's exactly a divine solution to the problem. You'd also have to consider the effort involved in calculating the displacement. I think the cask would burn out completely before you'd figure out how much air to remove to form your vacuum."

Master Nole rapped Miko's desk with his pointer. "What would you do? And I don't want to hear a peep about an elemental solution from you. We've had enough of that."

Petrah heard a few sharp intakes of breath from behind. Miko must have done something to upset the mage, some kind of catastrophic mistake. Miko's face was white and his lips a tight bead.

That didn't stop him from answering, as if he'd given the matter a great deal of thought. "Find a large-enough object nearby, levitate it, and smother the flames," Miko said. "Earth and sand would work well too. It would be a matter of scooping it out of the ground and containing it before burying the fire."

"You could use a shovel for that." A couple of snickers escaped the back row. Miko folded his arms. "I'm still not satisfied," Master Nole said. "Think, class. There are probably a thousand ways to do the job. How would you extinguish the fire? Surely, you can suggest something better than forming a vacuum or smothering the flames with an object or tossing sand on it.

"All right, last try. Who wants to suggest something else?"

Only one hand went up. Master Nole raised an eyebrow and gave the student the go-ahead.

"I would *will* the fire away, Master," Petrah said. "Just picture the fire and remove it completely with a single thought. I think that would be a divine solution to the problem."

Master Nole stood quietly for an unusually long time. Then something resembling a smile formed on his lips. "Interesting . . ."

MASTER MAGLO TOLD PETRAH that the soul could fly into the heavens if detached from the body. Why not do the same attached?

"Mind over body," he said to Petrah. "The body is but a vessel for the soul, and the mind is but an extension of the spirit. Together, they can lift the body, or anything else. Do you know what this is called?"

"No, Master."

"It's called levitation."

Miko had mentioned it as a possible solution to the problem Master Nole had posed to the students. Petrah thought it impossible until he saw Master Maglo's cross-legged form rise above the floor without the aid of his muscles. The mage glided upward until his head touched the ceiling.

"Mind over body," he repeated, looking down at his dumbstruck pupil.

A JOON SAT NEXT TO Petrah in the library. Afternoon light streamed through the shutters onto the table they shared.

They had a tome titled *Magus Corpus* opened to a chapter in the middle. The book was easily the length of Petrah's forearm, each page painstakingly written by hand, some adorned with full-color paintings of famous magi throughout the ages.

Petrah much preferred the louvers open above them, even though the students were encouraged to shutter them and study by lamplight, as natural light was a form of distraction and a catalyst for sinful thoughts. After all, Jah was the God of Light, and any god-fearing believer of San denounced the impure influences of the enemy god.

"I appreciate you helping me with learning to read," Petrah said. And he more than appreciated Ajoon's company. He understood why Kruush had enjoyed spending time with Ahleen so much.

Ajoon smiled, lighting up the entire library. She had different-colored eyes, one deep brown like her short hair, the other hazel. In a way, Petrah and her were the same: Ajoon with her two-toned eyes and Petrah with his blues.

"I think studying together helps us both," she said. "Besides, Taline and Nuk consider me a nuisance. Hamma doesn't have the time of day. And Miko, well . . ."

There was no need to spell it out. Petrah knew how much of a bully Miko could be.

Then again, Miko didn't like the fact that Ajoon had a soft spot for Petrah. It was as if he was . . .

Jealous.

"He's a bit sharp-tongued, I agree," Petrah said. "You and I make a good team."

A flicker of mischief danced in Ajoon's hazel-brown eyes. "Team, is it?"

"Yeah. Well . . . I meant to say—"

"No, 'team' is perfect. Unless you think it's a bad thing."

"Of course, not. I just meant—"

"I know what you meant. You're a boy and I'm, well, a girl. Not very many of us, I suppose, at least in our field."

As far as Petrah was concerned, women were every bit as capable as men, some more so. Ajoon was a perfect example. She was smart, giving, and a quick thinker like Ahleen.

"A number of Teradi are women," Petrah said. "They are great mage warriors and matriarchal tribal leaders. You're in good company."

"Good company, as in we're secondary in class? The Temple seems to think so. They've held us back for centuries."

Petrah didn't know enough about the inner workings of the Temple, although he knew its leadership was male dominated. "That will change."

"When?"

It was as good a question as any. "Um . . ."

"Exactly! No one knows. I'll be old and withered, and I suspect nothing will change."

"If it makes you feel any better, few are keen on my kind either."

"What, being a Prallite? Your accent is different, but you're a male. You'll do just fine. I have two strikes against me. I'm a girl and my parents are poor. Have you paid attention to our classmates and their pedigree? Their parents are wealthy or important. Some of them come from a long line of magi. Mine are, well . . . they're not anything, really. My father was a scribe for the Silver Blade, my mother a seamstress. Nuk's father is a magistrate, Tal's is the head of the Commerce Guild, Miko's the grandson of a Terad in a very prominent tribe, and his father is a Codex Keeper. The position of my family falls beneath theirs. It's unfortunate that I can't change the way things are for my family."

"But by coming to this school," Petrah said, "by bettering yourself, by becoming a mage, you *can* change things."

Ajoon's eyes sparkled. "Indeed I can."

"But I wonder," Petrah said. "How did you get accepted at Maseah, especially since your father is affiliated with another party?"

Ajoon mashed her fingers together as if deciding whether to answer. "He gave up his scribeship as part of an agreement with Master Joriah to take me on as a student. My father serves the Green Flame now, my mother too." She left it at that.

Not wanting to pry, Petrah fell silent.

Ajoon flipped to the next chapter. "Perhaps we should get back to our studies." She squinted at the text but then gave a satisfying sigh. "Ah, the Malaji. This is an interesting read. Why don't you take it from the top?"

Petrah placed his index finger under the first word. The calligraphy was beautiful, albeit in a different hand than in the previous chapter. "'The Mala'"—he frowned—"'Malaji?' Yes, that's it. 'The Malaji were once revered as the highest order of magi in Terjurmeh, able to channel divine power without equal. They were considered Mage Lords and operated in sec—'" Petrah looked up.

"'Secular,'" Ajoon said. "Keep going. You're doing great."

"'Secular capacity during the first millennium of Terjurmeh's history.' Wow, that's two-thousand years ago. 'In 1207, the Temple demanded they be absorbed into its hier'—um—'hierarchy as the Sacred Nine found the *auto-no-mous* nature of the Malaji to be a threat to the Temple.

Thus began a century-long war between the Malaji and the Temple, ending in a battle between the Mighty One and the—' I can't read this."

"'Malajus Exetor' He was the original leader of the Malaji, Mallavant the Cold. I've heard a story, rumor of course, where he killed a hundred priests in cold blood before facing the Mighty One in battle, hence the name. He's the most powerful mage in history. They say he almost destroyed the Temple." Ajoon breathed fast with excitement. "But never mind that. Finish the paragraph."

"'Ending in a battle between the Mighty One and the Malajus Exetor. The Mighty One killed the Malajus and imprisoned his soul in black diamond where it remains to this day, locked in the Shrine of San. The remaining Malaji were branded heretics and executed by the Temple. The second day of San-tel-moor commemorates their victory.'" Petrah scratched his head. "Do you believe this stuff?"

Ajoon lowered her voice, as if others might be listening in. "You know what I've heard? I heard the Temple never killed the Malaji."

"But the book says—"

"I know what *this* book says. It's supposedly canon, but I've heard there's another book that talks about the Malaji fleeing to the City of Night, where they rule to this day. You know where that is, don't you?"

The reference was vaguely familiar to Petrah. "Somewhere in the North?"

"Way north of Meerjurmeh, in the high desert," Ajoon said. "The ancient city of Kushan. It's also called the City of Night because no one has ever entered the city and lived or left. It's a black stain upon the world. They say the Malaji govern the people there with an ironclad rule, the old men kept alive by a fell power, each wearing a crown, like a king."

"Are you saying these Mage Lords are over three thousand years old? That's impossible," Petrah said. "The oldest person I've heard of is the Mighty One, who's said to be two hundred years old, which is plenty ancient. The Mighty Ones of history die off, just like anyone else, and then the next Articulate is voted into power by the Seers of the Temple."

"One would think," Ajoon said, pushing her knuckles into her cheeks. "But the Malaji survived. And I think you're wrong about the Mighty One. I think the same Mighty One has ruled since the beginning of the Temple, perhaps dying in flesh, but absorbing the soul of the next Articulate in line, becoming one with the original, and stronger each time. In fact, I'm willing to go out on a limb and say the Mighty One of today is the same as the one who defeated Mallavant. He is San's incarnate in Acia."

"How could any of them live so long, especially the Malaji?"

"There were eleven of them. Granted, they lost their leader. That left ten to rule in Kushan. The story goes they captured one of San's angels and fed off his energy to stay alive. Can you imagine the power of an angel coursing through your veins? I bet if they came back to Terjurmeh, no one could stop them. Well, maybe the Mighty One, if he truly is the manifestation of our god in the flesh. That would be something, wouldn't it?"

It was Petrah's turn to make sure no one was listening in. "You realize what you said is blasphemy. If the masters find out, they'll string you up, even if you are a girl." *And a pretty one at that*, he would have added.

Ajoon's face bloomed into a smile. "I like to live dangerously."

Petrah matched her smile. He let his gaze linger, taking in her eyes as they caught the light, brown-and-hazel jewels that brightened not only the library but his entire day. "Me too."

P ETRAH SAT ON THE floor of his room in the late afternoon, eyes closed, thoughts focused on the heavy book across from him. He had borrowed it as reading material to help with his studies. It made the room smell like the library, which made him think of Ajoon.

Concentrate ... or you'll never get this figured out.

With sweat brimming on his brow, he concentrated as Master Maglo had instructed.

Sense it. See it. Lift it, he told himself.

He'd tried this a hundred times without so much as a flutter of a page. He couldn't even make his writing quill twitch. It was frustrating and exhausting. He just repeated his mantra over and over, becoming lost in it. So he had no idea, when it actually happened, until he opened his eyes and saw the quill resting against his foot. As he raised his eyes higher, he saw the heavy book floating at eye level, spinning slowly.

I've done it!

A knock interrupted him, and the book fell with a loud smack.

Petrah opened his eyes to see Master Joriah poking his head through the door. The mage looked at the source of the noise, raised a brow inquisitively, and entered.

"Master Joriah," Petrah said, quickly coming to his feet.

Master Joriah gestured toward the floor. "You dropped something."

"Oh." Petrah picked up the book and quill and put them on the desk. Then, as Hamma had taught him, he stood straight with his hands behind his back, palms crossed.

Master Joriah nodded. "Good. Sit down so we can talk."

Petrah sat on his bed while the mage took the chair.

"It looks like you're progressing well," Master Joriah said. "It took me at least six months before I could grasp the concept of levitation. You've done it in two. How's your reading coming along?"

"Well, Master. Hamma's been a tremendous help, Ajoon too."

"Hamma's an excellent mentor. He would do well here as an instructor once he becomes a mage. Stick with him. There's a reason he's wearing the Green."

Master Joriah reached into his robe pocket and pulled out a small, leather pouch. "This is yours." He handed it to the initiate.

Petrah saw the familiar brass button and leather cord wrapped around it. It was the pouch Monta-por had given him. As it rested in his palm, he couldn't help but think it felt heavier than he remembered.

"I've added a little," the mage said.

Petrah unlashed the cord and opened the drawstrings. There were quite a few coins inside. The smell of metal tickled his nose.

"I'm giving it back to you because I want you to buy a new robe. You're coming with me as my guest to the annual Great Council. It will be educational for you. I get to choose one student each year. This year, I've chosen you."

It was an honor beyond words. Petrah asked excitedly, "When do we leave?"

"Tomorrow. Now go with Hamma into the city to purchase a new robe. I want you presentable." Master Joriah's eyes gravitated to the heavy book, then to Petrah. "Nicely done."

Chapter 12

The Great Council

I N THE EARLY MORNING, Petrah traveled with Master Joriah northeast of the city limits via coach to the Great Hall, dressed in his new white robe.

The horse-drawn carriage clattered as it rolled over the flagstone-paved highway. There were ten other magi in separate vehicles and close to a dozen soldiers on horseback.

"I'm looking forward to introducing you to our leader," Master Joriah said as they rode. "He's a prominent man; quite controversial too."

Petrah jostled in the coach. The smell of fruit was making him queasy. He didn't understand how his master could eat while they moved.

"Who is he?" Petrah asked, clutching his midsection and looking for any kind of distraction from the queasiness.

"His Holiness, Uhtah-Pei, Fifth Articulate of the Temple." Petrah's eyebrows tented in surprise. "I would have thought Masters Nole or Maglo would have mentioned him."

Petrah shook his head. His last encounter with an Articulate nearly got him killed.

"He's been our leader for over a year now," Master Joriah said. "It's a big change for us, a very positive one. His Holiness has incredible influence, especially among the tribes. Many other leaders are intimidated by his position in the Temple."

"I didn't know the Temple could get involved in everyday politics."

"As I said, it's controversial. We are a theocratic nation, Petrah, gov-
erned by the parties but ultimately ruled by the Temple. The Temple
might shy away from secular affairs, but who would oppose them if they
were to intrude on the mundane? Certainly not the citizens. Doubtfully
the tribes. A third of our military forces are under the Temple's control,
assigned to protect and enforce the will of the Temple. There are many
strands in this grand web we call Terjurmeh. As history has taught us, it's
better to side with the Temple than against it."

"What does this mean for the Green Flame?" Petrah asked.

"It means we can grow. The leaders of the top parties no longer look
at us as some kind of cult. We have leverage. By representing the cause of
the magus, we have the ear of many Teradi. And respect from the guild."

Petrah loosened the sash of his new robe. Maybe that would help his
stomach settle. "If we get the support of the priests, will it also allow us
to grow?"

"Unfortunately, it's not as easy as that. There are many factors when
it comes to aligning with a party, not all political. Take the Haj-bali, for
instance. They're a powerful and devout faction of the tribal community,
sympathetic to the Temple. Some would call them fanatics, but I admire
their devotion to their faith and their nation's religious establishment.
Their pro-theocratic view of the world keeps them from swearing allegiance to a single party."

"But with His Holiness as our leader . . ."

"Exactly. He can help us gain valuable allies like the Haj-bali." Master
Joriah produced a rare smile. "You're catching on."

W HEN THE CARAVAN ARRIVED at the Great Hall, the passengers exited their coaches. They were joined by a second caravan, bringing the number of Green Flame members up to thirty-five. Master Joriah estimated the total would increase to well over a hundred. He waved at several members and greeted a few by name but let them continue on to the Great Hall so he could speak to Petrah.

"The Great Hall has stood here for over a thousand years," Master Joriah said, presenting the ten-story coliseum of sandstone and granite. "It is the one place where all the parties have a voice and the one place where the most important decisions of our nation are made. It is the nexus of chaos and order, backstabbing and brokering, political posturing and underhanded diplomacy. And you will find nothing like it in the entire world. So," he said. "What do you think?"

Petrah took a long moment to take it all in.

The Great Hall stood as a single beacon in the sandy wasteland. Horizontal, electrum rods projected inward from the top, spanned by tightly pulled fabric that formed a large eave around the inner circumference to provide shade to the audience seated within while dousing the open center with sunlight. Each span of fabric was emblazoned with the insignia of a different party. Petrah saw the Green Flame's span fluttering above, a sea of green and black. A swell of pride filled him.

"It's amazing," Petrah said. "But—" He thought of what Master Joriah said about the politics and posturing. "What you describe seems so . . . unpredictable. And dangerous."

"Indeed," Master Joriah said with a gleam in his eye. "This is the most dangerous place in all Terjurmeh but also the most rewarding. It all depends on how well you play the game."

Petrah decided he would pay close attention to how the parties interacted. He would observe and learn and become a student of the inner workings of the country.

Master Joriah beckoned. "Let us head inside. Trust me when I say you will not be disappointed."

As they moved past the mass of tents to the side of the building—interim living quarters and meeting places for party members—Petrah noted slaves hard at work erecting new tents and pounding stakes into the ground. He smelled their collective stench, taking him back to his time working at the quarry in Kanmar. When he saw a Draad yelling at a lagger, he shivered and picked up the pace, eager to put the sight out of his head.

The standard bearer for the Green Flame led his procession through a giant pylon into the arena. As Master Joriah claimed, the interior was grand.

Majestic caryatids of ancient warriors, the height of the coliseum, supported the inside eaves with gargantuan, upturned stone hands. What must have been ten thousand seats climbed up from an open, sunlit center, running concentrically, intersected by aisles, walkways, and landings. There were plenty of seats left to be filled, with a steady stream of people continuing to fill the hall.

"Each party has a dedicated section," Master Joriah told Petrah as they walked. "Locations shift every year, the more popular parties getting the lower seats, the less popular the upper. We're headed over there." He pointed at a wedge of rows near the bottom, already occupied by a dozen Green Flame members. "To our right is the Silver Blade, to the left is the Black Arrow. The Fist, of course, is in the middle. Then you have other parties behind them, like the White Hand and the Copper Shield."

A chill ran up Petrah's neck when he saw the Black Arrow's section. He searched for Manis-cor, expecting the man to rise from his seat and point at him. He wanted to run the other way.

The party's standard bearer took his position front and center of the Green Flame section, standing on the floor of the arena like those of the other major parties. The Fist had three standard bearers to represent its enormous gathering, some three-hundred-plus members seated like imperial nobles. Slave runners darted about the Hall, working fast to situate the growing number of guests. There was a collage of other parties occupying the middle tier and an assortment of non-party guests in the top tier.

Petrah followed Master Joriah through a gated opening from the floor, up a flight of stairs, and onto a shaded balcony. The webbed eave hung high above, its dark fabric blocking out the dreadful sun.

Master Joriah took the time to greet several tribal leaders before settling in. Their colorful headbands bore the crests of their families. He locked forearms with other tribal members and exchanged verbal greetings with those out of reach.

Terjurmeh's history was steeped in tribal diversity, originating from its nomadic roots. The tribes continued that tradition today, traveling in bands across the desert plains in the cooler months.

Master Joriah greeted a few Terad-mari who sat officiously as priests wearing simple, red robes free of markings. Their seraks gleamed about their chests, reminders to the non-clergy of their station. Several acknowledged Petrah with cursory nods. The initiate reciprocated humbly.

Petrah gawked everywhere he looked. The movement of bodies, the clamor of voices, the sheer number of people—it was as intense as it was delightful. He couldn't wait to tell Ajoon about it. She should have come with him to see this spectacle. The more he thought about her, the more he realized he missed being with her. When he got back to Maseah, he promised to give her a full account of his adventure.

Master Joriah found his place in the second row, next to Masters Maglo and Nole. Petrah sat to Master Joriah's right. The seats were made of marble, worn from use, but ushers handed out planks of acha wood to sit on. Petrah thought the acha was a little less comfortable than the chair in his dorm room, but it was better than sitting on cold, hard stone.

It took another hour to fill the Hall. Most of the attendees were older, although Petrah spotted a few around his age. Perhaps they were special guests like him, novices of their parties, or aspiring students. He was honored to be the one student representing Maseah.

When Hamma had found out Petrah was attending, he'd shown more excitement than Petrah had ever seen from the older boy. "You know, I was chosen last year. It's a great honor." When Petrah pried him for details, Hamma had just grinned. "You'll see," he'd repeated, no matter how hard Petrah pressed him.

Four men garbed with red Temple headdresses carried a covered palanquin toward the Green Flame section. A single occupant sat beneath the framed cover, veiled by sheer fabric. Petrah leaned forward curiously.

"His Holiness, Uhtah-Pei," Master Joriah said. "Travels well, doesn't he?"

The Articulate was accompanied by a vanguard of attendants with shaved heads and a rearguard of Temple soldiers. One of the front litter bearers called out a command, and the four-man palanquin team halted.

A middle-aged man exited the palanquin. He was heavy and balding, and wore a decorative, crimson robe with triangular flourishes along the cuffs. He had a necklace with a hand-sized gold serak. A large box seat with plenty of cushions awaited the Articulate. When he made it to his seat, he waved at his party members, and a cheer went up.

"His Holiness looks our way," Master Joriah said to Petrah.

Petrah watched as Uhtah-Pei looked in their direction. For a moment, the Articulate's dark eyes met Petrah's. He smiled before turning away.

"You've won the favor of His Holiness," Master Joriah said. "This is most fortunate."

Petrah couldn't contain his smile. Had the leader of their party really noticed him? But he lost his smile as soon as he spotted Manis-cor arriving with his party. The Dark Arrow wore a black helm with an absurdly huge red plume and his infamous black cape. Petrah recognized Zen and a few other high-ranking Draadi. He prayed they wouldn't notice him.

A gong bellowed after the floor was cleared, and all eyes fell upon a large platform being wheeled in by thirty-plus slaves.

A man in a scarlet tunic, scarlet sandals, and a matching, red wig stood atop a dais in the center. He was accompanied by two men in black, one holding a wand and another a gong. When the slaves finished rolling the platform and stowing the ropes, the man with the red wig lifted his arms and cried out to the audience.

"Hail, brothers and sisters of the Temple, great leaders, and citizens of Terjurmeh. I am Norak, appointed Magistrate of the Hall. Welcome to the Great Council!"

The cheer of the crowd was deafening. Petrah soaked in the energy, feeling it sink into his chest.

It took at least a minute for the magistrate to wait them out. When there was order, he read off the roster of parties in attendance, beginning with the Fist.

All party leaders were introduced. They stood and waved to the assembly.

Petrah was most interested in seeing Andus-nai, the Iron Fist. When called, the man stood like an emperor. Although squat, he carried an immense presence. Of all the party leaders, Petrah considered his regalia the most outlandish, a compilation of intricately designed ceremonial, black diamond armor over black padding and a golden helm whose triple prongs jutted upward like desert lightning.

"Today," Norak announced, "we begin with a series of motions up for a vote in the council. The first motion is the Fist's request to respond militarily to a Meerjurmehan breach of treaty. Meerjurmeh has violated an international accord that forbids it to acquire lumber from the Northern Kingdom without consent from the Terjurmehan Trade

Council. The proposal at hand is to impose an embargo by seizing the city of Vergahl. The Fist has the floor."

"It figures the Fist would capitalize on that," Petrah heard Master Nole whisper to Master Joriah. "If we go after Vergahl, it'll drag the entire country into the conflict. Andus-nai doesn't care about Meerjurmeh violating a trade agreement. He doesn't care about anything but himself . . . and his oversized ego."

Master Joriah said nothing.

After several hours of boring speeches and arguing from a variety of party officials, Norak announced the verdict. "All votes are in and have been tallied. We have reached a majority decision. A strike force is authorized to attack Vergahl. The matter is now turned over to the ruling party for execution. Next motion."

Petrah looked at Master Joriah, who simply shook his head. It was apparent the Green Flame had not agreed with the decision.

Petrah's mind wandered as the next few items came up for vote. He overheard Master Joriah call one issue "trivial" and another "stupid."

When a matter came up about who would control shipments of produce out of Kanmar, Petrah expected nothing interesting to come out of it. But a debate between the Copper Shield and a minor party sitting right above them turned into a shouting match. Tensions escalated, and before Petrah knew it, a fight broke out between the two parties that turned into an all-out brawl. Soldiers rushed to the stands to break up the scuffle. In the end, several injured were attended to while three bodies were carted off, dead from what looked like stab wounds. Master Maglo shook his head at Master Nole, who simply shrugged.

Petrah expected both parties to be expelled, but Norak did no such thing. Everyone settled back into their seats to vote on the matter. The Copper Shield won, earning cheers and boos from the crowd.

Petrah leaned close to Master Joriah. "Why isn't anyone getting arrested? People were hurt, others killed."

"That's nothing compared to what I've seen over the years," Master Joriah said. "It would take much more than that for anyone to be removed."

"There aren't any consequences then?"

"The consequences have already been dealt. The Copper Shield won the matter."

"But—" Petrah said. "I don't understand."

"This is how it's always been, Petrah. Didn't I tell you this was a dangerous place?"

Magistrate Norak concluded the day's session by midafternoon.

Petrah was glad to leave. When he asked Master Joriah how things went, the mage simply replied, "We'll see."

The evening's activities were an unexpected treat for the White Robe. Magi apprentices and journeymen from other schools performed feats of illusion for the crowds gathered in the clearing between tents. There were also jugglers, musicians, and dancers. Petrah ate well and even got to enjoy some ale. He was treated to spicy, charbroiled manja served inside a folded flatbread stuffed with caramelized onions and topped with yogurt sauce. The aroma brought back bittersweet memories of his friends. Master Joriah kept him busy mingling, but after a while, it became too overwhelming.

Petrah needed a break. He left the area with his ale. As he rounded one of the outer tents, he ran into a contingent of Black Arrow members. To his dismay, the Draadlord was among them.

Zen stopped him. "Do I know you?"

Petrah's heart caught in his throat. "No, sir."

"My mistake then. You just look familiar." Zen lifted the large mug in his left hand and tapped Petrah's. "To mistakes!"

"To mistakes," Petrah repeated, taking a halfhearted swig. It was time to move on.

Zen seemed to have trouble keeping his body from leaning. He eye-balled the apprentice's cup and said, "You're almost empty. We're headed to the ale tent. How about joining us for a round?"

Petrah didn't want to linger any more than he had to and graciously declined. Zen tipped his head, bidding the young man farewell. But when Petrah turned, Manis-cor was walking his way. He, too, appeared drunk and nearly bumped into him.

"Pardon me, my lord," Petrah said. He tried to step aside, but the Dark Arrow grabbed him by the arm.

"You should be more careful, young one," he said and then released him. A strange look crossed his face. "Where do I know you from?"

"Nowhere, my lord," Petrah said. "I must get back to my master. He's probably looking for me."

Manis-cor's eyes flickered wildly. "That accent . . ."

"I must leave."

Manis-cor came within inches of Petrah's face, the odor of meat and alcohol heavy. "Who's your master?"

"Master Joriah of the Green Flame, my lord."

"Master Joriah, is it? I know that name." The Dark Arrow staggered back a step. "Maybe I should fetch your master and tell him what a liar you are. Would you like that?"

"No, my lord."

"Don't toy with me."

"I'm not, my lord. Please, I must go."

Petrah saw now that Zen was looking at him, not in the same drunken haze as before, but like a raptor eying fresh prey. Another man spoke into the Draadlord's ear, but Zen's eyes remained fixed on Petrah.

After a tense wait, Manis-cor finally waved Petrah away. "All right. Get out of here."

Petrah bowed his head and quickly retreated.

Chapter 13

Troubles

L EVIES AND BLOODSHED.

The passing of the first led to the other, and it took the magistrate and a contingent of soldiers almost an hour to sort the mess in the Great Hall.

What started as a ratified motion to increase taxes in support of the impending war ended in a feud between parties and tribes for and against the measure.

The arguing escalated, but it involved a much larger crowd than yesterday's deadly incident. Petrah watched finger-pointing turn to shoves, then the brandishing of daggers. Before soldiers could be dispatched to intervene, the conflict turned ugly. A man with a red badge embroidered onto his tunic stabbed a tribeswoman in a purple headdress. Her tribesmen retaliated, and a neighboring party with blue tunics succored their purple neighbors. Steel slashed and blood spilled.

By the time the soldiers had the skirmish under control, fifteen dead bodies were lifted and laid on the backs of horse-drawn carts. Not since his time as a slave had Petrah seen such senseless death. Unlike yesterday, arrests were made, and people were escorted out in manacles among a chorus of catcalls and jeers.

Petrah looked at Master Joriah for an explanation. The mage said, "The arrests were necessary this time. It sends a message to not just the troublemakers, but everyone present. Sometimes you have to remind people, even the powerful, that there are consequences for your actions."

When the area was cleared, crimson-splotched sand was the only evidence that anything had occurred. Flies buzzed the air, attracted to the sweating mass of men and women in attendance.

Uhtah-Pei, leader of the Green Flame, seized the moment to level a blow against the assemblage.

He riled the Haj-bali to a near frenzy with a speech condemning both the violence and the ruling party's ceaseless endeavor to destroy the country. The cost of the war would be another item to add to the nation's growing list of problems, highlighted by the previous year's financial fiasco.

"Division is ruining us," Uhtah-Pei told the energized audience. "How can a nation of holy people create such a schism as we've never seen in our history? We are crumbling within, and yet unilaterally, we are driven to war over a single commodity. There are reasons to spill Con-jurahn blood. A trade violation isn't one of them."

Uhtah-Pei addressed the tribal leaders. He spoke of increased famine, the spread of disease, and the dwindling of religious devotion as signs that San was displeased.

"You are the Teradi, the core of our collective spirit. Your nation needs you—not to squabble and split it—but to unite it and renew your connection with your religion, your faith, and your god."

The commotion brewing from the Fist's congregation threatened to drown him out. He spoke louder, his voice amplified by a means beyond Petrah's reckoning.

"The Green Flame calls for your allegiance. We call for you to put aside your political differences and join the one party that represents your interests. We are the voice of reason. And we are the only party to speak with spiritual meaning. What other major party in this Great Hall speaks thusly?" The Articulate pointed across the way. "The Fist? The Silver Blade? The Black Arrow? They are nothing but enemies of the state!"

Petrah felt the tremor of several thousand bodies rising from their seats. Fervent cheers met cries of protest and stamps of feet, shaking the Great Hall.

It was chaos.

A company of city soldiers charged into the coliseum with spears while dozens of Fist and Silver Blade attendees spilled onto the arena floor, ready to rush the Green Flame. The soldiers formed an armed wall between the parties.

"This is an outrage!" the Iron Fist shouted, his voice swallowed by the mob.

Master Joriah stood quietly for a time. Petrah was unsure what his master thought of Uhtah-Pei's contentious declaration or the unfolding bedlam or the potential consequences for their party. Or why he was so still when everyone else was so animated.

But when the mage looked at Petrah, an uncharacteristic smile grew on his face, letting Petrah know the Green Flame had just landed a small but crucial victory.

"THAT WAS MOST BOLD today, Holy One," said Felio, a senior Green Flame official after the council had adjourned for the day. He, Joriah, Maglo, Nole, Petrah, and others, including several new Green Flame members from various tribes, sat at a long table in the party's dining tent, with the Fifth Articulate at its head. "San is with you and with us."

An approving round of fists on wood revealed the high spirits of the gathering. After two draughts of ale, Petrah was feeling good too.

It was a triumphant day for the party, and he was glad to partake in the celebration among the Green Flame's elite. He had seen blood spilled over nothing. Now he saw ale spilled from overflowing cups and thought how much better he liked the latter.

Petrah stumbled toward the line of refuse tents. They were more like pillared sheets around holes in the ground. Six mugs of ale were to blame for the apprentice's off-kilter gate. He would have drunk a seventh had Master Joriah not stopped him.

Drunkenness invoked many feelings.

As Petrah staggered, they devoured him in a string of thoughts. He was sad one moment, thinking of his friends; ecstatic the next, imagining the future as a mage; and depressed the following, feeling like an orphan who would never know home or family.

You will be all right. You have a purpose now.

Petrah fumbled to find the entrance to one of the tents. Just as he found the seam, someone covered his head with a hood while another grabbed him.

T HEY STRIPPED HIM, PUT a collar around his throat, and left him in the dark, chained and blinded. His hot, ale-laden breath dampened the fabric of the inside of his hood. Every inhale pulled the moistened cloth tight against his lips, making each breath more challenging than the last. He was thankful when they removed it from his head and the cooler air struck his sweat-drenched face.

Petrah adjusted his eyes. Everything around him seemed to spin.

Still intoxicated, he struggled to keep from rotating with the room. An out-of-focus flicker in the middle of the tent danced like a hazy wraith, making it difficult to focus.

Petrah sat back and coughed violently. He cleared his throat and waited for the blurriness to subside.

He followed the collar's chain to the wooden post supporting the tent. A shadow on the floor revealed another presence. He looked up, and an ugly face looked down.

"Comfy, sweets?" the Draad asked. His nasty smile revealed a mouth full of twisted teeth. "Let me get your hosts."

Two men entered the tent, treacherously familiar faces.

Manis-cor approached the kneeling prisoner. "What do you think, Zen? Are we treating our guest to a deserving homecoming?"

The Draadlord reached over and yanked Petrah's chain, hauling him onto his haunches. "Mighty deserving, my lord."

The Dark Arrow circled the frightened youth slowly. "The scars on your back healed nicely. Almost time for some more, don't you think?"

The pulse in Petrah's neck quickened.

He watched Manis-cor pour himself a cup of water from a jug on a nearby table. The Dark Arrow took a swallow and let the rest trickle onto the ground.

"You know," he said, tossing the cup, "that escape of yours caused quite a scene. I wasted a lot of manpower on you and your cohorts. I'm sure we can devise a way to learn where the others went. We've already tortured some information out of one of the Jabah who helped you. You wouldn't believe how talkative someone gets when their fingernails are pulled out with pincers." Manis-cor pressed a finger into Zen's shoulder. "Make sure he tells you where the others are before we set sail for home. Rip him apart piece by piece if you have to."

When the Dark Arrow left, Zen grabbed a metal pail.

"Here," he said, hurling it at Petrah. "For old times' sake."

T HE GREAT HALL WAS filled to capacity. It was the last day of
the council, and according to the magistrate, thirty-four measures
were up for a vote. Joriah sat with Maglo to his left, an empty seat to his
right.

"Where do you think he went?" Maglo asked.

"I don't know," Joriah said. "I searched everywhere for him this morning. He just disappeared."

"Maybe he got himself a woman."

Joriah cast a disapproving look at Maglo. "We don't need this today.
Look at this place. I've never seen such hostility."

Jeers and shouting matches were rampant, creating pockets of discord.
Pandemonium was but a breath away. The only assurance against an
all-out conflict was the four-hundred-soldier contingent posted along
the gated entries on the arena floor. The magistrate was taking no chances
today.

"Let me ask you something," Joriah said. "Have you taught Petrah
how to perform a mind link?"

Maglo scrunched his forehead. "When have we ever taught initiates to
perform that? It's too dangerous at their stage of development."

Joriah groaned a sigh. "Then we'll have to search for him the old-fash-
ioned way. If I could just break away for an hour . . ."

"You can't. You're a voting member."

"That's the problem."

"What if I go?" Maglo asked.

Joriah tapped a finger against his lips and stared off into the opposing
stands. He waved the mage away. "Take Nole with you."

P ETRAH CONSIDERED EVERY TECHNIQUE the masters had taught him, but none seemed of any use for getting him out of his predicament.

Levitating the chain was useless, and lifting the embedded wood post was an impossible effort. He had never tried to raise something that wasn't freestanding. He closed his eyes and used his mind to feel the post, the chain, and the collar around his neck, using the technique Master Maglo had taught him to feel with his mind. None of the surfaces, metal or wood, gave him anything he could use to devise a way to free himself.

On top of that, he was thirsty, hungry, and hungover. He'd pissed himself once and needed to pee again. Zen made sure he was left with no food or water, but Petrah refused to use the pail to relieve himself. He'd rather soil his clothes than give the Draadlord the satisfaction of doing what he wanted.

"Still with us?" the Draadlord asked. Zen glanced at the empty bucket and shook his head. Then with a sneer, he added, "If you don't use that, you'll have nothing to drink."

Petrah didn't acknowledge his captor. He would remain defiant until his last breath, if that's what it took.

They can take away my freedom, but they can't take my will. Not yet.

The Draadlord dropped to a squat. "Let's make this easy. I'm going to ask you the whereabouts of your accomplices, and you're going to tell me what I need to know, right?"

Petrah said nothing.

Zen pulled on the neck collar, forcing the youth's face close. "Right?"

MASTER MAGLO CAUGHT UP with Joriah as he exited the coliseum.

The Great Council was concluded for another year. Thousands of weary participants filed out in a steady stream.

"Well?" Joriah asked, fatigue evident in his voice.

"I couldn't find him," Maglo said. "I spoke to workers, slaves, soldiers. Nothing."

"Damn it, Maglo. Today's been a disaster for us. I don't need to hear this from you."

"What happened?"

"The council passed a new law to cap Temple involvement in party politics: no priests or clerics allowed in policy-making activities. It's the first time something like this occurred. And here I told Petrah that the parties were powerless to prevent the Temple from interfering in layman affairs."

Maglo's eyes widened. "All because of yesterday?"

"Call it a coup by the Fist and its newfound allies. I can't even tell you how upset His Holiness is." Joriah scanned the area. "Where's Nole?"

Just then, the hawk-nosed mage walked up with a woman. The second individual wore a black robe with gray trim, a Silver Blade magus outfit.

"Consorting with the enemy?" Joriah asked.

The woman from the Silver Blade locked forearms with Joriah and patted him on the back. "Am *I* the enemy?"

"Perhaps," Joriah said. "It's good to see you again, Sef."

"You too. Nole tells me you've lost one of your White Robes."

"Yes. Would you know anything about it?"

Sef pulled Joriah aside from the foot traffic. "I've heard a rumor," she said. "It's about a Northerner who was a slave who escaped and was caught again by his masters. They say this Northerner was wearing white."

Joriah's dark eyes narrowed. "I don't know of any slave. What about my apprentice?"

"You didn't hear it from me, but if we're talking about the same young man, the Black Arrow has him."

"And how do I know we're talking about the same young man?"

Sef spoke into the mage's ear. "Have you ever seen anyone with blue eyes?"

J ORIAH PACED BACK AND forth in his tent, deep lines of concentration across his forehead.

Maglo and Nole sat in the back, each facing different directions and equally upset. After Maglo admitted knowledge of Petrah's past as a slave, the three got into an argument over whether to let the boy rot or attempt to bargain for his release.

"I say leave him," Nole muttered.

A man with a shaved scalp entered the tent. "His Holiness wishes an audience with you at once," he told Joriah. "Are you available?"

"Of course," Joriah said. Then, after seeing the man inspect the tent area, he said, "What, here?"

"Yes."

"Give me a moment to call for refreshments and—"

The man left before Joriah could finish. A moment later, the Fifth Articulate arrived.

Joriah bowed his head. "Holy One." Maglo and Nole got to their feet and followed suit.

Uhtah-Pei pushed past the magi, an unhappy look on his face. "This should be a day of triumph for us. Instead, I have a bitter taste in my mouth. Do you know why, Joriah?"

"I was there, Holy One."

The Articulate snapped the hem of his robe. "There's dissension among our membership. They whisper and speak of concerns that shouldn't be. I started hearing it after the Fist pulled that stunt at the end of the day. This must be handled swiftly. I want resolution."

"What can I do, Holy One?"

"Call for a meeting. Gather the magi and Teradi and have them rendezvous at the main tent in an hour. I must first meet with Baaka to prepare for the evening's blessing."

Joriah stared off for a moment, his eyes moving as if calculating something.

"What is it?" Uhtah-Pei asked.

"Nothing, Holy One. I have another situation with which we are dealing."

"What situation?"

"My apprentice is missing. We think he"—Joriah glanced at his companions—"might have been detained by another party."

The Articulate's eyebrows converged. "*Detained*? By whom?"

"The Black Arrow."

Joriah explained that the Black Arrow had taken Petrah captive and that it was because they claimed Petrah was their property. The Articulate's expression grew increasingly angrier as the mage spoke. Joriah expected his superior to rip into him for knowingly training a slave, especially when that slave belonged to one of the top three most powerful parties in Terjurmeh.

But the Articulate didn't seem to care that Petrah was a slave. Uhtah-Pei seethed as he said, "This is why the Temple needs to assume control of the population! Because of treacherous dogs like the Dark

Arrow. They've allied with the Fist to spit in our face today. And now this . . ."

Joriah let his party leader decide what to do.

"Enough is enough," the Articulate said. "Baaka can wait. I'm going to handle this matter personally. Get a squad of men and meet me outside the main tent in fifteen minutes."

T WELVE GREEN FLAME SOLDIERS followed Uhtah-Pei to the Black Arrow's camp.

Joriah, Nole, and Maglo trailed the Articulate, exchanging tense glances beneath the starlight. An aura shimmered around Uhtah-Pei in the night air, distorting the outline of his body and blending it with the dark. Joriah had witnessed such a sight on rare occasions and only among the most senior of the priesthood—a testament to the divine power they wielded, where the spiritual world pushed visibly into the physical world. It was beautiful as it was terrifying to behold. A shiver ran up Joriah's neck.

Three soldiers guarding the ring of Black Arrow tents came to attention as the Articulate walked up to them. "Where's Manis-cor?"

The soldiers eyed the armed contingent with unease. One gestured toward a large tent in the center of the camp.

Uhtah-Pei led his men past the astonished guards. Several soldiers were standing near a fire in front of the main Black Arrow tent. Two broke away and put themselves between Uhtah-Pei and the entrance.

"Move aside," Uhtah-Pei ordered.

"I'm sorry, Holy One," one of them said, "but we can't let you in. There is a private meeting. Is there something we can help you with?"

Joriah saw his leader's fist knot. He could feel the hostile energy radiating from the man's body. The Articulate's dark aura swelled.

Uhtah-Pei stabbed the soldier's chest with a finger. "Manis-cor. Is he inside?"

"Yes, Holy—"

The Articulate shoved the man aside, ripped down the tent flap, and entered.

Lamplight revealed the Dark Arrow and about a dozen party officials seated in a circle and engaged in banter. As soon as they saw who it was who entered, they stopped talking. Zen glanced at Manis-cor, who was seated on a throw of cushions. The Dark Arrow straightened his back.

"Holy One," he said, "To what occasion do we owe this honor? We thought the blessing wasn't until—"

The Articulate cut him off. "Spare me, Manis. I'm here to settle a matter."

A series of shouts were followed by a rush of feet outside. About ten Black Arrow soldiers came running. Joriah watched them form a perimeter around his men through the tent opening, hands on hilts, ready for action.

The Articulate didn't bother to look behind him. He walked straight through the circle of seated men and up to the Dark Arrow.

"I want my man back," Uhtah-Pei said, less than a foot away. "I was told you took him prisoner."

"We have a prisoner, but he's an escaped slave we recaptured last night. Black Arrow property."

"You're treading on dangerous ground, Manis. He was wearing white with a Green Flame insignia stitched over the front. Do I need to go into more detail, or should we just finish it?"

Manis-cor stood. He was taller than the balding Articulate. "And how should we finish it?"

"Do you or do you not have the man I described as your prisoner?"

Manis-cor inched closer. "I do. But like I said, he's Black Arrow property. Stolen property."

"I don't care how you categorize him. I want him released right now."

Both sets of party members grew restive. Outside, Joriah heard the unsheathing of swords. The situation was about to escalate out of control. The Green Party contingent was well outnumbered.

"I will do no such thing," Manis-cor said. "Party property is party property. The Codex is very clear about slave ownership, Holy One."

"I don't give a damn what your law states. I'm a member of the Temple. We do not adhere to that ridiculous law! Now, you either bring me that man or I will burn your flesh to ashes where you stand."

For a strained moment, the two stared at each other. Then, before either could speak, a loud commotion outside broke the stalemate, followed by the clash of metal.

"Order your men to stand down," Uhtah-Pei said.

"Stop the fighting!" Manis-cor shouted.

No one seemed to hear him.

The melee forced the Green Flame troops back against the tent.

Joriah was pushed down to the ground along with Nole and Maglo. Soldiers tripped and fell. Joriah saw one man fall by sword stroke, then a second, and a third. Everyone in the Black Arrow's court scattered to the side as the fighting drove inward.

Uhtah-Pei turned his back on Manis-cor and moved forward with purpose.

He crossed the fire pit and held out his hand. The air rippled from his fingertips.

Just as the first Black Arrow soldier stepped into the tent area, he was met by a tidal wave of invisible force. He fell to the ground, dead on impact, his midsection a burst of cinders. The others behind were blown backward by the residual force.

One soldier regained his feet and lifted his sword to attack but fell screaming, his chest blown open into a smoking crater. The air stank of burned flesh.

"I will not hesitate to kill everyone here!" Uhtah-Pei shouted. He snapped his head toward the rear, where a shocked Manis-cor looked on. "Have your men stand down or watch them all burn."

The Black Arrow ordered his troops to sheath their swords. He kneeled before Uhtah-Pei like someone who had seen his own death and survived. "Forgive me, Holy One."

"On your feet. We end this now!"

PETRAH STIRRED AS A hand shook him. He'd been dreaming of someplace dark and cold and—

His eyes flicked open, and he immediately pressed back against the wooden post of the tent. His chain rattled and the collar around his throat pressed harshly against his windpipe, spurring a fit of coughs.

They've come to get me. They're shipping me back to Kanmar!

"Petrah?"

Petrah's eyes watered, then focused. He saw a familiar bearded face, an impossible sight. He'd expected a Draad to come to haul him off to a slave ship.

But this was no Draad.

"Master?"

"Here, let me help you up," Master Joriah said. He helped Petrah sit upright against the post. Behind the mage stood a not-too-happy Zen and the Draad with the twisted teeth. "Unbind him," Master Joriah said to the Draad.

After the Draad removed Petrah's collar, Master Joriah offered him a skin of water. The mage examined Petrah as the apprentice emptied the contents of the skin. "Are you injured? Should I fetch a medic?"

Petrah shook his head. He wiped the dribble of water that had run down his chin.

Master Joriah turned to Zen. "Wait outside."

Zen gave the mage a daggered look, then complied and took the Draad with him.

Alone with Petrah, Master Joriah said, "You gave us quite the scare. And stirred up the hornet's nest too. Gods, you smell like a swine pen. Are you sure you're not injured?"

"How—?" Petrah began as a tickle in his throat threatened to unleash another coughing fit.

"A very fortunate set of circumstances is how we found you. You have His Holiness to thank."

"But—" Petrah said. "But you know about—"

"Yes, we all do now. Had Master Maglo divulged his knowledge of your secret back at Maseah, things would have transpired differently. I'm not happy he withheld such vital information from me. We could have avoided all of this."

Petrah couldn't allow Master Maglo to pay for Petrah's plea to keep his slave past a secret. "Please don't punish him, Master. Punish me instead."

Master Joriah's eyes softened. "No one's getting punished. Can you stand?"

"I think so."

Master Joriah helped him up. Petrah's legs and back ached, but he could stand, even walk.

"His Holiness wants to see us," Master Joriah said. "Specifically, he wants to talk to you. We'll get you bathed and fitted with a fresh tunic first."

Petrah swallowed. His mouth turned dry again.

Reading the pained look on Petrah's face, Master Joriah said, "No, it's not as bad as you think. If His Holiness wanted to discipline you, he would have let the Black Arrow keep you. And I wouldn't be here, would I?"

Of all the people who could have come to him in person, Petrah was glad it was Master Joriah. "Thank you, Master. Thank you for finding me."

Master Joriah gave his shoulder a gentle squeeze. "Come. Let's get the stink off of you."

B ATHED AND IN A clean white tunic, Petrah accompanied Master Joriah to Uhtah-Pei's tent.

Temple soldiers in red linen headdresses posted silently inside as oil lamps lit the lavish interior of polished wood furnishings sitting atop a richly woven tapestry of red and gold. Uhtah-Pei sat on a tasseled cushion in the center.

Petrah followed Master Joriah's lead and knelt, careful to avert his gaze and mindful of his previous encounter with the Articulate Septamo. It was a capital crime for a slave to look a clergyman in the eye.

"Holy One," Master Joriah said.

"Up, both of you." When Master Joriah and Petrah were on their feet, Uhtah-Pei ordered Petrah to look at him. "You've caused quite a stir, young man. And a mess as well. Has your master informed you of the trouble your recapture has cost us?"

Perspiration trickled down Petrah's nape. Master Joriah had provided Petrah with the details of the encounter between the Green Flame and the Black Arrow on their way over to the Articulate's tent. "He mentioned there were fatalities, Holy One. And that you had to get involved."

"Then you know the sacrifice made to get you back. Tell me, Petrah, are you as the Dark Arrow claims: the property of his party?"

The sweat not only soaked Petrah's neck but his brow too. His lips trembled, but they parted to give a truthful answer. "Yes, Holy One."

Uhtah-Pei looked Petrah up and down as if deciding what to do with him. "Do you know what the Codex says about slavery? It says a slave remains the property of its owner unless the owner sells or frees the slave. Yet here you stand before me in defiance of the Codex. According to Manis-cor, you were not released from bondage. By his right, you should have gone back to Kanmar. That means, no matter how you escaped, no matter your status as an apprentice, you are still a slave. Are you not?"

Petrah wiped the sweat stinging his eyes. Master Joriah had said this encounter wouldn't be as bad as Petrah thought. But standing here, being reminded he was but a lowly slave—

"I am," Petrah said in a voice that sounded distant to his ears.

Uhtah-Pei continued. "All of that said, I am an Articulate of the Temple. The Temple is not bound by the Codex. We stand above it. As such, I have decided on your doomed situation. Kneel."

Petrah knelt. He resisted bowing his head and kept his eyes fixed on the Articulate.

"As one of the Sacred Nine, it is within my right to commute your sentence of slavery. Such a deed is called holy manumission. Not even the Dark Arrow or the Iron Fist can contest it, for it is beyond reproach."

The Articulate got up from his cushion and walked over to Petrah. He reached down with his fingers and touched Petrah upon the crown of his head. The touch was warm, more than just the press of fingertips. Spiritual energy flowed, sinking into Petrah's skull, his neck, and his chest. "From this day forth, Petrah, you shall no longer be a slave. Rise as a free man."

A great heaviness lifted off of Petrah with the removal of the Articulate's fingers. Petrah came to his feet, lighter than he'd ever felt. Although he was taller than the Articulate, the man appeared as a towering giant within the tent, powerful as he was generous.

Petrah inclined his head. "Thank you, Holy One. Thank you for this priceless gift."

P ETRAH RODE SILENTLY IN the coach the morning after his release, his face misshapen with bruises and swelling, his mind occupied with the events from the past two days.

Wait until Ajoon sees you.

She would smother him with questions. What could he tell her? He certainly couldn't share that he'd been abducted because he was once a slave, could he? What would Ajoon think of him then?

She wouldn't judge me. She's not that way.

But what if she did? He couldn't risk their friendship over his past.

He was ashamed of his former life, even with Uhtah-Pei's gift of freedom. It was a stigma that would always be with him. Miko had smelled it on him like a krell. His fangs gleamed under the moonlight, ready to tear Petrah apart for any reason at all.

I won't allow him to know either.

Petrah took small sips from a water skin and nibbled on some fruit Master Joriah gave him. The rickety movement of the coach didn't upset the apprentice's stomach as it did on the previous trip, but his head throbbed like horses had run over it in a stampede.

"Don't dwell on it," Master Joriah said, looking up from the scroll he was reading. He peered at Petrah's cheeks and forehead as if counting the welts. "It's over now. If anyone asks what happened, you'll say you got into a fight with a student from another school who said something disparaging about us. Pride and poor judgment got the better of you, earning you a bruised ego and face. I gave you a stern talking-to for being so reckless, and Masters Nole and Maglo were there to witness me doing it. Agreed?"

Petrah nodded. "Agreed, Master."

"His Holiness has done a remarkable thing for you. You should pray and give thanks for his generosity."

Petrah gave an enthusiastic, "I will." Uhtah-Pei's intervention was more than a blessing. It was a life-changing act of kindness Petrah would not forget.

"And one more thing," Master Joriah said, rolling up his scroll. "You're going to continue your apprenticeship, and we're never going to speak of this matter again. Understood?"

Chapter 14

Tragedy

H EARTBEATS.

Their rhythm pulsed in his mind, riding a single thread of thought, pure and unadulterated.

Even with closed eyes, Petrah could tell the source and distinguish the animal and its location by sensing the unique signature of its life force, like listening to a melody.

He followed the heartbeats as they traveled above him. They were close now, perhaps a few feet away, rapid explosions of life among the branches. A bird taking a moment of respite from the heat in the canopy's shade, joined by a second whose wings fluttered with its landing.

A new rhythm made its presence known, slower than the first, and undeniably human.

Petrah opened his eyes.

He looked up from his bench at the tree shading him. The water doves were perched where he pictured them, cooing in the hot afternoon. One took to the air. Then it swooped low and away, followed by its mate.

"Hello, Master," Petrah said, standing, but not turning.

Master Joriah crossed into view. "How did you know it was me? Are my footsteps that obvious?"

"No, Master. It was your aura."

"Did Master Maglo teach you that?"

"A few weeks ago."

"After six months, I'd say you're making good progress. Now, if we could just improve your handwriting." Master Joriah gestured to the narrow dirt path behind them. "Walk with me. I want to talk to you about something."

The two traveled along the water's edge.

Fat-bellied peepers carried on in a disharmony of shrill chirps among the shielding growth while a black-eared potomus reared its bow-shaped head from the river and bellowed water from its flared nostrils.

"There's something that's troubling me," Master Joriah said, snaking around a patch of fallen palm fronds. "Normally, I wouldn't say anything, except that it's causing a bit of a problem with your peers. Perhaps you could enlighten me on why you're waking up your dormmates in the middle of the night?"

It took Petrah a moment to realize what Master Joriah was referring to. The decay of an animal carcass hidden among the reeds fouled the air.

"I can't sleep through the night," he said. "My dreams wake me up. Sometimes I catch myself talking."

"You mean screaming?"

Petrah slowed for a beat, trying not to let Master Joriah see the embarrassment on his face. "I can't seem to turn off my voice, Master. I don't know how to stop it."

"What do you see when you dream?"

Petrah wished he could have summed it up with two words—*bad things*—and left it at that. But he knew Master Joriah wouldn't accept a dismissive response, so he chose his words carefully.

"I see this barren place. A city, I think. No trees, no grass, nothing living. Often, it's already burned to the ground, and the villagers are dead; sometimes they're alive. There are tall, strange buildings made of metal, abandoned and twisted and in ruin. The sky's always dark with thick clouds. I can't tell if it's morning or evening. It's so . . . empty. But then this man appears on horseback with other horsemen following his lead, dressed like him, with black clothing over armor, and they're all carrying swords or spears. We never speak. He's older than me, about your age, with dark brown hair." *And blue eyes*, Petrah thought, but didn't want to say. "I try to hide from him. Sometimes it works; other times I run and they give chase. The man in black always hunts me, but he doesn't catch me, just as I never quite escape. It's maddening."

"What do you think this man wants from you?"

"To kill me, I suppose." Petrah kept the part about his mother trying to hide him to himself.

"But he never finds you?"

"No, Master."

"Does he do anything else besides hunt you?"

Petrah lowered his voice. "He and the others chase any villagers still alive, even the children, and when they catch up to them, they slaughter them. Every one of them. They—" Petrah halted by a knot of trees where an inlet carved inward from the shoreline. The smell of the rotting carcass was gone. "It's too cruel to say."

"Is that when you wake up?"

"Sometimes. Other times, I peek from my hiding spot in my dream and continue to watch. The man and his soldiers build mountains with the bodies. Then he climbs atop and sits on a throne made of bones. It's as if he knows I'm watching. He tries to draw me out and make me run. But I hide and watch. He never leaves me alone. Never."

Master Joriah patted the bough of an old, gnarled tree that tangled with the others. Somewhere among the branches above, a bird chirped, oblivious to the men standing below.

"Dreams have many meanings, Petrah. They're powerful tools for the initiated to understand the mysteries of the cosmos. I cannot say for certain what your dreams mean or what is causing them, but there's an obvious connection between you and this man, maybe something from the past you've forgotten, perhaps something yet to happen or something you're creating to mask what's really bothering you. Or perhaps your mind has formed a schism with your spirit, and the only way to cope with the division is by manifesting these intense visions. To discover a remedy can take considerable time. Some suggest long periods of isolated meditation. Others recommend abandoning the pursuit of magehood altogether. I doubt you'd agree with the second option."

"No, Master. Maybe we could try the first one," Petrah said hopefully.

"Nonsense," Master Joriah said. "I'm a patient man, but not *that* patient. I suggest a shortcut. I'm going to introduce you to our city Seer, Baaka. His perception of the unknown far exceeds any of ours. He'll uncover this dilemma of yours. Then we'll treat it and squash it. After we're done, your peers will get the rest they need, and I won't have to deal with this anymore."

The last thing Petrah wanted was for someone else to interrogate him about his dreams. Master Maglo had discovered his secret as an escaped slave by probing his mind. What else might Baaka find buried deep inside him?

"Can't we just forget about this?"

Master Joriah cocked his head as if Petrah's response was absurd. "And why would we do that?"

Petrah didn't have an answer. He swallowed and responded with a question that would suit Master Joriah. "When do we meet with him?"

"He's invited me to his table on San-tel-moor next week. I'm taking you and Miko. It'll be good exposure for the two of you, an opportunity to see how things work inside the Temple."

Petrah made a face. Miko was his least favorite person.

Master Joriah smiled. "Still not friends?"

S AN-TEL-MOOR WASN'T JUST ANY holiday.

It was Terjurmeh's biggest holiday, ushering in the new year.

Celebrations were to take place over the course of three days and nights. Petrah thought the conflict with Meerjurmeh would put a damper on the festivities for Elmar, seeing the country was at war, but it did nothing of the kind.

Master Nole stood behind his lectern in the canteem, orating on the current state of affairs of the Empire of Korin, the sovereign nation directly south of the Gōsh Mountains. Korinians, Petrah learned, spoke their own tongue, as well as Jurmehan, and had scant dealings with Terjurmeh, trading mainly with Meerjurmeh. It had only been within the last few centuries that Korinians purged themselves of paganism, adopting Jahism as their primary religion, although it was rumored their shamans still held onto the past, practicing necromancy and praying to the old gods.

Master Nole and the other instructors rarely spoke of Korin, as if the empire didn't exist, even though it occupied the greatest stretch of territory in the known world. Petrah suspected it had to do with the fact the emperor acknowledged the papal supremacy of the Prime Manifest, the pontiff who ruled the Jahn Church from the capital of Meerjurmeh. In previous dynasties, emperors and empresses had been deified as gods among their people.

Petrah wondered what it was like to be an emperor in this day and age. Surely it was magnificent, even if the emperor didn't earn the veneration of his predecessors. Did Terjurmeh even recognize the sovereignty of Korin? Since Terjurmeh and Meerjurmeh were bitter enemies, Petrah doubted it. Still, Korin was one of the six domains of Acia, and to dismiss it entirely was a "bounty of foolishness," as Master Maglo liked to joke. Petrah promised himself to study up on Korin and the federated states below her, the Provinces of the South.

"I have an announcement to make," Master Nole said, hawkish nose raised high. "We are in San's grace, for we are to receive another six students and a new instructor next month. We're also breaking ground on a new journeyman school."

Petrah perked up, as did his classmates. This was big news.

"As you know, the Green Flame's success is predicated upon its ability to expand. We must create the next generation of magi if we are to dominate as a party. This is good news for you, for you are a part of this growth—which is why I expect you to endeavor to lead the new students by example. I don't care if you are wearing the White. You will show the new initiates what it means to be a mage apprentice of the Green Flame. I expect no less. Do you understand?"

"Yes, Master," the students replied.

Master Nole held their attention with his unreadable gaze, although Petrah swore there were the underpinnings of a smile in there somewhere. "Very well. Dismissed."

P ETRAH WAS MEDITATING WHEN a shout broke the evening's stillness. He opened his door and ran into the dorm hallway, nearly colliding with Nuk.

"What's going on?"

"I think someone's hurt," Nuk said.

"Who?"

Nuk shrugged, and they headed outside.

Petrah saw Taline and Miko running ahead of them, Miko with a torch. Petrah and Nuk followed them.

When the four arrived at a clearing, they all stopped.

Hamma lay face-up next to a row of bushes, motionless, his eyes open and mouth agape with a wispy trail of smoke rising from it. There was a repulsive odor about him, like burned hair, but worse. Ajoon sat beside him, a stunned expression on her tear-streaked face.

Petrah knelt by her and put a hand on her shoulder. "What happened?"

Ajoon stammered. "I—I don't know."

"Are you all right?"

Ajoon said nothing, which told Petrah she wasn't. He wanted to wrap an arm around her, but this wasn't the time or the place.

Petrah said to the others, "Is someone going to find the masters or not?"

"Taline, you're fast," Miko said. "Why don't you go?"

Taline took Miko's torch and ran off.

Hamma's eyes were open, gazing emptily at the sky.

Petrah shook his head. "How could this have happened to Hamma?" He turned to Ajoon, then the others, stopping at Miko, who watched calmly.

"Maybe he had an accident," Miko said, looking Petrah in the eye.

"What do you mean? Like what?"

Miko shrugged nonchalantly. "Like the unfortunate kind."

Taline returned with Masters Joriah and Maglo and two soldiers carrying torches.

The added light gave Hamma's grotesquely frozen expression a surreal waxiness, as if he were a chimera from one of those folktales that spoke of the dead among the living.

Master Maglo dropped to his knees, perspiring and breathing fast. He touched Hamma's forehead and closed his eyes. When he was done, streams of sweat dripped off his face.

"Well?" Master Joriah asked.

"His mind is gone," Master Maglo said. "Destroyed. I couldn't retrieve a single thought."

"How's that possible?"

"There are many ways. This was done purposefully, I'm sure of it."

Master Joriah glanced at his students, one at a time. "Who could do this?" He looked at Petrah with his scrutinizing gaze. "Well?"

Petrah opened his mouth but didn't know what to say.

Master Joriah saved him by turning to the soldiers and issuing an order. "Take the body to the kiosk. Alert the watch. There may be someone loose on the grounds. Be careful. This person knows the arcane arts. Maglo, go with them."

The men carried Hamma off.

Petrah tried not to look at the Green Robe's dangling arms, but he couldn't help himself. *Gods, I hope you met your end quickly.* He couldn't stand it if Hamma had suffered. The student leader was loved by all. *No, not by all,* he thought sadly.

"Now," Master Joriah said to his pupils, "you're all coming with me. It's time for answers."

"I DON'T CARE," JORIAH said, slamming his fist on the table in his study. Nole and Maglo were in a closed session with the mage. They'd just finished questioning the students. None had admitted to seeing or knowing anything, but Joriah and his instructors didn't need any admissions to know who was responsible for Hamma's death.

"You saw his eyes," Nole said.

"I did, and we all know he did it. But that doesn't change my position on the matter."

Nole grunted his displeasure. "Joriah, it's your decision, but this is the second time we've gone through this. How many more dead students is it going to take?"

"As many as it needs to. Are we not at war? Do we not need warriors?" Joriah's face was turning red.

"We do," Nole said. "And Hamma would have made a fine one."

Joriah leaned over the table. "We do not reward weakness, Nole. If Hamma couldn't defend himself against a known enemy, how could he defend himself against one he never met?"

Nole's face was also coloring. "Then you're going to let this slide? No punishment?"

Joriah very much wanted to punish Miko. He had felt his chest tighten the moment he saw Hamma's lifeless form. Hamma wasn't just another student; he was part of Maseah's family, handpicked by Joriah to be among his first apprentices. Hamma had been a selfless soul loyal to his school, his party, and his Temple. A young man who'd earned Joriah's trust. A young man Joriah believed in. And one he'd hoped would excel and become a bright star for the Green Flame. But now—

Now Hamma was dead, and Joriah was left with a difficult choice: destroy Miko or keep him.

It wouldn't be enough to lock him up or whip him.

The punishment would have to be severe. Something befitting the crime.

These men knew as well as Joriah did that Miko's talent was extraordinary. That expelling him or even taking his life would be wasteful. Miko had the makings of a great mage warrior. He had the potential to become a formidable adversary on and off the battlefield. Why eliminate that potential? Why ruin a second life?

Joriah doubled down on his stance. "No punishment."

Nole glared. "You're serious then. You're going to do nothing."

Joriah jabbed the tabletop with his fingers. "Were you not listening to me? What did I just say?"

There was a moment of silence before Maglo chimed in. "This Miko of yours is far too dangerous."

Joriah nodded vigorously. "Extremely dangerous."

Chapter 15

Revelations

PETRAH TOOK HAMMA'S DEATH hard, but so did Ajoon, Nuk, and Taline, who sat with sagging postures in the canteem the next morning.

"Is there no one here who can answer my question?" Master Nole asked his class.

The absence of their student leader was as vexing to them as their silence was to Master Nole. Petrah kept stealing glances at Hamma's vacant seat, thinking the Green Robe would appear any moment to fill it. Miko was more bored than perturbed, fidgeting endlessly with his quill. Of course, he would be the one to not care that Hamma was dead.

Master Nole huffed. "Anyone?"

After several more seconds of quiet, Master Nole smacked his wooden pointer against the top of his lectern, jarring the class out of their doldrums and into the present.

"Now," he said, controlling his tempest of disappointment with measured words, "I know yesterday's tragedy has caused a rift in your young minds. Master Joriah was unsettled by it as well, as were we all. Hamma portrayed many fine traits we expect in an apprentice. Traits I expect of *all* my students." He lifted his pointer. "Hamma might be gone, but your path to magehood remains in front of you. Pray for his soul, light a candle at Temple in his honor, mourn for him in the wee hours of the morning, but do not mope around in my class as if your lives are forfeit. They are not. You must accept what has happened and move on."

Petrah dared not look at the others. He could only imagine their reaction to Master Nole's stern and heartless pep talk.

Master Nole inspires no one but expects everything.

Master Nole set his pointer down and stepped to the front of the lectern. He smelled like an old man's shave balm.

"Given your distracted minds," he said, "I'm giving you the rest of the day to yourselves. You will have a reading assignment to keep you engaged. You will remain in your dorm rooms and study until suppertime. After supper, you will return to your rooms and finish your work. When you're done, you will pray to San and give your thanks that he has blessed you with your apprenticeship. Tomorrow, I will quiz you. I expect you well prepared, well rested, and needle sharp. Fail my quiz, and I will strip you of your robes. I will not tolerate weakness. Do you understand me?"

As one, the class answered *yes*.

Master Nole allowed a protracted period of silence to follow, giving Petrah and his classmates ample time to bathe under his scrutinizing gaze. "Good. Now here's your assignment."

A JOON AND PETRAH TOOK the long way back to their dormitory, opting for the path wending toward the South Kesel River.

It was still morning, although the sun had risen to near its zenith in the sky, baking the dirt trail they strode upon but also releasing the perfume of foliage from the brambles that hugged the bank.

Ajoon startled when a fish broke the water, sending up a splash. Petrah laughed, which got her going.

"Master Nole isn't the only one who can scare you," Petrah said, teasing her. He was glad to break the spell of their dismal mood.

"I saw you quaking in front of him," Ajoon said, jabbing his ribs with a finger. "You thought he was going to whap you with his stick."

"Was not. But at least I wasn't spying."

"I sit behind you, silly. How do you consider that spying? For the record, I was watching Miko too. He wasn't himself either."

The mention of Miko brought Petrah to a stop.

Ajoon tilted her head, examining him. Her round cheeks were a healthy, deep tan, her inquisitive eyes searching his. "Did I say something wrong?"

"Everyone knows he did it," Petrah said, "yet the masters did nothing. It's like they're protecting him."

"Even if he did it, there's no proof. None of us saw anything. No one did. The masters questioned us. Remember?"

"I'm telling you, the masters have to know it was him. Who else could it be?"

"Why don't you talk to Master Joriah about it?"

"Me? What would I tell him, that I have a hunch?"

"You could at least ask him why he's being so lenient."

"You know Master Joriah. You don't ask questions like that. Master Joriah will put you in your place faster than you can draw your next breath." Petrah shook his fists. "It's not right. Miko got away with murder."

"Hush!" Ajoon looked over her shoulder, but no one was in the vicinity. Birds warbled, flitting happily among the brambles.

"I don't care if he hears me. He wasn't exactly hiding when he told me my predecessor had met an unfortunate end. In fact, he mentioned it proudly, like it was a badge of honor."

"He told you about Deven?"

Was that the student's name? No one had shared any details about the boy Petrah had replaced. It was as if he'd never existed. Would Hamma be forgotten too? "Not really."

Ajoon fussed with the hem of her robe. "Deven was incredibly smart. He acted innocent in front of the masters, but he was cunning and had a spiteful heart. Miko was cunning as well and prideful, and the two became rivals. I don't know who was worse. Inevitably, something was bound to happen to one of them by the other's hand. They were competitive to a fault and hated each other."

"Sounds like Deven was the star pupil."

"He wasn't. Deven had an affinity for channeling, but he wasn't as good as Hamma, and he was jealous of how quickly Miko was progressing. Still, he was good enough. If Deven was with us today, he'd be well on his way to becoming a mage."

Petrah suspected the worst but had to ask anyway. "What happened to him?"

Ajoon picked a wilting flower from the bush beside her. She spun it between her fingertips and let it twirl to the ground. Then her hand began to shake.

"You don't have to tell me," Petrah said.

Ajoon hid her hands behind her back. "No, it's all right." She looked at him. "I want to tell you, so you know." She drew in a deep breath, then let it out. "They found him washed up on the riverbank, torched to a crisp."

"Torched? Gods!"

"And that's not all." Ajoon fanned herself as if the sun had chosen to scorch just her. "The lieutenant who was second in charge of our militia at Maseah was also found dead. Supposedly, he and Deven were friends. The masters tried to convince us Deven and the lieutenant got into an argument that escalated into an altercation, but we suspected Miko was involved. There were too many holes in the story, too much emphasis placed on the unfortunate nature of a friendship gone bad, but no explanation as to the circumstances regarding the horrible way they died."

"Did you ever find out what really happened?"

"No, and I doubt I will. Poor Hamma took the incident hard." Ajoon looked down at the ground. "We all did. We all saw the smug look on Miko's face. It's as if he wanted us to know he was responsible."

"What did the masters do about it?"

She looked up at Petrah, eyes glistening. "What did they do about Hamma?"

"Nothing."

"There you go."

Petrah couldn't fathom why Miko would be permitted to murder not one student, but two. It had taken a toll on Ajoon, and rightfully so.

Was that the reason Master Nole was so hard on everyone? Was he frustrated because his hands were tied on the matter? Or did he condone the act of violence, along with the other masters, as if culling the weak was not only tolerated but expected?

Hamma wasn't weak. He was in Miko's way. Which means I'm in his way too.

Ajoon wiped a tear from her face. "Sorry."

"Don't apologize. I feel it too. In fact, I couldn't sleep a wink last night. I kept thinking about Hamma and how good a person he was, even if he tried to emulate the masters with his seriousness."

Ajoon laughed. "He was a pretender, wasn't he?"

"The best I know." Petrah liked how easy it was to talk to Ajoon. He could speak his mind to her. Her two-toned eyes were always filled with optimism, even during sad times, like today. The more he spoke to her, the more time he wanted to spend with her. "I have an idea."

"What's that?"

"Let's ditch our dorm room and find a place to study for Master Nole's quiz together. Somewhere quiet and out of the way."

"Master Nole told us to stay in our dorm rooms."

"Then I guess that makes us rebels. What do you say? Shall we defy Master Nole's orders and take our chances out in the wilds of Maseah?"

Ajoon beamed. Her smile was contagious. "Rebels we are then."

MASTER JORIAH TOOK PETRAH and Miko to see Baaka, Seer of Elmar, on the first day of San-tel-moor.

The mage dropped to his knees in the Seer's chambers and touched his head once to the marble floor. The smoke of incense clung to the air.

"Holy One, we are honored to be in your presence."

"Your homage is well received," Baaka said. "Rise."

The Seer was a short, plump man, soft and round in the face, with supple skin and a cleanly shaven scalp. Petrah had never seen someone so immaculate. He made Uhtah-Pei look like a vagabond in comparison. Baaka wore unwrinkled robes spun in fine, red thread with gold stitching along the sleeves and slipper-like shoes that looked as if they'd never touched the ground outdoors.

Petrah and Miko stood behind their master, triangles of oily Sercula on their foreheads, chins tucked as Master Joriah had instructed.

Petrah couldn't understand why Master Joriah had to bring Miko. To see if he and Petrah could get along? To see how much it bothered Petrah to be in his company? To see if either would instigate trouble?

Miko hadn't spoken a word the entire trip, except to interact with Master Joriah, who informed Miko and Petrah how to conduct themselves before the Seer of Elmar. The friction between Petrah and Miko remained palpable. Petrah was constantly aware of Miko's presence. It was as if Miko was watching him, like a river beast watching its prey, waiting for the right moment to spring. Was this how Deven felt?

Master Joriah knows we can't stand each other, yet he puts us together.

Perhaps the mage wanted Miko under observation and away from the other students for a while.

Then I'm the lucky one who has to suffer his company.

The visitors were in the rotunda of the Dome of San, the grand temple on Elmar's summit, right next to the Capitol Building. Against the wall, in the corner, was a raised dais and a throne-like seat with cushions—the Seer's seat. Three hooded figures stood along the inside wall holding staves of metal, their shadows flickering against the stone surface from the lamplight, their bodies still as fixtures.

After exchanging small talk with Master Joriah, Baaka turned his attention to the students. "Who are these fine young men?"

"Two of my apprentices," Master Joriah said. "Miko and Petrah."

Baaka appeared on the verge of laughter. "Petrah? What a name!" He signaled to the apprentice. "Come here, boy. Let's have a look at you."

Petrah came forward and bowed his head. "Holy One," he said.

The Seer looked the youth over.

Petrah smelled a sweet, floral scent, like water poppies. He'd heard of wealthy women wearing such fragrances, but never men.

When Petrah made eye contact with the Seer, it was as if a cold air battered him. The last time he'd experienced such a sensation was in the presence of Septamo, the First Articulate.

Baaka hovered an index finger just above Petrah's right eyebrow. "Hmm, this is curious. You are marked here. It looks like a scar, but it's not. It's a birthmark." He withdrew his finger. "People think birthmarks are mistakes. They're anything but. Each one is an act of celestial creation. Yours is an interesting one. There's a lot of history there. You may return to your master's side."

Petrah barely remembered having the semicircular mark. He always assumed it was a scar from a childhood accident, from when he was with his mother. He thought of her now, crying in his dreams. *Always* crying.

Baaka ran a hand down his robe, smoothing out a crease. "Miko, come forward."

As with Petrah, the Seer examined Miko meticulously. He closed his eyes, and his eyelids fluttered for a moment before he looked at Miko again.

"Interesting," he said. "You've got a lot of potential, young man. I sense great promise. But you're a little too thirsty, if you know what I mean. Slow down. Savor the journey to magehood. Holy warriors must show restraint. You may seek a path to a greater want, but you need to listen to your masters. They will guide you. Do you understand?"

"Yes, Holy One," Miko said.

"Good. I'm glad we had this opportunity. But"—he glanced at Master Joriah—"I sense there is more to our rendezvous than a chance meeting. You may go."

Miko returned to his place beside Petrah.

"So," Baaka said to Master Joriah, "why don't you let your pupils prepare to sup while you and I talk? I'm sure they would appreciate a tour of the temple before joining us in the hall. I'll have one of my clerics escort them . . . if that is all right with you."

"Of course, Holy One," Master Joriah said.

Baaka snapped his fingers, and a hooded cleric approached. "Take the boys to the washroom so they may cleanse their hands and feet. Then show them the grounds."

The robed man gestured to the exit, and Petrah and Miko followed.

W HEN THEY WERE GONE, Baaka ordered the remaining clerics to leave and seal the chamber.

Baaka led Joriah to an open window and leaned against the stone sill. The late-afternoon light draped his shadow far across the polished floor behind him.

"Times are changing," Baaka said. "The people grow restless. You should have seen them today: anxious, as if they hadn't slept for days. They don't understand why they feel this way. They don't understand why their anticipation of something inexplicable eats away at them. They sense something only a soul could sense." Baaka turned to the mage. "Do you know what it is?"

Joriah shook his head.

"It's all in the Scriptures. Come, let us have a drink and speak of these things."

Joriah followed the Seer to a wall with an inset of shelves. Baaka grabbed a crystal decanter from one of them and poured two drinks. Ruby-colored liquid flowed from the vessel.

"This is ju-ju." He handed Joriah a glass.

The mage took a sniff and nodded appreciatively. It smelled like cherries and cardamom. "Expensive stuff, I hear."

"Very. The liqueur comes from Vergahl. I should imagine the price will only go up after our troops withdraw from the city, assuming they don't do something foolish and burn the ju-man groves to the ground."

"I guess I'd better not enjoy this too much then. It might be the last time I have it."

"Indeed." The Seer brought his glass up in a toast. "Let us drink, old friend. To the future."

"To the future," Joriah said, tapping glasses and then taking a sip. Tart cherries and spice flowed over his tongue, with a hint of heat.

Baaka escorted the mage to a floor area covered with damask-patterned pillows. Joriah sat facing him on the other side of a knee-high table.

"Your students intrigue me," Baaka said, getting comfortable. "One is a mover, the other a thinker. Both have great potential. You've chosen well, despite the fact one isn't even a Terjurmehan citizen."

"Petrah's different, I agree," Joriah said. "But his mind is sharp, and his spirit is well suited for the craft. I brought him to meet you because he's having nightmares that are keeping his fellow students awake. It's interfering with their schoolwork and their concentration and has become a hindrance."

Baaka propped a pillow behind his back. "Have you tried divine norming?"

"No, it's too time-consuming. I'm looking for an accelerated solution. I figured since the boy is here . . ."

"You thought a Seer might spare a moment from his busy schedule to investigate such a trivial matter." Baaka's lips curled into a smile.

"I was hoping such a thing wouldn't impede on His Holiness's holiday schedule."

"You know me, Joriah. *Every* day is a holiday. The interesting thing is that I see you more than many of my clergy. How does that happen?"

"Our leader has a penchant for sending me on errands, it seems," Joriah said. Then, before the Seer could retort, he added, "So, you were saying something about Scriptures . . . ?"

Baaka's eyes lit up with childlike enthusiasm. "Ah, yes—Scriptures: tricky passages of gospel, penned by men whose quills were supposedly held in place by San's divine messengers. Do your students study them?"

"On San's Day and in their spare time. It gives them a good spiritual foundation, but unfortunately, their studies come first."

"Of course. You're not raising priests, are you?"

"Not until His Holiness changes our charter."

The Seer ran his hand back along the smooth baldness of his scalp. "Let me ask you something. What do you know of the *Book of Prophecy*?"

Joriah swirled the contents of his glass. "Only that it's the last book in our canon. I read it a long time ago."

"What do you remember?"

"Something about the children of San rising up at the appointed hour and swallowing our enemies like the dark swallows the light. It's an end-times prophecy."

"So you were paying attention in Temple, weren't you?"

"That, and my father made me read a lot," Joriah said, chuckling. "I've probably read the *Book of Prophecy* half a dozen times, although it was difficult. Complicated verses."

"The book was written that way on purpose," Baaka said. "Read between the eloquent text and you discover a karmic roadmap littered with signs. The question is, how do we decipher them among the long and often obscure passages?"

"Carefully, I would imagine."

"Very carefully. It takes a sharp eye and a scholarly mind to spot them. You have to consider, in every story, there's some amount of truth. In the holy writings, you can find bits of it here and there, if you disregard the literal translation of the words."

"What truth have you discovered?" Joriah asked.

"I've discovered that we're about to reach the end of our karmic road. It's a breath away, a few years at the most."

"A few years? Where did you read that? I don't recall seeing any timeline in the Scriptures."

Baaka swallowed the last of his ju-ju and placed the empty glass on the table. "Need it be spelled out for you? Events mark history. Cluster them together and reach a certain point, and there you have it: a timeline. There are specific events that have transpired in our lifetime that point to the Great Reckoning. I've seen them, and I'm not alone. The oracles have seen them too, just as the prophet Mahshat revealed in the *Book of Prophecy*."

Joriah gave it some thought. "Are you saying that we may see the end in our lifetime?"

"No," Baaka said, waving a finger, "not *may see*—but *will see*."

"How can you be sure?"

"The prophet wrote, 'And the Father shall beget a child, and his name shall be San-Jahad, for he is the Great One and the Great Son; and he shall rise up and rouse the masses and deliver his people from light into shadow and destroy those who would destroy him.'

"San-Jahad is alive. I've witnessed his birth in a vision. That's why I'm sure."

Joriah felt gooseflesh on his arms. "Alive where?"

"No place you could visit, even if you rode a bolt of lightning to it."

"That's impossible. No place is that far away, except the heavens."

"Not in the firmament," Baaka said. "Look to the sky and what do you see? You see a great gulf separating one heavenly body from another. But there is one point of light beyond the normal field of vision that is a world just like ours, a world of men. It's where the sacred son was born, about thirty-five years ago."

The mage's skin tingled all the way up his neck. "Then why hasn't the Temple shared this news? Don't the people deserve to know?"

"They will learn of many things soon enough," Baaka said. "For now, we keep it secret. That includes you. Only a select few know the truth."

"Then why did you tell me? I'm not a priest."

"I would have thought it obvious from our conversation."

Joriah wanted to say something, but his vocal cords failed to muster the syllables.

"Have you no recollection of the Great One from your readings? Was his countenance not among the words?"

Joriah thought about it. "The priests say the Great One would have a face so remarkable, even the angels would pause to take notice. As for what I've read, I don't remember much; maybe something about him having dark hair."

"And his eyes? What of them?"

Joriah nodded excitedly. "*Eyes of sky*: blue eyes. Just like Petrah's. I thought my apprentice's eye color an aberration, a mistake of nature perhaps."

Baaka leaned in with a smile. "Not a mistake; not if you're from where the Great One hails."

"But how could he have gotten here?"

"How, indeed! I doubt he arrived in any fashion we could fathom."

"Then perhaps he was born here, after all."

"Not born, but *reborn*," Baaka said, tapping the table. "There is something more to his being here than any of us realize. It was predestined, which is why I'm sharing this information with you against perhaps the better judgment of my fellow priests."

"So now what?"

The Seer poured them more of the precious liqueur. He held up his glass in a toast. "Now we have another drink. But tonight, when the boy comes to me, I will find the missing piece of the puzzle."

P ETRAH ENTERED THE SEER'S chamber with the same trepidation as his encounter with Septamo. It was the way Baaka had looked at him earlier, as if peeling away his skin and sucking out his soul.

Baaka was by himself, perched on a pile of cushions in the center of the room. Deep shadows made the lines on his face appear like trenches. "Sit over here with me."

Petrah took a seat across from him. It was too quiet, too intimate with just the two of them. Incense burned from a brazier, filling the chamber with toasted wood and warmed honey. Petrah wished Master Joriah had never insisted he come here.

"So," Baaka said appraisingly, "what do you think of our temple?"

"Very impressive, Holy One." Petrah wanted to keep his answers short and sweet.

"I would offer you some tea as a refreshment, but I'm afraid one of my servants mistakenly assumed I would be downstairs with the others and had prepared the tea service there." Baaka pointed at a table with a decanter of dark liquid. "Perhaps a drink more substantial then?"

"No, thank you."

"Your master tells me you're getting six more apprentices and that you're building a journeyman school on premises. Exciting times for your party. But with six new initiates, that would leave you at eleven, wouldn't it? Not a very fortunate number."

"Master Joriah told us six new students, but that was before we lost our lead apprentice."

"Yes, I heard. Tragic news. Who gets to replace him? You?"

Petrah made a face. "Me?"

"Someone needs to be the leader, no? Why not you?"

"I don't know, Holy One. I'm the newest apprentice. I'm sure Master Joriah would want someone who's been there longer. Hamma was the most senior of all of us."

"'Humility is best left to bake in the sun.' Then, they say, it would crack and turn into something more desirable. It's a proverb worth heeding." Baaka fixed him with a severe look. "A mage commands respect, not because the ordinary citizen admires him, but because the ordinary citizen fears him. Your student leader's death, while unfortunate, was necessary so that someone stronger could take his place. Are you that man?"

Petrah hadn't considered himself a candidate for the Green Robe. He assumed Miko or Taline ripe for the position. Ajoon had told him flat out she had no interest in such lofty positions, but she was every bit as qualified as them.

"I think I could do it," Petrah said.

Baaka scowled. "You *think*? Pah! You speak like an infant. If you were one of my clerics, I'd label you a man without faith. How can you convince your masters of your abilities if you can't convince yourself? It's said that a man who doesn't believe in himself or his cause is a dangerous man. Have you heard that before?"

Petrah knew his face had colored, but as to how red, he could only speculate. "No, Holy One."

"Can you guess what it means?"

"To me, it means a person who doesn't believe in anything is a liability, especially if others depend on him. He might fail at the wrong moment, endangering everyone. And because he's a disbeliever, there's nothing within him he can draw upon to get him out of the situation."

The Seer seemed amused, if not impressed, with the response. "You're not the man you were a moment ago. That was spoken with wisdom and conviction. If this is the way your mind works, then I retract my doubts."

Baaka got up and poured himself a drink. He raised his glass to the lamplight and examined the ruby-colored liquid before venturing a sip.

"This glass was made in the Andora province, just south of Korin. It's a gift from a family I've never met. It's traveled hundreds of miles north so it could find itself in my grasp. As you can see by the way my thumb fits in this divot here and the tip of my forefinger in this divot there, the glass remains perfectly in my grip, although the maker didn't know what size hand a Ter-jurahn such as I would have, or the purchaser what size glass to order from the maker. The question I pose is this: was it simple coincidence or fate? What do you think?"

Petrah didn't believe in fate. Nor could he get past the idea that the Seer's fingers fit because of the way he was holding the glass, an illusion made to illustrate a point.

"I would say I wouldn't be able to tell either way, Holy One. If it's luck, it makes sense. If it's meant to be, that also makes sense. Either way, in the end, you're a fortunate man."

Baaka toasted. "Ah, the politician emerges! You've been to the Great Council, haven't you?"

"Yes, Holy One. But"—Petrah frowned—"how did you know?"

"A certain someone told me. That same someone told me something else: that one of his top students has been causing a lot of trouble at night. Waking people up, it seems. Any idea who that might be?"

Petrah swallowed. "I—" His cheeks flushed.

"You needn't explain. Many priests go through the same thing during the time they're acolytes. I've heard some have dreams so violent, they set fire to their own beds. We call them *surati*, 'dreams of a higher power.' They occur when the soul outpaces the mind in its attempt to extend from the body into the spirit world. The physical self tries to compensate, and you get anything from nightmares to convulsions to even death."

Petrah had no idea his condition was so volatile. No wonder Master Joriah wanted to bring him here.

"Don't think of death as a bad thing. After all, you're trying to reach into the afterlife and draw back its ethereal power. If you reach too far, you end up permanently dead. Then what do you do?" The Seer chuckled, then continued, "The challenge you face is harmonizing the mind and spirit. One must modulate the other. If the stresses become too great, something breaks. You don't want that to happen, do you?"

Petrah began to really worry. How could his dreams cause such problems? "No, Holy One."

Baaka barely let the rim of his glass graze his lips. He drew in the alcoholic vapors with a connoisseur's grace. "Your master asked if I could look into the matter. I must confess, the request seemed odd at first. Surati are not at all that unusual, but your dreams do carry an interesting—how should I say—doomsday undertone, which I find most fascinating. Call me an aficionado of prophetic revelations. We know the future will arrive someday."

The Seer went to take a sip, then stopped and pointed the glass at Petrah. "Joriah says you keep seeing the same man when you dream, a warrior dressed in black. Is that right?"

"Yes, Holy One." Petrah saw the shadowed face and black armor. He felt the malice and hate. *He haunts me in my sleep and in my waking thoughts as well. I've no peace, not ever.*

Baaka sat for a while, contemplative while he studied Petrah. "Have your instructors spoken to you of the Trillian of Darkness?"

"Not yet, Holy One."

"I suspected they haven't. It's a set of tenets taught to clerics before they claim the Red and become priests. A cleric is sequestered to a sepulcher underground for three days and shut out from the light. Then an elder priest reveals the Trillian to the cleric in total darkness. Only in the dark may we see. Remember that." Baaka flapped the hem of his robe around his feet and shifted forward as if to conspire.

"There are three pillars of the Trillian: the dark that binds, the dark that usurps, and the dark that rules. Each one is a metamorphosis, like the way the black-horned moth goes from larva to pupa to moth. The moth, as you might imagine, is most vulnerable as a larva, falling prey to birds and other predators. At that stage, it serves the purpose of being consumed. It is weak, learning its way of the world. It must hide, blend in, and use every bit of instinct to survive its environs. Much like you students." Baaka laughed with his mouth closed, and Petrah smiled in an appeasing fashion.

"As a pupa, it is in the most dangerous phase, for it is neither child nor adult. It too can fall victim to a host of predators. In fact, it is most sought after in this phase, for the delicate meat is sweet and not yet poisonous. In its metamorphosis, it's stranded—between and betwixt, as they say. There's no going back and there's no way forward yet. It is digesting its own body to become what it was destined to become. When it emerges from its cocoon, may there be pity upon any who dare touch it. For it has become the killer, the deadliest and most venomous living creature in the four corners, and although it is small, it is mighty, able to take down any predator who brushes the poison-laced hairs on its body."

Baaka licked his lips as if he craved the carnage wrought by the tiny insect. "The path to apotheosis is also bound by rules. As a novice of the arts, you're vulnerable. To survive, you must bind with the dark, embrace it, and cloak yourself with it. You must glean the secrets of angels, borrow the stealth of demons, and tap into the unfathomable well of providence from the Father. Even so, it isn't enough." Baaka's tone became more urgent, as if he were racing against time to reveal the deepest of secrets. "You must usurp the dark, take of it, rape, ruin, pillage, and mutilate it to wear away at the mask blinding you, and don it as your mantle. Even then, you must dig deeper, to depths unimaginable. You must become your most vulnerable self to become your most capable self, and in doing so, consume your own flesh to shed your mortal cage and find the providence you so desperately seek. When you come out of it, when you slough off the chains of physical being, your physical self will be ruined and unrecognizable. But not your spirit. Not that most sacred vessel."

Baaka's eyes glittered predatorily. "And when you emerge—and you must!—you will rule the dark. You will know its infinite depths. You will know its limitless potential. Your enemies will fear you. They will shrink away, hide, and pray for protection. For you will be mighty and powerful, like a god. Only then will you be considered a master. Only then will you become one with the Father and one with the dark. Remember that."

Petrah soaked in the sage lecture, heeding the words, but fearing them. He had his hands full surviving his schooling. To "bind," "usurp," and "rule" were foreign concepts, but there was great weight in the Seer's lesson, heavy as a range of mountains.

"Now," Baaka said, switching back to the subject of Petrah's troubles, "let us find out who this stranger is, shall we?" Whatever hunger there was in the Seer's eyes was dulled again. Still, something was disturbing in the way he looked at Petrah—or more appropriately, through him. "Have you heard of the channeling technique, insurata? Some call it a mind join."

Master Maglo had used it to search Petrah's memories. With reluctance, Petrah said, "I do."

"If I'm to help you, I need to see what you see, and the only way to do that is to get inside your head. Will you let me in?"

Memories of brain-numbing vibrations left Petrah less than eager to say *yes*, but he did so anyway as he did with Master Maglo. Even if he wanted to protect the past, how could he refuse a man of Baaka's station?

"Good, now hold still," the Seer told him. "You might feel something . . ."

With a violent jolt, the process began. Petrah gripped the cushion beneath him and held on while his head endured waves of intense pressure. It was far worse than anything Master Maglo had done to him. Images blasted past at a dizzying pace.

When it was over, Petrah fell backward onto fabric.

He quivered, almost to the point of seizure. It took him a concerted effort not to fall sideways and convulse.

Seconds passed, and his muscles finally relaxed.

Across from him, the Seer sat quietly, mouth open, eyes glossy, expression teetering on gleeful. The combination was utterly grotesque.

Then his eyes moved.

He locked onto the apprentice; his rabid look unchanged. "You made a mistake," he said in a chilling voice. "The man in your dreams isn't some stranger."

Petrah's skin crawled. "Then who is he?"

Baaka's eyes turned savage. "Don't you recognize your own family?"

Chapter 16

The Offer

H E HAD A BROTHER. It was the first clue to an unknown past.

For months, he'd struggled to understand it, to splice the shreds of visual clues provided by his dreams. But the pieces told him nothing, and their montage far less. Baaka refused to say anything else regarding the discovery, dismissing Petrah before he could ask a single question. But he gave Master Joriah a parting suggestion to help Petrah curtail his outbursts while asleep.

"It's a meditative mantra called Copper Still," Master Joriah said. "Have you heard of it?"

"Is it different than Silkworm?"

"Silkworm soothes the mind, but Copper Still runs much deeper. We use it as one method within divine norming to balance the mind and soul. It won't get rid of the dreams. It might do nothing at all. But it should quiet your thoughts before you go to sleep. Perhaps that will be enough to get you through the night without waking everyone up. I'll have Master Maglo teach you the technique."

P ETRAH MET WITH MASTER Maglo the next morning in his underground office.

"Copper Still is not just another mantra," the mage began. "It produces a calm, almost tranquilizing effect the practitioner must be aware of. It won't harm you outright, but it might subdue you. And if you're overly eager, you might render yourself unconscious. Not a smart thing to do if you're, say, sitting too close to the river's edge." Petrah didn't like the sound of that. "To master it, you must achieve the right balance of too little and too much. How will you know? That's where practice comes in. Listen to my voice."

Master Maglo produced a sound that was deep but also hollow.

"It's a single bass note that produces resonance," Master Maglo explained. "We use the same frequency as the sleeping mind when it enters the dream state. Try it with me."

Petrah intoned the note until it matched the low sound Master Maglo made. As they chanted in sync, an odd thing happened. The glass lamp on the mage's desk seemed to hum, building and tapering, then building again, as if the mage were running a baton in a circle on the inside of a brass bowl.

"Now close your eyes and keep going," Master Maglo said.

Petrah did. The ting no longer came from the lamp but everywhere around him. A pleasing ringing filled his head. It cleansed the thoughts from his mind until only the sound remained.

Master Maglo snapped his fingers, and Petrah startled. "You fell asleep," the mage said.

"Sorry. I felt so . . ."

"Calm?"

"Yes."

"It tends to do that," the mage said. "Remember what I said about balance. Master Joriah wants you to practice every night. Keep doing it.

Then, as you did with Silkworm, I want you to internalize the mantra and perform it without making any sound in your throat."

Petrah practiced the mantra daily. While Copper Still relaxed him just before sleep, it didn't stop the nightmares, nor the screams. A week after he started, Nuk and Taline complained to Master Nole that Petrah was waking them up, and again Petrah found himself before Master Joriah. Petrah explained the man in black was still after him in his dreams.

"His Holiness said he's my brother. But I have no memory of a brother."

"As I speculated when we first spoke about this matter," Master Joriah said, "the connection between you and this man might be from your past, a hidden memory you can't recall, and one that is causing great strife. You need to move on from it. Meditate on putting it behind you and use what Master Maglo has taught you. If you can't remember your past, then bury it."

"But it doesn't make sense," Petrah protested. "How can I remember something that never happened?"

How can I just bury it?

"I don't have the answers, Petrah. You must make a concerted effort to still your raging mind. For the sake of yourself," Master Joriah said. "And your classmates."

Petrah continued his practice of Copper Still each night before bed. In time, the screaming outbursts became less frequent until they disappeared altogether. But the nightmares . . .

The nightmares remained.

W INTER AND SPRING PASSED, and once again, the unbearable
heat of summer returned.

Petrah turned sixteen on the day of the summer solstice.

He thought of his mother that morning. He couldn't help but believe
she was still alive. If he was a Northerner, then she was too. Perhaps she
had returned to Prall.

Other questions surfaced.

Was she thinking of him? Did she miss him? Did she cry at night,
wondering where he was?

I'll find you, Mama. Someday soon, I promise.

That San's Day, while attending service, Petrah lit a candle for her. He
had no notion of who his father was or what might have happened to
him or if he had any other brothers or sisters.

All he had were questions, no answers.

The war with Meerjurmeh concluded in a treaty between countries,
with the agreement that Meerjurmeh would relinquish all lumber trading rights with the Northern Kingdom to Terjurmeh.

Increased tension among parties took the forefront in the political
arena, causing a further divide between the Green Flame and its chief
competitors—the Fist, Silver Blade, and Black Arrow. The Fist was trying to expel the Green Flame from the Magi Guild, but Master Nole
assured the students no such thing could happen unless it was put forth
at the next Great Council. Even then, he said, he doubted the opposition
could swing enough votes, considering how influential the Green Flame
was among magi.

Whether Master Nole said that just to ease the concerns among the
students, Petrah couldn't tell. From Petrah's perspective, what happened
away from school seemed to have little impact on him and his classmates.
Maseah remained sheltered from the rest of Terjurmeh.

But within, Maseah was changing.

Master Joriah added seven new students to the school, bringing the total number of apprentices to twelve, twice the original number. With the increase came the decision to name a replacement for Hamma as the student leader.

"Miko is your new Green Robe," Master Joriah announced to his students. "You will follow his direction in the absence of your masters."

It was bad news. No, Petrah realized. It was the worst news.

Miko was a tyrant and a sadist. With his newfound position, he caused Petrah grief at every turn, making Petrah take up the rear of each march and perform menial tasks normally reserved for slaves.

That was on top of the public humiliation whenever Petrah made the slightest mistake.

Ajoon and Nuk often had to force Petrah to stand down when it looked like things would boil over.

Petrah's only salvation was his new friend, Taka, a young garrison soldier about his age. They partook in mock swordplay or explored areas where the apprentices weren't supposed to go. It was temporary relief for Petrah, but it did little to stem the pressure building within.

"Don't let him get the better of you," Taka said. "If you let him get under your skin, he wins."

"That's the thing," Petrah said. "He's already under my skin."

"Then you're letting him win. I don't pretend to understand the road to magehood, only that it's long and requires patience. We warriors have our own creed: 'Patience first, action second.' Only a fool engages his enemy with a headstrong attitude. Don't be a fool."

P ETRAH BUSIED HIMSELF BY studying in the library. The smell of old bindings and parchment filled the space, bringing with it an escape from the noise of the classroom, the pressure of fitting in among his classmates, and the stress of dealing with Miko. This was his island of tranquility, his place of happiness.

Ajoon made him happy too—with her company, optimism, and love for books. They endeavored to explore the history of Terjurmeh together. The busywork helped Petrah keep his mind on his craft rather than ancillary worries, like what additional torment Miko had in store for him.

Still, he was a bundle of nervous energy, not unnoticed by Ajoon.

"You need an outlet," she told him one boiling afternoon while they were studying. "You're too jittery."

"I have plenty of outlets," Petrah said. Ajoon looked down at Petrah's foot, which he bobbed relentlessly. He stopped. "Tell me then, what do you suggest?"

"Something creative."

"Like . . . ?"

"My father often suggested that I should take up poetry. That it was a civilized means of expression and one well suited for his daughter. After all, he was a scribe, so words were his business. Of course, he assumed the talent would transfer from father to daughter. Me, though . . ."

"Right, not the poetry type."

"You should try it," Ajoon said. "You're more eloquent with crafting things than I am."

"Channeling isn't the same as crafting poems."

Ajoon shrugged. "It was just a suggestion."

Petrah thought the idea silly, but then he gave it a go.

His first poem was utter rubbish.

Then he put a tune to the words and found cohesion to the blather, although it was far from polished.

Dawn, so painfully bright
Oh, what a treacherous night
Ale and mead and something red
Drowning in my aching head
Oh, how I wish to never drink again
That fiend, they say, will be my end
But no, my friend, not today
So be a sport and pour away!

It was a ridiculous rhyme, but it made him laugh, and the levity eased up some of the tension clawing at his throat.

Ajoon considered it crass but fun and suited for a tavern. "Not bad for your first attempt. What you need, though, is an inspiration. A muse, as they say."

"What, like the South Kesel River wending its way at night, with the marsh grass swaying?"

Ajoon frowned. "How's that inspiring? No, I'm talking about someone of the opposite sex."

"A girl then."

"Not just any girl, but a pretty one who catches the eye—and the imagination."

"Now you're talking like my friend Taka."

"I'm serious. You need someone to inspire great words. A young lady of substance, not a bar wench, mind you."

"Like who? I'm surrounded by adolescent boys and curmudgeonly old men. We're not permitted to go into the city, except on official business. It's not like I want to find a barmaid, anyway."

Ajoon's eyes brightened. "How about Taline?"

"What about Taline?"

"She's tall and athletic and . . . well, she's a girl."

Petrah had never considered Taline to be more than just a classmate. Her nervous energy suffocated him whenever they spoke. "That's not a very convincing argument. Have you heard her talk? She's like a windstorm."

"I agree she's a bit of a fast talker, but that just means she's a quick thinker . . . and smart. Smart is good, no?"

Taline was smart, but nothing compared to Ajoon. Ajoon had a way of taking her time when she spoke. Her words carried meaning and weight, and her cadence was effortless like her smile. And when she paused between words, Petrah held his breath just to see her lips shape the next syllable. "We hardly speak to each other," Petrah said. "She and Nuk are thick as thieves, though. Maybe she likes him."

"She doesn't."

"How do you know?"

"Because I know."

Petrah looked at Ajoon. Her eyes were perfectly mismatched, brown and hazel. He didn't even know what Taline's eyes looked like. They could have been gray, or purple, for that matter.

"I still think you should consider Taline," Ajoon said. "She's close to your height and slender too. I'm sure you like that."

Ajoon still didn't get it. Petrah didn't want Taline. She might be a good match for someone else, just not him. "Not at all. She has no hips. She's built like a boy and talks nasally. For what it's worth, I don't like tall girls. I prefer short ones." Ajoon was short, and she had hips.

"Like how short?" Ajoon asked, a smile creeping onto her face.

Petrah felt heat take hold of his cheeks. Ajoon had shifted closer to him as they spoke, now mere inches from him, her hair the scent of desert wildflowers.

He smiled back. "Short enough."

T O AID WITH THE now twelve students at Maseah, Master Joriah brought on a new instructor, Master Ecclesias. After a brief introduction from Master Joriah in the canteem, Master Ecclesias instructed the class on the importance of history and how it served as a teaching tool.

"The past informs us of the future," he told his students. "To forget the great deeds—and mistakes—of those who came before us is a travesty. How else can we learn what worked and what didn't? How else can we take the necessary steps to assure ourselves, our culture, and our nation of a better life? Now open your texts to page seventy-nine and heed well the second passage I'm about to recite."

Master Ecclesias was a long-bodied individual with a matching long face and a widow's peak that complemented the sharp corners of his eyes. Petrah thought him brilliant but not very personable. The new instructor had been a mage for the Green Flame for five years, working mostly with the Magi Guild and as a liaison to the ruling party, the Fist. Before that, he'd done a stint as an instructor at a journeyman school in Fangmordah. With Maseah's growing needs, Master Joriah had convinced Master Ecclesias to return to academia. Petrah hoped to learn a great many things from the mage.

Before their lunch break, Master Ecclesias gave them a research assignment.

"I'm challenging you to report on a channeler of great merit," he said. "This is a thinking exercise. I don't want you to just read about the past. I want you to experience it. For that, you must delve deep. You must read between the words to find the true meaning of each passage. Don't just tell me what this person did. Tell me why they inspire you. Tell me how they would make a difference in today's world as seen through your eyes.

And to make this project interesting, you're going to pair up. Choose a study partner. Work together. Decide together. You will submit your report as a team, and I will grade you as a team. You have one week to complete this assignment, so make it count."

While the other students groaned as if Master Ecclesias had given them the most difficult assignment in the world, Petrah and Ajoon exchanged smiles. This was exactly the type of project they would both enjoy.

Petrah and Ajoon set off to the library that afternoon. A couple of students joined them for a short while, then left. Alone among the stacks, they searched through the texts in the History section. Petrah looked for *Magus Corpus*, the book on famous magi, but it was nowhere to be found. Had someone borrowed it? Or put it back in the wrong section?

"I can't find it either," Ajoon said.

An enormous, dusty tome caught Petrah's eye, tucked away on the bottom shelf. Its blood-red, leather spine peeked out from an intricate, brass casing and was as wide as his hand. "How about this one? *Legends of the Black*. As in Black Robes. Looks interesting, doesn't it?"

Ajoon tilted her head to get a better look. "Sure, why not."

Petrah set the heavy text atop a table in the center of the library. The thick, brass cover was as formidable as armor plating, embossed with glyphs like those on Master Maglo's office door. Inside, colorful artwork of historical figures accompanied long passages, all done by hand. Several illustrations showed individuals dressed in mage robes, confirming in Petrah's mind they had found the right book.

"I'll make you a deal," Ajoon said. "I'll turn the pages and you take notes. That way, you can practice your penmanship."

Petrah smirked. "I'll make you a better deal. I'll take notes *and* write the report for us."

Ajoon grinned at that. "Deal."

She flipped through the tome while Petrah sat beside her with a sheet of parchment and quill at the ready. Petrah had grown to enjoy Ajoon's enthusiasm with research. More so, he liked her company. He wanted to tell her how much he looked forward to seeing her each day, that she made his life at school better, and that he had affections for her.

He didn't have the gumption, nor the experience.

Just tell her how you feel.

If it were only that easy.

"Wait," Petrah said, spotting a colored illustration on one of the worn pages. The image depicted a man dressed like a mage, except he had black body armor peeking out from under his robes. Across the front of his chest was a symbol that looked like a fiery serpent. "Who's that?"

Ajoon scrunched her forehead as she peered at the image. "The caption refers to him as San-Jahad. Hey, that's the Great One!"

"I thought the Temple forbid anyone from creating his likeness."

"You're right. No icons. No idolization. It's sacrilegious. I wonder how the artist got away with doing this." Ajoon blew on the binding, kicking up a small cloud of dust. "Old, I guess."

Petrah tapped the symbol on the figure's chest. "I've seen this before. I think it's called the Dragon."

"Or the Beast, depending on who you're talking to. Remember those paintings Master Nole showed us when we spent the week studying the Great War? The An-jurahn warriors had the symbol painted on their armor. They did it to scare off their enemies. Some good that did. They ended up losing the war." Ajoon reached for the corner of the page. "Can I turn it now?"

"No, give me a moment."

Ajoon sniffed her annoyance, but Petrah didn't care.

He studied the likeness of the Great One. Whoever the artist was, he was meticulous in his creation. The detail was remarkable, down to the serious expression on the man's face. That was when Petrah noticed the eyes.

He grabbed the lantern on the table and brought it close. "What color are his eyes?"

"It's hard to tell in this light, but they sort of look blue, like yours."

A rush of excitement coursed through Petrah. "Quick! Where's a copy of the Scriptures in here?"

"Which book are you looking for?"

"Something that mentions the Great One. What's that thing the priests are always preaching about, the Holy Transfiguration?"

Ajoon walked over to a bookshelf. Large tomes stood with their dusty spines out, packed together. She pulled out a book with gold lettering and a dark red binding and brought it back to the table. She placed it atop the open tome and swiveled it so Petrah could see the title. "Look in here."

Petrah squinted. *"Book of Prophecy?"*

"Yep. Last book in the Scriptures. The Holy Transfiguration talks about the transformation of the Father into the Son. If it's anywhere, it's going to be in the book that talks about end-of-days kind of stuff."

Petrah carefully pulled back the cover and started flipping. Ajoon came around and peered over his shoulder.

"Wait," she said to Petrah. "Turn back. There. Verses one through six. Read them."

Petrah had come a long way in his command of the written language, able to read Jurmehan as well as any of his classmates. "'. . . of a virgin woman this son was born. And it was said that he would have hair of black, face of a god, and eyes of sky, and in it all would see the Truth of the Father. And so he shall be named Great One and inherit the world.'" Petrah looked up from the book. "'Eyes of sky,' Ajoon. Remember hearing that in Temple?"

"Sort of," Ajoon said. "This is strange. It's about the future, but it's written in the past tense. Look at the way—"

"Stop! Listen to the words: 'eyes of sky.' What color is the sky?"

"Blue!" Then, Ajoon asked, "So, what does that have to do with anything? Are you saying you're the Great One or something?"

"No, it just means I know who that man is now." But with it, Petrah had many more questions, namely: how could a figure from the past be here in the present? *And in my dreams.*

Petrah looked at the drawing of San-Jahad. He tapped the man's face and whispered, "I see you too, Brother."

P ETRAH SPENT SAN'S DAY again in the library, this time alone, reading everything he could on the Great One. Every so often, he would look at the empty seat beside him before delving into the next passage.

A few times, he caught his thoughts wandering.

Stop getting distracted.

He couldn't help himself. He blamed Ajoon for his inability to concentrate.

If she were here, I might get something done.

But she wasn't, so he had to push her out of his mind.

He paged through the massive *Book of Prophecy.*

Ajoon was right about the book: it was downright impossible to understand. Petrah didn't know what he was looking for. If the man he dreamed of was this Great One, where did that leave him? The Watcher had called Petrah the *Key*, but there wasn't a single mention of a "Key" in anything he read. Nor was there a mention of the Great One having a brother.

With nothing accomplished, he closed the book and brooded in silence.

The door to the library opened. Juul, one of the newer students, entered. She had a lisp which affected her confidence, but she was as bright a student as Petrah had seen. As soon as she saw Petrah, she stopped and placed the tips of her feet awkwardly together.

"Hey Juul," Petrah said. When he realized she was here to see him, he asked, "What's going on?"

Her timid voice made her seem younger than she was. "Someone's here to see you."

"Who?"

"I don't know. He's outside the main gate, but the guards won't let him in. I think it's because he's with the White Hand."

Petrah bounded for the door.

He ran into the blazing light of the early afternoon, making for the main entrance to the estate. When he got there, he saw the face he had hoped to see.

"Kruush!" Then, to the guards in the adjacent watch tower, Petrah shouted, "Open the gate. Let me out!"

One guard frowned but then obliged. He pulled on a lever, releasing the lock. Petrah shoved the heavy gate open just enough so he could squeeze through. He gave his friend a big hug.

"Damn, it's good to see you," Petrah said.

Kruush laughed heartily and patted the apprentice on the back. "You too. What is that scent on you? It's . . ."

"Clean? They let us bathe, you know."

That earned a hearty laugh.

They looked each other over. Except for the beard, Kruush was about the same. He too smelled different, like perfumed oil. It seemed to come from the glistening curls of his beard.

"My, my," Kruush said, "you're a lot healthier than I last saw you."

"You too," Petrah said, poking his friend's expanded gut.

"Hah, this is what happens when you get married." He jiggled his protruding midsection.

"Married?" Petrah couldn't believe the good news. "You could have at least invited me to the wedding."

"Aye, I would have, but we've been out of the country for a while. We got married in"—Kruush glanced at the guards and then leaned over and whispered—"Sushtâh."

"In Meerjurmeh? They allow Ter-jurah to marry?"

"Not so loud," Kruush said, eyeing the guards. "And yes, they allowed it. They're not sticks in the sand like they are here, although they still dislike our kind."

"So, how's Tan? I assume he's still with you."

"Aye, like a third wheel, that one is. And quite the bachelor. I don't think he's going to settle down anytime soon."

Petrah gave Kruush a friendly punch in the arm. "I can't believe you're actually here. It's been months. No, longer than that. A year! Tell me everything."

"Here, in the dust and heat?"

"I'd like to invite you in, but you're wearing the wrong robe color, if you know what I mean."

Kruush aimed a finger at the insignia patch stitched over his right breast. "Because of this?"

"Normally, no one outside our party is allowed in. But hold on. I'll see if I can get permission."

Kruush started to protest, but Petrah left him standing there. The apprentice returned with a breathless Master Maglo in tow. The mage had rivers of perspiration flowing down from the top of his head. He barked an order at the guards, who seemed reluctant to let the White Hand member in. When he threatened to call their lieutenant, they relented.

"It used to be easier," Master Maglo told Kruush. "But with every-thing happening out in the world—" Master Maglo shook his head. "You understand."

"I do," Kruush said. "Times are tense. But thank you for allowing me in to see my friend."

"You're quite welcome." Master Maglo turned to Petrah and said, "Just make sure the two of you stay put where I told you."

"Yes, Master."

Master Maglo left the pair alone.

Petrah escorted Kruush to the designated area: an old, mud brick building overgrown with weeds. A lopsided overhang provided shade, and a table and two benches underneath offered a place of rest. They ducked out of the scathing sun. A moment later, a slave appeared with a water jar and two mugs.

"Courtesy of Master Maglo," he said, placing the vessel atop the table. The slave poured the drinks and left.

Kruush pointed at the soldier posted by a tall palm not forty feet away. The man leaned against the trunk with his arms folded, watching the two.

"Your party takes things way too seriously," Kruush said.

Petrah shrugged. "That's the way it is around here."

"I guess I'd better not say anything that could get you in trouble."

"Don't worry about that." Petrah poured his friend another mug of water. "So, tell me, what's happened besides you getting married?"

Kruush kept his voice low as he told the apprentice everything.

He and Tan were still together, equal partners in an international trading business backed by the White Hand. They had their own caravan route and made round-trip journeys to the Meerjurmehan capital city of Hōvar. It took weeks to get there.

"It's a tricky affair," Kruush said. "We bring dusk back to Terjurmeh and sell it for a profit. The spice is expensive and far more stimulating and addicting than that crap we drank back in the day."

"Is it still illegal?" Petrah asked.

"Aye, and it's a pain to get into the country, although customs is as corrupt as any part of our government. Let them keep a cask of the stuff as contraband, and they're happy. Business continues as usual."

Kruush said that he was still on the negative side of things with all the overhead. One or two more trips would change that.

"How is Ahleen handling the caravan lifestyle?"

Kruush downed his second cup of water. "She's a trouper and a smart businesswoman. She keeps Tan out of trouble; and me, well, she keeps me happy." Kruush brandished a toothy grin. "If you get the chance, come to the Travelers Inn just before sundown next San's Day. Ahleen and Tan would love to see you."

"If I can, I will," Petrah said.

"Good. Now tell me more about this apprentice business."

P ETRAH ARRIVED AT THE Travelers Inn a week later.

The taproom of the inn was a haze of smoke and charbroiled aromas. Petrah made his way between crowded tables littered with drinks. He was surprised by how easy it was to distinguish tribesmen from city folk and members of other parties. He was a lot worldlier since his last visit to a place like this. A couple of Green Flame members even extended him a courtesy nod, which he gladly reciprocated.

When he got to Kruush's table, Ahleen hugged him hard. "Oh my goodness, I missed you!"

"Me too," Petrah said. Ahleen looked as lovely as ever, with a deeper tan but still thin and petite. She smelled like the honeysuckle that grew in fragrant clusters on the north end of Maseah.

Petrah embraced Tan next, who had a budding midsection of his own. Like Kruush, he sported a beard. "I see you're twins now," Petrah told him.

"Indeed," Tan said with a vibrant flourish of the hand. "Except for the married part. I don't see that happening for a while."

"So I've heard."

They started with a round of ale and a platter of steaming hot kebobs fresh off the brazier.

"You know," Kruush said, pulling a piece of meat off a skewer and licking the juices from his fingers, "we could still use a third man on our team."

Petrah cocked a brow. "Are you trying to recruit me over dinner or something?"

"I'm serious, lad. Tan and I want you on board. Three's a good number. Very fortunate for business. Lots of money to share."

"You already have three with Ahleen," Petrah noted.

Kruush gave a pause, as if stumped by Petrah's statement. "True, but you're missing the point. Six years until magehood sounds like a prison sentence to me. Then what? You can be rich in a couple of years if you stick it out with us. I tell you, boy, I know this business inside out. And we've got some big things in the works. Don't we, Tan?"

His partner nodded enthusiastically. "It's true. We can increase capacity by adding workers, pack animals, and soldiers from our party to support larger shipments. Bigger trade deals mean lower costs and greater profits. Grease the right wheels and we can start cutting out the competition. Then we can add additional routes over time as we strengthen our contacts in the cities."

"It's about working as a family," Kruush said. "You're part of that family too. Tell him, Ahleen."

Ahleen smiled warmly. "We miss you, Petrah. You're our little brother. Our life isn't an easy one, but it's a rewarding one. I know you're making something of yourself here. I'm so proud of you for wearing the robe of a mage apprentice. But won't you consider coming with us, if not for just one season, to try it out? We could speak to your master. Perhaps he would allow you to study while on the road. If you don't like being on the road with us, or if being a trader doesn't sit with you, then you can return here. At least give it some thought."

Petrah looked at his empty mug. He was still too sober to let them talk him into anything, but Ahleen's words woke up a longing in him that made his heart heavy.

Becoming a mage was important to him, but so was being with his family—the sister and two brothers sitting with him right here. He missed them terribly, so much that he couldn't make eye contact with any of them. If he did, he was afraid he might say *yes*.

How can I say yes? How can I leave Maseah when I'm doing so well?

Petrah finally felt like he belonged in school. Pursuing magehood wasn't about money or prestige. It was about doing something he believed in.

And then there was Ajoon.

She made leaving Maseah that much more difficult.

"I don't know," he said, still staring into his mug. "The offer sounds good, but . . ."

Kruush flaunted his pirate's smile. "No worries. Drink some more, and we'll ask you again later."

The four carried on for hours over good food and many refills. In the end, although Petrah had too much to drink, he still refused their offer. The White Robe stumbled out of the inn with the help of his friends.

"When am I going to see you again?" he asked in a slurry voice.

Kruush rested a hand on his shoulder. "Soon. We'll be in the city until the end of the hot season. I'll come find you."

Petrah staggered backward. "Sounds good."

Tan caught him by the arm just as Petrah's knees buckled. "Whoa! Kruush, give me a hand."

Kruush grabbed Petrah by the other arm. "Looks like we're going to have to take you home."

"Aye," Petrah said with a goofy grin.

Chapter 17

Buildup

PETRAH AND AJOON SUBMITTED their research project the morning it was due. Petrah was proud of the fact that he'd written every word in the report, even though they'd collaborated on what to say. They'd agreed San-Jahad was not the right fit as their mage hero, so they went with a fourth-century magus named Varakkus they'd found in *Legends of the Black*. The mage had single-handedly staved off the Con-jurahn invasion of the original Terjurmehan capital city of Ekmed long enough for the young, elderly, and infirm to escape before the city was destroyed. He died during the conflict, but his sacrifice had served the greater good, which Petrah and Ajoon found inspiring.

"An interesting choice," Master Ecclesias said, raising a thin brow into a high arch. "I shall look forward to reading your account of this mage and the impact he's made on the both of you."

That evening, Master Ecclesias had the entire class gather in a clearing in a secluded part of Maseah. Torches illuminated them in the darkening twilight. The burning pitch overpowered the sweetness of the marsh grass.

The mage moved in a small circle, making eye contact with each of the twelve apprentices as he paced. "Who can tell me what the Kattra is?"

No one ventured an answer.

"You don't remember your lessons from Temple?" He eyed a few more students. "The Kattra was the first word ever spoken, the Word of

Creation. Its utterance divided the void from nothingness, the heavens from the firmament. You might have heard the priests refer to the event as the Divine Awakening. But what they probably failed to mention is that the significance lies in the cause—not the outcome—of the event. So what is the cause?"

He did a once-around view of his students who still seemed baffled, Petrah included.

"Think of a word. It's formed from one or more syllables. When vocalized, it carries meaning. In certain sequences, it carries power. The mage can harness this power if he or she vocalizes the combination of tones or syllables correctly. The effect is often immediate and profound. A mantra should be a familiar example of this, although mantras don't emit power to any great extent. You might ask, why speak when you can just use your mind? Let me show you."

Master Ecclesias pointed at a pile of mud bricks past the circumference of students. The wind gusted momentarily, fluttering his robe. He motioned, and the students parted, allowing him through. He went around to the back of the brick pile.

"Keep your eyes on the bricks," he said.

Master Ecclesias straightened and then uttered something unrecognizable. His voice seemed to multiply as the word left his throat.

No sooner did the last consonant resonate than the bricks sundered.

They cascaded to either side and tumbled to pieces. Gasps and murmurs cycled through the gathering.

"See?" the mage said. "One word, one result. An immediate and profound effect. Now, there's more to it than just putting together the letters. In fact, there are two parts to successfully invoking a word of power. The first is to use your soul as a conduit to channel the energy, just as you do with other techniques. The second—and this is the key—is to use the correct intonation. You need the proper resonance, inflection, and projection to create the desired effect. Otherwise, anyone could do it, right?"

Several heads bobbed.

"All right, class. We're going to perform a simple lift technique. Use your knowledge of levitation to assist you."

Master Ecclesias had the group fan out. He handed each person a piece of brick and spent one-on-one time with the student explaining the technique to be used for the exercise.

Petrah's piece appeared a deep brown in the torchlight. Night had swallowed the land.

Petrah noticed Miko watching him with a big smile on his face, the corners of his lips exaggerated into sinister points by the flicker of a nearby torch. The Green Robe whispered into the ear of the student next to him, and the two snickered.

He's always up to something, Petrah thought, annoyed that he was often the butt of Miko's jokes.

"Is there something the student leader would like to share with the class?" Master Ecclesias asked sharply.

"No, Master," Miko said.

"I didn't think so." Then, to the others, Master Ecclesias said, "That goes for the rest of you. This is serious business, not playtime."

Petrah subdued a laugh. *That's what you get for being an ass, Miko.*

When Master Ecclesias was finished with his tutoring, he demonstrated the lift technique to the class. He intoned a single word, and the chunk of rock at his feet shot up into the air. It hung in place a few seconds before dropping. He had the students repeat the word aloud.

"See? It's not as difficult as you might think. Remember, the key is to use your voice properly. Otherwise, the word of power is just another word. Now you try."

A dozen faces looked down. In a disharmonious attempt, they began. Petrah blocked out the sound of his neighbors as he concentrated.

A moment later, his piece of brick was suspended in front of him. The effort was easier than he'd imagined.

Miko was the second to get his object to float in front of him.

The other students struggled. Ten voices repeated the same word over and over, with varying degrees of change to the pitch or intensity of their voices. Occasionally, a piece would move or skitter, but no one else succeeded, except for the new girl, Juul, who finally got hers at eye level.

The three dropped their brick fragments while the rest kept at it.

"Stop," Master Ecclesias said. The mage explained the technique again and had the students pair off. "Pay attention to your partner. Listen to his or her voice. If your partner's not doing something right, stop and correct them. Again!"

Petrah had Taline for a partner. He wished it had been Ajoon. Ajoon kept glancing at them, and not too happy either by the furrow in her brow.

Was Ajoon jealous? Didn't she know Taline was just another class-mate, that Petrah had no interest in her?

Assuming Ajoon even cared. Maybe she was thinking of something completely unrelated that made her frown. But what could that be?

If Petrah could have switched partners, he would have. Taline was unfocused, and it took half a dozen attempts to get her to listen to him.

Then, as Petrah was observing his partner, his body suddenly tilted backward and lifted off the ground.

He cried out.

Up a few feet he went. He had no control over it. He flailed his arms as if doing so might help. It didn't. An astonished Taline stepped back, open-mouthed. The entire class stopped what they were doing.

"What is the meaning of this?" Master Ecclesias asked. He looked around until he spotted the culprit. "Miko! Put him down this instant!"

Miko did exactly as ordered.

Petrah fell to the ground, striking dirt back-first. Pain shot through his spine. He heaved, but no breath came at first. Then he gasped, sucking in air.

Taline and the other students stood by, frightened looks on their faces. Except for Ajoon, who knelt by his side.

"Petrah, are you all right?" she asked.

"I—" he started, cut off by the urge to cough.

Master Ecclesias came over. By the time he knelt beside Ajoon, Petrah was breathing normally and his coughing was gone. His eyes were still runny, though, and his back ached.

"Are you injured?" the mage asked.

"No." Ajoon and Master Ecclesias helped him to his feet.

The mage wheeled about and pointed a damning finger at Miko.

"You're coming with me *right now*!"

MASTER JORIAH HAD MIKO and Petrah alone by the outdoor dining area. The students sat on a bench while their master stood in front of them with arms crossed.

"I don't know what is going on between you two," he said, "but it's going to stop immediately. Do I make myself clear?"

Two heads nodded.

"As for you, Miko," Master Joriah said, "I'm deeply disappointed. The others look to you for leadership. Hamma never acted this way. He was a disciplined leader. I expect no less of you. But seeing how difficult it is for you to manage eleven White Robes, I'm going to ease your burden. Petrah."

The apprentice looked up.

"From this moment forward, you're to wear the Green as well. I'm giving you half the students."

Miko protested, but Master Joriah jerked his hand down sharply. "Don't even think about it! You're lucky I don't take away your apprenticeship." Then, to Petrah, he said, "One of the slaves will fit you for a new robe tomorrow. I expect you will not disappoint me."

"No, Master," Petrah said. He wanted to smile in Miko's face, but he maintained a serious, humble expression.

"Good. Now get out of here, both of you, before I change my mind."

MASTER JORIAH'S DECISION GAVE Petrah a much-needed boost to his confidence.

He went from being lowest in rank to being equal at the top. Wearing the Green was a significant step in his career, and he took the advancement with humility and gratitude.

Petrah breathed in the fresh scent of his new robe, felt the substance of the material, and allowed his fingers to run along the stitching on his sleeves. Annia had spent half the day tailoring and hemming. He swore the fabric was sturdier than his previous robe's.

"It's the same material," Annia told him. "It looks good on you, Petrah."

"You did a beautiful job. Thank you, Annia."

She smiled, then left him alone. Petrah wished he had the power to free her, to free all slaves. Could a mage ever rise high enough in station to make such a thing come true?

If I can, I will.

Until then, Petrah would apply himself. He would bring honor to his new status as Green Robe.

Petrah pulled the sash about his waist and went outside the dorm to lead his White Robes to dinner.

The evening meal was a quiet affair of grilled fish and roasted carrots. The aroma was wonderful and the flavors sublime. Petrah was careful to make sure the buttered vegetables didn't drip onto his new robe. Five respectful faces sat at his table, including Ajoon, Nuk, and Juul. None of them, including the students at the other tables, seemed dissatisfied with his promotion.

No one but Miko.

The disgruntled youth barely touched his meal. Instead, he stared stonily at his archrival.

Let him brood, Petrah thought. *Serves him right for everything he's done.*

Later, when the students were shuffling back into the dormitory, Miko barred Petrah's way. "I don't know what you think you're doing," he said, "but I don't like it."

Petrah shoved Miko's arm away. "After what you did yesterday, I'd keep to myself if I were you. The masters are tired of your antics, and so am I."

"Really?" Miko closed within inches of his opponent. "Don't read between the lines too much. They know who the real mage is among us. Your promotion is a façade. Don't think Master Joriah is on your side. He's a Ter-jurahn. And the Ter-jurah don't like foreigners."

"Just like they don't like backstabbing murderers."

A crazed look overcame Miko. "Are you accusing me of something?"

Ajoon was quick to put herself in harm's way.

"Move," Miko said.

"No, Miko," she said. She meant it too. "I'm not moving until you both stop."

"I see. You're protecting your boyfriend."

"He's *not* my boyfriend."

"No? Not even a little?" Miko laughed. "See, Petrah? She just feels sorry for you."

Nuk joined Ajoon to stand beside her.

Miko's grimace deepened. "What do you think *you're* doing?"

"The same thing as Ajoon," Nuk said. "Getting you to calm down. You too, Petrah. You need to back off." Petrah said nothing, but Nuk pressed him. "Right?"

"Right," Petrah echoed hollowly and folded his arms.

"Fine," Miko said. Then, pointing at Petrah, he said, "It's not over."

He walked off and disappeared inside the dorm.

Nuk poked Petrah in the chest. "This is getting dangerous, Petrah. Stop antagonizing Miko. You know what he's capable of. Next time, Ajoon and I might not be around to save you."

Chapter 18

Betrayal

P ETRAH THRUST HIS SWORD, perspiring in the afternoon heat. Taka blocked it with deft ease. Petrah swung again and Taka parried, delivering a riposte that stopped short at the apprentice's throat.

"Yield!" Petrah cried, feeling the dull point of the blade against his neck. Even though it was a practice sword, the metal could still puncture if pressed hard enough.

"Are you sure?" Taka asked.

"Yes, damn it!"

The young soldier withdrew his blade. A smirk danced upon his tan face.

Taka was husky and big-boned but nimble for his weight. He had a fluid way about how he moved, reflected in the graceful sway of his bangs. His smile widened, revealing a missing tooth.

"Next time you might lose your head."

Petrah knew he should have been studying or meditating, but he couldn't help himself. Hanging out with his friend was more important than staring at passages of boring text or absently keeping his eyes closed for extended periods of time. He could talk to Taka about things he couldn't with anyone else, even Ajoon. And learning how to improve his swordplay—something a mage would never do—was important as well. He was thankful Taka offered the lessons, even if it meant suffering humiliation at the benefit of his teacher.

Petrah rubbed his throat. "Why do you always have to do that?"

"Why not? If you keep charging like a krell, you're going to get cut down like one. How many times have I told you to measure before you lunge? You can't be sloppy, Petrah. A soldier lives and dies by his swordsmanship. Let's take a break."

"Yes, let's. Besides, you stink like bog water."

"I'll accept that as a compliment."

Taka set his practice sword against a palm tree and grabbed a water skin. He took a swig and handed it to Petrah.

They sat against the trunk, shaded from the cruel sun, perspiration pouring from their brows.

Taka wiped his sweat with the back of his hand and flicked the moisture away. "We'll rest a few minutes and go at it again."

"Maybe we should call it a day," Petrah said, thoroughly wrung out.

"Fine with me. You've already yielded. It wouldn't be fair of me to force it a second time."

"Hah, keep thinking that." Petrah mopped his forehead, but the perspiration kept flowing. "Do you want a lesson on channeling? It's been a week since you let me teach you anything."

"Petrah, I can't find the patience to meditate when I'm by myself, let alone after a round of honest melee. I don't know how you magi do it."

Petrah picked at the smooth trunk of the tree. "I'm not a mage yet."

"Still . . . I find it remarkable. I guess I'm only made for soldiering." Then, with a cutthroat's grin, Taka added, "Well, maybe womanizing too."

Think what you want, but you're no match for Tan. But Petrah didn't say that. He straightened his shoulders against the palm, interested to hear more. "You have a lady friend?"

Taka laughed. "*One?* Try *three.* But only Cena moves my heart. Petrah, you should see her: pretty henna eyes; skin the color of honey; face as fair as the morn. She's sweet, my Cena."

"Where did you meet her?"

"Her father's a potter. He has his own clayware store. I went to fetch a new jug one day for my lieutenant, and there she was, standing like a flower in the meadow. We're courting in secret."

"What about the other two?"

Taka waved a hand. "Just snacks in between. Maybe I could arrange to get you one."

Petrah looked down at his dirty fingernails.

"Oh, I see," Taka said. "You're in love with Ajoon."

"Am not!"

"No? Is it Annia then? Is she the one you fancy?"

"That's *not* funny."

"Tell me you don't like Ajoon just a little."

"Of course I like her. But we're both students. What am I supposed to do about *that*?"

"Nothing, I suppose. You'll die a virgin, and that will be that." Petrah folded his arms. Taka laughed with gusto but then apologized. "Sorry, I couldn't help myself. But seriously, though, I know a few brothels of note. We could break your—how would we put it?—*spell*. Then you could visit Ajoon as an experienced man, perhaps teach her a thing or two."

Petrah didn't find the offer amusing. "I'm not looking for a whorehouse. Ajoon is special."

"Have you told her that?"

"Told her what?"

"That you like her. That you have feelings for her. That you will both become magi and your children as well."

Petrah couldn't believe the gall of his friend. "What is wrong with you? Yes, I like her. Yes, I have feelings for her. But the rest . . . No, I'll not make a mockery of myself. I'm not you, Taka. I'm sixteen. I don't have your appetites."

"At sixteen, I was salivating like a famished dog in heat."

"You know what I mean."

"Fair enough. If you change your mind about becoming more *worldly*, I can help you. That's all I'm saying."

"I'm sure you could."

"There are many ways, my friend. Your fellow Green Robe, Miko, has indulged once or twice, although his tastes, I've heard, are quite eccentric. The point is, if he can have his fill, so can you."

The mention of Miko soured Petrah's mood. Why did Taka have to bring up his name?

"What's wrong?" Taka asked.

"Nothing." Petrah looked away.

M ASTER NOLE'S MORNING HISTORY class on the founding of the Korinian Empire had the entire class in a fit of glassy stares and yawns.

"Am I not entertaining enough for you?" Master Nole asked. "Does my lesson bore you to tears? Shall I dismiss you for the day so you can frolic among the weeds? Is that what your half-dead looks are telling me?"

At that point, Petrah was rigid in his seat, and he could tell his glassy-eyed classmates were as well.

"History is not for amusement," Master Nole said. "It provides immeasurable value. But seeing how little you care for it, perhaps we should switch to a more interesting subject, something with meat on the bone, yes?" The entire canteem was silent. No one dared to breathe.

Master Nole, with a now rapt audience, continued.

"Once you become journeymen— Correction. *If* you become journeymen, you will undoubtedly learn the more advanced forms of the arcane arts. One such discipline is one I've mentioned in the past but bears repeating. Especially today, when your bright young minds are at their dimmest."

Master Nole's hawkish nose swiveled left and right as if he was searching for someone to balk at his insult. No one dared.

"The art form you can look forward to is also one of the most dangerous and one suited only for the battlefield. Can anyone guess what it is?"

Hands went up. Master Nole chose Juul.

"Kantaka," she said.

"Yes. But why is it so dangerous? Why don't you apprentices get to learn this craft?"

"Because you can hurt someone," she said.

Master Nole wasn't satisfied. "Someone give me a better answer."

Nuk offered up a hand. "Because you can kill someone."

"Not *can*," Master Nole said, "but *will*. You don't use Kantaka unless you mean to neutralize your opponent. It's an ancient form of mental combat designed for warfare. But it's different from channeling or words of power. It requires these." He showed his hands. "What do you do with your hands?"

Ajoon volunteered. "You shape energy with them."

"Correct. Kantaka is the practice of shaping and releasing energy. A skilled practitioner uses their hands to shape the energy. Each shape forms a pose. Each pose is either offensive or defensive. There are over three hundred poses to choose from." Several gasps escaped the row behind Petrah. "Yes, there are many to choose from. How do you choose? It depends. If I do this"—he spread his fingers and curled the tips down—"it forms *ju-dem*, 'crab strike,' an offensive pose for attacking in close quarters. But if my opponent does this"—he cupped his hands away from his body—"it forms *sekka-sinsu*, 'saucer mirror,' a defensive pose to reflect and disperse the attack. Strike, counterstrike, and then strike again. Keep going until there is a victor. That is how it's done. It can take years to master Kantaka, but only seconds to win or lose."

Petrah wasn't the only one who sat on the edge of their seat. Everyone around him was engaged and wanting more.

"I know, I know," Master Nole said, enjoying the attention of his audience. "You are wondering: why must I wait three years to become a journeyman to learn such power? Why can't I learn it now? Let me show you."

The mage balanced his pointer atop the lectern so the bottom faced him and the tip faced the opposite wall, perpendicular to the students. He stepped back half a dozen paces. He looked at the students while bringing his wrists together and fanning his fingers like the roots of a tree. Then, turning back to the podium and squinching his eyes, he thrust his hands forward in the pointer's direction. It shot against the far wall, impacting with a pop that disintegrated the tip and fragmented the rest, sending pieces of wood everywhere.

The students flinched from the explosive pop, Petrah included. One even shrieked.

Master Nole walked over to the scattered pieces of the pointer and retrieved one about the length of a finger. He returned to the podium and held it up. "*This* is why you don't learn Kantaka as an apprentice. It's lethal. Yes, there are books in our library that speak of the practice, and even go into its theory. Some of you might have already snuck in reading time on the art form, thinking yourselves clever. But I will say this, and only once: do not practice this art form at our school. It is forbidden. Do you understand?"

A few nods and yesses escaped from around Petrah.

"I asked: do you understand? Say it!"

"Yes," the class responded as one.

"Good. I see you're not so dead after all." Master Nole scanned the room with narrowed eyes before relaxing his pinched face. "Now that you're awake, let's resume our lesson on Korin. I promise, it will be every bit as exciting as you hoped."

P ETRAH NOTICED THE LIBRARY was busier than usual that afternoon. Many students he hadn't seen before were buried in books borrowed from the stacks. He knew what drew their interest, if not from their smiles and whispers, then by the fact he was here for the same reason.

Ajoon sat across from Petrah reading up on Korin's first dynasties while Petrah read a short discourse on Kantaka poses, which included names and hand positions.

Ajoon leaned over the table to get his attention. "That doesn't look like our homework assignment."

Petrah smiled, a little sillier than usual. "Just practicing for when I make journeyman."

M ASTER JORIAH INVITED PETRAH to his home for tea the following day after class. To be invited was an honor, just as Hamma once said.

The dwelling was modest, a single-story residence centered around an open courtyard with a separate sleeping quarters, scullery, bathing stall, and room for entertaining guests. The courtyard was tiled in terracotta and lined with planters filled with fragrant honeysuckle. A continuous draft eased the heat.

Master Joriah's beard was cropped shorter than usual, just below the chin, and his mustache combed and waxed. He sat atop a plush cushion in the center. Petrah sat likewise, bare feet against the cool, clay tiles. Their cups of tea gave off a sweet earthiness, although the taste was on the bitter side for Petrah.

"I have a mission for you," Master Joriah said, blowing on his tea. "Now that you're a Green Robe, you're ready for your first assignment. Tell me, have you heard of the Great Act?"

Petrah thought back to his studies. "It's a Temple-sanctioned assassination." Then, realizing what he was saying, he asked, "You want me to do *that*?"

"Not at all. I was simply inquiring into your knowledge of the subject. Allow me to continue." Master Joriah took a sip. "Yes, the Great Act is a slaying sanctioned by the Temple. But it's more than that. It's the most revered action a clergyman can take. An outsider might call it an assassination, but it is not. To take a life in the name of San is a sacred act, especially when sanctioned by the top of the Temple order. No layman, not even the Iron Fist, may intervene.

"The way it works is interesting. A cleric paints an acolyte's face, hands, and feet red and black—the holy colors. The acolyte then carries out his mission in plain sight. To interfere warrants immediate execution. The acolyte brings honor to his Temple, his order, and his god. Nothing could be more important, as it boils down to faith and commitment, but just as vital, trust. Which brings me to you."

Master Joriah set down his cup of tea. "I want you to deliver a message to Master Keel in the Magi Guild headquarters on the morrow. The scroll will be sealed with my signet. You will deliver the message to him personally and no one else. Can I trust you with this task?"

Petrah let out the breath he'd been holding on to.

He was worried that Master Joriah had a more difficult mission in mind for him, something on the scale of the Great Act. Thankfully, his assignment was more mundane than that.

"Absolutely, Master."

"Good. I knew I could count on you." Then, with chilling certainty, as if to drive home the point that the task at hand was anything but mundane but rather of the utmost importance, Master Joriah added, "Don't let me down."

PETRAH CARRIED THE SEALED scroll Master Joriah had given him in a cloth-covered tube slung over his back. He minded it as if he were carrying the most treasured artifact in all of Terjurmeh.

He was grateful Taka had given him directions.

The guild headquarters was hidden in an obscure section of the city, two levels down from the summit. Master Joriah told Petrah to look for a building with the guild's insignia etched into stone above the main entrance.

The city came to life with the bustle of pedestrians packing the streets, shoppers and peddlers at odds over the sales of goods, a healthy aroma of cooked foods and exotic spices, and the occasional bloom of filth that snatched Petrah's breath away.

As Petrah walked, he recalled his conversation with Taka. His friend was abrasive, if not boastful, but at least he was honest. Petrah couldn't deny his feelings for Ajoon grew stronger each day. He thought of her often, just as he did now—in the middle of the noise and commotion while on a mission from his master. She was kind to him. She treated him as an equal, but she also looked upon him with more than that. He had no experience in this arena, but he knew it went beyond kindness.

Petrah wasn't sure how to quantify his feelings. Only that when Ajoon smiled, it brought him joy. When she spoke, he wanted to keep listening. When they were apart, he missed her.

How do I tell her these things? Should *I tell her these things?*

Ahleen would know. She would give him advice. She'd help him figure out his quandary.

But there was a matter that overshadowed everything.

Petrah's past as a slave.

Master Joriah and the other masters knew of Petrah's slavery. They'd turned a blind eye to the fact Petrah was once the property of Kanmar.

What if Ajoon found out? Would she think less of him?

A knot of fear took root in the pit of Petrah's being, threatening to branch out and anchor itself for good.

Then there was Miko.

Hateful, hateful Miko.

He pretended to like Ajoon, but it was superficial. He would rather drown Petrah in the river than gain Ajoon's affection.

Petrah shook off the dark thoughts and returned his focus to his surroundings and destination.

He tugged on the strap over his back to make sure the tube was secured properly, then walked around a line of people waiting outside an eatery with the hearty scent of stew and pepper in the air.

Petrah noticed, as he navigated the winding streets, that the same three men were behind him, albeit at a fair distance.

After several more blocks, it worried him.

Petrah thought them to be city laborers at first because of their dingy, camel-colored outer garments. By the sixth turn, he started to wonder. Then they disappeared into a pub, and he wrote off their following him as coincidence.

Get on with your task. Master Joriah is counting on you.

The guild headquarters was a large, two-storied structure with an all-seeing eye wreathed by a branch of the mirwood tree, whose leaves were said to bring wisdom when steeped in spring water and sipped slowly.

Petrah opened one of the double doors and peeked inside.

There was nothing but an empty, sunlit hallway that smelled of warmed stone. Another pair of doors stood at the end of the hall. Petrah passed through the second set of doors and entered a darkened waiting area where an old man sat hunched behind a desk. Lamplight danced on his wrinkled face. He looked up from the book he was reading and squinted.

"What can I do for you?" he asked gruffly. He reeked of peppermint oil, which was said to aid with achy joints.

Petrah unslung the scroll tube and held it up. "I'm here to see Master Keel."

The man tapped the desk. "Leave it here and I'll make sure he gets it." He resumed his reading.

Petrah stepped closer, getting a nose full of awful peppermint. "Excuse me, sir."

The man looked up again, annoyed. "What?"

"I was told to personally deliver this to Master Keel. Master Joriah was very specific about it."

The man rolled his eyes. "Gods, you children are so insistent." Petrah took offense to being called a child, but said nothing. The man grabbed his cane and motioned. "Follow me."

They stopped by a door near the end of the hallway. The old man rapped his cane against the frame. "Keel! Someone to see you."

Master Keel spoke something in return.

The old man jabbed Petrah in the arm and said, "He'll see you," and left.

Inside the quaint office, Master Keel sat behind a curved, marble table, quill in hand. Half-melted candles flickered against pale skin. The pleasing scent of beeswax replaced the godawful mint odor.

Petrah thought Master Keel a shrewd-looking man. His discerning eyes, gray patches of hair, and stiff posture made him appear rigid, but when he spoke, he was anything but.

"There are three reasons a young man would come see an old has-been like me," he said. "One, he's looking for a new career. Two, he's looking for a new master. Or three, he's looking for an excuse to have a good conversation. Which one are you?"

"I wish it was number three," Petrah said. "But I'm afraid it's number four: I'm here on an errand for my master."

Master Keel smiled. "Then we shall leave number three for another day. Now, what may I do for you, young man?"

Petrah explained the purpose of his visit and handed Master Keel the scroll from the carrying tube.

The mage broke the wax seal and read the contents. When he finished, he said, "That was interesting." He set fire to it and dropped it onto a brass tray where it turned to embers, filling the air with smoldering parchment and ink.

Petrah's mouth hung open. "You burned it!"

"Yes, I did. What else would I do with a confidential message?"

Petrah had no idea.

Master Keel gestured toward the door. "Come. Let me introduce you to some of my colleagues."

Petrah followed the mage upstairs, where it was considerably warmer.

Master Keel escorted Petrah to a room at the end of the corridor and introduced him to three of his associates. The magi were old men garbed in traditional, black robes. Petrah noted that everyone he'd seen thus far was as ancient as dust from a forgotten cave.

Were there any young men who belonged to the guild? Any women?

The elders seemed excited about the apprentice's arrival. They coaxed him into sitting with them and listening to their talk in the unkind heat. Master Keel joined the group but kept quiet, letting the others bicker among themselves over an assortment of subjects, mostly political. The last thing Petrah cared to listen to was an argument over whether the slave trade was as profitable as it was forty years ago.

You all should put your efforts into abolishing slavery, not worrying about its profit, Petrah wanted to say. Instead, he let the old men yammer.

Petrah grew fidgety as the minutes passed. He'd been gone from Maseah too long. Master Keel came to his rescue and bowed the pair out of the conversation.

"Off already?" one elder asked.

"I need to get our Green Robe back to his master," Master Keel said.

"Well, young man, tell your master to get his beard in here sometime. We've got serious business to discuss."

Petrah nodded graciously.

"Don't mind him," Master Keel said after they left the room. "Old Oeped rarely gets the chance to have a visitor less than a third his age. Believe me, having you was a treat. Plus, it was good for you to see what old magi do with their copious free time. Something for you to look forward to." He smiled, which lightened Petrah's mood.

Before letting Petrah go, Master Keel handed him a tiny scroll with a wax seal. "Give this to your master. Tell him to respond by the end of the week."

"Another confidential message?"

"If he burns it, you'll know. Either way, guard it with your life."

"I will," Petrah said, promising to give it the same care and attention as the message Master Joriah had given him. He slid the scroll into his canvas tube.

"I'm glad we met," Master Keel said, smiling with kind eyes. "Now that you know where we are, don't be a stranger. You're one of us."

"I won't." Petrah bowed his head respectfully and left.

T HE SCALDING SUN MADE the journey back tedious. Despite the heat, Petrah had a spring to his step, his spirits uplifted by Master Keel's parting words.

I'm one of them.

Master Joriah hadn't just given him a task.

He had given Petrah an opportunity to absorb the importance of magehood, of its necessity in the world, and the life ahead.

Petrah strode proudly, shoulders pinned back.

He was in the midst of a random thought when the feeling that someone was following washed over him again. He glanced behind and saw nothing but a steady stream of unfamiliar faces.

I'm either going mad, or . . .

On a whim, he changed direction. Petrah found an opening between brick buildings and slipped into an alleyway. The narrow passage ran straight through to the street on the other side.

He moved briskly, darting glances over his shoulder as he went. Above, the two-story buildings practically touched, blocking out all but a thin strip of sky.

Petrah was little more than a couple of dozen steps from the street when two men came into view ahead of him.

They had rough features, unshaven faces, and appeared to be the same men who had followed him earlier.

Except there were only two of them.

One was missing.

Petrah stopped, then took one step back, ready to sprint in the oppo-site direction.

The unsavory men produced daggers from beneath their long, camel-hide garments. They had hungry looks on their faces, like starving savages in search of food. Their blades were real, not practice ones like Petrah and Taka used. How could they have known he was going to enter the alley? There was no way to see between the buildings, unless . . .

You fool!

Petrah caught sight of the shadow among the rooftops just as some-thing sharp struck the side of his neck. He plucked the feathered dart out and looked at it incredulously.

His legs gave out, and the world turned black.

Chapter 19

Caught

PETRAH AWOKE TO THE shock of cool water against his naked body.

He was curled onto his side, his left cheek pressed against wood planking, his right cheek hot from the sun beating down on his face. The unmistakable scent of the South Kesel River rose from the evaporating water as screeching gulls assaulted his ears.

Why was the world spinning? It was as if he'd quaffed an entire barrel of ale.

Except he hadn't been drinking.

He had been walking home from the guild headquarters when—

A shadow blotted out the sunlight. A burly man straddled either side of his body with his sandals, holding a dripping bucket. "Hello, pretty eyes, remember me?"

Petrah didn't need to see the ugly face to know who was speaking. The name worked its way out from his hoarse throat. "Meska."

"You do remember. Here, let me help you."

The Draad pulled Petrah up by the chain manacled to his wrists, forcing him into a seat. The links rattled their awful tune.

Meska turned the bucket upside down and sat.

He wore the customary beige tunic of a slave master, with a red sash running diagonally across and a wide, leather belt with a set of keys clipped on. Although his broken nose was healed, it had a permanent crook that bent to the left in the middle, which made him look even more atrocious. If only Aggren could see his handiwork.

"Miss me? Come now, I know you do."

I miss you like the women miss your face.

Cruder words came to mind, but Petrah had other things to worry about. He shielded his eyes and took stock of his situation.

He was aboard a large galley docked in Elmar's crowded harbor, situated close to the bow, just below the foredeck. The craft was easily eighty feet long with a single, square-rigged mainmast. One bank of oars was occupied by naked slaves chained to benches. The ship's crew worked along the port side to unmoor the craft.

Judging by the sun's position, Petrah estimated it was near midday, which meant he had been passed out at least since the day before.

If anything, he'd be counted as missing, which gave him hope that a search party was out looking for him. Master Joriah would make sure of it. Not that it helped his immediate predicament, especially with the crew preparing to shove off. Who would look for him at the docks, aboard a slave galley no less? Both his wrists were manacled, secured to a ring bolted to the deck by a chain no longer than his arm.

He was going nowhere.

All hope evaporated along with the water on his skin.

"That's all right," Meska said. "We've got plenty of time to reacquaint ourselves. Nothing but time."

Petrah heard a familiar voice from the prow.

Miko!

The Green Robe was speaking to a man who appeared to be the captain. It removed any doubt about who was responsible for Petrah's ambush.

He yanked his chain in frustration.

Meska added salt to the wound. "Don't blame him, sweets. He's a businessman. He deserves to make a pretty ruh. Considering all the trouble you caused, the hefty price of getting you back is worth it. I admire a man who has the gumption to do the right thing."

"A traitor, you mean?"

Meska snatched Petrah's chain and pulled, forcing Petrah close enough to get a face full of spittle. "Now, you listen! You're our property, got it? No more being a tourist. You've caused our lord plenty enough trouble. Oh, I heard about what you and your master did at the Great Council. This is justice, lad. You're getting what you deserve."

A burst of anger shot through Petrah. "Once my master finds out you've abducted me, he's going to have your head."

Meska sneered. "You've got a new master now. Keep your eyes forward and mouth shut." He shoved Petrah away. Then, in a cooing voice, he said, "I'll be back to visit you real soon."

Meska headed toward the stern, keys jingling as he walked. He passed through the narrow gap between benches of naked rowers. The slaves sat in threes on either side, fifteen rows deep, oar handles across their laps. Their sunburned, despondent faces stared aimlessly, broken spirits reflected in their eyes. They were doomed, like him.

One seat near the front was vacant. Petrah's, no doubt.

We'll see about that!

Petrah felt his throat go dry when he spotted Meska conferring with a soldier from the Black Arrow. All the soldiers wore the party's crest over their breastplates, which meant the ship belonged to the Black Arrow.

Which also meant Manis-cor would find out about Petrah, if he didn't already know.

Petrah searched for the Dark Arrow, expecting him to appear any moment.

He didn't hear Miko's approach until the Green Robe was standing over him, flamboyant smile and all. "My, my, Petrah, you look a little out of sorts. I would have thought you'd be used to these accommodations."

"Master Joriah's going to flay you for this."

"Really? And how would that happen? Are you planning on telling him? Before you answer, you should know he sent me to find you. What do you think of that?"

Fire rose from Petrah's gut. "I don't believe you."

Miko tapped Petrah's chain with his foot. "It must be tough being a slave again. No more Annia to wash your robes or feed you. No more pretending to be a free man. No Ajoon to make you feel accepted." Petrah winced at hearing her name. "Touchy about her, are we? Oh, I've seen you two. I know you've been spending time together, locked up in the library for hours at a time. Don't think for a moment I haven't been watching you. But I also know you've been corrupting her, trying to move your relationship beyond friendship. The thing is, she doesn't want more than friendship."

"What are you talking about?"

"You don't know. How could you? Ajoon told me how you've been swooning, trying to work up the courage to express your affections for her. It's made her uncomfortable because she doesn't like you that way. It's me she cares for. It's me she wants."

Petrah shook his head. "You're lying. You're making this up. Ajoon would never want to be with the likes of you."

"That's where you're wrong. In fact, while you're rowing home, I'll be spending time with her. She'll be worried about your disappearance, of course. But don't worry. I'll be there to console her. I'm going to console her real good."

Petrah lunged but was caught short by the chain.

Miko stepped back, smile turning venomous. "My, what courage. Save it for the pits. From what I've heard, you're going to need all your strength."

"Master Joriah will learn the truth. When he does, it will be *you* who'll be going to the pits."

"Wrong again. I have to say, I didn't realize there was such an enormous price on your head. You must be really valuable to the Black Arrow. They're sending you to Kanmar; something about getting your old job back, they said."

"I'm no longer a slave. Uhtah-Pei granted me my freedom."

"He doesn't have the power to do that."

"Yes, he does. It's called holy manumission."

"Call it whatever you want. You're going nowhere."

"You're making the biggest mistake of your life, Miko. Uhtah-Pei will have you hanged when he finds out."

"Go tell that to the captain over there."

A whistle sounded from the stern.

"I'd love to keep chatting," Miko said, "but that's my signal. The crew's ready to shove off. Take care."

Petrah squeezed a metal link, but it was Miko's throat he wished he was squeezing. "I don't know how you arranged this, but I swear on my soul, this isn't the end."

"You're still wrong," Miko said, with certainty projected from his hateful eyes. "This *is* the end." He turned and walked away.

Petrah heaved against his restraints, using all the force he could muster. "Miko!" The iron deck ring held the chain firmly in place. "Get back here! I'm not done!"

Miko collected a leather pouch from the captain and left.

Petrah cursed. He banged a fist against the deck in frustration. He fought down the urge to scream. Clenching his eyes shut, he squeezed his hands over the chain until they hurt.

He let go of the chain and sat with his eyes closed, palm open.

The longer he sat, the less his hands throbbed and the more lucid his thoughts became. He coaxed himself to tamp down the rage.

Don't waste your energy. Conserve.

Petrah allowed the burning bitterness to filter out from his mind, then breathed in deeply through his nose and slowly out his throat. He repeated the slow breaths until he was no longer distracted by ill thoughts.

You can do this. Remember what Master Maglo taught you.

With a calm mind, he surveyed the ship.

There were six Draadi on board—two in the front and four in the rear. A helmsman, maybe a dozen deckhands, and three Black Arrow soldiers made up the rest of the crew. The soldiers were the apprentice's main concern. They stood on the raised foredeck near the helm, watching over the ship, each armed with a sword and two with crossbows.

"Shove off," someone called from the bow.

"Shoving off," another called from the stern.

The ship creaked as deckhands and dock workers pushed the galley away from the pier. Several more calls followed. A Draad shouted to the slaves to unship their oars. A whip crack reinforced the order.

Meska made his way back to Petrah. He squatted, grabbed Petrah's head, moved it side to side, and spread the prisoner's eyelids open.

"Still red. As soon as this crap wears off, you're rowing with the others. Here." He dropped a partially filled water skin next to Petrah. "Drink this and clear up that head of yours. I'll be back."

Petrah emptied the skin's contents. It wasn't much, but it helped him focus. If he had any chance of escape, this was it.

Petrah examined the shackles over his wrists. They were made of iron, each with a lock and keyhole. He'd failed to unbind himself when the Black Arrow had captured him at the Great Council and placed a metal collar around his throat. He would not fail again.

"Rowers!" called a Draad marching up the middle. "Get those oars in the water."

The slaves pushed the wooden looms through the gunwale openings, dropping the blades into the river.

A Draad with a scarlet headdress took position on a raised seat by the stern, in front of a large drum. He was the row master of the ship. When the slaves finished getting their oars into position, he pointed a baton skyward.

Everyone became still.

"Quarter speed!" shouted the helmsman.

A Draad in the rear repeated the order.

The row master struck the drumhead, sounding a large boom to start the journey. He set the pace, one strike after another.

The rowers brought the craft up to quarter speed to match the rhythm.

The ship cleared port. After maneuvering into the current, the helmsman gave the order to increase speed, and the cadence doubled.

There was a breeze now. Petrah closed his eyes. He let the steady beat and cool air calm him. He recited the mantra Copper Still and dropped into a meditative state.

Petrah focused on his wrists and pictured the metal encasing them. He channeled his senses into the locking mechanism and felt around, discovering without touching, following Master Maglo's technique of using mental feelers and tendrils of thought to navigate the causeways of the mechanical device and probe within. Tumbler pins gave off sharp signals, indicating jagged edges. He needed to push them in at just the right depth to rotate the plug and unlock the device.

"Running speed," called the helmsman.

Petrah moved the first pin until it aligned with the shear line.

The second and third followed.

Then, ever so slightly, he rotated the plug.

When it completed the turn, the latching mechanism sprung free.

One down, one to go.

Seconds later, he released the second lock.

Petrah opened his eyes and took a deep breath. The shackles were loose. One good shake and they'd fall.

Petrah planned his next move carefully.

The soldiers were still well within his sight, although their attention had lapsed into small talk among themselves. Deckhands were preoccupied with performing menial tasks. No one seemed to care about the blue-eyed captive, not even Meska, who was immersed in conversation with another Draad.

And why should they? He wasn't going anywhere. The only question now was how to escape without being seen.

The wind fluttered a canvas below the foredeck. Petrah saw casks beneath their protective cover.

An idea sprang to life.

If he could start a fire, he could cause a distraction. No one would notice a single naked man sneaking over the side of the ship when part of it was burning.

Combustion is like a recipe, Master Nole had once said. *You need air, tinder, and heat. Use your divine toolkit to create the heat. Then you'll have your fire.*

Petrah concentrated on the small barrel in the center. He caressed the wood surface with an invisible tendril and noted its coarse texture.

With the sun as his source, Petrah accumulated its warmth and focused it into a blistering point, using his body as a conduit.

Within seconds, a smolder on the barrel's surface sent a wispy trail of smoke into the air.

Just a little more.

Petrah worked through the calculation in his mind, considering the point of ignition.

Then a daunting thought struck him. Enclosures with fuel always held trapped gasses. If the gasses were to combust—

Without warning, the cask exploded, shooting shards of wood and flaming oil everywhere.

The blast rocked the craft. The soldiers above dove to the side and everyone else ducked low.

The tremor tossed Petrah sideways. If it hadn't been for the canvas cover, Petrah might be dead from the shrapnel.

"Fire on deck!" someone shouted.

Workers frantically grabbed lanyards and pails.

They formed a line when a second explosion blew out a hole beneath the foredeck.

The closest man screamed as oily fire set him ablaze. He ran shrieking, plunging off the ship in a smoking fireball.

Several workers hastily formed another water line opposite the first group.

Petrah flicked his wrists, and the bindings fell free. He crouched. The Draadi had their hands full with panicking slaves.

Now was his chance.

He ran to the edge and bunched his leg muscles for the jump. Another second, and he'd be in the water.

But the wretched pleas of the slaves stopped him.

He turned to see writhing humans, clawing, pulling, and yelling for their lives. Pure chaos.

Oh, no!

If the fire wasn't contained, the ship would be lost, and the slaves would burn alive.

All because of him.

"More water!"

Pails of liquid spattered the flames, but to no avail. The blaze flared up. It would be a raging inferno in minutes.

Petrah made for the chained men. The row master was busy beating down a slave with his baton when Petrah shoved the Draad sideways.

Frenetic slaves grabbed fabric and flesh and drew the man into their mad grips.

Meska charged down the center of the rowers. "You!"

Petrah pointed his hand and said the first thing that popped into his head, a word of levitation.

The Draad lifted into the air and then dropped on top of a bench full of slaves.

Meska kicked and punched at the clawing slaves, but there were too many hands upon them. "I'll kill you!" he screamed.

The slaves dragged him into their clutches by the hair and arms and beat him savagely.

Petrah pushed through the twist of limbs and unclipped the Draad's keyring. He endured an elbow to the chest, then unlocked the shackles of the nearest slave. Meska fought like a hellion, attempting to get loose.

"Hold him down!" Petrah told the freed slave.

The man, gaunt as a living skeleton, threw his weight onto Meska's back.

Past the mainmast, thick smoke obscured the front part of the ship. Petrah could taste the terrible char on his tongue.

Slaves yelled and pulled on their bindings. They screamed at Petrah to get his attention.

One slave, not much older than Petrah, gestured to him. "Give me a key! You can't get them all loose."

Petrah removed one of two keys from the key ring and handed it to him. Together, they worked the benches, freeing slaves. Most jumped overboard. A few remained to help their comrades.

Drifts of choking smoke blew past Petrah, stinging his eyes. The fire was burning out of control. In another minute, he wouldn't be able to see anything. He tucked his chin into his chest and tried not to face upwind.

"How many more?" he called to his partner across the aisle.

"Six, at least," the man answered.

The wall of heat closed in, and the crackling sound of burning timber grew intense.

With every pair of slaves released, the effort became twice as difficult.

By the time Petrah reached the last row, he was teary-eyed and hacking. He glimpsed Meska tangled in chains, yelling and thrashing. "Help me!" Meska screamed. "Help!"

For a moment, they locked eyes. Meska stopped screaming, stopped fighting. He beheld Petrah as if the former slave were an illusion, an impossibility. The smoke grew thick, casting a veil over the slave master, and his cries for help resumed.

Petrah doubled over from coughing, but a sturdy hand helped him up. The young man he'd given the key to guided Petrah to the railing to jump.

They leaped into the river just as the top section of the mainmast sheared off and landed in flames, crashing down where Meska was still screaming.

Cool water met the heat of Petrah's body. When he bobbed to the surface, he saw dozens of shapes moving in all directions in the surrounding river, including the young man that had helped him overboard. Petrah trod water for a bit, getting his bearings. He spotted Elmar in the distance and made a straight line for shore.

Partway into his swim, the slave galley became fully engulfed. Brilliant fire swirled skyward, followed by churning columns of black. Anyone still aboard was dead now.

At least the slaves had made it.

The rest, as far as Petrah was concerned, could sink to the bottom of the river, Meska included.

No, Petrah thought, remembering the Draad's final screams. *Especially Meska.*

Petrah worked his way through a bank of reeds onto dry land. A few steps in, he collapsed to the ground.

Covered in silt and soot and thoroughly spent, he flipped onto his back, breathing hard and looking up at the blue sky between stalks jabbing at the heavens.

He was alive.

Winded and with a bruised spirit, but he was unharmed physically. He hoped the same for the slaves that jumped from the ship.

He was freed, but it didn't mean he was free. The Black Arrow would not allow a ship full of escapees to go about their lives. There would be a search party . . . then consequences for those caught.

Get up, he told himself. *Your day is just beginning.*

Chapter 20

Choices

T ALL GRASS AND REEDS provided a fortress of welcome cover as Petrah listened for voices.

He heard nothing but the chitter of birds from one side and the death throes of the flaming ship from the other.

The surviving crew might not be in the frame of mind to give pursuit, but he doubted the tall column of smoke would go unnoticed. The city watch would be alerted, a contingent of soldiers dispatched, and the chase would be on.

As much as Petrah wanted to find a place to hide and rest, he needed to get back to Maseah. Unfortunately, the Green Flame's estate was clear on the other side of the city. He had no clothes, and he smelled like a campfire.

Petrah climbed to his feet.

He shook off the wetness and massaged his cramped, naked thighs with his thumbs.

Naked indeed.

A fine mess you're in. And you lost the scroll from Master Keel that you were supposed to guard with your life.

Petrah traveled inland until he found a dirt road running parallel to the riverbank. It seemed to head in the right direction. He ran along its course, mindful of anyone within earshot or eyeshot. Time was of paramount importance. If he dallied, he'd risk getting caught.

Then his escape would be for nothing.

The road curved west, and Petrah's jog diminished to a brisk walk and then a stagger. He passed farmland, feet aching and throat dry. Slaves worked the fields, but Petrah didn't see anyone supervising them, and none of the slaves seemed particularly interested in the naked man hobbling by.

Eventually, Petrah's progress deteriorated to a crawl, and he stopped. Cicadas whined madly from the twisting branches of bramblewood trees.

He was at a slight bend in the road.

Ahead, it widened into two lanes between large estates. He couldn't see much beyond fifty feet because of the tall bushes blocking his view. He'd get a better look once he rested a bit.

A voice startled him. "Hey, you."

Petrah turned to see a short, skinny, old man with wizened features, oversized ears, and desert-brown skin coming toward him. He was clad in only a loincloth. A faded black tattoo on his ankle assured the youth he was in safe company.

The old man aimed his walking stick at him. "What are you doing?"

"I'm heading into town," Petrah said.

"In the nude?"

It wasn't the question that made Petrah laugh; it was the indescribably comical look on the old man's face.

"What is so funny?" the man asked, sounding graver than his expression let on.

Petrah covered his mouth, but he was so tired and out of sorts, he was powerless to stop himself from laughing.

The slave gave Petrah a once-over and shook his head. He let out a crooked smile. "You look like you just rolled with the swine, but you smell like a burned field."

"It's a long story," Petrah said, snuffing his laughter. "Trust me, you don't want to know. But I've got to go, so it was nice talking to you." Petrah limped away.

"Wait," the man said. "You can't walk into town like that."

Petrah turned to him. "Then what do you suggest I do?"

"I guarantee if you go around that bend over there, you'll have to explain yourself to the Fist's men. They're about a hundred feet down the road. Saw them heading this way."

Petrah peeked around the bushes.

Sure enough, there was a patrol of soldiers. At the moment, they were talking to a man standing beside a cart whose wheel had come off.

Petrah limped back to the old slave.

"See? You keep going and you'll get caught."

Petrah sighed. He was weary anyway. "I guess I could use a bit of rest, maybe a spot of shade, if you don't mind."

"Not at all." The old man pointed away from the road. "There yonder is a good place to get you cleaned up. I even have a spare loincloth you can use. Probably not soiled either."

Probably? Petrah was too tired to care.

The man started down the slope into a field of wild grass. Petrah ambled after him. They headed toward a mudbrick hut in the middle of a clearing. An inlet from the South Kesel cut inland beyond a patch of high growth.

"Name's Lukka," the man said, looking over his shoulder.

"Petrah."

The slave cackled. "Now *that's* funny."

"So everyone keeps telling me."

A FTER BATHING IN THE river and donning a loincloth—which turned out to be clean—Petrah sat in the shade with Lukka, slumped against the brick wall of the small dwelling.

The stink of smoke was still about him but not as pronounced as before. Ahead, bees buzzed about a hive hanging from the arching bough of a tree.

Petrah's hands and wrists were swollen, his muscles beginning to spasm, and he couldn't rid himself of the taste of scorched wood in his mouth. But the breeze was therapeutic, and he hadn't the least bit of will to move from where he was.

Lukka entertained Petrah, speaking of his colorful life as a slave while the famished apprentice devoured a heel of bread and drank two skins worth of water. Petrah was surprised to hear how lax the man's master was. Lukka fared better than any Jabahn he knew.

"Reach a certain age and it can happen," Lukka said. "Depends on your master, of course. Mine is tough but fair. And rather than feed you to the krell because you are of no use anymore, or keep you bound because you might run away, you end up like me, free but not free. No, never free, but still." Lukka smiled a mouthful of teeth stained brown like nuuma nuts. "That said, I have plenty of scars from my younger years. You could say I've put in my dues." He showed Petrah the crisscross of scars on his back. "Not as pretty as yours, I'm afraid. Not that I'm comparing lashings."

Petrah shrugged. "I've put in my dues too."

Lukka pointed at Petrah's belly. "I can see that."

Petrah didn't know what Lukka was referring to until he looked down. He rarely thought about the faded scar below his breastbone. "That's from childhood. And no, I don't know how I got it."

"And here I thought you were going to tell me the story about how you fended off knife-wielding cutthroats. But enough about the past. Tell me how you ended up"—Lukka gestured at Petrah's nakedness with a bony hand—"liberated of your clothing."

Petrah would have preferred not to say anything, but Lukka appeared as harmless as a blade of grass.

He related the story of his trip to the Magi Guild headquarters, his short captivity aboard the slave galley, and his daring but foolish escape.

"This Miko set the whole thing up?" Lukka asked. "A bold move for one so young."

"More like brazen. I don't know how he found out that I used to be a slave, but I should have known he was up to something. He's cunning." Petrah didn't want to spend any more effort on being angry, but he couldn't tamp it down.

"The men that cornered you sound like mercenaries," Lukka said. "I might not know much about the workings of the world, but I know hiring these types doesn't come cheap. Where do you think Miko got the money?"

"His father, probably," Petrah said. "All the students come from good families, except for me and Ajoon."

"Yet Ajoon remains unscathed, I take it."

"He's left her alone so far. Miko fancies her, though. Or he pretends to, mainly to irritate me. I don't trust him to be alone with her."

Petrah didn't like the fact that Miko might try to take advantage of Ajoon in his absence. Ajoon was far from experienced in the ways of love, at least from what Petrah knew about her. He doubted she'd ever kissed a boy.

But Miko was vile, opportunistic, and a predator at his core. He knew things. He'd done things and would continue to twist the world and people around him, even his masters. Miko said he would console Ajoon. But would he harm her?

Lukka picked up on Petrah's trepidation. "You're worried about her."

"She means a lot to me. Miko is devious and deceitful. After what he did to me—" Petrah shook his head. "Who knows how far his treachery will go?"

Lukka gave him a sympathetic look. "I'm sorry this is happening to you. You seem like a good soul. Ajoon as well."

"Ajoon is an incredibly kind and caring person. She's very much a good soul. As for me—I don't know what to say. My master gave me a simple task, and I failed him. I should have returned to him, not fallen into Miko's trap and ended up on a ship."

"Yet you helped those slaves, Petrah. That was a great and selfless deed."

Petrah hoped all the slaves would find the freedom they deserved.

Lukka sat up as straight as his hunched body would allow. "Do you believe things happen for a reason, Petrah? Have you ever considered that it was all *supposed* to happen this way, that you were *meant* to become an apprentice and go through everything you did?"

Petrah tugged at a tuft of grass. "I'm not exactly a person of faith."

"Not a believer, I take it."

"Not particularly. To think that everything we do is part of some greater plan . . . I don't know." The Watcher knew, though.

Lukka pulled his skinny knees to his chest. "I think everything happens for a reason. Take what happened today, for instance. If your master hadn't given you the chance to become an apprentice and that boy hadn't double-crossed you and gotten you on that ship, what do you suppose would have happened to those slaves? Who knows, right? Maybe they'd still be rowing now, still prisoners. But you freed them. It took fire and a brush with death, but it was meant to happen. I believe that."

Petrah would never have thought of it that way. Lukka made everything sound so simple, so obvious.

Lukka continued. "We have a word to describe what happened: *destiny*. We all have it. It's like an arrow in flight. The bowstring is pulled at birth; you hit your mark at death; and in between, the arc tells the story of where you're going."

"What do you think you were meant to do?"

Lukka chuckled. "I believe I was destined to be a slave. Along the way, I was supposed to find a naked stranger walking the road in need of water, food, rest, and, of course, good company."

Petrah smiled. "I like that."

"I thought you would."

PETRAH AWOKE CLOSE TO evening. He lifted his groggy head and looked around. He must have been out for hours. The sun sat low on the horizon, and Lukka was gone. The ground beneath him was warm but cooling, the dried fields around him awash in the scent of hay.

Petrah stood and stretched his sore limbs. The swelling in his joints had gone down, but his muscles still ached.

Lukka appeared from the north. He traveled quickly across the field. When he arrived, he was breathless.

"I found out there's a large search party headed this way," he said. "You should stay here until morning. I have a hiding spot about a quarter mile away. No one would think to look there."

Petrah entertained the thought, but then dismissed it. He had to return home. Whatever havoc Miko wrought needed to end, once and for all.

"It's a generous offer," Petrah said, "but I have to get back to my master. He doesn't know what happened to me, and I have to square away a few things, if you get my meaning."

Lukka gave a reluctant nod. "I'll walk you out."

They ended up where they had met along the roadside. Long shadows stretched among thick brambles. Gnats swarmed the air in a maddening dance.

"Stick to the road," Lukka said. "If you see anyone, head for cover. The riverside is your best bet. Once you make it to the harbor, you'll want to walk on the inside of the road. If you must, swim. You obviously know your way from there."

Lukka placed a gnarled hand on the youth's shoulder. "Listen, Petrah. I may be old, but I'm no dummy. They say time is a thief, and wisdom comes to us only after we're sagging and creaking. But it doesn't have to be like that. I know that lad did you wrong and you feel compelled to finish what you started. But let your master take care of the situation. Don't ruin the arc of your arrow. Don't do anything you'll regret."

Petrah didn't want to promise anything, but he agreed Master Joriah should handle the matter. He thanked Lukka for everything and locked forearms. "I'll never forget this."

"Next time you're in the area, stop by and remind me," Lukka said with a wink.

But as Petrah headed off, and he gave his predicament with Miko more thought, he dismissed Lukka's advice to let Master Joriah handle the situation.

I must handle it myself.

A singular purpose took hold of Petrah, fueled by the day's events and months of mounting pressure. He'd make it back to Maseah, and then he'd confront his problem once and for all.

I'm coming for you, Miko.

Chapter 21

Showdown

P ETRAH NAVIGATED THE DARK barefoot, painfully aware of his scant garb, but more so of the task ahead of him: getting into Maseah unseen.

If he followed Lukka's advice, he would walk up to the gate, speak to the guards, and ask them to get Master Joriah. From there, Petrah would explain his disappearance to the mage and provide the details of his capture and escape and demand Miko be held accountable.

Miko would plead his innocence, deny any wrongdoing, and try to shift the blame to Petrah. He might even suggest Petrah had voiced second thoughts about being a mage and had seized the opportunity to run away while in the city. Then, after doubting his decision, Petrah had come back, only to concoct an absurd story about ending up on a slave galley.

With the galley burned to ashes and at the bottom of the river, and with the Draadi and crew either dead or scattered, what evidence could Petrah gather to prove he'd been a captive on the ship? What evidence did he have that Miko had hired mercenaries to subdue him or that Miko had received payment from the ship's captain? All Petrah had was his word.

Master Joriah might not believe me. He might say it's my word against Miko's.

If that happened, nothing would get resolved. Master Joriah would force Petrah and Miko to agree to a truce and put aside their differences.

Petrah thought of how Master Joriah had let Miko get away with killing Hamma. How his instructors had allowed Miko's crime to go unpunished.

Miko is a snake. Yet the masters are blind to his deceit.

But what if Master Joriah believed Miko? What if he believed Petrah was a liability or unreliable or a straight-out liar? Would he strip Petrah of the Green? Or would he do something more drastic and expel Petrah from Maseah?

Then Miko would win.

Petrah's cheeks burned from the hatred brewing. Lukka's advice dimmed in his mind, becoming fainter with each step.

Petrah couldn't see that well, nor too far ahead on his path, so he relied on the techniques he practiced at school—mainly the art of sensing the surrounding wildlife, the varied heartbeats and rhythms, and the flow of life.

It saved him on one lengthy stretch where a couple of soldiers materialized from the brush. Petrah hid in the thickets while the men relit their lantern and moved down the road.

The docks were quiet but not unoccupied. A dockworker whistled a sea tune that reminded Petrah of Monta-por and the way the captain would hum long into the night.

Petrah decided to swim to avoid the worker. He dipped into the cool river and swam from pier to pier, surfacing away from the oil lamps. He'd had his fill of smelling river water and having wet hair. He looked forward to drying off and putting on proper attire.

Petrah continued on his way home, stopping every so often to slip out of sight until he was sure the danger had passed.

When he arrived at Maseah, he was laden with sweat, his loincloth thoroughly damp and itchy. In his state of exhaustion, he was tempted to walk up to the guard post.

Petrah scaled the stone wall instead, using the uneven protrusions and grooves between the rocks and mortar as handholds and footholds. Upon arriving at the dorm, his senses picked up eleven sleeping bodies.

That meant Miko was among them.

He sleeps like a babe, shameless and without blame. He's in for a very unhappy awakening.

Petrah opened the dormitory door carefully. It creaked a little, which gave him pause.

When he was sure not a soul had stirred, he slipped inside and crept down the hallway. He discovered the door to his room was unlocked.

He paused, verified no one was inside, then shut the door quietly behind him and took a moment to catch his breath and still his racing heart. The room was dark. From what Petrah could tell, it was as he'd left it.

Petrah eased his deadened body onto the chair facing the window to the outside. The faint flicker of a distant burning brand danced off the sill and across his desk.

He wanted nothing more than to go to bed.

Or wash the sweat and grime away.

Or close his eyes and sleep in his chair.

You can't go to sleep. Not until you settle this business.

Crickets chirped outside while the familiar nighttime smell of moist earth and grass worked its way in. A slight breeze licked at the patch of perspiration on his brow.

Petrah turned to where the serak hung on his wall. Although he couldn't see but a rough impression of it in the darkened room, he could feel the presence of the cold iron and the sharp angles where it formed a delta—the symbol of Sanism, the religion of Terjurmeh. Petrah had tried to believe in what it stood for, its connection between man and god, the mortal and divine . . . and failed.

Now, the serak seemed to mock him in the dark.

As he reached up to remove it from its hook, he caught the faint outline of the chest at the foot of his bed that he hadn't opened in months.

Petrah abandoned the serak and felt along his bed until he got to the chest. He lowered his tired legs and set his bare kneecaps against the cool, stone floor. He fumbled until he found the hasp, then unlatched it. Once the chest was open, he pulled out the gunnysack. He laid it gently on the floor. Running his hands over the coarse material, he felt the lump of Jayeem's sword within.

Neckcleaver.

"Hello, old friend."

Petrah removed the scabbard inside and pressed his palm against the smooth pommel that contained the embedded bead. It felt right against his skin.

With a clean pull, he parted sword from sheath and wrapped his hand over the worn leather grip. With his other hand, he dumped out the whetstone and small well of lubricating oil, which stunk of fumes that reminded him of the burning ship.

Petrah lifted the weapon over his head and imagined wielding it in battle against an unseen enemy.

Or here, against a foe he knew.

What are you doing?

At first, he considered working out his frustration by sitting at his desk and sharpening the blade by feel. He wanted to relieve the tension trapped inside until his anger dissipated and his head cleared.

Lukka might have called it the sensible thing to do.

But the more Petrah held onto the sword and the more he felt its weight, the less inclined he became to let go. The fury that had ignited inside his belly flowed up his arm and into the metal, creating an odd sensation, as if a heat or energy field coursed between his fingers and the steel.

He flicked his wrist, and the field moved with him.

He sliced the air, and the field followed.

The more he moved his arm, the stronger the sensation.

Energy and matter came together, what Master Nole had referred to as "unity" in class. Petrah understood its theory—that the spirit could form an alliance with the body and mind to create a perfect union. If this was in fact the unity Master Nole mentioned, it was Petrah's first experience.

Then a peculiar thing happened.

Petrah discerned the texture of the masonry wall, the creases on his bedsheet, the scratches on his bedframe, the serak's soldered corners, all in crisp detail. A moment before, he could hardly make out anything in the room.

Now he could see everything with absolute clarity.

How is this happening?

Petrah blinked, shook his head, and closed and reopened his eyes. The details continued to resolve themselves without the aid of lamplight.

He thought it his imagination, the hallucination of an overactive mind. He was too worked up or too tired to rationalize it.

Petrah swung the sword. The energy field went with the movement, but the blade struck masonry, ringing out and sparking. He hadn't intended to hit the wall. The vibration coursed through his arm. His chest swelled with exhilaration, as if breathing in fresh air on a cool morning.

Petrah examined the sword for damage, but the edge remained unaffected.

He struck the wall again, this time intentionally. Fragments of stone flecked off.

He looked at the blade's edge again. Still no damage.

Petrah repeated the action, and the reverberation echoed with a dull twang.

"Hey," shouted a high-pitched voice that sounded like Nuk's.

"Keep it down," called another.

Petrah heard doors open.

Oh no, what did I do?

He hadn't meant to wake his dormmates.

Petrah slipped out the window as fast as he could and ducked below the sill. He waited and listened. Someone opened his bedroom door, mumbled, then closed it.

Petrah kept low to the ground and worked his way to the edge of the building.

Then he snuck around to the back of the dorm.

His face felt as if it were on fire. His heart strummed in his chest. He couldn't allow the others to know he was back.

Not yet.

I'll just wait here and—

The back door opened.

"Petrah?" It was Ajoon, dressed in a long nightshirt. She gawked at him.

He realized he was still holding Jayeem's sword. And that he still had on his loincloth.

Two more students came out through the back door.

Juul signed the holy delta in the air when she looked at Petrah. "San save us!"

Other students poured out of the dorm, many yawning or rubbing their eyes. Their faces filled with astonished lifts of eyebrows or gaping mouths when they saw Petrah, but none looked as surprised as Miko, whose bottom lip hung slack.

"Petrah, where have you been?" Nuk asked. "We heard you ran away. Is it true?"

All eyes fell on Petrah.

Petrah's grip on his sword faltered. He almost let it slip to the ground. He squeezed his legs together and brought his elbows in as if he could cover up his near nakedness. The worst part was the wounded look on Ajoon's face.

Taline said, "We've been worried sick about you, Petrah. What happened? And why are you holding a sword?"

Petrah stared at the weapon. His stomach knotted. How could he let them see him like this, especially Ajoon? He could feel her staring at him, questioning his mental state, wondering if he'd lost his mind.

Queasy embarrassment morphed into fiery rage when he looked at Miko again.

He aimed his sword at his rival. "Ask him."

Their attention turned to Miko.

All shock left Miko as his face settled into grim resolve. "This is between me and Petrah. Go back inside." Then, to the other students, he said, "All of you—inside!"

"No," Nuk said, stepping in front of him. "You two aren't fighting. We're not leaving you alone."

"Someone should get one of the masters," a student suggested.

Ajoon turned to Miko. "Miko, what's going on? What did you do?"

"What did *I* do? I'm not the one who ran away." Miko pointed at Petrah. "*He's* the one who ran away. He left the guild with a scroll from Master Keel but never returned to give it to Master Joriah. He abandoned his duties. In fact, he tried to leave the city. Why don't you ask him why? Ask our Green Robe about his proud history and why he would run away. Ask him what he was. The masters know. You should know too."

"Petrah?" Ajoon said.

"He's lying," Petrah said. "I didn't run away. Why don't you tell the truth for once, Miko? Tell everyone how you hired those men to poison me, how you arranged for my imprisonment, how you got paid for it. Admit that, and I'll tell them about my history. Then they can decide who's the real villain."

Nuk looked at Miko. "What is he saying?"

"He's talking nonsense," Miko said. "Now go inside before I knock you out."

Nuk folded his arms and stood his ground. "No. I'm staying put until you tell us what happened to Petrah. We deserve to know the truth."

"I'll say this once more, White Robe. Move aside."

Nuk's voice came out shaky. "I'm not going anywhere."

Miko punched Nuk in the nose, knocking him from his feet.

Nuk sat where he fell, stunned. He dabbed his nostril with a knuckle. It came away wet with blood.

Ajoon got in Miko's face. "Are you going to hit me too? Shall I show the masters a blackened eye to go with Nuk's bloody nose? I'll ask once more: what did you do?"

Miko sneered. "I gave Petrah back to his owners. Your little lovebird is a slave—Black Arrow property. He escaped from Kanmar, but he couldn't escape the price on his head. Do you understand the gravity of the situation, Ajoon? Petrah is in violation of the Codex, the law of our land. 'No slave shall ever rise above his station.' Those are the exact words. Do you know what else the Codex says? 'No slave shall ever be released from bond, unless through a public declaration by the slaveowner.' That means no escape. Do you know what liberties are given to an owner to exact punishment upon escaped property? Have you seen the scars on Petrah's back? Those are nothing!"

Petrah's mouth went dry. Ajoon was never supposed to hear these things. The sword tugged on his arm, becoming heavy and unwieldy, a great burden that wanted to be released. If he dropped it, if he ran off, he might yet escape the truth.

But his hand wouldn't let the sword go, even as Ajoon put her full attention on him, pity and hurt clear in the draping corners of her eyes. "Is he right? Were you really a slave? Are you still one? Are you Black Arrow property?"

"Listen to me, Ajoon," Petrah said, working to keep his anger in check. "The masters know. Uhtah-Pei knows. Our party leader told Manis-cor that I was no longer his property. Uhtah-Pei is above reproach and beyond the reach of the Codex. I might have been a slave, but I am no longer. Do you understand?"

"But you were . . ." she began.

"I can't change who I am—or who I was. But Miko paid to have me captured. He profited from it. He committed a crime, not me."

"I've committed no crime," Miko said, venom returning to his voice. "I was in the right, and the law proves it. If we are to settle the matter, then we should settle it here, right now. You and me, Petrah. Kantaka style. The old way."

"No!" Taline blurted. "You can't do that. Kantaka is forbidden. Someone will die!"

"Please, Miko," Ajoon said. "Let the masters settle this. No one needs to get hurt."

Miko ignored them, looking at Petrah instead. "What do you say? Shall we end this once and for all?"

Petrah knew what Miko was asking: a duel to the death.

Master Nole had forbidden his apprentices from practicing Kantaka at Maseah. Only journeymen and higher would be permitted to learn and practice the techniques. While many of his classmates had read up on the offensive and defensive poses of the craft at the library, he wasn't aware of any who'd actually learned how to use Kantaka.

"You know we can't do that," Petrah said.

"Why not? This is what you want, isn't it? A fight to the finish? Or did you bring that sword out here for fun? Come now, let's match your steel to my arcane abilities. Or better yet, toss it and challenge me like a mage." Miko bent his arms and lifted his hands so they were eye level and spaced apart. He was taking up position for battle.

Petrah tightened the grip on his sword. "I wouldn't do that if I were you."

"Drop your weapon and raise your hands," Miko said. "You know you want to."

"What I want is to cleave your head from your body."

Miko narrowed his eyes. "Pity." He curled his fingers into an offensive pose Petrah recognized as *ja-ben*, "tiger's claw."

Petrah jumped out of the way.

The ground where he was standing a moment earlier erupted in clods of earth. He barely had the chance to regain his balance when Miko took aim again.

Petrah retaliated with a lunge of his sword, forcing Miko to sidestep to keep from getting skewered.

The students backed away.

Petrah thought he heard Ajoon scream at them to stop. He had no intention of stopping. He used the momentum to whip his blade around, as Taka had shown him.

This time, he struck flesh.

Miko shrieked. Blood dripped from just above his left elbow. He retreated, clutching his limp arm.

Petrah moved in to finish him. He jabbed, aiming for Miko's chest.

It hit an invisible barrier, bouncing the blade back with vibration.

Miko retracted his good arm, uttered something unintelligible, and thrust it out, palm first. The air rippled. A wave of energy struck Petrah squarely in the breastbone, knocking him to the dirt. The blow sent his sword skittering.

He wheezed and cradled his ribcage.

Miko looked down at his arm. Streamlets of blood ran from the gash and dripped onto the ground. "Look at this," he told his downed assailant. "A slave who thinks he's a soldier! You barbarian. Now I'm going to teach everyone what a real mage does to his enemy. Swallow your last breath."

Miko pointed his finger at Petrah's head.

Petrah rolled away just as the ground exploded. He was too slow for Miko's second attempt.

Petrah clutched his struck leg and rocked back and forth as agonizing heat seared his tissue. The scent of burned skin filled the air.

Miko walked up to Petrah, blood streaming from his wound. "You think you're clever, coming at me with a sword? You think you're a warrior? You're nothing, just a slave. Someone's worthless property. And you try to *kill me*? You monkey!"

Ajoon held out her palms and stepped toward them. "Miko, that's enough. You've made your point. Lower your hands. Please!"

Miko looked at her wildly. "Enough? Who do you think you are, telling me it's enough? He's a slave. He's nothing!"

Ajoon pleaded. "Please, Miko. You don't need to do this. Petrah yields, don't you, Petrah?"

"There is no yielding in Kantaka," Miko said. "One lives, the other dies. That's how it goes."

"But we need to get you to a physician," Ajoon said. "You're going to bleed to death."

Miko glanced at his arm and scoffed. "It can wait. Now, I won't warn you again." He brought his killing claw upright. Ajoon stepped back.

Petrah clamped down on the pain and propped up on one elbow. His sword lay a couple of feet away.

Just as he began reaching for it, Miko stepped on the flat of the blade with a bare foot.

"For the record," Miko said, "you never had a chance. That's what separates the ordinary from the great. I'd tell you to remember this moment, but . . ." His face contorted into hate. "It ends now." He pointed downward with his index finger, forming *Turami*.

A sizzle of energy accumulated at its tip.

Petrah felt outward with his thoughts at the hundred-some-thing-pound body standing over him.

Living flesh.

Moveable.

Miko had done it to him. He could do it back.

Petrah uttered the word of power Master Ecclesias had taught him. Miko yelped as his body lurched up and backward.

Petrah used his mind to push.

Miko arced and landed several feet away, his body shuddering from the impact.

Petrah ignored the pain in his leg. He rolled to his feet as he had done many times with Taka and grabbed his sword. He ran over to where Miko was still flat on his back, coughing.

Petrah set his blade against Miko's throat, ready to slice it open.

"Petrah, don't!" Ajoon called from behind.

"If I let him live, he'll keep on killing," Petrah said over his shoulder. "Is that what you want?"

"Kantaka is over," Ajoon said, coming around to Petrah's front. "You won. Please, Petrah, for the sake of San, let the masters sort this out. If not for San, then for me. I'm begging you."

Miko twisted his lips into a snarl. "You should listen to her. Let the masters sort it out. Let them see you for what you really are."

Petrah pressed the tip of the blade against the hollow of Miko's throat. "Shut up!"

He wanted to push, to end it, here and now.

"Petrah, please," Ajoon begged. "Let him up."

Petrah couldn't do that. He couldn't let this animal go. "I can't."

"But you must!"

"You heard her," Miko said. "Do as you're told."

"I said shut up!" Petrah pressed down, creating a divot in Miko's throat. Any harder, and he'd pierce the skin. Miko's eyes widened—a first glimpse of fear, of anything even resembling a human being.

The field of energy from where Petrah's hand met the sword made his skin tingle all the way up to his neck, filling him with a primal craving. The masters had looked the other way in the face of Hamma's death, even though everyone knew Miko was responsible.

Miko was a murderer.

A murderer who needed to be put down like a rabid dog.

Ajoon was wrong. Petrah couldn't allow the masters to sort out the mess.

From his periphery, Petrah caught Miko knotting his good fist. Miko extended his forefinger into *turami*—the killing blow. One touch, and Petrah would die.

"Don't," Petrah warned.

Miko lashed out with his hand.

Petrah thrust down.

The blade punctured Miko's throat, jamming into his spinal column.

Blood gushed.

Petrah let go and staggered backward.

The sword twisted sideways, striking dirt, the blade still embedded in Miko's spine, the handle flopping up and down with a sick thump as he convulsed.

"What did you do?" Ajoon cried.

Petrah couldn't look at her.

Miko's convulsions ended, and a terrible silence stilled the air.

Before anyone could say anything, Petrah ran off and vanished into the night.

Chapter 22

Return from the Past

PETRAH INTENDED TO RUN away, far away, past Maseah and even Elmar, south perhaps, toward the Shrine of San or north to the most distant parts of Terjurmeh. But when he got to the muddy bank of the South Kesel that bordered the estate and listened to the river's ceaseless churn, he lost the desire to wade across, to hide among the reeds and keep going. It was as if the water had created a barricade to freedom, an impassable divide.

Among the shrubs and olive trees, Petrah hid.

He waited out the night, the dawn, and the cruel rise of the sun.

He sat among the croak of frogs and buzz of cicadas, watching the glitter of the river, wondering where he might find safe harbor—from his masters, his crime, even himself.

"You have nowhere to go," he told the water. "Now turn yourself in."

With defeat lodged in his brain, he did just that.

The four instructors—Masters Nole, Maglo, Ecclesias, and Joriah—presided over an inquiry, seated behind their table where they dined each day, shrouded by the shadow of palms in the late afternoon, with Master Joriah as the silent judge. Petrah confessed to Miko's death, even going as far as explaining his intention and use of his sword.

"Then whose idea was it to engage in Kantaka?" Master Nole asked, as if he didn't already know the answer.

"Miko's," Petrah said. "But—"

"He used offensive postures, did he not?" Master Ecclesias asked.

"Yes, but—"

Master Nole slapped a heavy palm against the table. "Then he insti-gated the conflict. Is that true, Green Robe?"

What could Petrah say to that? Everything they said was correct, but they refused to address Petrah's culpability in Miko's death, going as far as calling it an "unfortunate accident," not the willful cessation of life.

"I was outside with the sword first," Petrah said. "The threat was implied."

"But he proposed a fight to the finish," Master Maglo said. "Two combatants, one survivor. Your classmates corroborated that."

Why couldn't they see Petrah for the killer he was? Ajoon had im-plored him to back away. But did he?

"He challenged me to a duel," Petrah said, "and I accepted."

Master Joriah spoke for the first time, siding with his subordinates. "Kantaka is forbidden. Miko knew this. Yet he insisted on using it. And what you say about your abduction has merit. You were Black Arrow property at one time, and Miko capitalized on that. We confirmed the sinking of the slave galley, which corresponds to your disappearance. When we questioned Miko about it, he was quick to suggest you'd left Maseah for good, citing how you believed you didn't fit in and that the pressure had become too overwhelming. All lies, of course, knowing how poorly you two had gotten along. So where does that leave us, Petrah?"

Petrah stared at his instructors, wordless and unable to respond.

Master Joriah folded his hands. "Miko had a history of misfortunes started by him, well before you arrived at Maseah. This is the culmination of those events. And, yes, you engaged in a fight that left one of you alive . . . and the other dead. Such an unsanctioned, willful, and treacherous act should require a punishment befitting the consequences. One outcome is expulsion. Another is whipping. And a third, and the direst, exists in an obscure section of the Codex, giving us the power over life and death. Three outcomes, one choice. What shall it be, Green Robe?"

Petrah could have groveled, could have begged for forgiveness, but he believed himself guilty of the crime. He didn't want death, yet he couldn't bring himself to suggest the least of the punishments. "It should be whatever you will it to be, Master."

"You give us our pick of choices?"

The question sounded foreign to Petrah's ears, and his answer even stranger. "Yes."

Master Joriah spent a long time putting Petrah under his scrutinizing gaze. Petrah kept his shoulders back, ready for whatever verdict Master Joriah and his instructors would decide.

"We shall confer," Master Joriah said. "Find Annia and bathe. Then sequester yourself to your room."

On his way back to the dorm, Petrah stumbled into Ajoon.

They looked at each other, both with their mouths open. Petrah tried to apologize for his heinous actions. "Ajoon, I'm so—"

She brushed past him with a face of utter disgust before he could say he was sorry.

INSTEAD OF PUNISHING HIM, they rewarded him. Instead of stripping him of his apprenticeship, they made him a journeyman.

Petrah couldn't forgive himself for what he had done to Miko, to his classmates, and especially Ajoon. He was at fault. Yet the masters didn't see it that way.

"The four of us have made our decision," Master Joriah said. "You will wear the Gray. We will choose another Green Robe to lead the apprentices."

Petrah refused to believe he was inculpable for Miko's death. Surely, a grave punishment awaited him. "How can I wear the Gray when I killed another student?"

Master Joriah bristled, his dark eyes narrowing. "Are you not a mage warrior? A mage fights on the battlefield and wins wars. All the training you received, all the work you've done is not to use your mind to rescue a cat stuck up in a tree. It's for lethal purpose, whether to defend our nation or go after an adversary. Or have you not been paying attention? Wake up, Petrah! Death is a necessary part of battle. Would your enemy feel remorse after striking you down?"

"This was different," Petrah said, frustrated by the mage's apathy. "We weren't at war. The rules are strict regarding Kantaka. I violated those rules. Miko wasn't an enemy."

"But he was," Master Joriah said. "You refuse to understand it. Enemies lie without, yes, but they also lie within. Think about it." Petrah did, and although he wanted to find fault with the mage's reasoning, he couldn't. Master Joriah returned to his original point. "Four of your superiors questioned you, and four of your superiors made the same decision. Our decision is not a coincidence, Petrah. We deliberated and arrived at the conclusion together."

"What about Ajoon and the others? They saw me—"

"What they saw will make them stronger," Master Joriah said, growing testier with each breath. "Ajoon will learn from the experience. So will the others."

"But—"

"I will speak no more of this. You are a journeyman now. Report to Master Ecclesias after supper. He will see that you are fitted for your new robe."

T AKA ALSO SHARED MASTER Joriah's viewpoint. "You saw what that rat did to you. You shouldn't blame yourself. He had it coming to him, and he had it coming for a long time."

"Ajoon was right," Petrah said, not happy with Taka's perspective. "I should have let the masters handle the matter. I let it get out of control. Now I have blood on my hands."

"Your masters don't care. Besides, they're training you and the other students to become magi, not street sweepers. Magi use divine power to protect their party, safeguard their nation, and destroy their enemies. It's just as Master Joriah told you."

"You're a soldier," Petrah said. "Of course you would believe that."

"I *am* a soldier, through and through. I train with a sword, not to swat flies, but to be prepared in case I need to use it. If a fellow soldier threatens my life, don't you think I would be in the right to defend myself? And if he did something terrible to me, like pay mercenaries to drug me and put me on a ship, bound and in chains"—Taka lifted his wrists together to emphasize the point–"do you think I would report the soldier to my lieutenant and hope he disciplines him? No, I would do as you have done. I would take the matter into my own hands and rid myself of the problem. Then my lieutenant could decide what to do with me. But I bet you this: he would do exactly what Master Joriah did. He'd reward me for eliminating a terrible person from this world."

From the way Taka laid it out, it made sense. Miko had been a liability for the school. Talented, even gifted, but too dangerous, too much of a threat. As Master Joriah had suggested, *an enemy within*. Petrah started to understand the mage's perspective on the matter, even agree with it.

"Speaking of swords," Taka said, "your master let you keep yours, didn't he?"

The sword still lay wrapped where it had been delivered to his room, untouched by Petrah. "He did."

"Listen, Petrah. As your friend, I'm telling you: you will get past this."

"And my classmates? What about them? They're afraid of me now. Ajoon won't even talk to me. She hates me."

Taka patted his friend on the back. "I'm sorry about Ajoon. I know how much she means to you. She'll come around, you'll see."

They sat quietly for a while, backs against a sturdy palm in the late afternoon. Petrah was grateful to have a friend like Taka. To have someone who listened, who spoke honestly, and cared. When the shadows had gotten too long, Petrah got up. He yawned, weary as if he'd been up for days.

Taka placed a hand on his shoulder. "Get some rest. You need sleep." Then, with a smirk, he added, "You're starting to look like Annia."

Taka was right: Petrah needed sleep.

It was the dreams that left him fatigued in the morning, more vivid than ever before. *Surati*, Baaka called them, dreams of a higher power. Even though Petrah practiced Copper Still to keep the outbursts of his screams at bay, the nightmares lingered. And the more he dreamed, the more he saw his brother.

Then the Watcher appeared again.

He wore the same robe as before, cowl over his face, long, metal staff in his hand. He stood atop the craggy peak of a barren mountain buried in ash beneath bleak, gray skies. The valley beyond showed metal buildings in ruin amid towers of crumbling rock, overgrown and covered in soot.

"Where are we?" Petrah asked.

"At the end of the world," the Watcher said in his metallic voice.

"But not our world."

"You see before you another land, farther away than you can ever imagine, but only a step away if you have the Key."

The Watcher had referred to Petrah as the Key during their first encounter. "What happened to this place?"

"It was devastated by war, plague, and famine. But it was verdant and prosperous at its height. Jah the Maker abandoned her to fester and rot, a lesson to His children. Such is the tyranny of a proud god, of a Creator who creates but then turns away."

Petrah looked over the scarred landscape. It was as if a dragon had razed the land to cinders and ash. "This is where I'm from?"

The Watcher pointed a black fingernail toward the valley floor. "Down among those ruins. Your mother gave birth to you in the shadows, under a blood-red moon. The day you were born was a very special day."

Petrah heard a woman's voice, sweet but full of sadness. "I hear her calling me."

"She calls, even now, pining for her beloved child, the one she sent away."

"She's still alive?"

"Alive, but older now and alone."

Petrah concentrated on her voice. *Immael,* she said. *Immael, come back to me.*

"I can hear her. She called me Immael."

"Your birth name. The past returns to you," the Watcher said. "You're putting together the puzzle pieces of your childhood."

Petrah absorbed the gloom of the land into his words. "She didn't give me away. She tried to hide me from my brother. The Scriptures call him San-Jahad, the Great One. He would have slain me if he had found me."

"Quite the opposite. He wants you by his side, Petrah. You are his blood. There is no stronger bond."

"But the dreams . . ."

"Distortions of the truth," the Watcher said. "Your mother was scared when she was young—scared and foolish. The memory of it has influenced your deepest thoughts. What you need to know is that she feels immense regret for sending you away. The plight weighs on her. But all is not lost. You can still find her, if you wish, and allow her to make amends."

Petrah saw a woman tending a campfire with a long stick. She had pale blue eyes and dark brown hair with streaks of gray running through them, a waxen complexion with sunken cheeks, fine wrinkles around her eyes, and deeper lines above her brow. She hummed to herself and rocked back and forth, knees up to her chin, dirty feet pressed together and peeking out from the hem of a soiled, tattered dress. About her throat rested a necklace of stone beads, and dangling from it, a round silver pendant stamped with two fish on top of each other, facing opposite directions.

"My mother," Petrah said. "She looks so . . . fragile."

"She's not well," the Watcher said. "She mourns for her son. It has made her ill. Your mother needs you, Petrah. She wants to see you again so she can forgive herself. She speaks to the dark every night and begs for salvation. If, for just a moment, she could see her son, she would tell him how sorry she was."

Petrah was beset by a longing to seek out his mother, to console her, and tell her he wasn't angry with her anymore. He'd already made the promise.

He would make good on it.

"I remember now," Petrah said. "I—"

His view shifted away from the Watcher, pulled into a childhood memory with his mother where they huddled behind a partial wall of stone with a view of an avenue under cloud-battered skies. The wind moaned and whipped their hair. Soldiers in black on horseback rode up the avenue, the clop of hooves loud against the cobblestones. Petrah's mother clutched her son to her bosom, covering his body with her torn shawl, drawing him into a ball with her to make them small and unnoticeable.

After the horseman passed, mother and son ran across the empty avenue, darting into an alcove of a shattered building whose roof had disintegrated into rubble. From there, they entered the ruins of an adjoining building whose only outlet was through two walls that had collapsed into each other, leaving a slit that formed a constricted passageway. Petrah couldn't see anything past a few feet.

The passage gave Petrah pause. He resisted his mother's tug. Something felt wrong.

"It's just through there," his mother said to him.

"What is?"

"You'll see."

He didn't want to see, but his mother's grip was impossibly strong and the fierceness in her blue eyes unrelenting. She yanked his arm, forcing him in front of her.

"I don't want to go in there," he said.

"You have to—" Her voice was cut short by the whinny of a horse from the street. She put a finger to her lips.

They waited and listened. Men's voices. Then the sound of boots and the rush of soldiers toward them.

"Go!" his mother urged.

Petrah squeezed into the narrow passageway and stumbled in the dark. He tripped once on a blunt object and fumbled, hands out on either side, feeling the cold bricks grow closer, tighter. The suffocating darkness seemed to have no end, until—

He entered a courtyard open to the gray sky with a broken marble fountain in the center. Walls enclosed the courtyard. The one door Petrah saw, the only form of escape, was barred with a rusty grate.

But his attention went to the front of the fountain, where the air seemed to shimmer. When he angled his head, he saw it was the shape of an oval and the height of a man. It blurred along the edges and rippled over the surface, much like a misty lake tipped on its side.

Petrah's mother tugged on his threadbare shirt. She urged him toward the shimmering oval. "You have to go through."

He shook his head, unwilling to budge.

"You must. It's the only way."

The rustle of pursuit grew louder. Eddies swirled across the oval.

"I love you," his mother said. When he looked at her, he saw she was crying. Jeweled tears fell from ice-blue eyes. "I will always love you."

She hugged him, kissed him on the brow, then pushed him just as the first soldier emerged from the narrow gap they'd come through.

Petrah lost his balance, shoved backward, arms reaching out toward his mother, and—

The view returned to the Watcher.

Petrah's sadness changed to bitterness. "She sent me away."

"It was her wish at the time," the Watcher said, "but it was through ignorance and grief that she made the decision. She didn't understand your brother's intentions. She thought he was trying to take you from her. She thought he would harm you. She didn't know better. She does now."

"And what are my brother's intentions? To bring destruction to Acia? If it is, I want no part of it."

"You've mistaken destruction with liberation. The Con-jurah poison the world with their deceitful preaching. Their tongues are sugared with venom, their purpose false. Study their scriptures and you will know it to be so. They speak not of the Truth, of the Father's teachings, but of falsehoods. Your father's blood runs through your veins and with it, power and righteousness. His word is mighty and true. With your brother's sword, he shall smite the unworthy and rally the just."

Petrah surveyed the desolation of his homeland. The bleakness was never-ending. "Is San really my father?"

"Search your heart of hearts," the Watcher said. "What does it tell you?"

Petrah pictured a well of darkness, a void so deep that it stole the breath from his lungs. From its depths rose a voice, deep and terrifying, but also paternal and familiar.

The voice of a god.

The voice of a father.

"He whispers to me," Petrah said. "It's faint, but it's there, like a murmuring at the root of my soul."

"He whispers to all his children, but you more than most. You are his favored, stolen from your rightful place, but now restored. Your path to magehood has helped you open your eyes to this path. Once you are a mage, you will see it. As I've told you before, the path was chosen for you. It steers you in the direction of glorious inevitability."

Lukka had spoken of destiny, of the arrow that guided a person through life, from birth to death, the arc telling where it would strike. Petrah had shunned the flight of his arrow, yet it flew true toward its mark. Even now, nothing seemed capable of averting its path.

"I have no desire to find my brother. But my mother . . ."

The Watcher leaned his staff to the left. The landscape changed from barren wastelands to lush greens. "See those hills, yonder? There is forestland there."

Past the barren, pitted valley was a murky line dotted with shadowy protrusions along the horizon.

"This is Âhn, the northern part of Darkforth, over a hundred leagues from Elmar. In the wildwood lies a jungle, and in the jungle is an ancient pyramid," the Watcher said. "The locals call it *Hachaqua*, 'beacon of stone.' Atop the pyramid sits a portal that serves as a gateway between worlds. Step through, and you will return home. Go home, and you will reunite with your mother."

"But my brother lies beyond it too. Won't the portal let him through?"

"Only if you guide him through. You are the Key and he is the Sword, and together, greatness may be forged."

"What if I don't want it forged?"

The Watcher's voice vibrated with a strong hum. "Fate is an interesting thing. It tends to make certain things happen a particular way. I know your fate, Petrah. I know your future. You'll see it yourself soon enough."

P ETRAH AWOKE BREATHLESS.

The trill of scarlet crescents pervaded the predawn shadows of his room. The birds would repeat their morning rituals for the next few weeks before migrating south to Korin. He listened to their warbled calls while staring at the serak across the room.

It stared back, reminding him of who he was.

You are Immael, Son of Darkness.

"You bastard," he whispered, as if the Watcher were still there.

He tried to purge the dreams from his mind, but they lingered like the foul taste on his tongue.

What if the Watcher was a fabrication born out of his guilt, first of Jow-quu's passing and now of Miko's? Petrah had failed to save his friend and had purposely struck down his enemy. Where did that leave him as a man?

A coward. That's what I am.

There was a knock on the door, followed by Annia poking her head inside. "Sorry to bother you, but Master Joriah wants to see you at his home."

P ETRAH TIGHTENED THE SASH of his new, gray robe as he stood in the shadow of the loggia facing his master's courtyard. He noticed with distaste that his robe color matched the Watcher's skin and the desolate landscape he had seen in his dreams.

Fretwork lined the inside of the gallery of Master Joriah's home, an intricate, painted pattern of intersecting deltas. The journeyman closed his eyes, verbalizing a mantra to calm his nerves. He wasn't himself this morning.

Not by a long shot.

"Petrah," Master Joriah said from across the way, startling him out of his black mood.

Petrah bowed his head. "Good morrow, Master."

The mage took a seat at a stone table in the center of the courtyard. "I've asked Annia to have Ajoon take everyone to class this morning. You and I have some things to discuss." Mentioning Ajoon stirred up sour thoughts. Master Joriah nodded in understanding, more sympathetic than when he first gave Petrah the Gray. "She will adjust, worry not. I was beside myself as well when I saw someone killed for the first time. Death comes with the territory. You've witnessed your fair share of executions, have you not?"

Aggren had been the last, but he hadn't been the first. Petrah had seen many slaves lose their lives, not one for a reason that made sense. "I have."

"I was about half your age when a band of raiders killed my uncle. I was traveling north of Fangmordah with my family, not too far from the salt mining operations in Mingèl, when raiders attacked our encampment. It happened so quickly, just after dawn. We repelled our attackers, but not before one raider grabbed ahold of my uncle and sliced his throat. He was dead before he hit the ground. I couldn't eat for days after that. My mother showed pity for me, but not my father. Even though his brother had just been killed, he said there was a lesson in his death for all of us, and that we should give our thanks to San that only one life was lost that day. My father was far from kind, but I saw him grieve after my mother passed, so I know his heart wasn't as cold as many believed it to be. The point is, there are things one cannot unsee, acts one cannot undo, but death is a cycle of life that we must all endure and embrace. Ajoon will survive Miko's death, and she will be all the stronger for it in the long run. Do you not agree?"

Petrah didn't agree. He had inflicted irreparable damage on Ajoon through a single act.

Master Joriah was right on one front: the act couldn't be unseen or undone.

"I agree, Master."

Master Joriah clapped his hands overhead, and a servant showed up a moment later with two cups of mint tea and a platter of fruit and toasted flatbreads dripping with honey. The scent of mint leaves followed the trails of steam.

Master Joriah presented the platter to Petrah. "Let's eat."

Master and student dined quietly.

Petrah ate his breakfast in silence, working hard to hide his distress over his dream. He was present, but his mind was elsewhere.

When the meal ended, Master Joriah dabbed the air in three places, giving thanks to San. Petrah repeated the motion mechanically.

"One more week of summer," Master Joriah said, brushing his beard clean of crumbs with his hand. "You'd never know it from the weather as of late."

Petrah tugged at the collar of his robe. It was only midmorning and already it foretold another day of extreme temperatures.

"It'll be interesting to see what the tribes do if the weather doesn't let up by the end of next week," Master Joriah said. "They often leave after Hah'xallah." Hah'xallah was the holiday that commemorated the end of summer. It also heralded the defeat of the Con-jurah in ancient times, a triumphant moment in Terjurmeh's history. "Your friends with the White Hand will be on their way as well, I imagine."

The mention of Petrah's friends lifted his mood a touch. He was hoping to see them before they left Elmar.

He needed them now more than ever.

"They're supposed to head out the week after," Petrah said. "Too much traffic the first few days, with the tribes and all."

"It will be a mad exodus, as it always is. Your friends are wise to delay leaving the city."

Master Nole had given a dissertation on Terjurmehan tribes and their nomadic nature during the winter months and how they traveled great distances across the various deserts that made up the majority of the country.

Of course, a lot of it dealt with commerce.

Timber was to be gained from the Prallites to the north, ore to the west among several mining operations at the base of the Fural Mountains, and precious metals, jewelry, and glassware to the south, along the Gōsh mountain range. It was a necessary way of life for a landlocked desert country.

Master Joriah went on. "The Fist is sending an envoy to Hōvar the day after the holiday to meet with the Meerjurmehan ambassador regarding the trade embargo. It's interesting to note that representatives from all the major parties will be in attendance, except ours."

Petrah had assumed the Green Flame was involved in all international accords. "Why aren't we sending anyone?"

"We're not invited," Master Joriah said flatly. "It's a political game. Politicians vie among each other, the ones in positions of power cutting out their rivals. Get cut out of enough dealings, and you end up with no tribal support and no party. The Fist and its allies posture against us. This latest move is a ploy to see how we fare as outsiders. There will be a civil war long before we disappear from this world, believe me. For now, we play along. But the situation presents an interesting opportunity. Which is why I sent for you."

Master Joriah placed his fingertips together.

"His Holiness still wants someone from our party to go. That person's job will be to observe the negotiations between the Ter-jurahn and Con-jurahn delegations. Nothing more."

"You mean spy," Petrah said.

Master Joriah smiled as if impressed with Petrah's straightforward interpretation. "The challenge is to find one capable enough to do the job without being seen or recognized. We can't send any magi or party officials. They're too well known. The task requires a special skill set—something a journeyman might possess.

"I want to send you, Petrah. I trust your abilities. His Holiness already gave his blessing. I talked to him yesterday. He has favored you since day one, and that's not something to be taken lightly. This is an extraordinary opportunity for your career. Just imagine the potential." Master Joriah settled back in his seat. "What do you say? Are you up to the task?"

The Watcher had spoken of how fate made certain things happen in a particular way. Was this mission part of it, drawing Petrah east toward Darkforth? It was foolish to say no to Master Joriah.

Instead, he gave a professional response that would meet his master's expectations. "How do I get to Meerjurmeh?"

"It's all been arranged. You're traveling with your friend from the White Hand, the big fellow who visited you."

The journeyman's eyebrows lifted. "Kruush? You spoke to him?" Petrah couldn't believe what he was hearing. He attempted to hide his smile, but it was difficult.

"Your friend has agreed to take you to Hōvar. He also agreed to alter his departure to leave a week earlier than he'd planned so he could be on our timetable. He told me he's been trying to get you to go with him since he first joined the White Hand. It looks like he's finally having his way. In the meantime, Master Maglo will prepare you for the trip. There are some things he needs to teach you before you head out."

After the horrible series of events that had begun with Petrah's incarceration aboard the slave galley, this was joyful news.

Kruush, Ahleen, Tan, and him, together again!

I can't believe this. Surely, Master Joriah is jesting.

But he wasn't.

Master Joriah placed a hand on Petrah's shoulder. "I'm proud of you, son. This means a lot, not only to the party and His Holiness, but to me. May San be with you."

P ETRAH ARRIVED AT MASTER Maglo's office at first light. It was its usual mess, illuminated by two candles.

"So you have a mission I've heard," Master Maglo started off with a sly grin. "A secret mission, no less. Are you excited?"

"I am." The answer came out less enthusiastic than Petrah intended. "I mean I want to be. After all, I'll be with people I know."

The mage nodded, acknowledging Petrah's doubts. "It's your first real assignment. You have concerns, reservations. It's perfectly normal. With advancement comes more responsibility. But this is a good mission, Petrah. And an important one for the Green Flame."

"I just want to bring honor to our party." *And not mess things up.*

"You will," Master Maglo said. "I have full confidence in you. And by the way, I think the Gray suits you. I know you don't think you deserve it, after what happened, but I do. It's not a gift, Petrah. It's a step toward the next stage of magehood."

Petrah was still getting used to his new robe. He'd given Master Joriah ample opportunity to back out of promoting him to journeyman, but the mage had insisted on it. At first, Petrah thought the decision pure madness—one that flew in the face of reason. But then he realized it was a calculated move. That Master Joriah had given him the Gray to keep Petrah in his employ and to serve his agenda while also distancing Petrah from the other students.

The mage knew if Petrah stayed on school premises, his presence might create undue tension with his classmates, impede their learning, and even cause resentment that could boil over into unresolvable conflict. After losing Hamma and Miko, Master Joriah would not risk losing someone as capable as Petrah. Jolly-faced Master Maglo was in on it, the other instructors as well.

"I won't be coming back to Maseah, will I?"

Master Maglo shared a tight-lipped smile Petrah couldn't quite interpret. Was it sympathy? Pity? An attempt to ease the anxiety evident in Petrah's furrowed brow?

"We're just getting started on a new journeyman school here, but it'll take some time to complete. Worst case, you attend a school in Elmar when you get back. You can visit us anytime you wish, of course. But let's not get ahead of ourselves. Agreed?"

Master Maglo was being kind, even merciful, but the truth hung in the small office like the scent of melted beeswax. Petrah swallowed his disappointment and gave the mage a humble nod of agreement.

Master Maglo placed his thick hands on the desk. "Now, to the reason you're here," he said, "I'm going to teach you two disciplines for your journey, both indispensable and both techniques taught only to journeymen. The first is a listening technique that will allow you to amplify sound through solid materials such as metal, glass, and stone. Its purpose is to listen in on those who would rather keep their conversations to themselves—such as a closed-door session with delegation members from Terjurmeh and Meerjurmeh."

Petrah understood. "A spying technique."

"Yes."

"And the second discipline?"

Master Maglo smiled wide. "Have you ever heard of a mind link?"

Chapter 23

New Beginnings

PETRAH RUBBED THE COLD sweat from his palms and fingertips as he walked up the path toward the secluded inlet where Ajoon had agreed to meet with him. It was just before sunup, notes of jasmine in the air and the sky a dusty blend of deep blue and orange. Petrah was grateful for the opportunity to meet with Ajoon. They'd not spoken since the fateful evening of Miko's death. After Petrah's one feeble attempt at an apology, days earlier, he'd not had the bravery to try again.

He stopped abruptly when he spotted Ajoon sitting with her back to him on the bench facing the small inlet. His face tingled, and his legs refused to cooperate. It was as if he'd sunk into a quagmire. Ajoon's short hair caught the first rays of the sun, turning a brilliant red along the fringes.

How could he face her? Or find the words to ask for forgiveness?

Petrah thought that after a few days of avoiding Ajoon it might come easier to talk to her. That he could repair the damage and salvage their friendship. Now, with leaden feet and clammy hands, it was obvious that it wasn't easier, but a magnitude more difficult.

Master Joriah was wrong. She'll not become stronger from the experience. She'll become bitter.

"Petrah? What are you doing standing over there?"

Petrah gaped like a fish caught on land. He walked over to Ajoon but had trouble meeting her gaze.

He focused on her new green robe instead. "Congratulations on earning the Green. It looks good on you."

"As does the Gray on you."

He summoned the courage to make eye contact, but only briefly.

Taking a deep breath, he looked at the empty space next to her and asked, "May I sit with you?"

She moved over, and he joined her on the bench. Her hair smelled of spring blossoms. It seemed awkward to be sitting so close. It seemed just as awkward to hear her voice. It was as if he was meeting her for the first time.

"You can look at me," she said. "I don't mind."

Her brown-and-hazel eyes and smiling, round face didn't have the joviality he'd gotten accustomed to. There was a forcefulness to her smile. She'd always smiled with ease before. This was the smile of a stranger, and it gnawed at his belly.

He took another breath, then told her of his pending departure.

"We're heading out this morning," he said. "I wanted to make sure I said goodbye. Thank you for meeting with me. We'll stay the night in Elmar to celebrate Hah'xallah and then head out on the morrow."

"I'm so excited for you, Petrah. A real assignment! Master Nole gathered us around and told us you're leaving to take part in a special journeyman program sponsored by the guild. That's wonderful news."

Master Joriah had committed Petrah to secrecy. No one was to know his real "assignment" besides the other masters.

Petrah had hoped Ajoon would react less enthusiastically about him going away and a touch more . . .

Sad.

Maybe she was sad.

He couldn't tell if she was putting up a stone wall to shield her emotions, although she kept squeezing her left index finger, a thing she sometimes did when she was nervous. Maybe she wasn't sad as much as she was anxious.

I'm anxious too, but I'm not that good at hiding it.

"You don't seem excited," Ajoon said.

"Leaving is . . ." He couldn't find the right word. "Difficult."

Ajoon looked down at her hands as if the somberness of his words triggered her true feelings. She continued to pick at her finger, sadness seeping into the shaky tone of her voice. "You'll be missed."

Not as much as I'll miss you, he wanted to tell her.

He had many things to say, many things he'd rehearsed, but not the fortitude to say any of them.

"Listen, Ajoon, I came here to apologize. What I did was"—he swallowed—"inexcusable."

He paused, waiting for her to roll her eyes at his cliché excuse, but she didn't.

He forced himself to continue. "I've done more than ruin our friendship. I've hurt you. You're the one person who accepted me for who I was. But now that you've seen my ugly side, I'm"—he shuddered a breath—"ashamed."

Ajoon continued to look at her hands.

Petrah didn't expect her to accept his apology. He only wanted her to listen and allow him to say his piece. His pause went on too long, giving her the chance to respond to his declaration of shame.

"Miko was a bad person," Ajoon said. "He would have killed you. I saw him try to strike you at the end. Kantaka is a deadly art, which is why you should have backed away."

"I know. I wasn't thinking straight."

"You weren't thinking at *all*, Petrah. You egged him on with that ridiculous sword. You were so hateful. You weren't yourself. You were . . ."

"Like him?"

"Yes! And it hurts me. It hurts me deeply."

I've gone beyond hurting you. I've wounded you as if I'd impaled you with my sword. How can I say I'm sorry? How can I make this right between us?

He couldn't muster the words.

"Is it true he poisoned you and sold you to the Black Arrow? Master Joriah wouldn't tell us anything. He told us to accept what had happened and to put it behind us. But I can't put it behind me. I need to know."

She looked at him now, her hazel eye bright from the sunlight piercing the brush bordering the inlet, her brown eye muted in shadow. He was going to miss peering at her two-tone eyes each day.

"It's true," Petrah said. He gave her the abbreviated account of how Miko paid mercenaries to capture him and put him on a slave galley.

"How did you escape?"

Petrah smiled bleakly. "A mage uses his talents." He didn't want to share the grisly details.

"What about the part about being a slave? Was Miko right?"

This was the moment Petrah had dreaded since befriending Ajoon. He would have taken his secret to his last breath if it had not been forced out. It was time to give her the honesty she deserved.

"He was. I escaped, came to Elmar, and then Joriah found me. He didn't know I'd been a slave, not until the Great Council and my run-in with the Black Arrow."

"Then the masters knew and kept it from us."

"But Uhtah-Pei released me from bondage as a slave. The masters agreed to never speak of it."

"Uhtah-Pei could do that?"

"Articulates are powerful. They can do anything."

Ajoon sat for a few seconds, wiggling her toes. She'd removed her sandals. "What Miko did to you was atrocious. You both disliked each other from the start, but he had no right to do what he did. I'm sorry that happened to you, Petrah."

Petrah appreciated her understanding. "And I'm sorry about what I did to you. To Nuk, Taline, and the others as well, but particularly you." He rubbed his sweaty palms on his pristine, gray robe, afraid to ask the next question, although it was necessary. *You can do this.* "Can you forgive me for what I did?"

He waited for her to tell him *no.* Or that she'd think about it and let him know when he returned to Elmar.

She did neither.

"I want to," she said, biting her lip. She lined up the tips of her toes. Her feet barely reached the ground. "Getting together helps. Talking helps. Knowing how horrible Miko was helps. Knowing why the masters gave you the Gray also helps."

She didn't mention Petrah's past slavery, and he was thankful for that. Her response was as fair as any he could ask for, but she had more to say.

"Taking the time to process my feelings helps as well." She nodded at that, reinforcing its significance. "Now, if I can just stop waking up in the middle of the night in a fit of the shakes from seeing that fight with you and Miko in my dreams—"

"That's my fault," Petrah blurted.

"Let me finish." She narrowed her eyes at him, but it didn't come across as mean-spirited. "What I'm trying to say is, I need to get back to being myself. I've been out of sorts. It might be your fault, it might not. Maybe after our talk, I'll start getting back to normal." She turned toward him, folding her legs beneath her. She spoke slowly and deliberately. "To answer your question . . . I forgive you. Well, mostly."

He blinked. "Mostly?"

"Petrah, I won't lie and say our friendship can be what it was. I might not be angry with you any longer, or resentful, incensed, or the myriad of other dark things that I was feeling before, but my heart hurts. I feel the pain right here." She patted her chest. "Will it heal? Will the pain go away? I don't know."

Petrah wished he could use his channeling to heal her, to repair the deep hurt he had caused.

"For what it's worth," she said, "I'm willing to accept your apology. We can start anew when I see you again and take things slowly. Are you good with that?"

Petrah was more than good with it. Ajoon's forgiveness was all he wanted. The crushing weight he'd felt for the past few days lifted off him, and he found he could breathe easier.

She's a true friend.

It saddened him that all they might be is friends. He'd never expressed his fondness for her.

But he was encouraged by the possibility of creating a new foundation for their relationship—one that would last and one they could build on.

"I accept wholeheartedly," he said, and he meant it.

But the smile he expected from her wasn't there. It was missing just like the warmth in her eyes, that ray of sunshine he'd come to expect, now cool, distant, and shadowed. It was as if the sky had turned gray with the clouds from his dreams.

She added, "I still want us to visit Kushan someday and find out if the story of the Malaji is true. If you're up for it."

The invitation sat well with him, a connection to their past when they'd been giddy with the prospect of adventure. Her words, though, were flat, even if the intention wasn't. "You have yourself a deal."

"Pinky promise?" She held up her right hand.

He hoped for a smile, even a somber one, but accepted that he'd have to wait until another time to see it. "Pinky promise."

He curled his pinky around hers—one last contact between them—and they both shook to seal their agreement.

They stood and said their goodbyes.

"Thank you," Petrah said. "This meant a lot to me." They looked at each other for a long moment, mere inches from each other, but the gulf between them seemed impossibly wide. He memorized her eyes the way he wanted to remember them: kind and affectionate. "Best of luck as the new Green Robe."

"And to you with the Gray," she said. "See you when you get back."

"I CAN'T BELIEVE YOU'RE going to Hōvar," Taka said as he and Petrah headed toward Maseah's front gate. "You're a lucky bastard, you know that? Think of all those beautiful Con-jurahn daughters. They're probably dreaming of a strong Ter-jurahn to come rescue them from the lame men over there."

Petrah carried two satchels, a smaller one with a quill, inkwell, and roll of parchment, and a larger one for the pair of books he'd borrowed from the library. The first was *Channeling Linguistics*, a guide to divine intonations. The second was *Orumen's Phrases*, a compilation of inspirational words and phrases Petrah might find useful for his poetry.

He'd already decided to write a poem for Ajoon during his desert journey.

"I don't think their fathers would appreciate a womanizer like you snooping around," Petrah said. "You're doing just fine here with all your girlfriends."

Taka smiled like a scoundrel. "There's always room for more." He held up the cloth sack with Petrah's sword. "What are you planning to do with this?"

Petrah shrugged. "I don't know. Maybe bury it in the desert."

"You should keep it. First blood is sacred."

Miko's death was far from sacred, but Petrah didn't want to debate the matter, so he said nothing and kept walking.

They continued in silence.

The midmorning air was cool, the first break in the heatwave in over a month. Petrah paused by a pair of olive trees with twisted trunks. He and Ajoon had spent several afternoons under the shade of their branches. He still smelled the blossom fragrance of her hair from one such occasion on a particularly hot day.

Petrah would miss their talks, studying in the library together, taking walks, and joking around.

He would miss a lot of things about her.

Master Joriah said Petrah's trip to Meerjurmeh could last a couple of months. Petrah doubted the new journeyman school would be completed by then. Even if it was, would they allow him back?

They've made their decision. I'll be at a different school. Hopefully close by.

Saying farewell to his classmates was tough, made more difficult by their reserved hand waves and goodbyes. *They need time to change how they feel toward me.* And hopefully forgive him for what he'd done. With Ajoon's leadership, her schoolmates would be well looked after. There were ten of them now. Two more and they'd return to twelve, a fortunate number. Petrah was confident Master Joriah would find two superb candidates to fill the empty slots.

Petrah breathed in the warm air. Maseah had become home to him. Departing left a bittersweet taste in his mouth.

He'd miss Annia, who had always been kind to him, and all the other people who worked on the estate.

Kruush waited outside the main gate, along with a cheery and tearful Ahleen and a smirking Tan.

"It's about time," Kruush said.

"Don't you mean Happy Hah'xallah?" Petrah asked.

"Oh, that blasted holiday. Is it today? I believe I forgot."

Petrah introduced Taka to his friends.

"Try to keep this one away from the ladies," Taka said. "He's a bit of an animal."

Tan put an arm around Petrah's shoulder. "Worry not, young sir. I shall fend off the ladies with vigor on his behalf . . . and enjoy the spoils."

Kruush rolled his eyes, and Ahleen laughed. She gave Petrah a hug. "I'm so glad you're coming with us."

"Me too," Petrah said. He was afraid if he said much more, he'd match Ahleen tear for tear.

They worked together to place Petrah's belongings onto a cart harnessed to a donkey. Kruush had arranged lodging in Elmar for one night in celebration of the holiday. Petrah, along with Kruush, Tan, and Ahleen would take to the road the next day to mirror the ambassador's schedule and begin their trek across the great Bunai and Agobo Deserts that bridged Terjurmeh with Meerjurmeh. Then Petrah would begin his mission.

When they finished loading the cart, Taka locked forearms with Petrah. "Try not to get into any trouble over there."

"You know me," Petrah said with a grin.

Taka smiled in return. "Look me up when you get back. I've got the first round of ale."

Petrah gave Taka a spirited pat.

When Taka left, Petrah turned to take in the vast property one last time.

The Watcher had predicted a different life for Petrah than the one he'd known: the hand of darkness reaching out to pull him inexorably to its center as the gears of fate turned endlessly to make it happen.

I will make my own way, Petrah vowed.

Maseah stretched before him. Scarlet crescents sang their song in the distance. He wondered if he'd ever see this place again.

He gave it one last look.

Then he turned to face the long road ahead.

Preview of the next book in the series

K EEP READING FOR A sneak peek of **Book 2**, *The Dark that Creates*

Dark Prophecy

J ORIAH HURRIED DOWN THE winding stairs of the grand temple, sweat pouring from his brow, chest heaving to get enough of the stale air. He kept his left hand against the rough, stone wall to steady himself as he descended the precariously steep stairwell. One misstep, one false move, and he'd trip and tumble.

I'm always rushing, he thought, blinking the sting of perspiration from his eyes. *That's the crux of the problem.*

The temple, the Dome of San, crested the pinnacle of the capital city of Elmar as a beacon of faith. But it was larger than it appeared—much larger—plunging deep into the bedrock of the hill it sat upon. Torches danced in their sconces, casting mad shadows and releasing the smell of burning pitch.

Joriah slipped but caught himself, catching a crevice along the stone wall with fingers that clawed to find purchase. *Is there no end to this cursed spiral of stairs?*

There were few things Joriah despised more than being called to a meeting of the Temple elite. Not that he didn't appreciate their invitation. He was, after all, a mage of the Green Flame party, a layman in a country that bowed before the Temple's might. To be invited to a secret gathering of powerful clergy was deemed an honor of the highest level.

Yet I have no choice.

Joriah's duties seemed to grow by the day. As a senior mage of his party, he had the magi school at Maseah to run and new apprentices to recruit. He also found himself pulled into an increasing number of meetings with top officials within his own party. And then there was today, a holiday of all occasions, where he dashed to rendezvous with Uhtah-Pei, the leader of his party, a man touted as one of the most controversial figures in the country.

Uhtah-Pei didn't just head up the Green Flame. He also served as a high-ranking official in the Temple, a member of the Sacred Nine. In a nation where the clergy were supposed to keep their noses out of secular affairs, Uhtah-Pei had boldly—and some would say recklessly—seized hold of the country's political apparatus and turned it on its head. Joriah believed in Uhtah-Pei, but the Articulate demanded too much of his time.

He taxes me without end, but what can I do?

There was nothing Joriah could do, not if he wanted his star to brighten among the constellation of magi in Terjurmeh.

Joriah reached the base of the stairs, winded, with hair matted to his forehead and sweat running from the back of his neck down his robe. He combed back his slick hair with his fingers, straightened his black robe, and entered the temple's antechamber as composed as possible, given the circumstances.

Two clerics stood guard before a sealed entryway, faces reflecting the sooty torchlight. One pulled down on a lever inset into the stone wall, and the round door rolled slowly to the side with a deep, grating sound. Joriah stepped across the grooved threshold and into the windowless, vaulted sanctum.

Four faces looked up from high-backed chairs around a circular table. None appeared happy at his tardy appearance.

"Apologies," he said, quickly taking the seat beside Uhtah-Pei.

The door closed with an unnerving boom, sealing the granite chamber from the outside, and Joriah along with it. Candles lit the room from a chandelier over the table. More along the wall gave off the pleasing scent of melting beeswax. A cool draft filtered down from a hidden gap somewhere in the ceiling.

Joriah noted he was the only layman among the small gathering, the others comprised of the Temple's upper echelon: three of Terjurmeh's five Articulates—Uhtah-Pei, Septamo, and Nisheppeh—and Baaka, Seer of Elmar, one of three Seers in the nation. Although uncomfortable sitting with such powerful individuals, it was Nisheppeh who made Joriah the most unsettled. She was the only woman among them, Third Articulate of the Temple but as dangerous as they came. Her heartless, dark eyes belied a sinister core as she looked at the newcomer, tracking his movement as a krell might track its prey. Even her short hair, black as crows' feathers, ended in a choppy sweep across her brow and to either side of her ears, like fangs.

Baaka wrinkled his nose from across the table. "You're late."

"My apologies, Holy One," Joriah said. "It took longer than expected to get through the crowds."

"It's a good thing it's a holiday," Baaka said, grinning. "Otherwise, we might have you stand naked in the corner, as we do with the clerics."

Joriah smiled politely. Baaka liked to poke fun, but in no way invited him to do the same. Joriah lifted the mug in front of him and gave it a sniff. There was an earthiness to it. A sip confirmed black tea, lukewarm from sitting there. He drank his fill.

Uhtah-Pei whispered into Joriah's ear. "Is your Gray Robe situated?" He was referring to Petrah, who'd left Maseah earlier in the morning.

"He is, Holy One."

Septamo, First Articulate of the Temple, frowned at the late arrival. He was second in line to the Mighty One, the Temple's papal head, and he liked to flaunt his authority. "Now that we're all here, I'd like to continue, if that's all right." He looked at Uhtah-Pei.

"Of course," Uhtah-Pei said with a noble bow of the head.

Joriah appreciated Uhtah-Pei's ability to defer to Septamo, even though the Articulates were equals. If there was one thing Joriah admired about the Temple's elite, it was their willingness to work together—and share power.

Septamo went on. "As I was saying, I spoke to the Mighty One yesterday after midnight service. He gave his blessing for phase one of our plan. We're to pass word to the senior members of the clergy right away."

"It's about time," Uhtah-Pei said. "What about the measures we proposed? Do we have the go-ahead to fortify our troop positions in the cities?"

"We do," Septamo said. "Triple the number of Temple troops over the next twenty-four months, sooner if possible."

Joriah could tell where this was going. Even though the Temple maintained its own force of troops for protecting its people, monuments, and temples, the numbers were negligible compared to the forces under the control of the parties. An increase in Temple troops meant the Temple was posturing to impose its will and—if Joriah was reading into this correctly—eventually seize power and abolish the political parties altogether.

It was an interesting play. The country of Terjurmeh was already a theocracy, but with dozens of parties vying for domination, it left Terjurmeh weak . . . and fractured. A unified Terjurmeh under the Temple's absolute rule, including control of her military, would make it a powerful adversary.

"And what about the *San-mahadi*?" Nisheppeh asked. Her voice, cold as her eyes, made Joriah shudder. He'd met her only twice, but it had been enough. In here, her skin took on a deep, shadowed tone against the flickering candles. In the daylight, Joriah recalled the unusual cobalt tint to her olive complexion, as if she'd battled demons in the underworld and absorbed their essence.

Septamo wrapped his thin fingers around his mug. "Your fellow Articulates helped me convince the Mighty One to reinstate the sacred order. He's appointing one of our senior priests to the top post as we speak. Effective tomorrow, the new head will have the authority to recruit mahadi and send them out to any secular organization or tribe at will."

Joriah knew of the mahadi only from historical texts. They were a volunteer force made up of clergy, anointed by the Temple to root out heretics in the name of San, used in the past as an extreme measure to purge threats to the Temple. This occurred whenever the balance of power favored the secular, as it was starting to with the Fist's rise in prominence among parties as of the most recent Great Council. Joriah hoped the mahadi could do their work before civil war broke out, pitting the parties against the Temple, an event that hadn't happened in a millennium.

Septamo continued. "I will announce His Holiness's edict to the masses, following my sermon at midnight. You all know what kind of response we're going to get, especially with every key politician within earshot. Baaka, we'll need a strong showing of Temple troops."

"Consider it done," Baaka said, flattening a wayward thread against the seam of his impeccable scarlet robe. "No party will even think to denounce the proclamation."

Septamo turned to Uhtah-Pei. "Speaking of parties, it sounds like yours is getting put to the test. Last I heard, you're being excluded from sanction talks with the Con-jurah. What's that about?"

Uhtah-Pei waved his hand dismissively. "It's nothing. The Fist and the Black Arrow are playing a silly game, that's all. They think if they shut us out of their talks, it will send a message to the other parties that we're no longer needed in the political community. No one will believe such a ruse."

"I'm not worried about ruses," Septamo said. "I'm worried about civil unrest turning into something disastrous. If the Green Flame alienates itself completely, we'll have an unstable situation. I need you to keep your party members under control. We can't afford any disruptions to our progress."

Uhtah-Pei scoffed. "Brother, you worry too much. I'll handle it. Just concentrate on our funding. The rest will take care of itself."

The First Articulate crossed his arms and sat back, his expression unpleasant.

Baaka tapped the tabletop with his knuckles. "While I enjoy hearing us squabble over political posturing, what I'd really like to know is what's going on with our An-jurahn brothers to the east."

Nisheppeh spoke up in an icy tone that made Joriah squirm in his seat like sharp nails raked across slate. "I met with members from the newly minted Warlord Council in Âhn. They're going to choose a War Chief once they have enough warlords on board. The An-jurah still struggle to annex the southern states. Octapia, who came to visit us a few months back, told me the priesthood is getting involved in the matter. They're sending their Su-yi to deal with the unwilling warlords. Everything should be cleared up by spring."

If Nisheppeh had been in Âhn, it meant she'd journeyed to Dark-forth. Joriah began to understand this great plot being revealed and why the meeting had been called in secret. The An-jurah were allies of the Ter-jurah. Once, they were a single people. Now, they shared a common enemy: Meerjurmeh, the desert country that stood between Terjurmeh and the wilds of Darkforth. If the An-jurah were working to annex their warring states under one banner, as Nisheppeh suggested, it would be another step toward the prophecy of the An-jurah and Ter-jurah uniting to vanquish their enemy for good. Terjurmeh didn't have the strength to do it on its own. With Meerjurmeh's loose alliance with the Northern Kingdom and the Empire of Korin, Terjurmeh would require the full strength of the An-jurah to wage war against Meerjurmeh.

Baaka gave an amused nod. "Those Su-yi are nasty bastards. I hear they skin their opponents and hang them upside down while they're still alive."

"I'm not swayed by your high priest's assertions," Septamo told Nisheppeh. "What assurance do we have that the An-jurah will bring us our frontline fodder when we need it?"

"I met with our *friend* in Darkforth before I left," Nisheppeh said, dark eyes dancing in the candlelight. "He insisted all the pieces will come together when the time comes. I consider that as good as San speaking directly into my ears. Wouldn't you agree?"

Septamo nodded, an odd look of satisfaction creeping onto his face. The "friend" Nisheppeh referred to was a divine agent of San's. He was called the Gatekeeper in the Holy Scriptures, a powerful being believed to have once been an angel, destined to set key events into motion to aid the children of San to defeat their enemies. If he assured certain events would happen, Joriah believed it.

Nisheppeh turned her haunting eyes toward the mage. "Our friend asked about a certain someone in your charge, a young man with a peculiar name."

"Petrah," Joriah said. "He's one of my journeymen."

"Our friend wants to know when Petrah will complete his mage training. I plan to speak to our friend on the morrow. What should I tell him?"

"Let me answer this," Uhtah-Pei said, patting Joriah's hand. "You can tell our friend the young man is well on his way to completing his training. He's leaving for Hōvar after the holiday. We've given him a mission. He's to spy for us in Hōvar. It'll be a good use of his talents, which Joriah believes are extraordinary for someone so new to the arcane arts. From there, he travels to Tuur to meet Anandawa, who is returning from Darkforth. Anandawa will speed up our journeyman's training. Once his training is complete, we'll arrange for his travel to Darkforth. Petrah's abilities will be considerable by then. That's what our friend wants, isn't it?"

Nisheppeh pushed into the table with her long fingers. "Yes. Does your journeyman know of these illustrious plans?"

"No," Uhtah-Pei said. "Petrah knows only of his immediate task as a spy. He believes he's returning to Elmar to attend a journeyman school and resume his education. He doesn't know about Tuur or that our friend will send him home."

Baaka's eyes lit up. "Ah, so our young Petrah is going to have a family reunion."

Septamo frowned. "Why are we wasting time discussing this and why do we care if this journeyman reunites with his family? Aren't there more pressing matters than talking about some commoner under Joriah's charge?"

Baaka started laughing.

"You find that funny?"

"Not at all, Septamo," Baaka said. "I find it apropos. I'm sorry you've been kept in the dark, but our journeyman is San-Jahad's little brother. Hardly a commoner."

Looks of surprise filled the room. Even Nisheppeh arched an eyebrow. Joriah knew about Petrah's heritage from a previous conversation with Baaka. That Petrah and San-Jahad—the prophesied son of San, God of Darkness—shared the same father, making Petrah and San-Jahad brothers. Joriah would have thought Septamo would know of Petrah's divine blood and his relation to his brother.

Septamo came partway out of his seat. "That's quite the declaration. I know you have a fancy for prophecies, Baaka, but even this is a stretch, wouldn't you say?"

"You've seen his eyes," Baaka said. "The blue-eyed slave, if you recall? The one whose life you spared?"

"Him? He's the one?" Septamo furrowed his brow. "Manis-cor wanted him dead when I visited the slave works in Kanmar. It's rumored he burned a slave galley to ashes and helped the slaves aboard escape, costing the lives of the crew and her captain. You're telling me he's San-Jahad's brother because of the color of his eyes? He's just a slave. An escaped slave at that."

"*Was* a slave," Uhtah-Pei amended. "I released him from bondage."

"And he became one of your journeymen? How?"

Uhtah-Pei explained how Joriah recruited Petrah as a mage apprentice for the Green Flame, and Petrah's advancement to journeyman. "Imagine it, Septamo: our Gray Robe was a doomed slave when you first met him. Now, he's to serve a part in the greatest prophecy ever told. Have you ever heard of a slave rising to such prominence? It's unfathomable."

"Still," Septamo said, holding up a finger, "that doesn't make him the blood of the Great One. How would the son of a god become a slave, to begin with?"

"I've seen what Petrah sees," Baaka said. "Joriah brought him to me, and I looked into his mind. He's from San-Jahad's homeland, reborn here. His slavery is a matter of circumstance. He is without a doubt the blood of the Father, which makes him the blood of the Great One as well. His brother needs him. Fate calls and Petrah must answer. That's why our friend wants to send him home. If young Petrah can first conquer his channeling abilities and achieve magehood, imagine what a formidable warrior he will be by his brother's side when the Great One comes to Acia to help us defeat the Con-jurah and all the other believers of the false god."

Septamo seemed only slightly moved by the revelation. "San the Father begot many children over the ages, as we've all heard, although none among us today. Does the blue-eyed one share the same mother as the Great One?"

Baaka shrugged. "It's unimportant which vessel carried them into this world. Their mothers could have been whores for all we care. It's the children that are sacred and the ichor in their veins that matters. And, more importantly, it's their place in history that makes them who they are."

"What's your journeyman's place, then?" Septamo asked. "I've seen nothing in the Scriptures that speaks of a brother to San-Jahad. His part is apocryphal at best."

"Our friend is the Gatekeeper between the world of Acia and the Great One's, and Petrah is the Key," Baaka said. "He's the linchpin to San-Jahad's arrival. San-Jahad, who is the Great One, the Great Son, and also the Sword. You won't find the Key mentioned in the Scriptures, but you will find it written in the stars. I've seen it. Now that I have looked into Petrah's mind, I am certain of it." Baaka's lip curled into a contented smile.

Septamo nodded, finally giving in. "San indeed works in mysterious ways. We must recognize it when it presents itself in such a profound fashion. Your second sight is most welcome, Baaka."

"I agree," Nisheppeh said, teeth poking below her upper lip like a krell's. "We need to assure San-Jahad's brother is delivered safely to our friend. I suggest we keep him here in Elmar rather than send him off, at least until we can provide a proper escort after he's completed his training. I don't trust Anandawa. He's a loner and a renegade among magi, even if he's immensely talented in the arts."

Joriah waited for Uhtah-Pei to balk at the suggestion, which he did. "Petrah is *my* responsibility. He goes to Hōvar, as planned. Unless you can supply us with a spy unknown to the Meerjurmehan delegation. As for Anandawa, he's more than capable of keeping Petrah safe."

Nisheppeh folded her hands but didn't argue the point. Septamo abstained as well.

"Then it's settled," Uhtah-Pei said.

Joriah was thankful his leader stood up for their cause and pushed for Petrah to go to Hōvar, but the idea he might lose his Gray Robe didn't sit well with him. Still, the matter wasn't his to decide.

Quiet stole over the chamber, but only for a moment.

Baaka held out a finger and pointed it at each person at the table before hooking a thumb toward himself. "Every one of us has a purpose, a part in the Father's plan. Tonight, we proclaim it. Tomorrow, we set it into motion. We will cleanse our nation of heretics, and then we will go after the unbelievers who curse our god and make theirs supreme.

"This is a pivotal moment, brothers and sister. San is with us: his strength is in our hearts, his power in our souls, and soon, his vengeance at our fingertips. The Scriptures speak of the Great Reckoning—the end of days for the unworthy—as *his* time. It will be our time too."

The Seer stood and clasped his hands. "Pray with me."

Heads bowed.

"Father of Truth, hear our prayer. Guide us as we unfold your plan to purge the unbelievers from Acia. Enlighten us as we architect your mighty *Samath*. Strengthen us as we muster the courage to walk with you. Bless us as we sacrifice our captured enemies this holiday. Your divinity is ineffable, sacrosanct, and without measure. In your name, we ask these things. In the name of the Father, blood to spirit."

"Blood to spirit," repeated the group.

The Seer dabbed the air in the shape of the holy delta and sat down. The others remained quiet, absorbing the words with introspective devotion.

Samath.

Joriah knew the ancient word. It was the holiest of wars, whispered among soothsayers and zealots alike, the reclamation of the Truthful.

Armageddon.

Feast of the Hammer

P ETRAH MOVED THROUGH THE packed streets of Elmar under the glare of the midday sun, squished together with hundreds of people. It seemed as if everyone in the country had descended on the capital to celebrate the holiday of Hah'xallah.

Petrah let his friend Kruush lead the way toward the city center. Stocky and sturdy, Kruush carved a path through the congestion, making room for Petrah and their other friends, Tan and Ahleen, who walked single file behind him.

Petrah didn't want to be here. The swell of people flocking to the streets, coupled with their shouts of jubilee, constant motion, and un-desirable body odors, was too much for him. He'd gotten accustomed to the quiet and openness of Maseah during his time as a mage appren-tice, the great estate that belonged to the Green Flame party. Just this morning, he'd left the estate, saying heartfelt goodbyes to friends like Taka and Ajoon. He hadn't expected Elmar to be so hectic on a holiday. Even on San's Day, when the crowds gathered for prayer in the city, there was room to breathe and some semblance of order. Today's crowds were pushy and suffocating. Maybe his friends would consider abandoning this madness and leaving the city ahead of the ambassador's schedule.

But first, he had to convince Kruush. "Can't we leave today?"

Kruush maneuvered around a donkey cart jutting out into the road. Like Petrah, he wore a simple beige tunic and sandals. The donkey brayed as Petrah passed, breath scented of hay, the bell around its throat ringing. "You know we can't do that," Kruush said.

The traffic eased for a few paces before forming another bottleneck. Tan and Ahleen were right behind them. Hawkers from vendor stalls tried to take advantage of the slowdown, competing for attention with wild hand waves and calls, adding to the chaotic jam of pedestrians. One old man with missing teeth dangled beaded necklaces with serak pendants in front of Ahleen, trying to negotiate with Tan to buy one for his "pretty lady."

Petrah pushed forward so Kruush could hear him. "But why can't we?"

Kruush cast dagger eyes at the hawker, who backed away. "Do you see all these people? It's a madhouse. We'd never make it out. Besides, I've already paid for a room for us, so that's that. And you forget, we're not traveling alone."

"But—"

"It's already decided. We leave tomorrow. Now let me concentrate on where we're going." Kruush squeezed past a pair of men who were standing in the middle of the street shouting at each other and pushed ahead.

Petrah knew better than to argue any further. And he knew Kruush was right and that Master Joriah would agree with him.

At first light on the morrow, Petrah and his friends would join the caravan of nomads and filter out the city gates. They'd trail the Terjurmehan ambassador's party and head across the desert to Hōvar, Meerjurmeh's capital, where Petrah would spy on behalf of the Green Flame—his first assignment as a mage journeyman. Master Joriah had coordinated with Kruush to ensure Petrah had a safe escort to Hōvar and would have everything he needed for his mission. Petrah didn't inquire how much Master Joriah had paid Kruush for this arrangement, but he'd asked Kruush if Ahleen and Tan knew about his mission.

"Of course they know," Kruush had said. "Did you think Tan and Ahleen thought you were traveling to Meerjurmeh on holiday? And before you get your head in a fuss about it, I told your master that I would tell them, but no others, and he agreed. To everyone else, you're a merchant's apprentice of the White Hand, working for me."

Petrah looked forward to proving himself to both Kruush and Master Joriah, but leaving Maseah—his home for the past year—left his stomach in knots. Was it because he'd be gone for almost two months, as Kruush had estimated? Was it the sheer responsibility of performing to Master Joriah's expectations? To Kruush's?

But as a young lady in a white tunic passed Petrah, with the same short hair and wide hips as Ajoon's, he knew. The young lady made eye contact with Petrah, furrowed her brow as Petrah's eyes lingered too long, and hurried along. Petrah's pulse quickened and his stomach clenched even tighter.

Ajoon's face remained etched in Petrah's mind. He remembered how her two-toned eyes had reflected the pain and confusion just a few hours earlier when he'd apologized to her. For the deadly incident involving Miko. For showing Ajoon his ugly side. For breaking their trust.

Her words came back to him with heaviness. *Petrah, I won't lie and say our friendship can be what it was. But my heart hurts.* His chest constricted, making each inhale more difficult than the last. *I forgive you,* she'd told him. He wanted to believe her. To believe he could repair their relationship. But to wait two months until he saw her again . . .

It's too long. Much too long.

Petrah practiced his mantra, Copper Still, to calm his runaway thoughts. With each step, the constriction in his chest eased; with each inhalation, the knots in his stomach loosened.

Being with his friends helped. Ahleen, like an older sister, shared a kind and comforting smile with him. Tan, acting his usual, playful self, flirted with not one but two ladies selling wares in stalls beside each other. Kruush, with a confident but comical flick of his wrist, fended off another hawker adamant about peddling his trinkets to Ahleen. Petrah loved his friends for who they were—and as they were. They were family, and they would always be his family.

The four arrived at their destination in the early afternoon: the top of an ancient quarry shaped into an amphitheater. It sloped down to a large oval arena buttressed by a sheer sandstone wall that enclosed it. Already, hundreds of bystanders had settled in among the many rows of stone seats, although none sat, as was the custom on Hah'xallah. Kruush led Petrah, Ahleen, and Tan a third of the way down to a vacant space that could accommodate them.

Ahleen said to Petrah, "It's quite something, isn't it?"

Petrah hadn't taken part in a gathering of this size since his visit to the Great Hall, the ten-story coliseum that served as the meeting center for the annual Terjurmehan Great Council. The noise and constant movement here were just as intense and no less grand.

"It is."

Petrah thought he spotted a couple of his classmates in the crowd, Nuk and Taline perhaps, but it was hard to tell with all the commotion. Everyone was here for the Reenactment, the centerpiece of the summer's-end holiday celebration. The magi who ran the school at Maseah encouraged their students to attend so they could learn the meaning of Hah'xallah firsthand.

"Hah'xallah reminds us of our heritage," Master Nole had said in class the week prior. "It reminds us we are Ter-jurah. Just as important, it reminds the Con-jurah who we are. We do that by reenacting the day they almost forgot."

It was a painful reminder, too, as Petrah understood it. Each year, the Ter-jurah reenacted the fourth-century Terjurmehan victory over the Con-jurah in a vivid portrayal of the famed battle, concluded by a ceremonial sacrifice of actual Con-jurahn captives done the "old way."

Hah'xallah had earned the name "Feast of the Hammer" because of how the Ter-jurahn actors would bludgeon their captives using war hammers. Petrah thought the act sadistic and reprehensible. What was the purpose of venerating a bunch of warriors who were dead for over two thousand years?

There is no purpose. It's just an excuse to carry on a meaningless tradition.

"Look at them," Kruush said, shaking his head. "They're like a sea of vultures. They can't wait for the blood."

"The good news is we leave tomorrow," Tan said.

Tomorrow, the city would empty, as Hah'xallah signaled the end of the hot season. The nomadic tribespeople of Terjurmeh would leave for the desert, where the cold season's more temperate weather would make their travel tolerable.

"Aye," Kruush said. "And not soon enough. I should have listened to Petrah and forsaken this insanity."

From where Petrah stood, the amphitheater eased down several dozen feet to a ring around the quarry floor, girded by a ten-foot vertical drop. Families crowded around him, talking excitedly among themselves, with anticipation of the day's main event taut on their eager faces. Up near the top, Petrah noticed a line of Temple soldiers with their customary squared, red linen headdresses and spears. They outnumbered the city troops two to one, which Petrah thought odd.

"Why do you suppose there are so many Temple troops?" Petrah asked above the din, gesturing to the soldiers. Petrah had gone into the city many times, both to attend Temple and to carry out tasks for his masters. He'd seen the Temple troops scattered about, only a handful at a time. He counted nearly thirty here.

"There must be a delegation from the Temple in town," Kruush said. "Someone important, I'm guessing."

"But so many soldiers? No, it must be something else."

Kruush shrugged.

Petrah changed the subject. "Where are the actors and slaves coming from?"

Kruush pointed at the far wall of the quarry. "See that opening? A tunnel leads from the slave barracks to the floor. They'll come through there."

Petrah spotted a shadowed entrance hewn into the blond-colored rock, covered by a metal grate. He pictured the wretched slaves huddled and then forced to walk out, only to meet a horrific ending. At least as a city slave in Kanmar, Petrah didn't have to worry about being executed, not without bringing it on himself.

These poor souls were doomed from the start.

A crying child drew Petrah's attention behind him. The boy was perhaps six or seven, with teary, red-rimmed eyes and a round face. An older man on his right—his father most likely—and a woman holding his hand on his left accompanied him. The woman shook a finger at the boy and then said something to the man, who slapped the child hard across the face. Petrah flinched as if his own face had been struck. The boy started to sob, but a threatening raise of the arm from his father reduced it to a whimper. When the father saw Petrah looking at him, he shrugged and said, "Boys."

Petrah turned back toward the quarry floor, teeth gritted and heat flushing through his body. The way the father hit the boy stirred the painful memories of the times Petrah had gotten flogged as a slave. The man's mannerisms reminded him of Meska, the Draad who had made Petrah's life miserable. *Meska got what he deserved.* The slave master had lost his life to the very slaves he'd oppressed, a fitting end.

Kruush picked up on Petrah's irritation. "Don't pay him any attention. It's not worth it."

Petrah folded his arms and tried to heed what Kruush said. Yet the situation chaffed Petrah the wrong way, and he couldn't shake it.

Actors dressed as Terjurmehan soldiers poured out onto the quarry floor. They trotted around the perimeter of the site, waving to the audience with mock swords, rousing cheers, and laughter. They wore red-dyed leather breastplates over camel-colored tunics and carried elongated shields embossed with flames. A second group of actors in ancient tan, Con-jurahn armor came out. The crowd booed them, cursing, shouting, and making derogatory motions with their hands.

The actors split up into Ter-jurahn and Con-jurahn camps on opposite sides of the arena floor. A red-robed priest, accompanied by two clerics, walked out into the center. He ascended a podium midfield and held up his hands. The crowd fell silent.

"Children of San," the priest cried. "Behold the battlefield of Andelah, the ancient site of the greatest victory in our history. The year is 394. Our ancient capital of Ekmed has fallen. The Con-jurah believe their lands unassailable, their borders impenetrable. But lo! Our warriors have crossed the great desert into their homeland. The Ter-jurah surprise the Con-jurah and take them by force. Behold the Reenactment!"

A cleric issued a battle cry, and the Ter-jurah charged across the field to the crowd's roar.

The actors engaged each other in a mock melee. They hacked and thrust dramatically with their blunt swords. The crowd hooted and jeered in response. One by one, the Con-jurah fell. Their leader, a man with a wing-tipped helm, lifted his shield in a yielding fashion and dropped to his knees. His soldiers followed suit and laid down their weapons. The battle was over.

The crowd chanted, "*Ufah! Ufah!*" Hammers! Hammers!

The priest and clerics on the podium waved their arms up and down, whipping the spectators into a frenzy. People stamped and shouted "ufah" in cadence. Petrah and his friends were among the minority who withheld from the fervor.

Petrah felt a tap on his shoulder. He glanced behind and saw the boy's father glaring at him. The man shook a fist at Petrah. "Say *Ufah!*" His son was next to him, half-heartedly doing his part, with a swollen face. It made Petrah want to punch the man.

"Mind your own business." Petrah turned around. How dare this man tell him what to do? The muscles in Petrah's shoulders quivered and a bloom of heat washed over his face.

Below, the actors waved goodbye to the crowd and left. Draadi came out, pulling a train of naked men and women shackled and chained to one another.

Slaves.

Real Con-jurahn slaves, shaking and terrified.

Petrah's throat tightened.

We shouldn't be here. This is wrong. Wrong!

Soldiers entered the field carrying heavy war hammers. As soon as they lifted the oversized weapons above their heads, the crowd went wild.

Ufah! Ufah!

Workers wheeled out long stone blocks and latched them to the end of the podium. The Draadi positioned the slaves in a single line. By fours, they dragged them over and chained them to the blocks, chin down. Petrah heard accusations of "murderers" and "bastards" and more sordid names from the crowd. The slaves whimpered and cried and begged, but the energized crowd overtook their pleas.

Petrah pulled on the collar of his tunic as if he couldn't breathe, couldn't swallow, as if he were himself shackled.

The presiding priest raised his hand, and the spectators quieted down.

Ahleen looked away. Petrah would have too, but the macabre display below drew his eyes, much the way one might watch a slave galley go up in flames.

The first round of hammers fell, and the crowd cheered.

The soldiers carted off the bludgeoned slaves and secured another group for execution. Parents and children alike shouted in glee around Petrah. *What's the matter with these people?* He wanted to claw his way to the front, jump down, and yank the hammers from the soldiers, perhaps use them on the soldiers instead. Behind him, the boy's father was lost in a fit of bloodlust. The smell was also getting to Petrah: sweat, stone, and gore reminiscent of the day Aggren died at the hands of Draadi.

Ahleen held Petrah's arm, firm but not too tight. It was exactly the support he needed. His eyes traveled to hers. They were shaped with concern.

Had they been alone somewhere quiet, he could have expressed to her how this place—these people—were affecting him. How they were dredging up terrible memories and squeezing the breath from his lungs. Ahleen was someone who would listen but never judge. She was as good a person as any he'd known. But there were things best kept to himself. Between Miko's death, leaving Maseah, and this depraved display of brutality, Petrah wanted to find a hole and vanish.

Petrah raised his voice over the cheering. "We shouldn't have come here."

"Try not to watch," Ahleen said. "It's better that way."

How could he turn away when everywhere he looked, lewdness ran rampant? These people were a sepsis with putrid hearts and misguided rapture. Petrah's face and arms tingled. It was the same sensation he'd felt when he faced off against Miko. He was ashamed to be among these animals.

Ufah! Ufah!

The blaring of the chanting assaulted his ears. Petrah looked over his shoulder at the father of the boy, who was shouting with all his worth. The boy's father was no different from the rest, perhaps the worst of them all.

He caught Petrah staring and motioned with his hand. "Turn around!"

Petrah continued to stare.

"What did I tell you?"

Petrah's masters taught him never to strike an unarmed man without cause. They taught him never to use divine power without necessitation. They taught him many things, but he forgot them all in that instant.

Petrah grabbed the man by his tunic and hauled him around. He uttered a single word of power and sent the shocked man cascading downward. People tumbled into one another, driven forward by invisible momentum, tangling together. The man landed a few rows down, his fall broken by spectators who shrieked and yelled.

Kruush snatched Petrah's arm. "What are you doing?"

Petrah yanked his arm away. His anger turned to humiliation as he noticed the stunned onlookers around him.

"We need to leave," Kruush said. "Right now."

Kruush led the way, shoving past irate bystanders. Ahleen and Tan went next, Petrah last. The boy's mother cursed after Petrah and even spat at him, but he kept his head down and moved forward. Along the top of the incline, he spotted a pair of Temple troops pointing at the chaotic disruption and laughing. Other troops seemed preoccupied or mildly amused. None left their posts. Petrah braced himself for one to reach out and grab him, but he made it past the exit and kept going.

He didn't look up until they were well clear of the quarry and the angry mob. When they had distanced themselves from the commotion, they stopped.

Petrah apologized to his friends. "I don't know what came over me. First the hammers, then what they did to the slaves, and then—" He was getting worked up again. At least the tingling was gone. He shuddered to imagine what might have happened if he'd had Jayeem's sword with him. "It's no excuse for my actions. I'm sorry."

"It's over now," Kruush said, as far from happy as Petrah had ever seen him. "You could have gotten yourself arrested and us with you."

"If we linger, that might still happen," Ahleen said. "We should head to our room."

Kruush bobbed his head. "Aye. Thank goodness we head out in the morning. We'll finally be away from this place."

Even at their distance from the amphitheater, the sickening cheer from the crowd carried into the streets.

Tan gave a vigorous nod. "Right. It's time to leave. And not a moment too soon."

Visit https://www.stevepantazis.com/lod2 to get ***The Dark That Creates***, **Book 2** in the series, or scan the following QR code.

Acknowledgments for The Light of Darkness series

This series has been decades in the making and has taken on many forms, culminating with the book you just read and the other books in the series.

As many an author can attest, writing is a lonely pursuit, but bringing a work of fiction to life and making it the best it can be requires a team. For those who've helped me along the way, I am truly grateful. What follows is a list of extraordinary human beings who have lent their sharp eyes, astute minds, and brilliant suggestions to me during my journey with this series.

Because *The Light of Darkness* started many moons ago—back when I thought my nine-book series would be a duology; then, a trilogy; and finally, the nine books it has become—I need to acknowledge three talented editors: First, there's Michael Wolf, who made all his amazing edits using a red pen and printout of the manuscript. Then there's Joshua Essoe, who tackled the beginning of the story. And, finally, Jonathan Miller, my current editor, who went above and beyond with his masterful edits and thoughtful suggestions, and pushed me to take my story to the next level.

Then there are my alpha and beta readers, starting with those who helped with the earlier version of my work (in no particular order):

Daniel Piangerelli, Roy Hamilton, Janis Flax, and Andrew Alberti. My alpha (first) reader for this latest version of the series, Leslie Bridgwater, who dove into uncharted waters and offered indispensable feedback. And the beta readers who volunteered to read and comment on my work: Karen Harrison, Jerry White, Kate Julicher, Candice Lisle, and John Parus. A many thanks to you all.

Of course, we mustn't forget the gorgeous cover art and interior artwork.

The covers would not have been close to where they are if not for the critical eye of my good friend, Wulf Moon—an author and artist in his own right—who helped me choose the best color palettes, action poses, and lighting, and advised me on "guiding the eye of the reader on a journey."

For the cover design and creation, I want to thank my cover artist, Les (Germancreative), who worked tirelessly to make the eBook and print covers for all nine novels and the prequel novella. She created a brand for the series that offers an engaging and consistent look and feel. No matter how many revisions I requested, Les rose to the challenge to produce her best work.

While I can claim credit for creating the maps of my fantasy world, my artist, Sam (Samsul Hidayat), turned them into masterpieces, each with an engraved look that's both classical and timeless. He also made the background art you see at the start of each chapter. Ten custom pieces of art, one per book, based on the book's theme.

Because of my long voyage at sea with this series, which began as a watercolor map I painted in 1992, there will be those who helped me but whose names have slipped through the cracks of my ship. Know that your kindness and generosity are not forgotten and that your contribution is forever bound to this enduring work.

About the Author

STEVE PANTAZIS is an award-winning author of fantasy and science fiction. He won the prestigious Writers of the Future award and has published short stories in leading anthologies and magazines, including *Nature*, *Galaxy's Edge*, and *IGMS*. He is the author of *The Light of Darkness* epic fantasy series. When not writing (a rare occasion!), Steve creates extraordinary cuisine, exercises with vigor, and shares marvelous adventures with the love of his life. Originally from the Big Apple, he now calls Southern California home. You can learn more about him at www.StevePantazis.com.

Connect with Steve

Get a **FREE eBook** just by signing up for Steve's newsletter: https://www.stevepantazis.com/subscribe

Support Steve at **Patreon** and receive early access to his short stories and novel chapters, along with cool swag: https://www.patreon.com/StevePantazis

To find out more about Steve and his happenings, check out these links:

Facebook page: http://facebook.com/SFFAuthor
Twitter: https://twitter.com/pantazis
Website: https://www.stevepantazis.com

Also by Steve Pantazis

Visit **https://www.stevepantazis.com/books** to see Steve's current and forthcoming releases or scan the following QR code.

Short stories and novellas:

A Matter of Time

A World Without Flowers

Aliens Anonymous

Apostate

Before I Let You Go

Between a Rock and a Fireball

C'est la vie, Humans

Chameleon

Cold as Space

Curse of the Goddess of Kaanapali

Cursed Magic

Daddy's Girl

Daughter of Time

Decadent Deception

Earth for Sale (Sold!)

Eternity's Traveler

Gods of War

Hex

Honor Bound

Humanity's Last Hope

I Dream of Stars

Illusions

In a Blink

In Darkness Lies

Infernally Yours

It's Only Skin Deep, Darling

Light in the Shadow of Worlds

Magic in the Land of Oppression

Murder on Moonbase 9

Odin's Daughter

Out of Print

Race to the Relic

Purple Orchid Eater

Reset

Surrogate

Switch

The Abernacle

The Daughter You've Always Wanted

The Devil Walks into a Bar

The Hunt

The Legacy
The Longest Mile
The Old Man and the Sea Siren
The Prize
The Sacrifice
To Be Human
Universal Problem
Unlucky
Untamed

Boxed sets:

Alien Worlds
Dragons & Magic
Human 2.0
Miscreants & Mayhem
Modern Magic
Robot Dreams
Space & Time
The Alien Within

The Light of Darkness epic fantasy series:

Prequel: The Dark That Ignites
Book 1. The Dark That Begins
Book 2. The Dark That Creates
Book 3. The Dark That Binds
Book 4. The Dark That Usurps
Book 5. The Dark That Defies
Book 6. The Dark That Burns
Book 7. The Dark That Destroys

Book 8. The Dark That Rules
Book 9. The Dark That Ends

Science fiction novels:

Blackout
Godnet